About the Author

Levi Samuel was born in 1986 in Elk City Oklahoma, though he was raised in Springfield Missouri. While in high school, he discovered the game, Dungeons and Dragons, as well as a Live Action Role Playing group, where he truly discovered who he was. Graduating high school, he joined the Army, but quickly realized that wasn't the life for him. He returned home and went to work in manual labor jobs. Being a quick study, he became a skilled tradesman in a number of fields, but the quest for happiness and purpose evaded him. In 2008 he became a father and has raised his daughter by himself ever since. In 2009, he decided to write a book, which was the start to a lifelong and rewarding career. His first book was published in 2013 under a penname. He's since established a laundry list of qualifications and achievements. Levi lives with his daughter and their cat, Alona.

Please subscribe to my newsletter for first access to all new content. http://eepurl.com/dxRUvL

What you hold here is the product of several years of growth. This was his first completed book, though it's since been revised many times and is far from the original concept. Whether you enjoy this book or not, leave us a review at any online retailer. Reviews help open the door for other readers, as well as teach the author new ways to entertain.

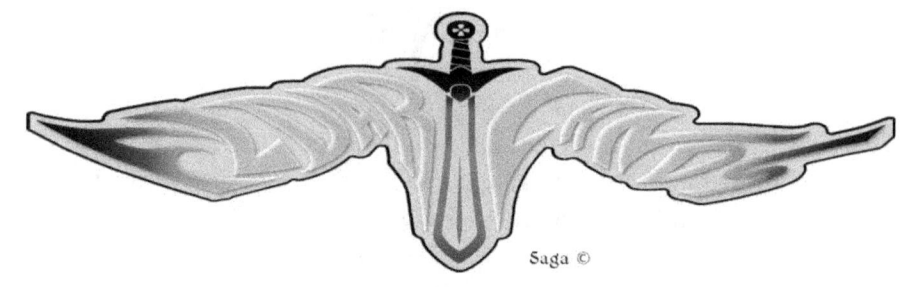

Saga ©

Heroes of Order Trilogy

by Levi Samuel

Izaryle's Will

Izaryle's Prison

Izaryle's Key

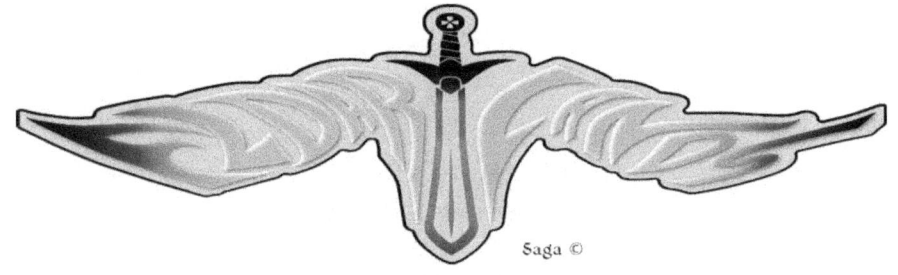

Saga ©

Heroes of Order Trilogy
Volume One

IZARYLE'S PRISON

Levi Samuel

PUBLISHING

ELDARLANDS©
Heroes of Order Trilogy – Volume Two

IZARYLE'S PRISON
Eldarlands Publishing
Copyright © 2015-2019

The story, cover art, and illustrations by Levi Samuel.
Edited by Edward Gehlert
Foreword by Bob Dixon

Genre: Fantasy / Series

ISBN: 1-7321471-3-2
ISBN-13: 978-1-7321471-3-3

Find all the author's projects at http://www.LeviSamuel.com

Foreword

I had the pleasure of meeting Levi a few years back at Tri-Con in Evansville, Indiana. In the dealer's room, he had the misfortune of being seated at the table next to mine. Setting up our tables, we struck up a conversation, as many authors do. The conversation would soon be joined by fellow author, Ed Gehlert and his wife Eva. At some point during the day we decided that since author, Shane Moore was late to the con, it was our civic duty to decorate his table with as much trash as we could find. It escalated quickly. How odd it was for the con goers to make this easy by adding their own garbage to the ever-growing pile. Throughout the convention many more shenanigans happened, more than the courts will currently allow me to speak of. That's a joke by the way. Courts were not involved. But there was one thing that did come from that amazing and eventful weekend. The friendships I made with many of the guests and staff.

This past fall, 2016, I reprised my role of comedy superstar and general goofball at Tri-Con. I was in the midst of my own book release, Snafu Fubar: Nothing Heroic when my first sale approached the table while I was setting up. It was Levi. He handed me a ten-dollar bill, to which I had to laugh a little. The reason being, Levi was releasing his own novel, the predecessor to what you now read. I'd already intended to pick it up from him, and for the same price no less. My humor aside, and a brief explanation on my part, we agreed it made more sense to just trade books. It wasn't until I started reading that I realized how truly gifted of a writer Levi was. Over the past few years, since our meeting, we'd had plenty of talks, either in person or via internet messages. I knew he was a down to earth, intelligent, and good person, but I never realized how well he made a story come to life until I read the words within that book. I found myself in awe as I read each page so naturally. As you can imagine, when he asked me if I would write the foreword to the second book of the series, I considered it a great honor.

One of the things I like to do as an author is to help promote those friends who are on this creative adventure with me. That being said, I'm usually seen at events sporting a T-shirt that features a local band I like, or an artist, or what have you. At the 2016 Tri-Con release, I noticed Levi had shirts printed up for the event that sponsored both the convention and his new novel. It was about one in the morning, after we'd both been to the Mojo Brothers Party (a party one must attend if ever given the opportunity) when I realized I hadn't had the chance to grab one of the shirts. I wanted to help support my fellow author and the convention, to which we were both welcomed to with open arms. But unfortunately, the dealer's room was closed and I was scheduled to leave extremely early the next morning due to the long drive back home. Levi literally took the shirt off his back and handed it to me.

When I suggest authors or musicians to people, especially if I know them, my recommendation is based on two criteria. The first, obviously being talent, and the second is how good of a person they are. Levi meets both of these categories in high fashion. If you ever have the pleasure of meeting him at a signing, you'll see exactly what I'm speaking of. He treats the patrons just as he does the main attraction, each with respect and a friendly, welcoming smile. When you approach his table, you'll feel as if you're talking to an old friend that you haven't seen in a while. And I promise you, before the event is over, he'll be that friend. Rare in today's world do you find such an amazing talent, not only as an author but as a human being.

Bob Dixon
January 2017

I struggled, longer than I care to admit, with the decision of who to dedicate this book to. I've so many people that have shown interest in who I am and what I do that I had trouble picking just one in the long list of names that raced through my head. These people push me to keep moving forward. They ask me how to get involved and help spread my name. They've earned a place in my life, and for that, I'm eternally grateful. I truly wish I could list each and every one of them, but alas, this page is intended for a single person.

As this will not be my last book, I'll have many other dedications to send out into the world, but I believe this book needs to be solely dedicated to my mom. She's a wonderful, strong, twenty-nine-year-old woman, or at least that's what she claims anyway. I wouldn't be where I am if I didn't have her guidance throughout my life. She always inspired me to be unique and creative, especially when the rest of my world tried so hard to crush my desires. From her, I learned to fight for myself, and to stand for what I believed in. So, thank you, mom. I'm happy to have been raised by you. And even though we've had our problems in my younger years, I'll always love you!

Highlor
Ryse
Ice Fall Pass
Ice Fall Mountains
Canfield
Port mark
Rest
Drumlen

GALMAK
IceLands
ICEFALL
Karabour Mountains
Idenor
High Point Bluff
Adariel
Fields of Shanar
Kencar Pass
Tiernoor
Kadil

Contents

Chapter 1
The Shadow's Rise

Rolling clouds of gray soar across the heavens leaving an eternal darkness over the world below. Far to the south an explosion of energy washed across the land, not seen, but felt. The mystical wave traveled in all directions, announcing its arrival to all capable of understanding.

The city of Idenfal was the largest for months in any direction. Its northern face was protected by a wall of mountains wrapping around and swallowing the ancient fortress settlement. A large chasm blocked the south limiting access to a handful of snow covered bridges stretching across the deep ravine.

The clank of swords and guttural laughter echoed from the west where a massive army of orcs engaged in their training. They displayed thick armors and heavy weapons, built for purpose rather than show. Crude structures stood around the orc grounds. These were lined with fur against the harsh winter winds and steady snowfall. It was a city in its own right on the outskirts of Idenfal.

A great many orcs stood in a large circle cheering those within. Of the two castes, the veterans were easy to identify. They wore trophies of fur and hide over their crude armors. Their gray-tinted flesh was marred, serving as both resume and medal in their battle-hardened society. The younger orcs wore no such markings having not earned that honor yet.

Several unarmored orcs fought back to back, fending off their circling aggressors. Lashing out, they struggled to keep them at bay. As one fell, the others engulfed them, tightening the ranks.

The strongest of orcs watched from his perch of bone. He wore the pelt of a black bear over his shoulders. Its head mounted atop a helm, giving him the appearance of the large creature. The weathered skin clinging to his face displayed scars of victories long past. He sat in his chair watching the younglings train. Only the strong would survive. They had no use for anything less.

The elder orc looked up from the fight, sniffing at the air. Pressing his calloused hands against the arms of the rugged throne, he pushed to his feet, towering over the others. "Stand down!" The booming voice echoed across the field, halting all within earshot.

A somewhat smaller, but equally marred, orc approached. "Warchief, what do you command?"

"Time for training is over. Gear and group them. No more than four paired. Something's coming. We need to be ready." The grizzled warchief stepped from his platform and into the layered snow. He felt the pain of his years starting to catch up with him, though he was still strong enough to hold off any who dared challenge him. Glancing over his shoulder, he gazed upon the orc once again. "That one on the end is a bit scrawny. See how he fares against the rest. Make sure they know their place."

"As you command, Warchief."

The old orc marched across the field, listening to the snow crunch beneath his boots. Reaching one of the towering archways of the ancient citadel, he pulled the wooden door open and stepped inside.

The chiseled ashlar of the looming fortress was weathered from time and element, but it held strong. The massive cathedral was formed into the mountain, stretching up into the rolling clouds.

Near the peak of the tallest spire, a figure stared out the stained-glass window, watching the commander leave the field. The orc was nearing the end of his days but he was too stubborn to die in his sleep. He'd have to go with a weapon in hand. But none of the orcs were strong enough to surpass him. New blood was needed, though it seemed a disservice to get rid of him through simpler manners. No, the old orc would die. But it would be in service to him. He'd been a loyal servant. That was the least he was owed. The shadowed figure felt a sensation erupt a great distance away. There was only one thing that could be responsible for such an outburst.

"Time has come." Spinning on his heel, Rezerik marched across the throne room and into the grand hall. The walls were decorated with black and white tapestries. Each one embroidered to show an antlered face stretched and overlooking the world. They fluttered as he passed, falling back into their stagnant status afterward. Between each hanging cloth, a sconce was mounted to the wall. Orange and yellow flame danced across the top seemingly to its own rhythm. Not even his passing made them alter direction.

His boots echoed along the bare, stone floors announcing his approach long before his arrival. Rounding the corner, Rezerik passed into a narrow stairwell and rushed down, circling several times. Reaching the bottom, he watched the dust fly from his steps. It'd been so long since he'd visited this place. Taking a deep breath he continued on, staring at the large doors of black stone in the distance. They seemed so far away despite the relatively short walk.

Cautiously making his way forward, Rezerik placed his gloved hand upon the ancient stone. It was cold to the touch even through the thick leather. He took another deep breath and closed his eyes. For the briefest moment, Rezerik was unsure if he was ready for what awaited him on the other side. Clenching his hands around the pitted rings he pulled, watching the seam between them split. Stale air and dust rushed through the widening crack showering him in its stench. He wasn't surprised. It'd been a millennia since he'd last opened them. None of the others would dare, even if they knew where it was.

Opening the doors just enough the pass, Rezerik stepped through. While it had been gone for an eternity, the lingering presence of the divine might that once occupied the room felt remnant. The twelve towering statues glared down at him, their faces gone long before his time. Rezerik marched through their pensive gaze stopping in front of the dull mirror on the far wall. A thick haze drifted over the surface like a cloud of smoke in the dust filled room. Placing his hand against the dirty reflection, he pushed.

Magics swirled within the reflective surface and it flexed slightly, swallowing his hand. The tension was that of a pool of water, waiting to claim him whole. He pushed harder, forcing his arm into the mirror. Buried to the elbow, the resistance increased. His arm quivered against the force, unable to pass further. "Izaryle, damn it. Let me go!" He strained with all his might trying to pass through the standing portal.

A dark shadow fell over the room. The lilliputian light breaching the open door was snuffed, out leaving the ancient chamber in total darkness.

Rezerik felt the abundance of power surround him. It twisted his insides making him feel sick. So much evil in one place was too much for anyone, even him. Burying the pain as best he could, Rezerik held his resolve against the entity. "I'm surprised it took you this long."

"Why do you use my name in vain, Rezerik? You should have known you can't leave me so easily. None can." The words resonated in his mind, more than he heard them. Though the power behind each syllable shook the foundations of the towering statues, knocking dust from the ceiling.

"Save it. Why can't I go through? It's open. I feel it."

The expanded shadow rolled into a single orb and began to take a humanoid form. The misty tendrils solidified and took on features. Within a few moments, a woman stood the chamber beside him. Her long, brown hair was pulled into a tail at the back, draped over her lavender plated robes of ivory. The booming voice silenced, replaced by smooth, compassionate vocals. "It's true that it's been opened. But you're bound to this place, as am I."

Rezerik trembled beneath his armor. As a shadow, she couldn't touch him. But like this— in this form, he was helpless against her. She could destroy him with a mere thought if she so desired. Dropping to a knee, Rezerik bowed deeply. "My apologies, Izaryle. I didn't mean to offend."

She stepped toward him and placed her hand on his shoulder. "Rise, you own me no apology. I've come to help you."

Help me? Why would she do that? Rezerik stared up at her, lost in the words. "You brought me here to rule? Why would you help me leave after all this time?" Rezerik picked himself up. Even in his larger stature, he felt dwarfed by her.

"We want the same thing. To return home. In a roundabout way you serve as a part of my lock. So long as the nightkings remain, I'm trapped." Izaryle turned away from him and approached the mirror, looking deep into the hues of speckled shadow.

"My Lady? If we're what's keeping you here, why don't you just kill us and take your revenge? You're more than capable now that the way is open." Rezerik studied her movement. It was as if he was looking upon the essence of existence, slowly losing himself to her glory.

She turned to gaze upon him once again. "Things aren't so simple. Even if I wanted to harm you, I can't. This body is mere illusion. It can't physically act in this realm without a host. That's why I speak through my devoted."

Rezerik noticed a tear roll down her cheek. He knew it was in his best interest to remain silent.

Breaking away, Izaryle glared into the mirror once again. "If you're to use this gateway, you must appoint a new nightking. Though not just anyone will do. Only a select few have the potential to harness the power coursing through you. I'm afraid you won't find many in this—" She paused, selecting the appropriate word. "—prison. Even rarer will be one who can free me."

"Do you know where I can find such a being?" Rezerik kept his eyes locked on her. Despite her caring demeanor, he'd fallen prey to her tricks before and wasn't about to fall again.

"There isn't one. At least not yet."

His face solemn, Rezerik schemed against her. *I may not be able to find one to free her. But I can find one to free myself.* "How will I know when I've found someone capable?"

Izaryle closed her eyes, forcing the tears back. There was so much she wanted to say, but couldn't. Stowing herself, she spoke, refusing to look at him. "Memories of your past will guide the way. Though I warn you, perception has a way of tainting what we thought we once knew."

Rezerik watched her form shift back into shadow and fade away. The sparse rays of flickering light returned to the chamber. "You're leaving me with riddles? Why can't you just tell me what I need to know?"

The booming voice returned, dropping him to his knees. "Not all answers are black and white!"

Heavy flakes of snow rained from the clouds, layering into heavy drifts along the forest's edge. Beyond the tree line, frozen leaves could be seen protruding through the light layer of white, most of it blocked by the thick canopy.

The whinny of horses echoed from the open wasteland, frantic in their unease. Several figures rested in the blackened saddles staring into the dark woodland. A legion of orcs stood behind them, quiet in their ranks, refusing to draw the attention of their masters.

Rezerik stood in the stirrups and threw his leg over the black-haired steed. Jumping down, the powdered snow exploded around him adding to the constant flurries. It clung to his black cloak and smoked armor, contrasting against him for the briefest moment until it melted from his body heat and soaked into the fabrics. Handing the reins to one of his mounted companions, he turned and marched into the forest.

The chilling wind rolled against the tree line creating a vortex of snow at the edge. Pressing through, Rezerik took his first steps into the dark wood. The crippling breeze fade away, blocked by the slightly warmer forest air. He stared into the natural darkness, glancing into the tree tops. He had no illusions he was being watched. In fact, he'd be a bit disappointed if he wasn't. Such a failing wouldn't speak well for the thousands of men he'd lost to the forest. A faint smile on his lips, Rezerik marched into the depths listening to the frozen ground crunch beneath his boots.

The hair at the back of his neck stood on end. He could smell the power radiating within this place, though he couldn't identify much else. It was simply a wellspring of the mystical energy overflowing all around him. It was a shame his men hadn't been able to claim these lands. Such a site would grant untold advantage over the other nightkings.

A familiar scent reached his nostrils. Rezerik stopped, sniffing the air for its direction. Finding his query, he altered path and marched along the dark forest, stopping just outside the unseen barrier. Extending his hand, he touched it. The glimmering waves of magic swirled around his blackened glove.

Stepping through the protective dome, a large fortress stood just ahead of him, wrapped in a fortified wall. The ring of a hammer echoed in the distance, accompanied by the scent of cooked meat.

"So this is Haidengal?" Rezerik questioned aloud, casually walking toward the sealed gate. He didn't expect them to let him in. Were their roles reversed he certainly wouldn't.

Levi Samuel

"Halt at the gate!" The guards froze at his sight recognizing who he was.

Rezerik could smell their fear. It had a sweet stench. Like that of rotting flesh. His cheeks tightened, smirking his superiority over the frightened collection of humans and elves. Certainly his presence had circulated their little sanctuary by now. Not so much as a whisper could be heard on the other side of the towering wall.

"Wha— What do you want, Rezerik?" The guard choked on his words, clearly unhappy that he had been the one to speak.

Rezerik suspected the man had lost a game of chance, leaving him the duty of addressing him. He stared at the man, holding complete silence. It wasn't that he didn't have words to say. He simply found it amusing to watch the man squirm in discomfort. He could feel the unseen archers trained on him. He imagined their shaking palms struggling to hold the string of their bows, drawn and ready to fire. It was good they were on edge. It would make his task easier. "Send out Elalon. I'll have my words with her." Rezerik turned, presenting his back to the gate and took a few steps away.

Moments later, he heard the gate creak open slightly. Slowly turning, he locked eyes on the elf standing a few feet from him. Her steps were so light he hadn't heard her approach. She wore fine garments of white silk. The oversized cuffs draped past her waist, blending into the flowing material. Her long, golden hair was braided and hanging down her back. He didn't have to see a weapon to know she was armed. If not with unseen steel, he could smell the magic flowing through her. "Lady Elalon." Rezerik greeted, offering a mock bow.

"Why have you come here, Rezerik?" Her voice carried into the thinning tree tops like spring flower on the wind.

"Can't a man visit with his old friend without having ulterior motives?"

"We're anything but 'old friends'. We fought together once, a long time ago. Any friendship that may have flourished has long since shriveled into a husk of remorse. I'll ask again, what are you doing here?"

Rezerik sighed heavily. "Down to business then. I've come to offer a truce. My men will never again step into this forest, under my command. Any who do will be subject to your penalty."

"And what do you want in exchange for such a deal?"

"Oh, nothing much. I simply require the services of your scouts. My own are unsuitable to the task. However, yours know how to acquire their target without killing them."

"And who would my scouts be seeking?" She kept her eyes locked on the nightking. He was conniving and deceptive. Even the slightest shift in his eyes could alert her to his schemes.

"Travelers from a land different than this one. I can't say what they'll be wearing or what they may have with them, only that they'll be unfamiliar with these lands and coming from the ruins outside of Alegon." Rezerik hid his intentions knowing she was searching for them. Truth was it didn't matter who found them first, only that they were found. If the resistance got to them before his men, it would allow him to kill two birds with one stone. Of course, he didn't expect her to agree. She'd try to play him just as he was playing her. "So, do we have a deal?"

"I'll consider it."

"I'm afraid I need an answer now. You know as well as I, you don't have time to move your little settlement here before my men can be upon it. And I'm sure your scouts have already reported the army parked right outside the forest's edge."

Elalon considered her options. He was right. She didn't have time to evacuate, at least not without calling the sharliets to their position. They could hold them off for a while, but there was no way to save them all if his men came. *Damn him for forcing me into this position. I should have seen it coming!* Refusing to betray her demeanor, Elalon let her emotions subside. "Very well, Rezerik. You have a deal. I'll have my men search for these travelers. If we find them I'll send word by way missive."

"That doesn't quite work for me. I'll leave one of my men in your custody. Beat him, lock him up, torture him— I don't care. Just make sure he lives and is able to travel when the time comes. Release him with their location and you'll never have to fear assault from me again."

She took a deep breath. "Fine. When you reach the field send your man in. My scouts will pick him up from there."

Rezerik spun around and headed for the unseen barrier.

"Oh, and Rezerik. Don't bother coming back. We'll be long gone before you'll have the opportunity to get this close again."

Chapter II
From the Ashes

The roar of a waterfall echoed through the spathic landscape. Tiny beads of water sprayed from the base creating a mist of color in the beaming sunlight. The walls of the shallow ravine were covered in bright green grass and dark colored mud at the water's edge. Two children ran along the top of the narrow canyon laughing in the spring morning.

"Whoa, did you see that?" One of the children slowed to a stop looking down at the river bank. Refusing to wait for an answer he made his way to the source of his focus, careful to keep his footing.

"Is— Is that a body?" The other child asked following after her friend.

The boy reached the bottom and knelt beside the damp figure, half buried in dirt. He reached out and grabbed the man by his shoulder. Pulling hard, he rolled him, exposing a mud-covered face. The body bounced lightly with the rushing water suspending the lower half.

"Is— is he alive?"

"I think so. He's still warm." The boy pulled him further onto the shore and shook him. "Hey, are you alive?"

"Joshua, don't touch him. What if he's diseased?"

"He's laying in the water, Susan. If he's dead, I think it's more likely from drowning." The boy pulled the man's tan vest open, searching for any clue to his identity.

Susan pointed to a leather sash strapped to his right hip. It was emblazoned by a golden shield with a black trident in the center. "I think he's a dreuslayer. You see the trident?"

Ravion felt the sun on his skin. Muffled voices echoed around him. He could feel something touching him. Panic set in. He couldn't breathe.

Coughing, his mouth filled with water. Spitting it, he took a deep breath. The air made its way into his lungs, offering relief. He opened his eyes seeing the two small children kneeling over him.

"Are you alright, mister?" Joshua asked, both surprised and delighted at the man's awakening.

Ravion coughed again, forcing the last bit of water from him. Catching his breath, he rolled over and pressed his hands into the muddy earth. Getting to his knees, he weakly stood. "Where am I?"

"Northern Krondar." The girl calmly stated.

"Where's the nearest city?"

"Fender's Spear is the closest city, but you're about a week from there by horse. You might be able to catch a wagon from Tamora. It's just over the ridge." Susan continued.

Ravion gathered himself, checking to make sure he still had his father's sword. Happy it remained in its sheath, he looked around finding the direction the kids had pointed. "Is it safe to assume it's a human settlement?"

"Mostly. We have a couple half-orcs left over from the occasional raid. And the myrkalfar pass through sometimes, but it's mostly human."

Ravion gave an extended bow offering thanks. Standing to his full height, he scanned the top of the hill. He couldn't see anything at this elevation, but the landscape was fairly straight forward. He was certain he'd be able to see something when he climbed from the crevice. Assurance in mind, Ravion turned to face the children once again. "Thank you for your assistance. If you ever make your way to Marbayne, be sure to visit the keep. I'd be happy to repay you for pulling me from the water."

"It's no problem, mister. Just remember our faces when we're old enough to join the army. I want to be a border warden." Joshua smiled, barely able to contain his excitement.

"Do you now? Well, come visit me when you're old enough. I'm sure we can work something out. Until that day, be well." Ravion smiled and turned to make his way up the incline. Reaching the top of the hill he could see for miles. The land was remarkably flat. He recalled the bits of research he'd done on the area. How they ever had to worry about raids was a mystery. Any advancing army was sure to be spotted hours, if not days, before arrival. This was the only area that held any form of natural defense and that was simply because it bordered Evinwood. As the children directed, he could see Tamora resting between two branches of the winding river. It was a small settlement, little more than a dozen buildings comprising the entire town. It'd be a miracle if they had a single horse available.

Ravion passed a split rail fence lining the single road going through the center of town. Several of the rails were broken and lying half rotted in the dirt. He couldn't help but feel like they were a metaphor for the entire village. Every building was rundown, missing many of the essential components to make it a comfortable residence, let alone a safe one. The population wasn't much better. They appeared next to starving. They wore dirty and tattered clothing, barely suitable for rags. How they could live in such a capacity was beyond him. The children of this place had done him a favor though. If able, he'd see to it that they got what they needed to live comfortably. At least until their fortunes shifted and they were able to fend for themselves. One thing was plainly certain, this place had nothing to offer him currently.

Continued on, Ravion crossed the wooden bridge just on the other side of town. It was a rickety thing matching the upkeep of the other structures he'd seen in the area. Stepping into the browning grass of the unkempt road, he found the sun and headed south.

Ravion walked for what felt like hours. The golden field was just over knee-high and unusually dry for the time of year. Tiny bits of grain clung to his dark blue pants, still damp from the river. Growing tired from the trek, he spotted a small forest in the distance. If he could reach the shade of the trees he could take a short rest to regain his strength.

As if the fates were aligned against him, a deep, guttural tone sounded in the air.

It churned his stomach. Ravion froze, lowering his head with the horn's recognition. Sighing heavily, he drew his longsword and spun to face the approaching war party.

At least a hundred orcs charged toward him. Their axes raised and ready to cut him down. Green-tinted flesh blocked out most of their features, but there was one detail he could make in the closing distance.

The rage in their eyes announced intent, stronger than he'd seen them display. This was personal. If only he knew what they were after.

Ravion took a defensive stance and waited, knowing they would swarm him within minutes. *I've never been the praying type, but gods, if you're listening, I sure could use some help right about now!* Timing his attack, Ravion brought his sword low catching the first orc in the stomach. Spinning around, he slashed another while twisting to avoid the deadly edge of an axe.

Another horn sounded behind him, this one much more pleasant. It had a gentle melody, much like the alfaren horns, but this was different. It had a sharpness that couldn't be mistaken.

What is that? Ravion couldn't look back to see who, or what, approached. To do so would lower his guard to the advancing orcs. Sword at the ready, he silent watched the large, brutish creatures rush past him giving wide girth. It wasn't their way to ignore a threat. That meant only one thing. The source of the unfamiliar horn had to present a much larger danger. He'd have to proceed carefully. Lowering his guard, Ravion watched the last few orcs pass by, leaving him baffled in the shadow of the forest's edge. Curiosity growing, he turned to see what he was dealing with.

Hundreds of pink-skinned humanoids stood along the edge of the trees. Their crude scimitars, rapiers, and other weaponry raised and ready for battle. They swept across the field with blinding speed, clashing against the smaller war party in a shower of death. The two armies roared against one another like an ocean wave against a cliff face.

Taken back at what he was seeing, Ravion watched the battle from the distance. The newcomers tore into the orcs with ease, washing over the first several ranks in seconds. There was something familiar about them. Something he knew he had seen before. They fought with the grace of the alfar, but looked more human than anything. But they were neither. They were more like him, like dalari. The realization hit him. How could he have forgotten what his own people were like? Gripping his sword. Ravion charged into the rear of the embattled orcs. He cut them down mercilessly, slicing his way toward the front line.

Orcs fell in troves, helpless to the superior numbers ahead of them, and the lone attacker at their rear.

Ravion spun around, slicing another orc in half. For the first time he could see the army in clear detail. His stomach churned from excitement, nervousness coursing through his veins. His hopes nearly beyond containment, he studied them, lost in their unique beauty. They weren't what he'd thought. At least not in the traditional sense. These were different, broken in a sense. Calming himself, he cut down the next closest orc, hoping his actions would label him an ally. If these unknown creatures were hostile he needed to show them he was there to help. That was quite possibly the only way to escape with his life if things didn't go according to plan.

The last few orcs grouped together, trying to fend off their execution. They sloppily moved backward, trying to retreat into the field, but it was no use. There were too many of the pink-skins. They were surrounded. Nowhere to run, they fell to the tarnished, once elegant weaponry.

A strong gust of wind blew across the plains flinging Ravion's long, red hair about his face. He held his sword low, but at the ready to assure he meant no threat unless provoked. His beaming blue eyes were locked upon the remaining force.

They stared at the lone ranger, standing his defiance against them. He was brave to say the least, but likewise foolish. There was no way he could hold against so many, regardless of skill. They knew who he was. Just because they'd changed didn't mean their memories were robbed.

"Do you speak common?" Ravion asked. "My name is Ravion Santail, Dreuslayer and Co-founder of The Order. I'm afraid I've never seen your kind before, therefore I hope you won't take it as sign of disrespect if I refuse to lower my guard."

A beautiful woman stepped forward and took position at the head of the large group. She moved with such grace and elegance, her form never betrayed her. Standing midway between the formation and the lone combatant, she surveyed him from head to toe.

The dreuslayer watched the woman make her way toward him. Perhaps he'd be able to learn something about these people and their society. She was beautiful by all standards, her platinum hair pulled into a tail and hanging low down the back of her black, leather armor. She carried a polished, silver rapier on her side, and had a bow strung across her back. Ravion studied her for a brief moment, knowing she was doing likewise.

"We know who you are, Ravion. My name is Senaria. We're refugees. Our kind has been broken. Us few no longer sharing the beliefs of our ancestors. As outcasts, we seek a place to call home." Her voice was strong and unwavering. She spoke as a warrior, but had a soft harmony underlying the musical tone.

He studied her face. There it was again. That familiar trait he'd thought he saw earlier. Looking beyond her appearance, Ravion searched her energy. *There it is.* The light blue aura, like the one surrounding Kane, only this was brighter, unblemished. But these— creatures— they weren't like Kane. These were pure, not like the memories from his childhood. That was able to be seen without looking. These were a different kind of pure. Like something that once was, had returned to its former grace. They had to be dalari, didn't they? His mind raced with the possibility. If they were, that meant he was finally in position to rebuild their legacy. "Please don't take offense to this, but what are you?"

Senaria smiled briefly, considering his question. "We've chosen to call ourselves Mul'daron. The first of our kind." The answer, while accurate, wasn't what he meant. And she knew it.

"You said you're outcast from your people. What were you before?" Ravion didn't need to ask. The pieces clicked into place. But he needed her to confirm it.

Senaria shifted uneasily, unsure if she could trust the seemingly young human. Sighing heavily, she adjusted her stance. Trust had to start somewhere. And who better to trust than one that could possibly understand. Steeling herself, she spoke. "You knew us as dreualfar." Senaria froze, ready to defend herself if he attacked blindly. Seeing his reserve, she continued. "The corruption was pulled from us a few weeks ago. We fought to escape the catacombs, taking arms against those that weren't changed. We knew we couldn't remain among them, not that we'd want to. The taint was broken, and while we have the memories of the pain we've caused, we're no longer the enemy you've spent so many years battling."

Ravion heard her words. They were like a heavenly voice narrating a dream. He recited the ancient stories his father used to tell him. Both stories aligned into one truth. That meant he'd found what he was looking for. These mul'daron were the first of a new generation of dalari. Ravion sheathed his sword and looked upon her in a new light. A commanding and assured presence built inside him. "You have nothing to fear from me. If you'll accept, I'll guide you to a safe location where you can begin your lives without fear of persecution. It won't be a pleasant existence, but it'll be safe until you can find better accommodations for yourself."

Senaria considered his offer. He had the potential to aid them, his status alone was verification. But it was a huge risk. If she was mistaken in his intention, he could easily betray them. Was trusting him, a previous enemy of her kind, worth the possible extinction of her family? Glancing at several hundred homeless figures behind her, each one looking for guidance, she weighed the options. *I hope I'm right about him!* Turning back to Ravion, she stared him in the eye, offering silent warning. "Your assistance would be greatly appreciated."

A single arrow spun through the air, aimed for its target. The hardened-steel head struck with such ferocity it tore through the man's armor, sinking deep into his chest. Losing his footing he slammed into the reinforced wooden wall. He was dead before he hit the ground.

Over a dozen dreualfar roared from the shadows of the hidden cavern. They rapidly engulfed the unsuspecting guardsmen. Their green and black tabards sprayed red in the slaughter, leaving them to bleed out on the dirt covered road. The small band rushed through the unprotected gateway and into the incognizant city.

Lythus stepped through the opening, shoving his sword into the back of one of the defeated guards. The man went limp, crying out in his death throes. Hearing the horns echo in the distance, announcing their attack, Lythus sheathed his blade. "This way!"

Unaware of where they were going, the dreualfar followed. Never before had they dared enter the heart of the forbidden city. Such a thing was believed to be a death sentence. Yet this man, this masked figure, showed no fear of the dreuslayers or their tactics which had led to the deaths of so many. A number of guards charged toward them ready to reclaim the security of their beloved land.

The two groups crashed against one another, each holding their own. The dreualfar were out manned and out skilled, but they fought with a resolve that tested the commitment of their enemies. Uncaring if they fell in battle, they tore into the guards, claiming nearly three to one.

The masked rogue stood behind the dreualfar, watching the battle play out. They were little more than a tool at his disposal. Several were going to die here. There was no question of that. He didn't need them all anyway. But at least a few had to survive. Hearing the clank of chains in the distance, Lythus glanced to the west. The massive Dreuslayer Keep, perched at the mountain base was spewing soldiers through the heavy portcullis. That meant word had reached The Order. He was nearly out of time. If the army made it here, all of this planning would be for nothing. Returning his attention to the battle in front of him, Lythus quickly counted the fodder. Less than half remained. This had gone on too long. "Enough!" His voice carried over the battle, silencing both sides. All eyes on his, he drew his sword and stepped to the forefront.

The remaining dreualfar stepped back allowing their commander access.

The guards stood ready, unsure what was going to happen. Their eyes locked on the shadowed and pale orc skull covering the man's face. They permeated fear. It was one thing to battle the vile black-skins when they were being commanded by one of their own. Quite another when they didn't know who was commanding them. It made the entire situation unpredictable. Raising their weapons they readied to face the disguised man, hoping they could hold long enough for the border wardens to arrive.

Lythus smiled beneath his mask. These were the men chosen to keep the city safe? They're frightened little puppies, awaiting their master's protection. Silently drawing on the powers within himself, he flipped his sword around and raised it to the sky. A bright flash of blue and white erupted from the heavens. It jumped to the blade and split off shooting into the opposing men. He watched the static charge rip through their bodies, scorching them each time it exited. They collapsed on the well-kept road, unable to delay him any longer. "Come!" Refusing to wait a moment longer, Lythus he led the way along the eastern road, ignoring the cowering citizens and frightened merchants.

The roads turned from dirt to stone, both sides lined in staggered wooden posts. Every other one had a glass shield mounted to the top, an amber glow beaming from beneath. The lanterns didn't offer much in the daylight, but at night they lit the streets quite nicely. Street signs intersected occasionally, marking the way for visitors and traders. Each one displayed a carved trident, serving as a silent promise of protection inside the city. A promise that was currently being tested.

The dreualfar launched themselves at the few patrolling guards that approached. They were little more than a minor inconvenience in the grand scheme of things. The ring of battle died down leaving all the market guards dead or dying.

Lythus looked around at the defeated men. He had no doubt there would be more very soon, but he wasn't overly concerned. So long as he reached his destination before the army reached him there was nothing to fear. He glanced at the exhausted dreualfar. There was a sadistic pleasure in their eyes. As if they treasured their current trespass more than anything. It made sense. An assault against a group that specialized in the killing of their people had to be liberating. He just had to be careful. If he gave them too much reign they were likely to waste time on the townsfolk. That would do nothing but waste his time. And his time was too precious.

They rounded the market square and stepped into a fair-sized courtyard. The cobblestone street intersected another, leaving a large landing at the center where the road curved around. In the middle, several stones were stacked to form a large fountain with a perched dais at the center. Water sprouted from the top tier, splashing onto the stone ring, and trickling down to the lower levels. The reflective liquid left an emerald mist in the fading sunlight.

The dark cloaked figure approached the fountain and jumped onto the ledge. The crystal-clear water soaked into the back of his pant legs. Staring down at the gathered dreualfar, Lythus ensured he had enough to complete his task. Confident in their number he returned his attention to the fountain. "Circle around and get ready."

The dreualfar moved into position unsure what was going to happen.

Lythus reached beneath his cloak and drew a dagger. Kneeling into the water, he traced the edge of one of the stones and pried up. The transparent liquid filled the compartment almost instantly. Stashing the blade away, he peered into the hole, spotting the hidden lever at the bottom. Grabbing the metal handle, Lythus gave a light tug, feeling it click into place. The fountain rumbled to life shifting the base stones in a counter clockwise direction. The mid layer spun opposite, while the top tier stopped spouting water and dropped into the base.

The dreualfar watched nervously. The water drained from the pool revealing a series of tracks and gears hidden among the stone. One by one the molded granite slabs slid into place, revealing a spiraling stairway leading down.

"What are you waiting for? Let's go." Lythus jumped from his perch and rushed down the stair before the final stones had settled. Reaching the bottom, he stopped at a heavy, wooden door with several rings embedded in the face. Glancing back to make sure all the dreualfar were present, he returned his attention to the door and reached out, spinning the outer ring.

An echo of moving stone radiated in the narrow chamber. The dreualfar jumped, watching the stairway shift into a solid wall. No sooner than the passage closed fully the grinding resumed and the walls slowly moved toward them, threatening to crush anything in the room.

Lythus wrinkled his nose, smelling their fear in the enclosing space. *Cowards!* He quickly shifted the remaining rings, arranging them into the image of a large, jagged trident. The walls retracted and settled into place. A resounding click echoed on the other side of the door and it swung open to reveal a long tunnel. He marched into the dark path. The mounted basins ignited with each step, illuminating his way.

They passed several doorways and connecting tunnels. Lythus ignored them completely. There was no telling where they led, or how far they went. Some connected to the catacombs, some held other secrets. But discovering which was little more than a shell game in the underground labyrinth. Only his current path mattered.

Lythus made his way to the far end of the tunnel, approaching the final door. Quickly unscrambling the puzzle as he had upon their entry, it sprang open revealing a large room. The wall to his right was lined in barred cells. Many of them occupied by a number of dreualfar, orcs, and other creatures too dangerous to hold in the surface prisons. Even the occasional human rested comfortably in the underground jail. The center of the room was dished, forming a large ring. Training dummies made of wooden posts with simulated swords and shields were grouped around the edge. The left wall held an independent room with its own stairway leading up, and the far side of the room was sectioned off, sealed by a large, reinforced door and an odd-looking disc positioned over where the latch should have been.

"Free your kin if you must. When you're done meet me in the ring." Refusing to wait for them, Lythus marched across the room and approached the disc mounted to the sealed door. It had a faint aura surrounding it and five finger-sized holes embedded in the surface. Removing his glove, Lythus extended his peach colored fingers and pressed them into the holes. He felt the cold mineral ebb from his touch. The stone-like material started to glow a bright green. Twisting his wrist, the disc rotated and clicked into place. He pushed the door open and stepped inside. The exterior walls were lined with tables and shelves. Racks were fixed to the walls, displaying a variety of weapons. Upon the shelves a number of items rested peacefully. They were sectioned by type. One layer was stacked with runed chests, nearly locked against one another. One shelf was filled with books. Their multicolored bindings coated in dust from disuse. Numerous artifacts rested where they'd been laid gods knew how long ago. There was even a wooden divider organizing thousands of sealed scrolls and what appeared to be rare spell components.

Lythus made his way around the room, running his bare fingers over the placards, wiping away enough dust to read what they said. He found it amusing how many of the items were labeled 'Unknown'. He sighed. "Such is the way of pompous do-gooders, always claiming treasures they know nothing about." Rounding the isle, Lythus stopped, finding the treasure he'd been seeking. Reaching down, he held his hand over the finely crafted blade. He could feel the power within, yearning to be released. The dagger itself was made of a rare ore embedded with crystalline fragments. Very few knew of its existence. Even fewer had ever seen it. Recalling the mineral's history, he carefully grabbed the handle, ensuring the blade didn't contact his flesh. Looking over the room a final time, he made for the door.

Twice as many dreualfar stood in the center arena awaiting the fearful figure.

Lythus approached, glancing over at the empty cells. Not only had they freed all the dreualfar, they'd murdered the other prisoners, leaving them to bleed out on in the caged cells. It was no loss. This prison was for the special few that had no chance of rehabilitation, yet were too valuable to execute. They would never have seen this place otherwise. Lythus casually approached the group, unable to contain the smile beneath his mask. Stepping to their center, he reached into the pouch hidden beneath his cloak and retrieved the fist-sized emerald, once the crown jewel of Shadgull. He extended the gem, holding the crystalline dagger over the top. Several sparks of energy jumped from one to the other draining the color from the emerald. His fists shook, struggling to contain the power transfer. It took every ounce of strength to keep them in place, like trying to push two opposing pieces of magnetite together. Feeling the last bits of power transfer to the blade, he tossed the empty gem to the slate floor. It shatter into several fractured pieces of clear quartz and scattered across the pit. The enchanted blade glowed a deep purple, pulsing in the basin lit chamber.

The dreualfar stared in wonder and impatience. The power of the blade demanded their attention, but the lingering presence of their mortal enemies left them uneasy.

"Now for the final ingredient." Lythus smiled beneath the mask. Striking like a bolt of lightning, he sprang forward, slaughtering the assembled mass with the pulsating blade. Each death made it grow brighter. He watched the final dreualfar hit the ground, barely able to look upon the beaming weapon. The blackened skin of the bodies faded to a light pink, draining them of their identity. The weapon burned so brightly. He could feel it trying to penetrate his armor.

Holding the dagger away from him, Lythus pulled the straps of his bracer and exposed the tan colored skin beneath. Taking a deep breath, he chanted the spell. "Yawa nrub eht hsaw llahs luos sih, etas ot liaf I dluohs. Mrof siht ot em dnib nrub sti yam. Edalb yloh siht eubmi I ssenkrad htiw."

Without hesitation, Lythus pressed the tip against his flesh, hearing the sizzle burn deep into him. Screaming his torment, he fell to his knees, careful to keep the weapon in place. The corrupted magics wrapped around him, crawling beneath his skin. It felt as if his soul was being scorched, burnt beyond recognition. He strained against the pain feeling the magics take hold. Arm quivering, he struggled to finish. Breathing heavy, Lythus angled the tip and drug it through his charred meat to inscribe the rune.

Levi Samuel

Chapter III
The Bigger They Are

A thin layer of flaky rust covered the pitted, iron bars. Krenin's thick, green hands were locked around them watching the spectacle upon the other side. The large human straddled the defeated alfar. Reaching down he grabbed the agile creature's matted, brown hair. Lifting his head, the human drug his sword across the alfar's throat, cutting him to the spine. The dead creature dropped, his face slamming into the damp sand. Roars filled the air at the scene. They couldn't get enough blood to sate their appetite.

The half-orc released the bars, inspecting the red dust clinging to his skin. Wiping them together, Krenin turned and secured his twin axes. The keen weapons were polished to a shine. Sunlight gleamed on their edges. He'd grown fond of the weapons, forged from the great sword his brothers had given him. Krenin shook the memories from mind. They wouldn't serve him here. Staring at the light weight axes, he could nearly feel their desire for blood. The same desire the crowd craved.

Returning his attention to the arena, the thick chains clanked along the huge sprocket, raising the portcullis. He watched the human approach, his beady eyes locked on him. The man's bronze skin was shiny, partially from sweat, but it was more than that. He looked as if he'd been oiled from head to toe. His face bore no emotion, simply a lingering glare that burned into the half-orc's soul.

Krenin couldn't help but feel like the man wanted to lunge at him. It was a silent challenge. But they were both too smart to start anything outside of the sands. Krenin's eyes followed the man until he was out of sight. Returning his attention to the golden, blood soaked sands and,

Krenin marched up the ramp. The roar of orc cheers funneled into his ears. Guttural laughter and joy washed over him, a sense of bliss burning its way into his gut. He reached the center of the large stadium and threw his axes into the air, greeting his audience.

They erupted at his gesture, shouting their praise.

The portcullis clanked open on the far side of the arena. Krenin turned to see who he'd be fighting. It was always a surprise. If he could prepare it'd make the whole process much smoother, but as it were, they never knew until they took the sands. The gate stood wide open yet nobody passed.

The crowd grew restless, booing the absence of his opponent.

He had to do something. They were growing restless. Raising his axes once again, Krenin shouted, letting his words silence their chants. "Seems the mighty Krenin too scary for him. He hide in cell, pissing himself! These, the little things in life worth fighting for!"

Receiving his boasts, the crowd roared louder than ever. It was short lived. A massive quake echoed through the stands shaking the very ground beneath them. Locked in silent anticipation they stared intently at the large opening on the far side.

Krenin turned to face the monster slowly making its way onto the sands. How such a beast could even fit in the tunnels was a mystery in of itself. He could hear his heartbeat thundering away inside him. Not so much as a gasp could be heard from the spectators. Only the echoing footsteps of the approaching behemoth sounded. He'd never seen one of its type before. It was twice the size of the largest orc and drug what looked to be a huge club that may as well have been the lower section of a tree. Even the thick ridges along the sides and head reminded him of tree roots.

Processing the sight, Krenin saw the crowd in the corner of his eye. They returned to their usual, primitive selves though he couldn't hear them. Only the beat of the drum in his chest and the earth-shattering foot falls were audible. He was frozen in the sight. How could such a creature exist? He'd been told of all manner of beasts, many of which he'd never seen. But this one, this creature, it was something familiar but unknown. Memories flashed, recalling a specific book Ravion had been looking through. Krenin hadn't paid much attention at the time, but what he saw looked just like this massive beast. It was a mountain troll if memory served. Though what he saw in the picture was somewhat different. It had flesh of stone, where as this one had dark green skin and layers of moss for hair. If region named them it stood to reason, this was a forest troll.

Will to live growing, Krenin gripped his weapons, feeling his knuckles pop around the leather wrapped bindings. Taking a deep breath he prepared himself for the fight of his life.

The troll spotted the small orc in the center of the arena. As if it awoke its brutish nature, the beast let out an earth-shattering roar, drowning the echo of the crowd. Raising the tree-like club it charged.

Krenin let his rage grow, feeling each thundering quake barrel toward him. The sand hopped from the massive weight impacting it. His heart pounded in-time to the rhythmic beat. Watching the behemoth, Krenin waited for the perfect moment. *Now!* He broke position and charged straight toward the beast, releasing his own battle cry.

The thick club cut through the air as if it were moving in slow motion. A single impact was likely to kill him. The huge, wooden cudgel slammed down.

Krenin jumped just before it connected. He felt the wind from the impact rush around him. His feet landed atop the massive club, balancing ever so slightly. Refusing to wait a moment longer he charged up the weapon and jumped, bringing his axes around.

Chunks of blood-damped sand flew into the air. The troll saw the tiny orc in the air headed straight toward him. Bringing his hand up, it swatted the pest away, knocking him from the sky like a bee in search of pollen. The sharp edges of the chopping blades bit into his arm, shooting pain through his body. Anger on the rise, the troll ripped his weapon from the sand.

Krenin crashed into the sand. He had to have drawn blood, but it was too soon to tell. The swat came out of nowhere. Jumping to his feet, knowing he didn't have much time, Krenin searched for the creature. Fortune favored him. He was behind it. Heaving his axes he brought them down, sinking the blades into the troll's back. Bright-green blood erupted from the wounds, coating his weapons. Ripping them free, the back spray splattered across his face. The florescent spray was in deep contrast to his darker complexion.

The troll howled in pain, spinning around to find the tiny orc. Raising his club he reared back to crush the pest.

It moved much faster than he'd expected. Momentarily frozen at the sight, Krenin tried to move but couldn't. He was too close. Regaining control of his body the half-orc lunged, hoping to avoid the blow as best he could. The trunk-like club caught him in the side and launched him from his feet. Krenin felt the air rush from him. He couldn't breathe. Flying through the air his body popped painfully. No doubt his ribs were broken. He landed roughly on the arena floor, momentum carrying him through the wet sand. Every part of him hurt, but it told him he was still alive. Though if he didn't get up he wouldn't be much longer. Forcing himself to his feet, Krenin spit the sand from his mouth and exhaled in short, rapid breaths trying to control himself. Adrenaline pumping, the damage hadn't fully registered. It would keep him going a while longer, but it did little for the pain. His muscles tensed and his bones cracked. Taking his first deep breath, Krenin forced his eyes to remain open. Turning to find the troll, he spotted his axes lying in the sand where he'd been standing.

The troll watched the little orc fall to his back several steps away. To his surprise, it got back to its feet. Roaring his anger, the forest troll spat his twisted words at the orc. "Pu kcab teg dna tih Rakuu's ekat ot elba cro ynit woh?"

Krenin forced the pain aside. Clearing his head of all distractions he recited Malakai's words. "A distracted mind is a dead mind." He had to get his weapons if he was going to survive. "Don't know what you say and don't care. You going to die!"

The troll approached the defiant orc, raising his club to finish the job. There was no way he could withstand another hit.

Krenin felt the shadow engulf him long before the brute reached striking distance. He glared at the ugly, green head silhouetted in bright sunlight. It made it difficult to see anything, but it was better than being completely blinded. Watching the club raise, ready to deliver its final blow, Krenin readied himself.

The crowd fell silent, awaiting the fate of the half-breed. He'd done so much to bring them entertainment. It would be a shame for him to fall. But that was the life of a gladiator. Some would win big from his death, others would go into debt. It was orcish politics in the north. Had the lesser races known the true extent of their ambitions there was no way they'd think them nothing but muscled brutes.

Waiting for the right moment, Krenin kept his eyes on the beast. He might die, but that day would not be this one. The club rocketed toward his head. Diving between the troll's legs, he ignored his pain at all cost. Throwing every ounce of strength into a single blow Krenin slammed his shoulder into the creature's crotch. The club slammed down, showering sand atop of them both.

Rakuu cried out in pain. Dropping the club, he grabbed himself, hoping to dull the throbbing ache.

The axes were too far away. There was no doubt of that. Searching for option, Krenin spotted the embedded club. He couldn't lift it even on his best day. Out of choices he spun around and jumped on the troll's back throwing his arms around it's midsection as best he could. His arms weren't quite long enough to lock his grip, but perhaps he could hold on long enough to do some damage. Squeezing as hard as he could, Krenin felt several pops in his insides. An unbearable pain exploded in his side. He couldn't tell if it was more of ribs breaking or the already broken ones resetting. It didn't matter. It hurt. Holding his breath to keep from passing out, he squeezed. He had to weaken the beast if he was going to survive.

Feeling the orc latch onto him, Rakuu forced his composure. He wasn't sure how he was going to get him off. He was just at that spot that always itched, but was just out of reach. And there was no way grab his arms. Troll joints were too stiff to bend that far. He could try to fling him off or he could crush him under his weight. But squishing him was dangerous. The tiny orc had already proven it was faster. And there was no telling what kind of tricks it would try to play if they were on the ground. A decision made, Rakuu flailed about, trying to throw the orc off of him. It was no use. He was attached too well. Howling his frustration, a rush of anxiety flooded him with the unwanted growth.

Krenin strained to keep his hold. He was growing tired and his grip was slipping. If the beast kept spinning, he was going to fall. Running out of time he scanned for his axes. They were close, but still out of reach. Out of options he buried his face in the creature's arm pit. The stench made him want to vomit, but it was nothing compared to what he was about to do. Opening his mouth, he bit into the soft flesh of its underarm, ripping his head from side to side. Bright green blood erupted in his mouth, filling it as he tore a chunk of flesh away. It tasted nearly as bad as it smelled. Spitting the meat and fat to the sand, an oily film clung to his mouth.

Unable to get away, the troll roared in pain. He couldn't sooth the hole in his arm, not while the orc had ahold of him. Lost in panic, Rakuu charged toward the side wall. If he could smash him against it, he'd be free. Anxiety urging him, Rakuu tripped over the thick, wooden club and slammed face first into the sand.

Feeling gravity shift, Krenin saw his chance. Letting go, he rolled away from the troll, letting him fall in solitude. Rushing over, he snatched up his axes and spun around hoping he could finish the beast before it could rise.

Rakuu rolled to his side to sooth his underarm. He could feel the edge of the torn area at the tips of his calloused fingers. Careful to keep sand out of the wound, he pushed against the blood-soaked ground to pick himself up.

Krenin charged. Jumping as high as he could, the keen edges ready to strike deep. Landing on the troll's back, it buckled under the unexpected weight. Letting loose, Krenin swung hard, burying blades of death into the beast's neck.

A sharp pain cut into the base of his skull. Rakuu tried throwing his attacker from him, but it was too late. The second axe found its mark. All strength fled him and he collapsed in the tingling numb.

Krenin stood atop the dying troll. His fists were locked around the submerged axes. The first was embedded in its spine, the second stuck between the vertebrae passing straight through the flesh and bone. The troll's head fell from its shoulders, bouncing on the sand before coming to rest a few feet away. A pool of bright green ichor leaked out, soaking into the already moist ground.

The crowd erupted in cheers, amazed by the battle they'd just witnessed.

Krenin plucked his embedded axe free and tried to raise them in victory. They were so heavy. Exhausted and full of pain, he felt them slip from his grip. The heads sank into the churned sand. Abandoning them, he weakly marched toward the portcullis. He needed rest, and gods willing, a healer.

A gentle breeze caressed the waist-high stalks of dancing, brown wheat. It was a calming roar, one that went unnoticed unless listened for. Agonizing screams echoed through the crack in the air, filling the open plainlands with their despair. A shimmering orange tear appeared, ripping apart the fabric of reality. It widened, allowing room for a single figure to pass.

Perrimen stumbled through the magic vortex, tripping against the tall grass. Pulling himself up he pushed through, clenching the mask sealed against his face. "How could I have failed? It wasn't my fault. I couldn't stop it!" A trampled path followed in his wake. Struggling against the latched appendage the voices echoed their retort, taunting his already fragile sanity. *You failed! He's coming! Why didn't you stop him?*

Unable to take the abuse, Perrimen dug his fingers beneath the edge, hoping to dislodge the source of his torment. His head throbbed against the echoing chorus, refusing to abandon him. His nails cut into his jaw line, but he found the nearly seamless edge. Forcing every ounce of will into a single cognitive purpose, the aged wizard pried it from his skin. "It wasn't— my— fault!"

The golden shroud peeled away, growing easier in passing moment. The voices silenced, leaving him to himself. The red and blue tendrils atop his head shriveled and disappeared. His brown duster faded away leaving the tattered robes of white and gold in its place. Tightening his hand into a fist, Perrimen forced his body to obey for the first time in as long as he could remember. Free of the controlling power he felt a vulnerability in himself. One he'd never noticed before. He was a weak old man. While his years of study trained him in the arcane arts, making him one of the most power magi in Dalmoura, it was a candle compared to the sunlight the mask provided.

Dropping to his knees, he stared into the reflected sunlight feeling the rays upon his face. The relevance was not lost on him. Perrimen tensed, accepting the sudden freedom bestowed upon his broken mind. It was a blessing and a curse. To be free meant responsibility, which in itself was a prison. The truth was there was no such thing as true freedom. Only shades of an illusion. True freedom was true chaos. The question became how much was it worth? He glanced at the wicked kris tucked into his waistline. Drawing the blade he could feel the darkness within, begging, pleading, asking to be used. Were he inexperienced in resisting such temptations he had no doubt the blade would have claimed him as its next victim. Stuffing the weapon back in the sash he exhaled, letting his stress fade away. The wind embraced him, gently caressing his face. A shadow in the back of his mind demanded attention. Acknowledging its presence, the realization of his actions hit him. "He's coming! I need to let the tower know."

Sighing deeply, Perrimen pushed himself up, decided in his future. Turning west, he pressed the mask against his face, letting it thrust its freedom upon him once again. The golden, expressionless cover enveloped his head completely, locking itself to him. The red and blue tendrils sprung with force, resuming their ever-seeking dance. His clothing shifted, reverting back into the brown, leather duster, covering clothing he couldn't see, but clearly felt. He knew what needed to be done, but he couldn't do it like this. As if his thought were command, the duster morphed, taking a fluid like appearance. His gold and white robes returned, though not the tarnished and stained one he'd been wearing. These were long and elegant, seemingly new. The power flowed through them like a sheet of water in constant flux around his body. The mask and cap faded into him, revealing his round, freshly shaven face, and shoulder-length hair, groomed and sun-faded brown. His receded hairline left a slight peak in the center of his aged face, though the years of his youth returned.

Knowing where he needed to go, the wizard took a single step toward his destination. The orange crack appeared and, as quickly as he'd arrived, he was gone.

Stepping from the swirling energies, Perrimen marched through the arched doorway ignoring the guards posted on either side. Passing through the reception hall, he didn't bother looking at the decor. It hadn't changed in centuries. Such admirations belonged to apprentices and visitors. Ignoring the receptionist, he stepped into the teleportation shaft and pictured the destination in his mind. The magic swirled around him. Turning around, Perrimen marched into an expansive chamber filled with tomes and scrolls as far as the eye could see.

"Perrimen?" Uirial asked, rushing over to take his brother's hand.

"I've come to warn you. The corruption has been released. It's already begun to spread into the realm. The tower will not be around much longer."

Uirial paused, studying his brother's face. He'd been gone over a decade, yet his youth had reversed. Something was different about him, but it was clearly him. The fact he'd been able to enter the chamber without summons was proof enough. "Brother, tell me. How'd you come by this knowledge? When last we spoke, your mind was broken from the weight of the crown."

"I'm not here to talk about my time as baron!" Perrimen snapped, slamming his fist down on a pile of books. It was no wonder The Tower's reputation had diminished over the years. They always over analyzed everything instead of taking immediate action. "Something must be done. I can feel the tendrils lashing out, wrapping themselves around the base stones. You must act!"

The magnis looked his aged brother up and down. "You don't feel like yourself. But I've learned enough to know when to take your advice and when to turn cheek. I will do as you ask." Uirial placed his hand against his brother's shoulder, giving him a reassuring pat. "I'll look into the oculus. Perhaps I'll be able to find this corruption before it sets in. He released the elder mage and turned toward the shaft. Spinning around, he took in his brother's sight once again. "Perrimen, I'm glad you're back. This place hasn't been the same without you." Uirial disappeared in the swirling tunnel.

Wasting no time, Perrimen pulled the hidden dagger and laid it upon the table. Running his hand over the wavy edge he closed his eyes, focusing his energies. An image came to him. An image of a man familiar, yet concealed. "He's in Krondar!" Snatching the dagger, he stuffed it away, allowing the dark torrent to surround him. Energies spinning, Perrimen vanished.

Chapter IV
Chosen Regrets

The air was warm with a musky scent. Though he'd been in it so long he couldn't note the difference anymore. Exhausted and out of breath Gareth opened his eyes, looking up at the ceiling overhead. Several chisel marks told the story of when the tunnel had been carved. Tiny droplets of water had eroded it in places leaving long jagged columns hanging down, threatening him. The slightest tremor could dislodge any one of them, spearing into his body. Shaking the thoughts of doom from his mind, Gareth took a deep breath, feeling the compressed clay beneath him. Summoning his strength, he rolled over and pushed himself up.

Crawling to the underground pond, Gareth scooped the dark water into his hands. Staring at the reflection looking back at him, he hated the visage. It was him, he knew that much, but he was dark and twisted. The vile beasts he'd sworn to exterminate stared back at him. Not just one, but all of them. He was haunted by their corruption. Closing his eyes, Gareth forced the image from his mind. Bringing the collected water to his mouth he sucked it in, washing the dry, gravely film away. The cool liquid soothed his throat, pouring down his esophagus. He felt it hit his stomach like an explosion. Pain shot through him, convulsing his innards. Instinctively he clenched his midsection, hoping to somehow control the fluctuating pain inside him. He hadn't even felt the impact of falling over. Curled up, cradling himself, the hunger pains began to fade.

Gareth took a deep breath, exhaling through his nose. It seemed to calm him. Pulling himself upright he scooped another handful and anxiously swallowed, hoping it wouldn't react as it had before. He sucked the water down, glad it went smoothly. Slowly having his fill, Gareth hoped it would sate him until he could find some food.

Staring into his twisted reflection, he couldn't see past the caked blood. It had grown crusty with the addition of dirt. Dipping his hands into the cold water, he quickly washed himself, careful not to reopen the gash over his eye. The water stung, but it felt good to clean the area. He felt as if it returned a small amount of his humanity. Probing the swollen skin around the wound, he was certain infection hadn't yet set in. As best he could tell, the skin yellow, and it wasn't warm with fever. He hated to admit it, but he was already getting use to its loss. His perception was shot, but he was adjusting much better than he would have predicted. It seemed his other senses were compensating for its loss.

Gareth grabbed the stolen satchel, pulling it to him by the dirty strap. Flipping it open he peered at the black book within, unsure if he should look upon it again. It was clearly not meant for him. Such power could take him down an even darker path than the one he was already on. Yet he was drawn to it. There was something inside that called to him. Unable to deny it any longer, Gareth pulled the shimmering binding free and opened to the center pages. They were blank as ever, refusing to display the smallest detail. "So we're going to do this shit again?" Reaching across himself, he squeezed the wound in his shoulder, forcing the broken skin to split just enough to seep. Securing a droplet on the tip of his finger, he wiped it on the page, watching it dissolve before he could remove his finger.

The page sprang to life, displaying the markings he'd already skimmed. Their meaning was lost upon him, but he didn't mind. Deep down he didn't want to know what it said. Knowledge was power and power corrupts. He had enough corruption in his life. There was no sense in adding more. Content that the words were still available to him, that he hadn't imagined them, Gareth closed the book and stuffed it into the leather bag. Pulling himself to his feet, he shook the water from his beard, letting the tiny streams run into his torn tunic. He threw the strap over his ruined shoulder and turned to find his way out.

Echoing footsteps bounced off the walls, sounding an alarm to his safety. Spinning around, Gareth listened for them, trying to find their source. He wasn't sure how many boots there were, the echoes distorting their number. But they were clearly growing louder which meant they were getting closer. He focused on them, trying to extend his reach. Calm, collected drums rang in his ears. Several sets echoed in his mind. *Why would they be sounding drums down here?* He'd never heard war drums quite like them. Almost as if they were— heartbeats! The realization hit him. If what he was hearing was indeed their heartbeats, they had to be much closer then he'd realized. Using what little time he had, Gareth stepped against the cavern wall and held his breath. Focusing every ounce of will into the action he calmed himself, feeling his own heart slow to a near stop. If he could hear them it made sense they would be able to hear him. Waiting for his prey to show itself, Gareth clenched his fist, letting his hatred for the dreualfar fuel him.

A lone sentry stepped into view. He was surprised by its appearance. It knelt beside the river and dipped a waterskin into the slow flowing current.

Gareth paused, looking upon the faint blue aura surrounding the creature. It was hidden beneath the surface, but plainly present. He had no doubt, had he not been studying the beast, he wouldn't have seen it. It's a trick. It had to be. Only Ravion had what he was seeing. The dreu were deceiving him. It'd be plain as day if they were not. "You black-skinned bastards can't fool me that easily!" Gareth charged forward and locked his arms around the deceptive dreualfar. Refusing to give the others time for attack, he sank his teeth into the creature's neck, tearing at the exposed arteries. Dark red blood exploded in his mouth coating it in the sweet, coppery substance.

The mul'daron screamed his pain, unable to escape the crazed dreuslayer. His cries were muffled by the thick, clenching hand over his face.

Gareth ripped free the chunk of flesh and spit it into the water. Covering the creature's mouth, he grabbed the back of its head and twisted hard. The snaps echoed out leaving a blank, fearful expression staring back at him. Gareth slowly lowered the body, hoping he'd silenced him before the others heard the screams. His hopes were short lived, seeing several others step into sight and rush toward him. Setting his feet, Gareth threw his hands up, ready to fend off the approaching aggressors. "I don't care how you've disguised yourselves, you can't fool me. It's death you seek and I'm happy to oblige."

Gareth clenched his fist, his knuckles popping in protest. Rage coursed through his body watching the deceptive creatures surround him. He felt alive, more alive than he'd felt in a long time. It was as if somehow his rage had manifested around him, protecting him. He didn't feel hunger, nor pain. In the blink of an eye the broken warrior was rejuvenated, ready to fight to the last breath.

Bringing his fist around, Gareth punched the closest creature. He felt the blood spray long before he realized what happened. The creature collapsed at his feet, its head cut in half from the defensive blow.

The other mul'daron slowed, unsure how to proceed against the dangerous dreuslayer. Watching him closely they inched forward, hoping to stay out of reach.

Gareth's face contorted in surprise as much as his attacker's. *How'd I do that?* Noticing their concern, he realized he had a few moments to figure out what it was and, with luck, how to do it again. Glancing at his clenched fists, blood and brain fluid clung to the blade-like appendages protruding from them. He studied the transparent weapons for a brief moment. They were unlike anything he'd seen before. Even the few dreuki that used similar weapons didn't have anything quite like this. Running his thumb along the edge, he felt the keen blade threaten to slice his flesh. A wicked smile broke, exposing his blood-soaked teeth. "Who wants the other eye?" Gritting his teeth, Gareth stepped into the fray, swinging the unexpected weapons wildly.

Fear and confusion radiated from the group. Using anything they could to deflect the invisible swords, they closed in on him in a desperate attempt to subdue the wild man.

Gareth spun around, punching and slashing. He could feel the unseen blades cutting into his opponent as if they were a part of him. Every block, deflection, and hit felt as if they were against his arms, though it didn't hurt. It was more a feeling of pressure than pain. Trusting his new-found weapons would protect him, Gareth pushed onward, cutting them down. His rage poured into each strike, delivering one lethal blow after another.

The bodies piled around him but there were many more to add. Gareth deflected a strike from one of the crude swords, opening up its wielder. Stepping into the creature's threat range he slashed in, cutting it in half. He felt great, but his hatred was quickly waning. Each death sated his blood lust, draining him a little more. He felt the blades weaken, their power nearly diminished.

"No!" Gareth screamed, forcing himself to push harder in a vain attempt to refuel his rage. He saw one of the rust colored scimitars headed for him. Throwing his arm up to block the potentially deadly attack he felt it connect, slowing the blade slightly. His ethereal weapon shimmered and dissipated, leaving him defenseless. *How was that possible? Where'd they go?*

The slowed scimitar bit into his shoulder, crippling him. Gareth dropped to his knees, unprepared for the painful strike. Panting heavily, he glared up at the swarming beasts, their pink colored flesh unable to fool him. "I may die this day. But I'm taking you bastards with me!" Gritting his, Gareth lunged forward, hoping to get his hands on as many of them as possible. Punching, biting, kicking, scratching— nothing was beneath him in his final moments. He watched helplessly as his unarmed fist smashing weakly into their armored forms. Out of breath and exhausted, he tumbled forward and fell to the cavern floor. He couldn't move. Was he poisoned? Why was he so exhausted? It didn't feel like the dreuki venom. This was worse. Unable to pick himself up, Gareth collapsed, feeling his heavy eyelid threaten to close. He tried to fight it, tried to stay awake, but it was no use. He had to sleep. Darkness overcame him. He felt as if we were floating. He was all alone, no one to comfort him. Nothing but shadow in the night. He was lost in an eternal void. Not even his thoughts would answer him.

Staring at the unconscious warrior, the mul'daron inched forward, unsure if it was some kind of rouse. One of the creatures broke through the ranks. It took a long look at the bodies piled around the lone man. "Bind him. We've lost too many already. When he wakes, I don't want a repeat of what happened here." The mul'daron turned, leaving the soldiers to obey his command.

They carefully wrapped the ropes around the dreuslayer's wrists pulling them together. Locking them behind his back, the secured him, assuring the mysterious weapons would not be used against them again. Every limb bound, they lifted the deadly dreuslayer and carried him off.

A cool breeze passed through the trees rattling branches and leaves alike. The sun was fading fast, leaving more shadow than anything in the dwindling vibrant light. Two horses waited patiently, tied to the hitching post planted at the camp's edge. Upon a wooden bench made of split cedar, a young noble sat, picking his fingernails with his dagger. Another stoked the fire in the center of the rock ring.

"Are you sure you want to go through with this?" The stockier man asked, poking at the embers. He wore a black cloak over his heavy iron breastplate. A shield rested across his back and a sheathed longsword hung from his hip, scratching at the dirt from the awkward angle. He wore no identifying colors, save for a small sash of blue and green concealed beneath the heavy cloak.

"I wouldn't be here if I didn't. We need change. My father is too blinded by duty to see that." Erik stuffed his dagger away, straightening his cloak. Like his armored companion, he wore all black, concealing his identity as best he could. Adjusting against the smoothed bench, Erik let out an annoyed sigh. Glancing at the fading sun, he wondered how much longer it would be. It disappeared behind the trees signaling the final minutes of daylight.

"And change you shall have!" An unfamiliar voice echoed from the shadows, chilling them to the bone.

Both Erik and Jem jumped, searching the shadows. Hands resting upon weapons, awaiting cause to draw, they couldn't find to whom the words belonged.

"Show yourself!" Erik demanded.

A dark figure appeared in the flickering firelight not a foot from where the young price had been. The red and yellow glow danced across a pale white face, shaped like that of an orc, but lacking flesh. "There's no need to fret. If I intended to kill you, you'd already be dead."

Jem held fast, keeping his hand on his sword. If this figure tried anything he'd fight to the last breath. "My Lord, can you trust him?"

Erik ignored the question. Releasing his swords, he took a step toward the masked man. "You're the one that sent me the message about the dagger?"

"Indeed, I am. Have you brought what I requested?"

The young prince reached under his cloak and pulled a small, leather bag dyed blue. The top was tied together by a pieced of green lace. Holding it up for the man to see, Erik continued. "I have. And do you have what I need?"

Lythus studied the young man for a moment. He was confident for his age, though that trait wasn't uncommon in humans. They had a certain arrogance in their upbringing. More defined in those of status than the common man. The boy had trained all his life, and no doubt he was skilled with his blades, but he lacked a certain creativity. "I have what you seek. Though I warn you, your path requires great sacrifice. Are you sure you're ready for such burden?"

Jem stepped forward to whisper into his commander's ear. "My Lord, I've heard rumors of this man. He can't be trusted."

Erik raised his hand, silencing the young knight. "What price can be too great for the protection of my lands?"

"Very well." Lythus reached under his cloak and retrieved a rolled scroll. The edge was sealed by black wax and bore a generic stamp in the center. Tossing the parchment to the young nobleman's feet he patiently awaited his payment.

Erik tossed the sack to the masked man and bent to retrieve the scroll, keeping his eyes locked on the figure.

Catching the bag, Lythus bounced it a few times, weighing the contents. Stuffing it under his cloak, he returned his attention to the two men. "Remember my warning. Even for a kingdom, some prices are too high. You've made that choice for yourself." The fire flared up, throwing several sparks into the night sky.

Erik and Jem searched the darkness for the figure, but he was nowhere to be seen.

Returning his attention to the parchment, Erik broke the seal and unrolled the scroll. Gaze locked, his eyes danced upon the words written within.

My dear young noble of Shadgull,

The dagger occupying your obsession is forged of a power greater than your comprehension. To wield it would be to lose yourself. I understand your desire to obtain it, however I'm afraid it's currently beyond even my reach. Until it changes hands, and it will, it always does, it's a fool's errand. But I'm a man of my word. You asked for a power to help you turn the tide and ensure the survival of your lands. I offer you just that.

When your wall was created, during the first Dreu War, the base stones were enchanted with a power unlike any other. At the same time several runestones were buried throughout Dalmoura. Their system as a whole acted as a barrier against the very magics that created it. This is what has kept the wall intact all these years despite the numerous battles it's faced. Unfortunately for your people the wall has been fractured. The magic has faded and left you open for attack. The very magics that currently tear your lands apart are the same ones that once protected it. If you're to save your people you must restore the stones to their former glory. But I'm afraid it's something you cannot do at this point in time. Only the one true baron has the power to restore the ancient runestones and stabilize the network. If you achieve that status, take the crown to the site known as Heroes Gate. In the center of the archway you'll know what you have to do. Good luck in your endeavors.

Lythus the Black

"Son of a bitch!" Erik crumpled the message and tossed it into the fire.

"What is it, My Lord? What'd it say?" Jem studied his commander's face, unsure what unnerved him so much.

"It's next to useless. It said I can't get the dagger right now but offered a consolation that's still out of my reach. Only the 'one true baron' can restore the magics that protect us."

"I suppose that's better than nothing. Did it say what the baron has to do?"

Erik plopped down on the bench. It creaked under the sudden weight. Running his fingers through his dirty-blonde hair, he buried his face in his hands. "The crown has to be taken to the center of Heroes Gate. It says I'll know what to do from there."

"Well, you're not at a total loss. Perhaps you can convince your father to ride to Heroes Gate. I'm sure he'd be more than receptive if you explain it to him."

"Have you met my father? He doesn't believe magic should be used in such a way. He thinks all battles can be won from the tip of a sword. I fear he won't act until it's too late."

Jem approached and sat down next to his friend. "My Lord, if I may speak freely?" He stated more than asked. "Your father is a wise and noble man. I'm sure he has his reasons for believing the way he does. But I believe you underestimate his faith in you. If you give him a chance, I'm sure he'll come around, as I have."

Erik looked upon the man in charge of his protection. The two had grown up together, Jem being named his guardian when they were toddlers. Smiling, Erik released his worries. "All setbacks aside, I'm fortunate to have a friend as loyal as you."

Levi Samuel

Chapter V
The Price of Trust

Several basins hovered near the wall of the underground chamber, dimly lighting the room. The red brick and mortar was free of dirt and moss. Unlike the other chambers of The Tower, this one was exceptionally well organized. Despite its small appearance, book shelves stretched on as far as the eye could see, leaving nothing out of place.

Uirial crossed the threshold, watching the basins flare upon his approach. The arch-magus paused, feeling the darkness around him. Searching its source, he knelt beside the entryway and inspected the cornerstone. It was deep-red, nearly black in color. Running his fingers along the odd stone he stood, clearly disturbed by his findings. "Scigam enivid fo noitpurroc!" His words boomed through the seemingly small chamber, echoing in their ferocity.

The shelves sprang to life, moving throughout the room. Coming to rest, a collection of tomes dismounted and landed in a stack on the central table. It was free of dust, a silver candelabra resting peacefully in the corner. The tiny flames burned bright, roughly halfway down the melted stick. Yet the strands of wax held fast refusing to drip beyond their current position.

The arch-magus marched toward the table, waving his hand. The books flipped on end and floated out around him, displaying their ancient covers. He ran his hand over each one, skimming the contents without opening the pages. Deciding which was worthy of his attention, Uirial gestured.

Three of the books returned to the table while the others flew across the room, retaking their positions upon the shelfs.

Uirial opened the first tome, scanning the scribed words within. The ink was smudged in places from where a heavy hand had lingered a bit too long. But overall the script was fluid and neat. Taking in the words, no telling how long they'd been recorded, he read on searching for the knowledge he sought. One passage in particular caught his interest.

"—and the breaking of slaves will bring forth the agents of shadow. For they are known, not through their visage, but by their actions. And on that day, the strands of corruption will lash out and engulf any who stand opposed!"

Uirial looked up from the book feeling an unnatural cold brush across him. Watching the steam roll from his breath, the magical lamps flickered, like a torch in heavy wind. His gaze shifted to the basins, hovering not far. Never, in all his time as arch-magus, had he seen them react is such a manner. "Something's not right!" He whispered to himself. "Books, away!" He commanded.

The heavy tomes flew from the table, rejoining their brethren upon the shelves.

"Laever suluco!"

A swirling orb, nearly a foot in diameter, shimmered into existence floating over the table. Storm clouds rolled inside the white opal casing keeping it in constant motion.

Uirial held his hands on either side of the oculus, careful not to touch it. There was no telling what would happen if one such as he connected with the eye. At the very least he feared eternal sight. That was a curse he didn't wish on the greatest of adversaries. "Show me the source of the corruption."

The clouds darkened, swirling inside their housing. They grew black as night blocking out all sight.

Unable to see the details he rephrased his request. "Show me the dangers of which my brother spoke."

Thousands of images flashed into view, not lingering more than a brief moment on any single one. The arch-magus felt his eyes strain against the sights, unable to fully comprehend any of them. Incapable of taking anymore, Uirial closed his eyes letting the oculus return to its idle state. Unanswered questions filled his mind, dampening his senses.

Forcing a single question to the surface, he looked upon the orb once more. "Show me who corrupted the base stones."

A figure appeared in the clouds, shrouded in darkness. The image began to clear, burning away the shadow with a beaming breastplate with a coiled dragon on the belly.

Uirial already knew the answer, but he had to be certain. "Who is this man, this visage of the High Templar?"

The clouds rolled, as if they were searching for the answer. The arch-magus wasn't surprised. He knew Kane. He was an honorable man who would never willingly serve the shadow. Such a response could only mean one thing. He wasn't himself. Looking deep into the cloud, he asked more directly. "Who controls the High Templar's body?"

Quicker than he could finish the final word, the clouds rolled black, slithering inside the casing like a giant serpent. Uirial felt something brush his bright red robes. He glanced down seeing a thick tendril of black and purple shoot out, wrapping itself around his legs. He hit the floor, air escaping his lungs. Another tendril shot from the wall surrounding his midsection. The vise-like grips tightened around him. Time was running out and he didn't have anything available to protect himself. If he could reclaim his breath he could use his stronger magics. Simple parlor tricks wouldn't do much to help him against such darkness.

The corruption drug him toward the wall, pulling him into the pitch-black stones. Nearly half devoured, Uirial's skin began to harden. The tainted power was seeping into him. He was running out of time. Forcing what breath he could, he shouted what was possibly the last spell he'd ever chant. "Rewot eht morf sgnieb lla tropelet! Rewot eht morf sgnieb lla tropelet!" He had to be certain the spell took hold. The loss of a single life was too high a price. "Rewot eht morf sgni—" His words were cut short from another tendril wrapping itself around his face. All but his upper torso remained outside the wall.

His skin took the texture of stone, graying and marbling, cracking where the tight lasso constricted. His time was up. If the tower was going to survive this it would have to do so on equal ground. The corruption had penetrated too deep in this land. There was no saving it if it remained. A tower of darkness would do nothing but corrupt the people it was sworn to protect. He couldn't allow that. Abandoning all fight, Uirial retreated inside himself, letting his battle become an internal one.

The arch-magus body was yanked fully into the wall, only his face remaining on the surface. The darkening skin shifted, claiming the red of the tower's stone walls. His eyes opened one final time to look upon the room of archives. "Eno emoceb I, htaed ym yb!"

Hundreds of confused magi picked themselves up, staring at the crumbling outer walls. The main structure ripped itself from the earth, taking the sub levels with it. Several blackened stones, trimmed in red, shifted their position reforming into multiple stilts. As if it were alive, the suspended tower turned toward the west and started walking, careful not the step on the helpless bystanders at its base. With unnatural speed it was gone, leaving only the churned dirt and broken walls where it had been.

The fading sun made the brown fields seem to stretch forever. In truth it wasn't so much of an illusion. Krondar was largely open field with small patches of forest. The only real exception was the southeastern mountains separating them from the coast.

Ravion could see the tall, snow cover peaks in the distance. He hadn't spent much time in the mountains, but he knew enough to navigate them. It was one of the many things he'd learned about the land in his search for the catacombs. Turning to look upon the army of mul'daron behind him, he approached their leader. "My Lady, Senaria." He offered a slight bow, showing respect to her position.

"You know you don't have to formally greet me each time we speak. I was forged in battle, I'd appreciate the same courtesy you'd give to any other soldier."

"Understood, My Lady." Ravion started to bow once again, catching himself. "We're about a day's travel from the base of the mountains. Given your desire for discretion, I'd advise we march through the night and reach them by morning. I believe I know of an abandoned fortress that would serve your needs until we can find you better accommodations."

Senaria paused for a moment, considering his words. "I appreciate your concern, but my men are tired. They need to rest. And I for one have spent too much of my life living in darkness. I want to travel by day." She turned, addressing the hundreds behind her. "We make camp. Break into groups of ten. Bury your fires and tend your needs. I expect each group to assign a watch. Get some rest. We move at first light."

The mul'daron broke into smaller groups and began setting up tarps, while others went to work digging fire pits.

Ravion watched the small groups spread out to provide the most protection for the camp as a whole. Several of the soldiers marched off into the night, taking bows and spears with them. He was surprised at how well organized they were. Those were skills that took a great leader and years of training to master, yet these people acted as if they'd live this way their entire lives. He wasn't sure how much time he'd lost in the catacombs, but one thing was certain, it wasn't long enough for these people to develop their skills from nothing. They'd either worked together long before the breaking or there was more to their story that Senaria wasn't telling him. He guessed the latter, but it wouldn't be polite to openly ask. Not that she owed him answers in the first place. After all, he clearly wasn't going to tell his own secrets. At least not yet.

Senaria pulled a large tarp from the bottom of her pack and unrolled it. Stretching it out across the dry grass she held her hands out, channeling the energies into the thick canvas. It expanded, growing in height and taking the form of a small house. She connected the corner posts and tied it off, ensuring it would remain against any strong winds.

Ravion was a bit surprised by her trick. It was no surprise she possesses magic, it was something all his kind were born with. But its use required training. That was something he had never had. Sure he could do a few small incantations like healing a minor wound or connecting with the plants of a small area to find the location of something he was tracking, but that was nothing compared to what she had just done. That kind of magic required training, yet he was sure she was a swordswoman. Shaking the thoughts from his mind, he found a small shrubbery and took a seat next to it. He wasn't fully trusting of these new people yet and it was best to keep a wary eye open throughout the night.

47

Approaching footsteps roused him from his sleep. Keeping his eyes mostly closed to avoid suspicion, Ravion squinted from beneath his lids. He saw a pair of brown, leather boots standing before him. Refusing to allow time for an unwarranted attack, he sprung up and drew his dagger. The blade connected with the mul'daron's throat, edge pressing firmly into skin. A trickle of blood rolled from the shallow would, disappearing beneath his tunic.

The man stared back at him, a look of uncertainty on his face. Carefully considering what actions would result from the outcome of his predicament he spoke, feeling the blade's edge against his windpipe. "Shhh! Don't draw suspicion!" The mul'daron calmly spoke, just over a whisper.

Ravion pulled the blade away, but kept it ready. Taking a step back, he spoke in a hushed tone. "Why do you wake me?"

The mul'daron gestured toward the command tent. "We don't have much time. I overheard some of the guards talking a little while ago. I wasn't sure who I could trust. But Senaria seems to trust you. That means I can as well." He paused letting the dreuslayer comprehend the importance of what he was about to say.

"Go on."

"It seems not all of us share in Senaria's vision. For as long as I can remember I've had this insatiable craving for power. It was something we all shared. Yet many of us could not rise above our masters to taste more than we were given. When the curse broke, we were freed of that desire, or so I thought. Some of our number are planning a takeover tonight. Senaria is the strongest of us. She held that status before— everything. If they can kill her while she sleeps there won't be anyone to stop them. We'll be thrust back into the world which we fought to escape. I don't want th—" He choked on his words and fell forward.

Ravion caught the mul'daron, seeing an arrow protruding from his back. Several shouts erupted from camp. Ravion could see figures running, striking any who reached for their weapons. It was too late. The coup had already begun. Dropping the dead mul'daron, he drew his longsword and rushed toward the command tent.

One of the attacking guards slashed out, aiming to cut the outsider down. Ravion easily deflected the strike, driving his sword into the man's heart. Ripping his blade free he continued on, reaching the tent. He could hear voices inside. Slowly pulling the flap to the side, he peered in.

The room defied the laws of nature. It was nearly four times larger than the exterior and fully decorated. The walls looked to be made of wood and the floor was lined in fur. Three figures stood inside, their weapons drawn, yet at ease.

Senaria was bound to her bed. The wooden posts were too sturdy to break. She'd was gagged, her hands pulled overhead. Her legs were bound separately, tied to the opposing corner posts. It didn't take much to discern their intentions.

One of the men laid his sword against the table and drew a thin, curved dagger. Slipping the wicked blade beneath her nightgown, he easily cut the thin material from the bottom hem, splitting it up under her arm.

Senaria squirmed and fought, trying to get free but it was no use. The ropes were too secure. Glaring her hatred at the men, she knew she was helpless. Helpless and unable to fight back.

He quickly cut the straps over her shoulders and pulled the ruined garment free. Taking a step back, he admired her bare form, imagining all the things he was going to do to her. Lustful intentions filled his eyes, striking fear into hers.

Ravion had seen enough. He couldn't stand by and allow this to happen. Taking a deep breath, he threw the canvas flap open and rushed inside. Finding the closest voyeur, he drove his sword into his back. The would-be rapist was dead before he hit the ground. Retracting the sword, Ravion drew his dagger and flung. It embedded itself in the other watcher's esophagus. The blade sank deep, burying itself to the hilt.

The last mul'daron turned to see the approaching dreuslayer. He placed his dagger against the subdued woman's throat, daring him to continue. "Take another step and I'll kill her!"

Ravion paused. He knew he didn't have much time. This man, this scum would probably to kill her anyway. If he didn't act quick, her chances of survival would diminish rapidly.

"I've seen how you look at her. Tell you what. Stand watch. When I'm done, you can have a turn."

Ravion let his own sinister smirk breach the surface to his deadly serious face. *He actually thinks he can barter with me. That puts things in my favor!*

The mul'daron smiled, seeing the dreuslayer's response. Now all he had to do was defile her, and then kill him once he started.

"There's one little problem with your offer." Ravion added.

"What's that?"

"She's not a toy you can willingly pass around!" Ravion flung his sword, watching the long blade flip end over end. It passed into the mul'daron's shoulder, launching him back and pinning him to the wall.

The illusionary magics inside the tent shimmered and disappeared, leaving stained canvas in its place. The pinned mul'daron struggled against the blade, but it was no use. He couldn't pull it free of the support post.

Ravion approached the bed. Reaching down he grabbed the wicked, curved blade and threw one of the fur blankets over Senaria. Carefully, he cut the ropes and handed her the dagger. Turning around he made for the exit, leaving her to do what she had to.

Senaria smiled. She was right to trust him. Pulling herself up, she wrapped the blanket around her naked form, tucking the tail inside the wrap to hold it in place. Approaching the helpless mul'daron, anger and vengeance burning in her eyes, she raised the blade.

"Please. It was just a joke. I wasn't really going to—"

"Shut up!" Her energies flowed forth, silencing the man.

He moved his mouth trying to speak, but the sounds wouldn't come. He tried to move, but was bound. She watched tears flow from his eyes, feeling no remorse for him. Slipping the tip of the curved dagger under the edge of his woolen breeches, she sliced the retaining band, uncaring if the edge bit into him. The belt and top band split, allowing his pants to fall free. She glanced at his under endowed member. "You were going to use this thing to cause me pain. You were going to take pleasure in it. Well, I've news for you. I'm going to use it to cause you pain, and I promise, I'll take pleasure in every drop of blood I draw from you."

He cried out, but was unable to give his fear voice. He tried to fight, his body was unresponsive to his pleas.

Senaria pressed the tip of the blade into him, watching blood and urine trickle from the wound. Slowly dragging the razor-sharp edge upward, she split him, destroying his manhood. Returning her attention to his face, she stared deep into his eyes. "You had a chance at a new life, Mareis. One free of inflicting pain and misery upon others. But you had to revert back to your old ways. I wish I could simply threaten you to never try this again. But I'm afraid it too late for that. Your kind will never learn their lesson. The best I can do is put you on display for any others. If lessons can't be taught, then fear must serve as a deterrent." Finishing her statement, she brought the dagger around, burying it in his throat.

He gurgled in protest, unable to escape his fate.

Taking comfort in his demise, Senaria watched the life leave his eyes. She pulled the longsword from him, letting the body crumple to the ground, bleeding out into the trampled grass. Turning from the dead man, she laid the sword upon her bed and grabbed her clothes. Quickly throwing them on, she strapped her armor into place and sheathed her own sword. Grabbing Ravion's weapon she made for the opening.

Ravion stood patiently outside. He held one of the crude scimitars at the ready, standing defensive against any approaching attackers. Senaria tapped him on the arm with the flat of his sword and flipped the blade around to hand it to him. "Thank you for what you did in there. Most would have walked away and let it happen, or taken his offer. I'm indebted to you."

Ravion tossed the stolen sword to the ground and took his own. "You don't owe me a thing. No one has the right to make another person feel trapped inside their own body. If this is the last time I have the ability to prevent such from happening I'll consider it a life well lived. But the world is an ugly place. Sadly, I fear I'll have many more chance to right that wrong."

She smiled. "Well, for what it's worth. I truly am grateful. Now if you'll excuse me, I have some problems to deal with."

Ravion bowed, gesturing toward camp, forgetting her earlier request. "By all means, My Lady."

She marched past him, taking in the full extent of the battle between her men. Raising her hands to the sky, Senaria summoned the energies letting them flow from her. Dark clouds rolled in, blanketing the area. Flashes of lightning illuminated the field, striking the ground in several places.

Ravion watched the strikes target the attacking groups. They struck with such ferocity that charred bodies flew through the air, crashing down into the waist-high stalks.

The battle roared to a halt. Both sides recognizing the danger the storm represented.

Senaria dropped her arms letting the clouds dissipate. She looked over the group, a mere fraction of what it had been. Sorrow and pity filled her. Her voice boomed across the field like thunder shaking the ground. "Enough!" She felt sorry for them. Why couldn't they let their past go? The only thing that came from darkness was more darkness. Why was that so hard to understand? Taking a deep breath she spoke again, letting her words sound just loud enough for the dwindling army to hear her. There was no sense in drawing unwanted attention. "Mareis is dead. Those who followed him, lay down your weapons and surrender, or face immediate execution."

Several of the groups slowly tossed their weapons to the side and raised their hands overhead. She looked over the men, silently judging them. It was impossible to ensure all opposition was eliminated, but perhaps enough could be separated to prevent any future plots. "Gather and bring them to me."

The loyalists engulfed the prisoners and pulled them toward the command tent. Placing them on their knees in front of their commander, they backed away just enough to show support while preventing a crowd.

Senaria watched the numbers grow. One by one her army diminished, leaving her with less than half of what she started with. There was no telling how many loyal soldiers had fallen during the attack, but judging from the number still in their beds it had to have been upward of fifty in the initial assault.

She shook her head, scanning the faces before her. The sun was on the rise, illuminating the carnage of the small camp. It was much worse than she had feared. "I had such high hopes that we could live in a world not bound by greed and oppression. But you had to go and jump on the first wagon back to all of that." Senaria sighed. It was painful, seeing how many clung to the old ways. "As I'm sure you're aware, I cannot allow you to coexist with those of us in search of a better life. To allow such poison into our home would be to destroy us all. But I'm also not without mercy. I'll offer you this one final chance. Abandon the corruption and seek out a better life with the rest of us, or face exile from our ranks. Either choice will not be an easy one. If you stay, you'll have to work twice as hard to reclaim lost faith. If you go you'll head east, away from these lands. You'll face unknown risks, with the promise of death if you ever return. Think carefully, for I will not tolerate another outburst such as the one that occurred this evening." She turned, abandoning them to their thoughts. Pausing outside her tent, she looked upon Ravion. "Will you please join me?"

Stepping into the tent, Ravion glanced at the dead mul'daron lying against the wall. "My apologies for ruining your tent."

She approached the table and tossed her sword onto it. Glancing to her guest, and down to the body, she returned her attention to her armor. "It's a small price to pay for knowing the truth." Senaria laid her armor to rest over the small, wire stand and turned to face the man. "You mentioned an abandoned fortress last night. Do you believe it large enough to house upwards of three thousand?"

"I believe it would. It'll more than likely need work. I don't know when it was last used and I'm sure time has taken its toll. Though I'm afraid I don't fully understand. Even before the attack, you had maybe five hundred. You're down to roughly a third now. Forgive me, but that's a long jump to the thousands."

"You're a smart man. I know you have secrets of your own. I can tell when you're obscuring details. Do you really believe I would do any different? I had to be sure I could trust you. This is but a single unit of our people. The rest remained in the catacombs, awaiting my word. We've been locked in a bloody civil war since the curse broke. The dreualfar want us dead as we aren't them any longer. And we want a home of our own."

"I see. Well, I've already promised you my assistance. That promise holds true, regardless of how many of you there are. But I would have one request, if you'd be so gracious to accept."

She arched an eyebrow, waiting for him to continue.

"You knew who I was, so I'd assume you're familiar with Gareth. I haven't seen him in over a month now. If your men happen to come across him, could you make sure he's okay? Though I'd recommend they use caution. I can't promise he won't attack on sight, especially if he's faced his own challenges."

"I'll send word immediately."

"Thank you." Ravion turned to leave, pausing a moment longer. "Oh, and your assessments weren't wrong. I do have details I'd like to share with you. But I feel now it not the time, though if you have the resources I urge you look into a race called the dalari." Ravion stepped through the flap, leaving her to her duties.

Chapter VI
Fantastic Beast

Blue and silver light beamed from the large stained-glass window overlooking the ancient throne. The colored rays splayed out forming a perfect sigil across the marbled floor, interrupted only by the blue carpet running the length of the room. Baron Remle De Leon's voice echoed across the grand hall from his elevated perch.

"Son, how many times must I tell you? Magic is not what our people need. They need to be led from a position of morality and strength. Not some fool who rushes after the next Holy Grail. Or do I need to remind you of the outcome to that fable?"

"Father, hear me, please. I've done all the work. This is not some fool's errand. I had the information authenticated at The Tower before it left. This is what our ancestors used to protect our lands. I'm just asking you to follow in their foot prints." Erik pleaded, holding out a stack of parchment.

Remle sighed heavily and took the stack. Flipping through pages he skimmed the hundreds of scribbled words and occasional depictions. He was surprised at how much information was available on the subject. Strange that he'd never heard of it before. Though his people were known to be prideful at times, it was likely they didn't wish to admit that they needed help. Handing the parchment back to his son he stood and stretched his legs. "Very well. I'll accompany you to Heroes Gate. We'll explore this little fail safe. Though I want you to promise me that if it turns out to be hog wash, you'll drop this pursuit and learn to lead as I have."

Accepting the stack of research Erik felt a tinge of success flow through him. "You have my word. I'll have the horses readied. How many men do you wish to accompany us?"

Remle paused, thinking over the question. Heroes Gate was just over a week's ride and he didn't wish to leave the throne empty long. If they head up Kings Road, they could stop over in Aldridge, and again in Marbayne. From there it's three days to wall and they'd reach the gate on the final day. "Start with fifty men. I'm sure others will join us along the way. Steward, send an emissary ahead to Aldridge. Tell them to expect us in two days' time. From there we make for Marbayne and to the wall. After our stop at Heroes Gate, we'll run the eastern pass back home." Entrusting his order were received Remle marched along the blue carpet, muffling the sound of his boots. Reaching the entryway he turned and disappeared. It was a long journey and he need to gather himself.

Dust fell from the rafters, rousing Krenin from him slumber. Staring at the shaking beams he could hear the cheers overhead. It was no doubt an exciting match. He could always tell from the volume. Sitting up Krenin felt the healing wounds along his torso stretch their displeasure at the movement.

Leather soles echoed off stone, announcing visitors. It was a bit early for another match. Why were they here? Attempting to act as if he wasn't listening to their approach, Krenin reached over and grabbed the wooden bowl resting beside his cot. Scooping the paste-like soup into his hand he stuffed it into his mouth, feeling the crunch between his teeth. No doubt a beetle had gotten in with the grubs. He hated when that happened. The shells always clung to his teeth when he chewed. Though it wasn't like he could refuse it. Food was food and it would sustain him. Looking up from the bowl he watched two guards approach his cell.

The closest one drew a large brass ring and began searching for the proper key. Krenin watched the other one. His hand rested against the head of an axe. It was rare for them to gather him armed. This had to be a special occasion. Speaking the guttural tongue of his ancestors, the natural words felt good in his mouth. "Why are you taking me out? I'm not scheduled to fight today."

"Plans change. You been summoned. Special request from the chieftain." The armed guard clearly wasn't happy with the arrangement, but he wasn't going to be the one to go against the chieftain's orders.

Finding a small, silver key the orc dropped the others, letting the ring catch them. He shoved it into the lock and twisted. An audible click sounded and the barred door swung open.

Krenin laid the bowl where it had been and pulled himself to his feet. His muscles were sore and the bandages around his midsection were stained with blood. "I haven't yet healed from last fight."

"Doesn't matter. This your last fight one way or another. You win, you go free. You lose, you die."

"Why?"

The armed orc reached behind him and pulled the twin axes from his belt. Tossing them on the straw covered bed he nodded to the other guard to leave the room. The orc did so, hurrying to avoid penalty.

"You were brought here as punishment for crimes against the Kuren Clan. None expected you do so well in pit. You made a lot of coin, which went to the clan you wronged. Victories have paid for the life many times over. And since you refuse to die in battle, clan decide to let you go with a final exhibition."

Krenin stared in disbelief. He'd lost track of how long he'd been trapped and forced to fight as a gladiator. Now they were just going to release him? "Who do I fight?"

"You face Drognau, Terror of the Sands."

The half-orc had heard the name in whisper, but it held no lingering meaning. He'd never seen the man before, though his stories were legendary. If he could kill this man it would bring him honor for the rest of his life. No orc would refuse him station with such deeds attached to his name. Perhaps this was how he was going to rid himself of his cursed heritage. He reached down, securing his axes and marched toward the door. "Lead the way."

They marched through the twisting labyrinth of tunnels held up by wooden supports and clay. Krenin couldn't help but dwell on the anxiety building inside him. He was torn between hope and fear. This would be the fight to decide which one ruled him. He'd recalled the few tales he'd heard of Drognau and, truth be told, they scared the shit out of him. If this man was truly as powerful as they claimed, he would be a difficult adversary, but he was the key to freedom. That alone would see him succeed. Turning toward the large gates, Krenin watched the chains slowly pull the heavy portcullis up.

The guard grabbed the piled armor off the table and held it out for the half-orc to step into. Krenin laid his axes down and poked his head through the central hole, placing his arms one at a time. The movement was torture, but he had to endure. If anything, it would loosen him up. He felt the heavy layers of leather clap around him.

The guard buckled the sides into place and took a step back. "Be well, slave. Fight with honor and you'll spend the rest of your days outside these confines." He offered a final salute to the half-blood and turned, leaving him to his fate.

The orc's actions sent a sense of pride through him. It meant he'd made an impact. That alone was enough to boost his confidence. Krenin took a deep breath and secured his axes. Marching up the ramp he heard the crowd erupt in cheers at his sight. He searched the large arena, hoping to get a glimpse of his opponent. The empty ring seemed odd. He was the challenger in this battle. That meant he would be last to enter. *Where is he?* A deafening roar tore into his ears sending shivers down his spine.

Krenin could have recognized that roar anywhere. Glancing up, he noticed the massive wings circling overhead, though the dragon didn't look quite right. *Is that him? Nobody said anything about a dragon!* Taking a deep breath, Krenin placed his axes beneath his arms and knelt down, grabbing a handful of sand. Rubbing it into his palms, he let the coarse grit dry and add friction to his sticky grip.

The chains lowered behind him sealing the reinforced portcullis.

Krenin wrapped his fingers around the leather wrapped handles of his axes and marched toward the center. If this beast was his opponent there was no sense in delaying further.

Another ear shattering roar echoed overhead and the creature began to lower. It touched down in the center of the ring, looking upon the small half-orc.

Krenin watched it land. It was the strangest creature he'd ever seen. It stood on hind legs, roughly eight-foot-tall giving it about a head and a half over the largest orc. It had the head of a dragon, and a long, thick tail. Several black spikes ran from its crown, down its back, and to the tip if the tail, jutting out like vicious weapons of death. Serrated scales of dark green covered its body, overlapping at the joints. Its talons were complete with razor-sharp claws. Though the most disturbing thing of all was the bat-like wings folded neatly behind it. As if it wasn't enough to be able to kill with every part of its armored form, it had to be able to fly as well. In all rights it had to be a dragon, but what kind of dragon stood upright like a man. The creature stared into him as if it were accessing him, as he was it. If dragons had the ability to look smug this one certainly managed to pull it off.

A high-pitched hiss escaped its mouth, revealing a blood-red forked tongue. Krenin felt the pressure threaten to pop his eardrums. He had to find a way to escape it or risk going deaf. Covering his ears he watched a mist-like fog roll from the creature's nostrils. It pooled on the ground, making its way toward him. How could he survive this? He didn't even know what it was capable of. The urge to do something, anything, overcame him. Abandoning all reason, Krenin charged, raising his axes. A battle shout echoed across the arena exciting the spectators beyond control. Unconcerned with the need for air, Krenin darted across the growing pool. It separated like a cloud in the breeze.

Drognau hadn't expected him to charge. Most opponents fled from his toxins. They were always too afraid to risk entering. This one was different. He didn't seem to care. The half-orc was upon him quicker than he was ready for. Watching the axes speed in toward him, Drognau spun around, whipping his barbed tail.

The armored tail caught him in the ribs. Krenin felt them break once more, shooting pain through his body. Surely the fresh wounds had reopened from the impact as well. Slamming hard into the sand, he landed on his back. The ground shook under the creature's massive weight. It was upon him before he could move. Staring the beast in the face it towered over him, confirming its nefarious plot. "Why is it always my ribs?" Krenin cried.

The dragonkin broke its gaze, rearing back to stretch his thick, muscular neck. Sucking in large bouts of air, his lungs filled. It was ready to spew lethal toxins atop the downed orc. His snout shot down, aimed at the pathetic half-breed. *Why do they continue to give me such pathetic toys?* It didn't matter. He'd end this one quick enough. Then he'd claim his treasure and return to his lair where he could count them again. They did't have anyone good enough to best him. The green-skins were lucky he chose to play their little games in the first place. He could slaughter every single one of them if he so desired. But that would do little to fill his coffers. No, it was best to let them break themselves against him. He'd gladly take their riches. Who didn't like resting upon a bed of jewels and gold? Not to mention the precious virgin sacrifices they occasionally threw at him. He licked his lips, lost in the thought.

Krenin watched the creature's maw open slightly. He could see green smoke boiling behind the pointed teeth. He had to move. If the dense fumes touched him, whatever it was, it most likely wouldn't be good. Searching for an escape, something caught his eye. A small gland rested near the underside of its jaws. It wasn't any bigger than a walnut, but it looked soft, unlike the rest of the large monstrosity. It was a long shot, but he had to do something. He had to survive. Ignoring his pain, Krenin lashed out, swiping his axe at the beast's throat. The blade tore into the soft scales, nicking the fleshy sac. A yellow fluid drained out, soaking into the sands.

Drognau roared in pain. *How did he cut through my scales?* Even his softer belly scales were too dense for most weapons to pie*rce. The abomination must have keen weapons.* They clearly weren't magic. Anger flooded him. He stepped back, sniffing at the small beast to make sure he hadn't missed anything. *No, not magical. Not anything for that matter. What are they made of?* He'd never smelled that ore before. Shaking his head, Drognau soothed the torn venom sac. His forked tongue shot out, wetting his scaly lips. "You're going to pay for that. And once you're dead, I'm going to add your weapons to my collection. Something that rare doesn't deserve to be in your filthy hands. Maybe I'll put your head between them so I can remember you."

Krenin couldn't deny the intelligence the creature possessed. It was clearly more astute than the orcs gave it credit. But how did it know his axes were made of drastol? More importantly, how was he going to defeat it? It was strong, fast, and smart! And he couldn't match one element, let alone all three. Picking himself up, Krenin tightened his grips. The last thing he wanted was lose his only advantage. Calmly strolling toward the beast, he searched for any weakness, hoping to find one before he arrived.

Drognau tried forcing the poison from his throat, but it was no use. The muscles were cut. They couldn't contract enough to force the venom into his windpipe. He would have to do this the hard way. Flexing his wings he stretched them to their full width. The cocky half-breed was taunting him. If he knew what was in store for him, he'd run to his death, not walk. "You'd be smart to throw yourself upon your axes now. It'll be less painful than what I'm going to do." Drognau brought his wings in, flapping them harder and harder. The amount of force put into the motion was amazing. Such a display of brute strength was nearing the boundaries of natural. The heavy gust of wind lifted him off the ground, showering the half-orc in abrasive sand. He didn't have to try so hard once he was in the air. Pacing his wings, Drognau lifted himself higher and rocketed into the sky. Nearing peak height, he leveled out and locked his sights on the abomination below. He was but a speck at this distance. Adjusting his eyes, his vision shifted to give a much closer look. His death was going to be agonizingly slow. *No one hurts me and lives to tell about it!* Drognau folded his wings, letting a free fall claim him. Twisting around he brought the wings out to guide his attack. Extending his claws, he prepared to snatch the orc into the air.

Krenin had trouble seeing through the sand cloud. The powerful gusts were fading, telling him the creature had taken flight, but he was blinded. Squinting against the flying debris he searched the sky. A dark shape caught his attention. He could barely make out the creature's outline, but it was growing larger, headed straight toward him. It was moving too fast. There was no way he could withstand the impact. Glancing at his weapons, Krenin twisted and leaned back. Bringing his axe around he threw it as hard as he could, letting loose at the apex of his swing. The light weight, well-balanced weapon tumbled end over end pausing briefly each time the head was at the lowest point. Krenin watched it tear into one of the fleshy wings, sinking to the handle.

A sharp pain tore into his right wing. Drognau glanced over, seeing a gaping hole in the web. One of the blackened axes was lodged in the bone. He hadn't expected the half-orc to sacrifice one of his weapons. Though it seemed there was much he hadn't expected. He was coming in too fast. He had to slow himself. Flapping to control his descent, the wing couldn't catch the wind. Off-balance he spun, unable to stabilize himself. Falling faster, dizziness took hold. Adjusting with his good wing, Drognau slowed the spinning, but couldn't do much else. The ground was rapidly approaching. Pulling his limbs in at the last moment, he crashed into the arena floor. A wall of coarse dust exploded around him.

Watching the incoming creature, Krenin rolled out of the way. He felt bits of sand hit him. He popped up on his feet, gripping his remaining axe. The pain in his ribs was great, but he had to ignore it for now. He could deal with it if he survived. Cautiously approaching the fallen dragon-man, he searched through the cloud, hoping he could finish it before it got up. It was unlikely the fall killed it. He would have to land the final blow for himself. Climbing the mound of sand, Krenin surveyed the half-buried beast within. Its eyes were closed and one of the wings was jaggedly folded at an awkward angle, broken. A fair amount of blood seeped from the punctured bones. He spotted his axe near the creature's tail. Only the handle was sticking from the sand. Raising his weapon he inched closer, ready to remove the beast's head.

A slit-like eye shot open, expanding to focus on the half-orc. Drognau sprang to life, raking his sharpened claws at the approaching abomination. Pain shot through his body. The fall must have damaged him more than he'd hoped.

Krenin jumped back narrowly avoiding the deadly swipe. He tripped over the uneven ground, tumbling down the small mound. The sands shifted beneath him telling him the beast was freeing itself. They slid into the hole, filling the crater and trying to bring him along with it. Krenin clawed at the loose sand, trying to stop himself. To his fortune he escaped the draw. Picking himself up he turned and backed away, watching the broken beast crawl from the pit.

"Oh how you will pay. I've faced hundreds of adversaries of every race and never before have I bled. When I get my claws on you I'm going to peel your flesh from muscle so you can experience every ounce of pain I have to inflict. Only after I've eaten every part of your body you can live without will I let you die!" Drognau stabbed his talons into the sand, balancing himself. One limb at a time, he made for the half-orc.

Fear grew inside him. The beast was furious, and he its only target. He knew he couldn't hold against it in melee. Taking a deep breath, Krenin watched the creature approach, unsure how he was going to win this fight. He felt a heavy droplet splash against his bare arm. Looking down, he watched the water collect the dust and run off. Another drop hit, followed by a dense downpour. The rain soaked into everything, all but eliminating the cloud of floating dust. As if a sign from the gods, Krenin spotted the handle of his axe sticking from the sands just in front of the beast. Apparently, he wasn't the only thing that got caught in the sandslide. He felt his lips tighten, revealing a knowing smile to the approaching creature. "You'll have to catch me first." Laughing in pleasure, Krenin charged, leaping into the air with his axe overhead.

Is this orcling stupid? Why's he charging me? I can shred him with ease. Bringing his clawed hand up, Drognau watched the half-orc jump. He was too far away to hit him. "Ha! Too soon you pathetic half-br—."

Krenin slammed into the ground in front of the creature, bringing his axe down with all his might. It hit the handle of its twin slingshotting the blade straight up and into Drognau's chin.

The sharp edge penetrated his brain, silencing his words. Drognau staggered, unsure what had just happened. He tried to catch himself, but something was wrong. He couldn't move. His limbs gave out and he crashed face-first into the sand, jabbing the war axe deeper into the underside of his skull.

The torrential downpour slowed to a stop, emptying the last few droplets over the battleground.

Krenin picked himself up and dusted the clinging sand from his bloodied leathers. Approaching the dead dragon-man, he straddled its long neck and raised his axe. Bringing it down in a solid, fluid motion, he severed its head.

"Krenin the undefeated! Krenin the Dragon Slayer! Krenin the Almighty!" The crowd erupted in cheers of praise and excitement having never seen such a battle.

Grabbing his embedded axe, the head along with it, Krenin calmly marched toward the gate, watching it raise for his approach. He was free now, provided the orcs didn't try anything underhanded and kept their word. Exiting the arena, he paused just inside the gate. It clanked down, trapping him in the small confines.

Over a dozen orcs stood in the room, awaiting him. They were armed with large axes and hammers, proudly displaying their thick, metal armors. Many had bear pelts secured to the shoulders as protection against the chilling winds, or so he guessed. These weren't guards. These were soldiers. And from the look of them, they were his executioners.

"Drop your weapons and remove your armor, slave!"

Krenin looked over the orc. He was older than the others and wore a finer armor with quality furs and hundreds of markings etched into it. He wasn't sure what it all meant, but if he had to guess he was an orc of power. "I was told I'd go free if I won. That means you no longer refer to me as 'slave'!" Krenin tightened his grip, knowing the embedded axe was next to useless in its current state.

The elder orc cracked a smile at his rebellion. "True enough. You've earned your name. Krenin, relinquish your weapons and armor. They'll be returned to you when you leave the city."

Krenin stared at the old orc for a long minute, unsure if he should trust him or not. "How do I know you won't kill me the minute I pose no threat?"

"You're a warrior. Even unarmed you pose a threat. But I'm an orc of my word. Your victory over Drognau has granted freedom, status, and wealth. Not only over yourself, but over this city. The beast has been hording treasure for decades. With his death that treasure has become yours. Most of it anyway. So please, drop your weapons. I give you my word, as chieftain of Tulgrimm, they'll be returned to you once you're outside the city."

A heavy sigh escaped him. "Guess that has to do." Krenin dropped his axes. The free one clanked to the ground, while its twin hit with a thud from the weight of Drognau's head. Unbuckling his armor, Krenin laid it across the table and returned his attention to the chieftain.

The orcs calmly approached and collected his belongings. Stuffing them into a large bag they moved aside, exposing an open doorway he'd never been through.

Krenin marched past their number and into the corridor. It was nicer than the other ones he'd seen. This one actually had smoothed walls and was decorated beyond nailed planks. They escorted him through the underground labyrinth and to a set of sealed wooden doors. Sunlight beamed through the seam where they met.

Awaiting the orcs to open them, Krenin stepped through, lost in the sights around him. He'd never seen the orc city before. It was strangely wonderful in a harsh sort of way. Were it not for his history with them he could have found it a wonderful home. Outside the tunnel, orcs marched on all sides of him, led by the chieftain. He kept watch on as many as he could. If they were going to execute him, they were going to be in for a surprise.

Making their way through the heart of the huge city, Krenin found himself studying the structures. It was a style of craftsmanship all on its own. The citizens were another story. For the most part they ignored him, going about their daily lives. It was the younger orcs, the children, that made him smile. They stared as if they knew who he was. Many joined the ranks marching alongside the group, trying to keep him in their sights as long as they could. He found it amusing. Occasionally one of them would work up the courage to run between the soldiers and slap his leg. Followed immediately by running away, fear in their eyes. He guessed it was some sort of challenge between them, an innocent way of proving bravery. It felt good to inspire them in such a way. It was certainly going to be one of the things he'd remember for the rest of his life.

The group rounded the corner, stepping into a wooden tunnel. It twisted and went back the other direction as if it were some sort of defense if the city were under attack. Stepping through the other side, Krenin spotted a large steel reinforced gate. It towered over them, even in the distance. Reaching the massive portal he could hear the chains inside the wall rattling. The twin doors cracked, displaying a large road on the other side. A wide bridge made of wood spanned the long chasm. It was lined with a single rope run through the center of the rail posts.

The chieftain stopped at the edge of the bridge and turned to address the newly freed half-orc. "Your freedom lies on the other side. You've proven yourself worthy of being called an orc. From this day forward, you're welcome among our kind." He nodded to one of the soldiers.

The orc dropped a large sack at Krenin's feet. It was nearly bulging at the seams.

Krenin grabbed the bound opening and heaved the sack to his shoulder. It had to weigh at least a few hundred pounds. Nodding to the chieftain he took his first steps of freedom and marched across the bridge. Stealing a glance over the edge, his stomach churned at the sight. It had to have been several hundred feet to the deep-blue waters beneath. Returning his eyes to his path, he reached the other side. Glancing back, Krenin looked upon the orcs one last time. In unison, they offered salute and turned to reenter their city.

Dropping the sack, Krenin pulled the leather binding free. Looking inside he found his armor had been folded neatly and tucked around his axes. Removing his equipment, he readied for the long journey home. Beneath there was a smaller sack with hundreds of coins and gems piled around it. Opening the smaller bag he found Drognau's glazed eyes staring back at him.

Chapter VII
Slipping Shackles

A cool breeze drifted through the cavern entrance carrying the briny scent of stale seaweed. Gareth had spent enough time on the sea to know when he was near one. He could see filtered light through the cloth clinging to his face. A rag had been stuffed into his mouth and tied in place, keeping him from talking. His hands and feet were bound behind him, forcing him face down on the rocky terrain. His body ached, as if he'd completely exhausted himself and hadn't had the chance to recuperate. Footsteps echoed past, telling him he wasn't alone. Gareth tried to focus on his anger, but it wouldn't flow. He was too worn to linger on the pain.

Another set of boots approached, pausing near him. A forceful grip latched hold of his bound arms and lifted him from the cold ground. Gareth didn't know where they were taking him, but surely weren't stupid enough to give him a chance at escape.

The temperature dropped slightly, but he remained warm. That meant they were going deeper into the caverns. It was odd. Dreu didn't normally camp so close to an entrance. The sunlight would burn them. Released, the impact of the cold, hard ground was jarring to his unsuspecting form. It was gentle all things considered, but he was sure they wanted him to feel some pain. Additional ropes engulfed his arms, burning into his flesh and cinched tight. It didn't make much sense. He was already bound, what were they hoping to accomplish? To his surprise, his arms sprang free of his legs, allowing the sore muscles to return to a more natural position. Gareth pulled against the bindings, realizing what they had done. He was still bound, just not in a manner preventing movement.

Being yanked up, his weight was placed on his own two feet, a welcome change from his raw stomach and chest. Gareth staggered, disoriented in the sensory deprivation. Not to mention the fact that he hadn't walked for at least a few days. He wasn't sure how long they'd had him, but it was certainly long enough for his body to lose some of its muscle memory. Guided backward, Gareth felt something hard impact the back of his knees, buckling them. To his surprise there was a bench awaiting him.

The mul'daron ran the ropes through the holes in the wooden seat, pulling tight to keep him seated. Assured he couldn't move they ripped the bag from his head and untied the gag, stepping aside.

Gareth was able to see for the first time since he'd passed out. It wasn't much of a sight. The bright, yellow entrance blocked most of the details his single eye could normally give him. Though he could make out a lone figure seated in front of him, the man's back to the entrance.

"Gareth Dreuslayer. I must say I never expected to have you in such a position. Moreover, I never expected to be in the position I'm in either."

His throat was dry from lack of use, but he forced the gravely words out anyway. "Then why don't we switch? You sit here, and I there. I'll promise to cut your ears off before I run a blade through your head."

The figure let out a light chuckle at the prisoner's rebellion. He truly was everything the rumors claimed. "Oh, I don't believe that to be necessary. You and I aren't so different. We both want the same thing." He nodded to one of the mul'daron.

The man approached, extending a waterskin to the parched dreuslayer. Gareth glanced at the uncorked container. "You really think I'd drink anything you gave me? For all I know it's poisoned."

"Look at it this way, if I wanted you dead we wouldn't be having this conversation. I could simply leave you bound. Starvation would claim you within the next day or two. So ask yourself this, if I wanted you dead why would I waste perfectly good poison to make it happen?"

He had a point, Gareth couldn't deny that. Nodding to the pink-skinned figure beside him, Gareth tipped his head back to take a drink. It soothed his throat, but hurt when it reached his stomach. It wasn't nearly as bad as before, but it certainly reminded him how long it'd been since he'd eaten. Clearing his throat, Gareth returned his focus to the silhouette. Features were beginning to appear against the backdrop of light. "So, if you aren't going to kill me, why am I here?"

"As I said, we want the same thing. The dreualfar are no friend of mine. They're just as likely to kill us, as they are you. What's the old saying? The enemy of my enemy is my friend?"

"We're not friends. For all I know this is some trap to get me to reveal something."

The figure laughed once again, sitting back in his chair. "And what do you think you have that isn't already known? You're a little too full of yourself, I'm afraid. You're of little value when it comes to information. Your life on the other hand, that's greatly valued and it just so happens that you have valuable friends. One of these friends has applied this value to my commander and our people. That in of itself has granted you salvation, especially since you killed so many of my men. Though I can understand your confusion under the circumstances."

"So you're just going to let me go?"

"In due time. I have a couple questions I'd like to ask you. First off, do you know what this is?" The shadowed mul'daron held up a brown satchel, exposing the shimmering black book inside. "We took it from you while you were out. My men have looked over it from cover to cover, but haven't been able to find so much as a single scribe mark. We know it's magical. Hell, a blind man would know that much."

"I don't know. I found it in the tunnels. Thought it'd be good as kindling if I needed to make a fire."

"I see. Well we're going to hang on to it for the time being. Wouldn't want it getting damaged until you have need of your fire." He smiled, suggesting he knew more than he was letting on. "Secondly, when you killed my men, you were using a magic none of us have ever seen before. Do you know how you did it? Or perhaps how someone could learn it?"

"I don't know what to tell you. It started a couple weeks ago. It just happens sometimes, usually when I get mad. As for teaching someone how to do it, I wouldn't know where to start. I don't even know how to control it myself."

"That's a shame. Perhaps those answers will be revealed to you soon. That's all I have for you right now. I hope you'll understand that I can't risk letting you loose upon my men. I wouldn't want you to get mad again. We both know what happened last time. We move in the morning. Until then, you're to be kept separate from my men. Food and water will be provided. Once you're done, you'll be bound and gagged for the duration of your stay. When we reach our destination, I promise you'll never be kept against your will by my people ever again."

Gareth watched the light fade feeling the thick cloth take its place over his head once again.

The towering wall stretched across the land running one hundred miles in both directions. At the center a massive bastion stood erect, overlooking the approaching army of men.

The majority wore the blue and green tabard of Shadgull, though a fair many were dressed in black and green of Marbayne. Those few hung to the outskirts of the group, serving as added protection in the unlikely event they were attacked.

Remle pulled the reins of his horse. The majestic creature was a mixture of brown and white, as if the white patches had been splattered across and eventually took dominance. Looking over the ancient post he surveyed the guards posted atop the structure and on foot at the closed gateway. Glancing at his son he gave a reassuring smile. "Center of the tunnel. Is there anything I need to look for?"

Erik dismounted his horse and approached his father's. "I'm told you'll know what you're looking for when you get there. I'd guess it's something only the owner of the cornet would recognize."

The fair-haired man threw his leg over the steed and jumped down. His armor shifted under the weight of impact. Adjusting it, Remle stood to his full height and grabbed the crown from atop his head. Spinning it between his fingers he looked into the colored gems, seeing the reflection of his aging face. "Erik, I'll do this one last thing." Pausing, he glanced up to look into his son's eyes. "When it's done we return home. At that point I plan to retire. I've had too many years. It's time you take my place."

Remle placed his hand on Erik's shoulder, giving him a light shake. Spinning around he marched toward the sealed gate, replacing the cornet.

"Baron Remle, what brings you this far north?"

"I made a promise to my boy. Would you open the gate for me?"

The guard paused for a moment. Keeping his eyes locked on the towering man, he yelled his command to the wall. "Raise the gate! Baron Remle requires entry!" He stepped aside allowing access.

Remle approached the portcullis, watching the reinforced steel lattice raise into the stone and out of sight. He stared into the empty tunnel faintly seeing the opening on the other side. It had to have been at least a quarter mile to the other side. Why anyone needed such a wide wall was beyond him, even in times of war. It did have some logic to it. Its size made in nearly impossible to scale with any real force of number. It would be next to impossible to destroy even the smallest section. Despite the amount of resources its construction had taken, it was a valuable tool when facing an invasion. It could limit the largest army to little more than a handful at a time, turning an otherwise impossible battle into one of endurance.

Taking a deep breath, Remle marched into the dark passageway watching the closest torches flare in response to his approach. The sound of his men standing idle faded, replaced by the echo of his leather soled boots against the stone floor. Reaching what he guessed was the middle, Remle removed his crown and searched for any sign of his query.

Erik watched his father fade into the distance. He was little more than a speck in the middle of lingering shadow. A familiar thud echoed to his left. Glancing over, he spotted the red and black fletching of an arrow protruding from one of his knight's chest. The man toppled from his saddle and landed in the grass.

Roars echoed from the ancient bastion and dense grass around the army. Men sprang up from nowhere, lashing out at the unsuspecting caravan.

Erik drew his swords, looking around for the closest attacker. "It's a trap, be on your guard!" He parried a sword, bringing his offhand around to run the man through. Spinning, he stabbed into another, saving one of his knights that hadn't gotten off his horse yet. He quickly surveyed the

numbers. The ambush was well laid out, but they lacked the man power
to overrun such a large force. Had they just been the original riders
perhaps, but they'd picked up many from Aldridge and Marbayne. His
mind raced. Did they have a mole? How else did they know how many
left Shadgull?

Retreating from his thoughts, Erik blocked another attack. He looked
into the face of the man. I recognize him. Recalling where he'd seen him,
the visions flooded his mind. There it was. This was one he'd arrested not
a few months back. He was caught cutting purses in the market square.
Yet he was dressed as one of the wall guards. The young prince ran the
man through. Pulling his weapon free, he glanced around to see the
fading battle coming to its end. The bandits never stood a chance against
so many, yet they were well organized. This meant there had to have
been a higher plan to all of this. A distraction maybe?

Erik squinted into the tunnel, finding his father. Their eyes met for
the briefest moment. His heart sank seeing a shadowed figure in the
tunnel behind him. There was no way to get there in time if the figure
was a threat. Abandoning all tact, Erik charged, rushing into the stone
archway.

Lythus watched the deceived baron search for the doorway. The man
was off by several feet, though he'd never know it. He didn't know what
he was looking for. Seeing his opportunity, he quietly made his way
behind the man, raising his dagger to finish the job. Blade in hand, he
selected the perfect location and plunged the weapon toward its mark.

No! You will not kill him!

Remle ran his fingers across the stone unable to find the slightest
marking. The clink of blades echoed along the dark corridor, reaching his
ears. He froze, listening intently. He turned toward the entrance, seeing
the signs of battle outside. His son stood in the distance, frozen in fear.
He had to get there. Their men needed to be commanded. Taking his first
step toward the exit a sharp pain shot through his spine. Remle crumpled
to the cold, stone floor, unable to move. Staring up at the arched ceiling
of perfectly aligned brick he saw the pale, orc-faced mask step into view.

Kane struggled against his body forcing the blade lower than it was
aimed. He was too late. It sank deep into its target, burying itself to the
hilt. He slowly approached the dying man, feeling remorse for what had

happened. Kneeling beside the dying baron, Kane propped him up, hoping to make his final moments comfortable. Pulling the mask away he stared into the fading eyes, seeing a mixture of emotion in the gaze. "I'm sorry. I tried to stop him." Kane pleaded, hoping Remle could forgive him.

Remle silently wept. He couldn't find the strength to speak. His body was growing cold with each passing moment. Lip quivering, he wished he could tell the noble warrior that he forgave him. The words couldn't reach his mouth. Fear and nervousness flowed through him, claiming a bit more of his conscious mind. He knew he wouldn't last much longer.

Holding the man tight, Kane watched the life leave his friend. He wished there was something he could do, but even he was a prisoner to all of it. Anger flooded him. How could he have allowed himself to be trapped as he had?

You shouldn't be able to do this. You're mine. I did the ritual. You cannot power through it!

The enraged prince ran as fast as he could. He was out of breath, but he had to keep going. He watched his father fall, unable to do anything about it. Seeing the prefect opportunity to claim vengeance, he brought one of his swords overhead and flung it at hard as he could. The weapon flipped end over end, flying toward its target.

Lythus forced the rebellious warrior back down. Glancing up, he noticed the incoming sword. Timing it, he flung his dagger, knocking the sharp weapon off its trajectory. The wild blade flew past him, sending a sharp pain through his side. He glanced down, realizing it had grazed him. What was worse, the orc-skull mask lied broken beneath the blade at his side. Sighing his irritation, Lythus snatched up the crown and stood, peering down the tunnel at the approaching prince. A sadistic smile came to his lips. Twisting the coronet he aligned the reflected torchlight off the colored gems. The focused beams reflected on the wall, finding their mark. He listened to the hidden doorway open and turned to face the prince, knowing the shadow was too dense to reveal his face. "I told you such pursuits came with a heavy price. You should have listened."

Erik couldn't make out the man's identity. He was human, that much was clear. But the distance and shadow made it difficult to make out details. He had one chance. Exhaling, he brought his remaining sword up and threw it, hoping he could right all of his wrongs with one fatal blow.

Lythus stepped into the open doorway hearing steel on stone behind him. Glancing at the unarmed prince he smiled one final time. "Thanks for doing all of this for me. I might have had a difficult time with it by myself." Stepping through the threshold, the stone shifted behind him and sealed the hidden tunnel away.

Dark green moss clung to the jagged stones and aged mortar of the abandoned keep. The wooden ceiling was torn open revealing an array of deep blue clouds and twinkling stars in the distance.

Ravion felt the cool air rush through the crumbling room, biting into his thin clothing. He watched the lantern flicker, its glow dancing across the warped table. The wood was solid but weathered, leaving deep grooves where the grain had dried. Dipping the tip of the feathered quill into the tiny vial of ink he scribbled words onto the rough parchment, watching the black liquid soak into the page. Dotting the final line containing his name, Ravion laid the quill in its stand and gently blew across the lettering, letting it dry. Tearing the parchment to size, he rolled it and lifted the shield on the lantern, exposing the orange and yellow flame. Grabbing a stick of red wax he twisted the melted end into the flame, watching it turn from a solid stick to a dense, glossy fluid. Wiping a corner of the melted wax over the loose end of the miniature scroll, he quickly pressed his seal into it and watched it retake its solid state. Approaching the window, Ravion let out a sharp whistle.

A moment later a raven flew into sight, taking perch on the rotted sill. Ravion carefully tied the scroll to the bird's leg and held out his finger. The raven climbed on, balancing himself.

Staring into the bird's beady eyes, Ravion held a silent conversation. Raising his hand out the window, the raven took flight and disappeared into the night sky. A shadow took form on the wall beside him. He turned to look upon Senaria leaning against the worn and warped door frame. The door had long sense fallen off its hinges, but the frame seemed to be in good shape despite the moisture it had obviously suffered. "Lady

Senaria, I trust you're finding everything to your liking?" He let out a light smirk, assuming she held similar opinions.

"You weren't lying when you said it needed work. Though it will suffice. We have trees and stone nearby. Given a few months I believe we can rebuild good as new." She paused a moment, staring at her friend. "Do you believe he'll help us?"

"He's a good man. I believe he will, though it may not be in the most direct manner. His type prefers indirect action. At least that's how they like to make it seem. I'm sure we'll know something by morning."

"I'm grateful for all the help you've given. I don't believe we'd be in as good of shape as we are without your guidance. Recent events considered." She smiled.

"You honor me. Though I believe you'd do the same were our roles reversed."

"I'm not so sure. You forget the pain we caused before the breaking. Were I in your shoes, I don't think I would have been so lenient, let alone taken action to aid the creatures responsible for so much death." Senaria's tone shifted, recalling the memories that tortured her.

Ravion stepped forward and took her hand. "When you've seen as much as I, you learn to forgive easily. It doesn't do any good to dwell on the past. The only thing that matters is how you proceed into the future."

"Some things can never be forgiven." She stared at the floor, solemn in her words.

Ravion slowly reached out, pressing his finger against the bottom of her chin. Gently lifting her head he stared into her almond-shaped, brown eyes. "Anything can be forgiven. The trick is never forgetting. The two go hand in hand."

Senaria smiled and stepped close to him. His warmth felt good in the cool air. Staring into his eyes she felt his arms wrap around her. "And you think we can be forgiven?"

"I know you can. You've already started down the correct path. It's up to you where you go from there."

"Will you be there to right me when I'm wrong?"

A smile breached his lips. "I'll be around whenever you need me. Though I've faith you're strong enough to find your own—."

She pressed her lips against his, cutting him off.

Rays of sunlight beamed through the open roof landing on Ravion's face. He opened his eyes feeling their warmth on his skin. Coming to his senses he recalled the night's events and studied the beautiful woman lying next to him. Her skin was perfect in the morning light. She was curled up beside him, buried in the fur blanket. He felt lost in her sight. Her light silver hair was scattered about her face and split, revealing a single slightly pointed ear. He didn't want to get up and risk waking her. This was the first time he'd slept in an actual bed in as long as he could remember. That was reason enough to stay. He took a deep breath and carefully climbed out of bed.

"Trying to sneak away?" Senaria opened her eyes, smiling at the naked man.

"Not exactly. You looked comfortable and I didn't want to wake you. I need to see if my message was received." Ravion pulled his clothes on and leaned over the bed, kissing her softly.

Quickly making his way back to the study he found a scroll lying on the worn table. A familiar stamp rested in the green wax. Ravion snatched up the message and broke the seal. The fine parchment unrolled, pulling itself from his hands. Floating in front of him words echoed in their author's voice.

"Son of House Santail,

I appreciate you reaching out to me with news of these findings. I would like to know more detail when time permits. As per your requested information, I'm afraid only the Lord of Krondar has the ability to grant such deed. Fortunately for your needs, no man currently holds such title. Krondar is unique in the sense that it has no noble lineage. Its populace is comprised entirely of refugees and outsiders. Therefore any plot of land that has not been claimed is available, though there are no legal proceedings to its true ownership in the absence of a lord. I will tell you the barbarian people hold one sacred law higher than any other. Strength rules supreme. If someone is not strong enough to hold onto what they have, they don't deserve to keep it. This has both benefit and penalty, depending on which spectrum you fall. Thank you again for reaching out. It's been far too long and I look forward to meeting you in the near future. Additionally, if one desired to claim lordship over Krondar one must simply evoke the Rite of Godrick at the city heart of Fender's Spear. Though do not do so lightly. Rarely, does one make it past the first day.

Sincerely,
Perrimen Sarandar, Former Arch-Magus of the Tower, Former Baron of Dalmoura

Ravion watched the scroll burst into flame and gently float to the warped floorboards. The red embers disappeared in the flaky ash, breaking apart from the light breeze. "Huh. Is that all?" He chuckled at the thought, wondering how far this endeavor would take him.

Senaria approached, wrapping her arms around his chest. Resting her chin on his shoulder she quietly spoke. "You're going to do it, aren't you?"

Ravion placed his hand atop of hers, feeling her warm, soft skin. "I fear I have to. Your people could make a home here, and chances are they'd be just fine for many years. But people are greedy. One day someone could come and demand you leave. I know the outcome of such an order. There's no sense in future bloodshed when I have the ability to staunch it now."

Senaria kissed his neck, whispering into his ear. "You're a noble man, Ravion Santail. This land is lucky to have you. I'm lucky to have you."

Spinning around to keep her arms in place, Ravion pulled her close and kissed her. "I think I may be the lucky one. I've wandered this realm longer than I can remember. Never in all that time have I found someone quite like you."

Levi Samuel

Chapter VIII
Proving Ground

Broken wagons lined the sides of the road, strung together with wooden planks into makeshift stands. People pedaled their wares, dressed in little more than rags.

Ravion walked along the isles eyeing the less than desirable merchandise on display. He couldn't help but feel sorry for them. Most were malnourished and covered in dirt. They were far from the worst he'd seen in this nation, but they clearly weren't the best either. How they could live this way was beyond him. It seemed so primitive compared to the comforts he'd grown accustomed to in Shadgull. Even Marbayne, small as it was, had paved streets. This was little more than a glorified village acting as a capital city. Perhaps if all went according to plan he could make some changes and improved these people's lives.

Making his way to the city square, Ravion climbed a stack of wooden crates and turned to face her citizens. Clearing his throat he spoke, letting his voice carry over the chatter. "People of Fender's Spear, hear me! My name is Ravion Santail. I've seen the quality of life the people of this land face. I wish to make a difference. I believe I can help to ensure your families are fed and clothed. I can establish trade routes with the rest of Dalmoura. I can ensure the protection of your homes from the frequent orc raids. I do not seek to rule you! I simply wish to make your lives easier. You do not need a ruler. You need someone who knows a thing or two about economics and government. Though I don't expect you to take my word for it. I'm aware of the customs this land holds to the highest value. With that knowledge I wish to enact the Rite of Godrick. Any who wish to oppose me, please step forward."

Every man, woman, and child within earshot turned to face the dreuslayer. They were captivated by his words. Never before had one addressed the issues they faced on a daily basis. Many had come to claim the rite, but never one so educated. It was usually some kid fresh out of training and seeking to make a name for himself. Unfortunately the only name they ever made was on their headstone.

One of the citizens, an elderly woman, hobbled to the front of the crowd and extended her wrinkled hand to the young dalari. Ravion took the woman's hand and stepped from his stage. "What may I do for you, Ma'am?"

She spoke in a weak, yet sweet voice, only heard due to the silence of the world around them. "Young man, the Rite of Godrick grants you room and meal during your trials. I'd be honored if you'd stay at the inn."

"It would be my pleasure, though I hope you'll do me the honor of allowing me to compensate you for your hospitality during my stay. If you feel the need to show charity, please apply the meal toward someone in need."

She bowed as deep as her frail body would allow. Pushing against her walking stick, she pulled herself up and made way for the inn a step at a time.

Ravion escorted the woman to one of the larger buildings. It was one of the few two-story structures in town and the only one with a collection of glass windows along the upper floor. A single wooden door, painted red, stood near the center of the wide establishment. Despite its aged appearance it was in much better condition than the other buildings surrounding it. Ravion grabbed the brass handle and pulled the door open, gesturing the woman to enter.

She smiled, patting him on the arm and stepped inside.

The interior had the strong scent of pine. Ravion glanced around at the wooden furniture carved of cedar and other soft woods. They were coated in heavy layers of flax oil, leaving a glossy sheen on their smoothed surfaces. Looking around at the occupants he noticed a few elderly men sitting at one of the tables playing a game of cards. They didn't bother looking up from their game. A portly man was hard at word in the back room rolling out dough on the counter top. He was covered in flour and glistening beads of sweat clung to his forehead. Overall, it was a fairly relaxed setting. Roughly twelve tables made up the common room, with a dining room on the far side and the kitchen beyond that. To his right, a small section was elevated by a platform just wide enough for a band to find comfort. Across from the stage, leading above the dining room, a waxed banister wrapped around and disappeared into the layer above.

The elderly woman turned to him, weakly balancing herself. "Take a seat. I'll get you a key." Refusing to wait for a response she pressed onward making her way across the common room, toward the kitchen.

Ravion picked a table near the stairs ensuring he could watch the entrance. If he was going to spend any time here he needed to scout the place and find any other exits. Taking his seat he stretched his back against the wooden supports. It was a comfort he desperately missed. Reaching into his belt pouch, Ravion pulled a stained leather bag and a long-stemmed pipe. Packing it full of the stale tobacco, he put the stem in his mouth and searched the room. Spotting his query he quickly stood and made for the fireplace to the left of the entrance. Reaching up he grabbed a spill from the ceramic jar and carefully stuck it into the fire, watching the end ignite. Gently drawing on the pipe, the tobacco turn black and started to burn. Ensuring it would remain lit, Ravion tossed the thin stick into the flames and returned to his seat. Blowing a large puff of smoke into the air he watched a man step through the entrance, pausing in search of the occupants.

His eyes locked on Ravion. Approaching, he pulled out a chair and took a seat across from him. "That was quite the speech you gave. I must say, I'm impressed."

"And you are?" Ravion quickly assessed the man. He clearly didn't belong to the commoners of this land. His dress was too fine for that. Smooth skin covered his face, suggesting he'd recently had a shave. His dark brown hair was clean and combed over.

"Ah, forgive me. I sometimes forget my name has little meaning elsewhere. I am Wallace Thurmoau. I've made it my personal duty to aid the fine people of this land, much as you yourself have proclaimed. The Rite of Godreu is a nasty business and you'll need all the help you can get."

"Godrick." Ravion corrected.

"My mistake. So what do you say? Do you feel like making an ally?"

"Mister, Wallace, was it?" Ravion leaned for forward in his chair, removing any idle language from his stature.

"That's correct, Wallace Thurmoau"

"Well, Mister Wallace Thurmoau, what is it exactly that you do?"

"I deal in new beginnings. Let's say you've had a run of bad luck. You come to me, I take a look at the problems you're having and make them go away. For a modest fee, of course."

"And these problems, am I to assume they're of a monetary nature?"

"Is there any other kind?"

"I see. Well, Mister Wallace Thurmoau." Ravion paused, leaning against the backrest. "I do not find myself in need of your services. In fact, I feel you're very presence and position in this city is one of the many problems that requires fixing. When these trials are up, I'll be taking a close look into your business endeavors. Take that as you will, Mister Wallace Thurmoau. Though I hope you'll have the foresight to straighten your affairs before I find myself in a position to do something about them."

Wallace jumped up, knocking over his chair. It crashed to the floor, echoing out a loud pop. "Now wait just a minute! I'm a reputable business man. You'll show me the proper respects."

A mild smirk formed at the sight of the enraged man. He looked like a child throwing a tantrum for not getting his way. Ravion casually took another drag off his pipe, blowing the smoke to the side as if to prevent further insult. "Let me stop you there before you say something you're going to regret."

"I might say the same to you! Just who the hell do you think you are threatening me like that?"

"Ravion Santail, Dreuslayer and founder of The Order, Councilman of Marbayne. And former escort for the previous Baron of Dalmoura, Arch-Magus Perrimen Sarandar." He offered mock salute with his pipe, refusing to stand.

"I... You're... But... You have no status here, Dreuslayer! What makes you think you can interfere in my affairs?"

Ravion sighed heavily, laying his pipe on the table. Leaning forward he spoke as clear and calm as possible, hoping the man would get the hint. "Aside from the treaties signed by all the lords of Dalmoura, my border wardens have legal right to enter any land for the purpose of justice. If that weren't reason enough, I'll soon complete these trials and I'll have lordship over this land. At which point no amount of groveling or bribery will be able to protect you from me. Now, I suggest you either pay these fine people for their services and have a meal or go about your day."

Wallace's face flushed red. Short of drawing the dagger stuffed in his waistband, there wasn't much he could do in response to the insolence this man offered. And a single dagger against a trained warrior? There was no way he could win. "Good day, Mister. I suggest you keep a set of eyes behind you. Never know when someone's going to make a move."

Ravion smiled at the coward. "Is that a threat?"

"Just a friendly reminder." Wallace offered a half-hearted salute and turned, making his way out the door.

The woman returned carrying a small, brass key tied by a piece of twine. She laid the key on the table and bent down, picking the chair up and returning it to its proper location. "Wallace Thurmoau. She shook her head. He's nothing but trouble."

"Did you have some experience with him?"

"Aye, a few years ago. Just got him paid back last summer. Took every bit of savings we had, but we're done with him now thank the gods. What can I get you to eat?"

"Anything without turnips, thank you."

She nodded and made her way back toward the kitchen.

A few moments later a young man brought out a platter with sliced meat and stewed vegetables piled around it. A large hunk of bread rested on the edge of the plate, the bottom side slightly soggy from the collection of juices. The man sat the dish on the table, sliding it across to the seated warrior. "What can I get ya' to drink?"

"If you have any available, I'll have tea. Though if not, water's fine."

He bowed and rushed off.

Ravion moved the bread in hopes that it wouldn't collect any more moisture. Spooning the vegetables he took a bite, tasting the butter melted into them.

The young man returned a moment later carrying a small, glass mug and ceramic pitcher. Steam rose from the top. He laid the cup on the table and poured the water into it. It swirled, turning a murky brown from the minced leaves resting at the bottom. He slid the cup across the table and set the pitcher on the edge. Pulling out a chair he took a seat. "So, yer' gonna help us get out from under ol' Wallace, huh?"

Ravion wiped the food from his mouth and regarded the boy. He had to have been in his late teens. More than likely trapped in such an existence, tending to his parent's needs. There was no shame in it, though he never desired such a life. "One of many issues I'd like to assist with."

"Well, good luck with em'. Guy's a snake. Wouldn't surprise me if he's throwing money around right now. Probably gonna' hire someone to come after you. That's what he does to people that can't pay em'."

"He fancies himself too righteous to get his hands dirty." One of the men playing cards said from across the room.

Ravion glanced over at them. Their game had ceased. Now all eyes were on him. "I assume you've seen this?"

"Don't have to see it. Been through it. 'Bout five years back, I owed him a handful of silver. He hired some kids to come beat on me every day for a week. At the end I was still two silver short. He had my leg broken. Wouldn't do it himself. Always sent someone else to deliver the message."

"That ain't all." The boy interjected. "He's got a whole group of guys workin' for em'. One of these shops misses a payment, he sends em' to rough the place up."

Ravion took a sip of the tea. It had just a hint of citrus mixed with barley. "I see. Sounds like I may have my work cut out for me. Do any of you know what I'm looking to face during these trials?"

The elderly man shuffled the deck of cards and began dealing them out again. "I've never seen anyone finish them. It's a week-long trial. The sole object is to survive. Nothing is off limits. If you last the week, the position's yours. I don't recall anyone other than the mage completing them."

"I thought you said you've never seen anyone finish."

"I did. I've been around a long time and never seen it. The mage was before my time. He was the last lord we had. Though nobody's sure why he left. Some say he went on to bigger things. Others say the seat is cursed. Hard to say. But nobody last long."

"This mage. Did he have a name?"

"Sure did. Though they say the chair strips it from you. Don't know if there's any truth to that. He was called Primeren when I was a boy. Never heard it spoken again after he disappeared. Throne's been empty ever since."

"Good to know."

"No problem." The man shifted to face his friend, clearly growing impatient with his lack of attention. "Oh, one more thing. You'd better learn to sleep with one eye open. When I said anything goes, I meant it. The last kid who tried had his throat slit while he was asleep. These people don't hold anything back."

"Thank you. I'll keep that in mind."

Staggering from the powerful blow, Ravion caught himself before he fell. He exhaled, forcing his senses into submission. His blackened vision returned revealing the head of a large mallet headed straight for him. Relying on his agility he twisted, narrowly dodging the crushing blow. A fence post collapse in his stead. Noting the large man's broad side, Ravion thrust his palm outward, shoving firming into the fleshy part of man's shoulder.

Caught off guard by the unexpected pressure point, th man staggered sideways, the buried hammer slipping from his grip.

Ravion spun around, using the distraction to position himself. Stepping behind the man he jumped on his back, locking his arms around his thick, muscular throat. He could feel the throbbing pulse beneath his grip, increasing against constriction.

Dozens of spectators cheered from the outskirts of the battle, careful to keep their distance. They didn't want to risk getting caught in the fight. Some feared for the smaller, more agile man. While others in the crowd cheered the brute, begging him to spill blood.

Ravion could hear the mixed cheers. They were the least of his concerns at the moment. So long as everyone kept their distance he wasn't overly concerned.

The barbarian panted heavily, staggering against the added weight. His already red face was beginning to turn purple from lack of oxygen.

Ravion felt the man growing weak. "Did Wallace hire you?"

Choking on his words, he managed to get the single syllable out. "Yhus!"

Ravion squeezed as hard as he could, feeling bones pop beneath his arms. He wasn't sure if they were his own or his prey. Clinging tight, he felt the man stumble.

The brute fell face first into the dirt, sending a cloud of dust into the air around them.

Ravion felt the impact. Even softened by his cushion it didn't help his arm any. His elbow throbbed, but he'd survive. Ensuring the fight was finished, he slowly released his hold, hoping the man would stay down. Ravion ensured the man was still breathing. There was no sense in killing him over something so trivial.

The barbarian drooled into the dusty road, unaware of the world around him. His chest heaved, compensating for the lack of air he'd suffered.

Smiling, Ravion stood to his full height, knocking the dust from his clothing. He rubbed his bruised elbow, feeling the broken skin at the nub. It was bruised and tender, but relatively minor all things considered. He wiped the sweat from his forehead and looked at the mixture of glossy perspiration, blood, and smeared dirt clung to his fingers. Instinctively, he wiped it on his pant leg and searched the crowd for any other challengers. He took a small amount of pleasure locking eyes on the several he'd already defeated. They hadn't expected him to be ready for their ambush. Their whole plan fell apart having underestimated his superior dexterity.

A sharp pain shot through his side. Caressing his ribs, Ravion softly pushed, hoping it would ease the pain. He couldn't be sure, but it was possible two of them were broken. Though he wasn't going to give them the satisfaction of knowing that. Slowly making way for the water trough, Ravion dipped his hands into the cold water and cleaned his face.

The cool liquid rouse his senses. He glanced at the sheathed sword stashed beneath it, happy it was still there. Eyeing his father's hilt, he took a large gulp and turned to make his way toward the center of the crossroads again. It was foolish, but he declined the use of his weapon. If he didn't have to kill anyone, maybe he could keep it that way. There was no reason to take a life over such silly sport. Besides, doing the rite barehanded would prove he was the strongest among them.

Ravion marched to the center of the crossroad, burying his pain. Throwing his hands up despite the shooting agony in his side, he shouted above the chatter of the voyeurs. "I've bested every man that's had the courage to face me. I've done so without weapon, for the glory and honor required of me by the parameters of the Rite of Godrick and the sacred laws of Krondar. Is there anyone else who will face me?"

The crowd erupted in deafening roar of shouts and celebration. Not a single word could be heard above the commotion.

Ravion searched their rank, unsure where the next one was coming from. He needed to find him quick. It wouldn't serve his purpose to be hit before he was ready.

A glimmering head towered above the rest, pushing its way through to the front. Clear of the line, an even larger man than the last was revealed. He wore a blood red tunic and tan, leather breeches covered in soot. His bald head was offset by a long, handlebar mustache. He didn't carry a weapon, but from the look of his bulging muscles he didn't need one. The challenger stepped into the opening, pressing his knuckles against each other.

Ravion heard them pop from the distance. Wiping the blood from his face, he took a deep breath and prepared himself for the fight.

The man charged, ramming his shoulder into the dreuslayer's gut. Lifting him into the air he carried him across the clearing and rammed into one of the fence posts. It splintered beneath their weight and broke, sending Ravion to the ground with it.

Panic enveloped him, stealing his breath. Forcing himself to remain calm, Ravion sucked through his nose, hoping to avoid taking too much at once. It was hard to breathe through the dried blood collected in his nasal passage but it was required if he was going to be methodical.

The huge man grabbed his dirty, loose fitting, blue clothing. Pulling him from the dirt he lifted him a few feet and slammed him back into the ground. Wasting no time he drew back and punched, hoping to break the smaller man's will.

Ravion saw the incoming blow. Throwing his hand, he caught the man's arm and slowed the attack. Seizing the opportunity he kicked out, wrapping his legs around the man's shoulders and head. He squeezed with every ounce of strength he had hoping to drain him of his raw power.

The challenger easily lifted and slammed him back down. He was severely limited in his current state. Lifting again, he repeated the process, unable to break the agile dreuslayer's hold.

Ravion exhaled each time he hit the ground, keeping his body under control. The pain was excruciating, but he had to endure. *For Senaria!* Squeezing tighter, the man began to weaken beneath his grip. He had to compliment the man on his tactic. It was a good attempt, but he'd planned for such by using each blow to strengthen his hold. It wouldn't be much longer now. His legs were compressing the man's throat. A moment longer and he wouldn't be able to breathe. That would give him the upper hand he'd been waiting for. The man slammed him into the ground again, heaving between his legs. It seemed he lacked the strength to pick him up again.

The grip tightened around his throat. He had to break free. He couldn't hold his breath for long and even if he could, there were other ways to shut a man down with access to his neck. He was already beginning to slow and his arms were getting heavy.

Ravion tightened, taking the slack from his exhausting opponent. He'd already won, so long as nothing changed in the next few seconds. But it would. It always did. Ravion forced a premature smile beneath the surface. Not because he wasn't entitled to it, but because it was possible his nose would start to bleed again. Feeling the last bit of strength leave his opponent he stared into his pleading eyes. "Are you one of Wallace's boys?"

The man shook his head as best he could.

"I thank you for that. You have my respect." Squeezing a moment longer, the man fell limp. Releasing his hold, Ravion ensured no permanent damage was done to either himself or the unconscious man. He stretched his back, feeling his ribs pop back into place. If anything they felt better now. Knocking the dust from him once again, he turned to the crowd. "Is there no one else?" Searching their faces, he hoped no one would step forward.

Moonlight reflected off the glazed window illuminating the room in a pale white. The wooden door slowly creaked open revealing a cloaked figure. It stepped into the room and closed the door. Cautiously making its way toward the bed it stared at the gently rising and falling blanket made of thick, green-dyed wool.

Ravion heard the floorboards creak. Gathering his senses he listened to the footsteps, slowly making their way closer to him. He could feel the warmth of a body hovering over him. Waiting for the perfect moment, he cracked his eyes just enough to see the figure. "Senaria?"

"Shhh, you should be sleeping. You've had a rough day. You need to rest."

"What are you doing here? It's not safe for you yet."

Senaria gently caressed his cheek. Smiling, she took in his sight. He was one of a kind. A noble warrior unlike any she'd met before. "I had to see you. I wanted to make sure you were alright."

A smile came to his face. Throwing the blanket to the side, Ravion reached out and pulled her beside him, kissing her deeply. His ribs argued in protest, but it was worth it.

Lost in his embrace Senaria cuddled beside him, forgetting herself for the briefest of moments. Memories rushing back, she pushed him away hearing him wince in pain. "You need to rest. We can be together once you've healed."

"It's not that bad. Just a few bruises and scrapes." He lied.

She sighed and unwrapped her cloak. Tossing it on the table she pulled off her armor and weapons, laying them on top of it. Crawling into bed beside him, she kissed his forehead. "Tonight we sleep. You don't know what tomorrow's challenges will bring and I don't want to risk losing you do to some foolish exertion."

Ravion chuckled and pulled the blanket over them. "Yes, ma'am." Wrapping his arms around her, he pulled tight feeling a bond he'd never experienced before.

Hours passed and Ravion awoke seeing a figure standing in the shadows a few feet from the bed. He could feel Senaria's head lying against his chest. Glancing at the table, their weapons were too far out of reach. And he couldn't readily get to the dagger stuffed under the pillow, having not expected Senaria to join him.

The figure stepped forward brandishing a rusty dagger. "I— I'm sorry!"
The voice sounded like that of a child. The words shot fear through him. He ripped the blanket away, searching Senaria for a wound.

She awoke, jumping from his sudden outburst. Finding the intruder she reached over and grabbed her sword. The blade was unsheathed and at the figure's throat in the blink of an eye.

"Wait!" Ravion called out.

Senaria froze, keeping the blade outstretched and ready to strike.

"Lower you hood." Ravion sat up and kicked his bare feet off the bed, pressing them against the chilled floorboards. He wore a pair of loose fitting gray pants and no shirt. The figure slowly reached up, keeping the dagger in view. Grabbing hold of the hood it fell, revealing a young girl maybe twelve years in age.

Senaria looked from the girl to Ravion unsure what to do. She lowered her sword. "You're— You're just a girl."

"You said you were sorry. What have you done to be sorry for?" Ravion couldn't explain why, but none of this felt right. He was just happy Senaria was okay. He wasn't sure what he'd do if she came to harm because of him.

"I— I was supposed to kill you while you slept, but I couldn't do it. Not when I saw her with you."

"Who told you to kill me?"

"Wal— Wallace Thurmoau. He said if I did it, he'd forgive my ma' and pa's debt. I didn't want to, but I didn't have much other choice." The girl broke into tears unsure what she was going to do. "Since I couldn't do it. I don't know what's gonna happen to my folks now."

Senaria sheathed her sword and laid it back on the table. "You're welcome to stay with me, you and your parents, until this whole thing blows over."

Ravion laid his hand on her shoulder. "Are you sure that's a wise decision? I understand the reasoning. Just— Are you ready for that already?"

She smiled at him, placing her hand atop of his. "It'll be fine. If this is to be our new home we have to set an example. Besides, what other options are there?"

"I could send a missive to Marbayne and have a unit of border wardens sent this way. They could act as peace keepers until I'm able to deal with Wallace."

"And what would these people do in the meantime? It's obvious he's not going to stop until he has no choice. None of them are safe until he'd been dealt with."

Ravion smiled and kissed her forehead. She was a natural tactician. "You have a point."

"You'd really take care of us?" The girl was visibly shaken, though it was difficult to tell if it was due to fear or relief.

"It's the least I can do. You didn't kill the man I love. I can show kindness in turn." Senaria reassured the girl. "Gather your parents. We'll leave before the sun rises."

"Love, huh?" Ravion smiled, hearing the word.

"Shut up. We'll talk about it later." Senaria lightly punched his arm. Standing up, she quickly threw her armor and weapons into place and wrapped the cloak around herself. Leaning in, she kissed him once again. "Be careful. I don't want to lose you to something foolish."

Levi Samuel

Chapter IX
To Know Thyself

"Wake up! It's time to move."

Gareth opened his eye, staring into the darkened bag over his head. His back side was numb from the compact clay floor. His arms were sore from being bound. He felt someone grab him, pulling him to his feet.

"Hope you've got your rest. We've got a long way to go."

Stretching as best he could in his immobilized state, Gareth felt his spine pop several times, soothing the built-up tension. Extending his hands, he signaled he was ready.

The guard grabbed the bindings, guiding him through the underground corridors.

"Gniog er'ew kniht uoy od raf woh?"

"Taht rof ecnatsid yna levart d'i. Emoh a su dnuof Senaria. Rettam t'nseod."

"Hush up back there. Be on your guard. We're passing through dreu territory."

Gareth perked up hearing the name. If those bastards showed it'd give him the strength he needed to break free and slaughter every last one of them. Listening to the hushed voices he couldn't help but feel like he knew what they were saying. Clearing his mind he waited, listening to his surroundings.

"I really hope this place is as grand as she said it was. It'd suck to walk all this way only to find a shithole no better than these damned tunnels."

"Just a little further now. They should be lying in wait just around the corner. Come on! Remember, stab and back away. Don't want to get caught in the ambush."

What the hell? Why would he openly talk about an ambush? Why isn't anyone doing anything about it? Surely, he said it loud enough. Gareth felt a trickle of liquid drip from his nose. Raising his arm he pressed it against the thick sack, trying to wipe it way.

"They're just on the other side of that bend. Be ready!"

Gareth tensed unsure of what was about to happen. Bracing himself for anything, he listened intently. The familiar sound of an arrow's thud rang out in his head. He heard the death throes of one of the men around him.

"We're under attack!"

The clank of swords echoed off the cavern walls around him. He couldn't tell where anybody was, friend or foe. Struggling against the bindings Gareth shook his head in all directions, trying to dislodge his cover to no avail. His excitement and anger grew. He could feel it inside, threatening to spill forth. He had to channel it. He had to control it! Focusing rage toward desire, his senses expanded revealing his surroundings. He could see the walls and people. They weren't as he'd expected. They were cloudy, like figured in the fog. It wasn't much, but it was more than he had before. Glancing at the ropes he traced their shadowed form, locating the end. Marching toward the battle, gaining as much slack as he could, Gareth spotted one of the dreualfar hidden behind a rock. It had a short bow in hand and an arrow nocked, ready to fire. Focusing on the creature, a heat unlike any other engulfed him. It was as if he were holding flame, though it didn't burn.

Screams echoed around the bend. One of the dreualfar charged out, his clothing aflame. Desperately seeking anything to save him, he ran straight into a wall, dislodging one of the loose stones. It crashed down, crushing him in an instant.

"They're falling back. Regroup and find out how many we've lost!"

The ropes pulled taut, recalling Gareth to the group. "Wan ol eis otls th oa thawar. Ol ilw oon ol oar eeol oln ooh owte wa anwol!"

"What'd he say?"

"I don't know."

"You think we should remove his gag and find out?"

"You really want to risk him using that magic against us again?"

"What if it's important? It's not like Aerol's around to give the order. He didn't survive the fight."

"Rangar, what do you think? You were second in command. Should we let him speak?"

"Go for it, but he walks in front. If he flips his shit again it'll give us time to put a blade in his back."

The cloth tighten against his face for the briefest moment. Gareth recognized they were untying the cinched cord around his neck. His vision was blurry in the underdark, but it felt good being able to see again. Feeling the cool cavern breeze on his skin he glanced at the men before him. They truly were enemies of his enemy. Only one question remained, was that enough to excuse them for holding him prisoner?

"What the hell? You been headbutting the wall?" The mul'daron untied the gag, pulling it from his mouth.

"What do you mean?"

"Your face is covered in blood."

Gareth wiped his face on sleeve covering his shoulder. It was difficult to reach, but perhaps he could remove enough to keep it from being sticky. "No clue why."

"Whatever. You better not have the plague or nothin' like that. I've been through too much shit to die from something as ugly as that."

One of the other mul'daron spoke. He had a commanding tone about him and stood ahead of the rest. "You had something you wanted to say?"

Gareth glanced around, uncertain which one was guilty. Ready to defend himself, he repeated his previous statement. "One of you is a traitor. You knew about the ambush and stabbed your commander in the back." He searched their eyes looking for any sign of guilt.

"I highly doubt that. How would you even know? You've been in that sack too long. It's starting to mess with your head."

"I'm serious. I can prove it!"

"How?" The commanding mul'daron asked.

"Give me a moment." Gareth closed his eyes, focusing on the lingering rage inside him. Channeling it, he listened to everything and nothing at the same time. Voices flowed into his head revealing the darkest secrets imaginable. One in particular caught his interest.

"This guy can't prove nothin'. He didn't see me stab him. There's no way he could have."

Opening his eyes, Gareth continued listening, searching their faces for the owner of the voice. "Him!" The subdued dreuslayer nodded to the one that questioned his appearance.

"What! I didn't do nothin'! You can't prove it!"

"Check his dagger. I bet the wound will match that of the one in your commander's back."

Rangar approached the accused mul'daron. "Secure him."

Two of the others grabbed his arms to keep him stationary.

Rangar reached for the dagger at the mul'daron's waist. Snatching it, he could see the fresh blood clinging to the blade.

"What's this going to prove? What is this guy, a mind reader? You can't prove anything other than you're escorting a lunatic!"

Carrying the blade to the body of their fallen commander, Rangar carefully inserted the blade into the wound, making sure he didn't alter it in any way. "It's a perfect fit. Even the color of the blood matches."

"Oh come on! You're buying this shit? For all I know, you just stabbed him yourself to make it look like a match! You can't do this to me. I've got—"

Rangar flung the small blade, burying it into the captive mul'daron's throat. He choked on his own blood and went limp. The other mul'daron released him, letting his body fall to the cavern floor. Turning to Gareth, Rangar gave a light bow. "I thank you for exposing him and revealing who truly murdered Aerol. He was a good man and an even better friend."

"I only met him the once, but he seemed—." Gareth paused, selecting a fitting word. "— Trustworthy."

"Nonetheless, you have my gratitude. In return, I'm going to release you of your binding for the remainder of our trip. When we get close I'll have to blindfold you again, but I promise it won't last long."

"Understood. Just know, if we run into any more dreu I want first blood!"

Rangar chuckled. "I believe I can agree to those terms." Turning to his men, he gestured toward the bodies. "Quickly check them for anything of value. There's no sense of leaving anything behind for the dreu to lay claim."

The inn was bustling with patrons. Everybody wanted to get a look at the man on track to become their new lord. Despite the early morning, a band was on stage playing their newest tune in celebration of their savior.

"He walked into town, not a hero or a gent. He made his stand and claimed the Rite of Godrick. But look at him now, unmarred, nor in pain. Ravion's our savior, the savior of slaves. He took a stand against a tyrant. A man that weaseled his wealth. The people of Krondar were shaken. Bruised and beaten, and left to bad health. He said, 'Hey, your business is done here. I'll face every goon that you've got. A week full of trials is nothing. I may as well give it a shot.'

He walked into town, not a hero or a gent. He made his stand and claimed the Rite of Godrick. But look at him now, unmarred, nor in pain. Ravion's our savior, the savior of slaves.

The weasel wouldn't turn tail so easy. He had to put in his two cents. He hired every thug this side of Shadgull, and even hired a sickly old wench. But Ravion saw it all coming. He stared them all in the eye. In doing so empty handed, he still hasn't taken a life.

Went on to fight a brute, a bard, a scholar, and a mage. His strength of will defies the very dawn of this dark age. But look at him now, unmarred, nor in pain. Ravion's our savior, the savior of slaves.

But look at him now, unmarred, nor in pain, Ravion's our savior, the savior of slaves!"

Ravion chuckled at the song. It was a bit embellished he thought, but such was the nature of bards. No tale was good enough as it truly happened. Grabbing his tankard he tipped it back, tasting the final drops of broth. It had an unusual taste to it, but it was probably just the spices of this region. They all seemed different than the one's he'd grown accustomed to.

The room was nearing capacity. Everyone wanted to be near him, as if somehow his proximity brought them hope. The band started another song, drowning out the constant roar of conversation.

Ravion felt the beads of sweat clinging his forehead. He wasn't sure if it was the constant clutter of people or something else. Whatever it was, he didn't feel well. Exhaling, he closed his eyes, trying to focus. Dizziness claimed him, as if his insides were churning. Staggering from his seat, Ravion balanced against the thick, wooden table. Finding his resolve, he pressed through the crowd he made for the door.

The cool outside air assaulted him, chilling his flesh. It was both a comfort and torture. On one hand it soothed and dulled the nausea. It was the sweat clinging to him that was the problem. The breeze sent a chill straight into him, freezing beneath the surface. Ravion shivered, rubbing his arms in hopes it would warm him. Something wasn't right. He was growing weak. Was it the food? The spices? Involuntarily, he heaved, expelling the acidic contents of his stomach. It splattered in the dusty ground outside the tavern's door. He felt better, but it was far from over.

Stepping from the wooden ramp at the entrance, Ravion noticed a strange scent in the air. There was a familiarity to it, one he couldn't recall. But he knew he'd smelt it before. An unseen force slammed into him, knocking him from his feet. Rolling from his back, Ravion searched the street in hopes of finding his assailant.

"I'm glad you came outside. I was worried I'd have to blast you through the wall of the inn. There's no telling how many innocent bystanders would have been caught in the crossfire."

Ravion glanced at the approaching figure, his vision blurry from the blast. Details slowly took form, revealing a man in his late twenties. He wore brown robes and had the look of a mage. He clearly wasn't of the Tower, if such a thing was of importance since its disappearance. "It's nice to see that you had the decency to blindside me when I was alone. Are you one of Wallace's people?"

The man chuckled at the question. "Let's just say that I know of him. And his money is greatly appreciated, but no. I have my own reasons for being here. Who could pass up the chance to put Ravion Santail in his place? Though I must say, you haven't aged a day."

What? "I apologize, you have me at an impasse. Have we met before?" Ravion push himself from the ground, finding his feet. It took every ounce of strength he had, but the illness was letting up since he'd vomited.

"I wouldn't expect you to remember me. It was a long time ago. Just know that I've spent years searching you out. I can't begin to express my excitement when I learned that the infamous Ravion Santail had landed in a place called Krondar and he was fair game to anyone who wished to face him. I want you to know that when I kill you this day, my father will have finally been avenged."

His skin was cold despite the pouring sweat seeping from his body. His clothes were drenched, clinging to him. Each chilled gust of wind, cut to the bone. Ravion wanted to vomit again, but such an action would present opportunity for this man to strike. Closing his eyes in an attempt to block out the cramping pain, he found his words. "I'm afraid I have no clue who you are or what you're talking about. If I killed your father, I offer my apologies. But you must understand if I'm responsible for his death, I had good reason."

"Damn your reasons! I was but a boy when you showed up. But I remember your face like it was yesterday." Thrusting his palm forward, another burst of energy erupted. The spell flew straight into the weakened man.

The force surround him. Ravion tried to withstand it, but it was too powerful. His feet left the ground, launching him backward several feet. Landing hard on his back, Ravion rolled and jumped to his feet. "That's the last one you get!"

The man laughed at his taunt. He was already defeated, he just didn't know it yet. Pointing his palms together, fingers nearly touching, the man summoned the energies inside himself. A ball of flame formed between his hands. The further he separated his hands, the larger it grew. Bringing them overhead, he flung forward and launched the torso-sized fireball at his target.

Ravion watched the flaming sphere soar toward him. He didn't have the agility to dodge it currently. He was too weak to run. Out of options, he did the only thing he could. Ravion side-stepped as best he could and twisted, letting the flame graze him. He could smell the heat burning into his clothes, but to his surprise it didn't hurt. The ball flew past, narrowly brushing him upper body and face. It exploded behind him, engulfing one of the dilapidated wagons lining the road. Marching as quickly as he dared, Ravion watched the man summon another fireball.

"You won't be so lucky this time!" Flinging the newly formed ball, he watched in anticipation.

Ravion continued forward. There was no way he could dodge. He was too close. Holding his breath, the flame collided head on. His clothes burst into flame, warming him in the chilly morning air. It felt good, as if the remaining illness was burning away in the heat. He was getting stronger. Closing his eyes, Ravion felt the flame wrap around him, shrouding him in their comfort. He could feel the aura of his people. It felt brighter, stronger, as if it was absorbing the magic of the spell and strengthening him. The warming energy reached his core, burning away the last of whatever plagued him.

The fireball crashed, exploding upon his chest. Instead of burning him to a cinder, it twisted and fell apart, as if it had been dispelled after detonation. That was impossible! He stared dumfounded at his opponent. How'd he do it? If the fire couldn't hurt him, he'd have to use something less nobody could withstand!

Townspeople came running, hearing the commotion. They crowded around the pair, hoping to get the best show. Packed shoulder to shoulder, they watched the spectacle, silently cheering their unarmed savior. He was out matched in every way, yet he always prospered. If he could survive this final day he'd be their new lord. Such a prospect was both reassuring and frightening. They'd been unregulated so long, how much of their lives would change? Yet it was exciting to witness the trials first hand.

His dexterity returned. Ravion held his pace, hoping to use it sparingly. He didn't know exactly what made him feel better, and there was no sense in wasting the second wind to find out. "You're running out of time. When I reach you, this will be over." Truthfully, he didn't want to hurt the man. He had no quarrel with him, aside from his attempted murder, but that was a technicality. It seemed most people wanted to kill him these days. But he wouldn't allow this man to stop him. If it came to it, he'd do whatever he had to in order to survive.

The man flung his hands forward letting his magics loose. A dark liquid appeared on the ground beneath Ravion's feet.

Ravion slipped and slid the syrup-like substance, but he didn't fall. Unfortunately, it slowed him drastically. Which meant he had more time to be targeted. The thick oil beneath his feet felt akin to walking on glossy ice with hardened soles. Each step forced him balance or risk falling. At least the oil didn't seem to stick. That was good in the fact that he wouldn't have to clean it off his boots.

Reacting on impulse the mage formed another fireball. This one didn't have to be huge or special. Launching it into the grease, he watched it ignite with ease. The flame spread like wildfire engulfing the entire area in a burning magical heat.

Flames flared to life reaching chest height. Ravion felt the wind tear through the holes in his clothing. Much more of this and he'd have to finish this fight naked. He was fortunate that the heat didn't bother him. It was a welcome surprise. Carefully making his way through the flaming oil, Ravion stepped onto the dirt patting the charred holes in his clothes, hoping to save them a bit longer. "This is your last chance. You'd better not mess up."

"You arrogant prick!" Closing his eyes the mage forced every ounce of will into a single, deadly attack. He had to ignore the approaching man. Any distraction would take away from the full effect of his spell. He could feel the torrent of magical energies flowing around him. Just a bit longer and he'd have his revenge.

Ravion watched the dark power swirl around his opponent. He wasn't sure what was happening, but he knew it wasn't good. It was as if the world around them was being destroyed. The air darkened and the ground cracked, ripping itself free. The jagged chunks crumbled, disappearing into the void. Only the man at its center, could be seen. The tear in reality grew ever closer, swallowing everything in its wake. "You're losing control! Abandon your spell or it's going to kill you!" Ravion pleaded.

He heard the words echo in his mind. *Don't listen to him. He's trying to distract you. Kill him. Claim justice for all you've lost!* Pressing the spell ever larger, the man felt the energies reach their full potential. He was almighty. Nothing could stop him now. Opening his eyes fear enveloped him. The dark energies continued to grow, pulling at him. *What have I done?*

Ravion backed away. The power was unstable, threatening to devour everything. He had to do something. If it continued to grow, there was no telling how much damage it would cause. Quite possibly, it could suck the entire city into the void. Looking around, Ravion spotted one of the rail post of the broken fence beside him. It was lying in the dirt, but looked solid enough to help. Snatching up the rough-cut lumber, he fed it into the void, keeping hold on the end. The swirling current drew it toward the center. "Put aside your anger and grab hold. It's going to kill you!"

"Then I'll take you with me!" Grabbing the thick post, the mage yanked, pulling the unarmed man into the sundered darkness. Taking victory in dislodging his enemy, the man lost his balance and tumbled into the tear. His body was ripped apart and gone before he had time to scream.

Ravion felt the draw pulling him further into the rift. He had nothing to grab hold of. Nothing to stop himself. Surrounded by shadow, he felt a familiar presence. As if a hand pressed into his back, he stopped moving toward the rift. A broken light appeared in the heart, growing brighter by the moment, similar to how his aura reacted to the magical flame. "Kane?"

"You can't be here. You have to find a way to get me out!" The armored warrior stepped into view. He looked stronger than ever, standing proud in the twisting energies. They wrapped around him, licking the glowing light.

Ravion felt the pull soften, though it was far from gone. "How'd you get here?"

"We don't have time to discuss that. I'm trapped on the other side. I tried to escape, but he pushed me back down. Get out of here and save me!"

Glancing at the broken aura, Ravion noticed it pulsed, drawing in the shadow. A ring of normality formed around the armored warrior, as if the two were canceling each other.

That gave him an idea. "I need to absorb it!" Ravion declared. Focusing on his own aura, he let the power rush through him. It wasn't as he'd imagined it would be. The chaotic energies of the void both fed and drained his innate magic. He was growing stronger, but fatigue was starting to set in. Letting his thirst expand, Ravion opened his eyes. The rift shimmered, seeming weaker by the moment. Suddenly, it faded and snapped shut, disappearing from existence and sealing Kane inside. The current subsided and the darkness disappeared revealing a large ring of barren earth where grass had once been.

Cheers reached his ears, the unharmed spectators singing their praise. "Ravion! Ravion! Ravion!"

Taking a deep breath, he let out a sigh of relief. He just hoped no more showed up today. He wasn't in the mood. Glancing around, a familiar face greeted him. The man stepped forward, silently parting the mob of excited spectators. His white and purple robes were clean as ever, moving as if they defied the winds. "Well done, Ravion."

The exhausted dreuslayer dropped to his knee, locking sight on the ground in front of him. "Baron Perrimen, you honor me with your presence. If you're here to challenge, you know as well as I that I would never fight you, even in friendly competition."

Perrimen placed his hand on the kneeling man's shoulder. Lost in the lengthened, red hair he stared at the back of his head. "Find your feet, Ravion. I'm not here for competition, nor am I the baron. You know I've not held that role for a very long time."

The young dalari stood and looked upon his friend. "Then why, may I ask, are you here?"

The aged, yet youthful wizard smiled. His voice echoed around them as if magically amplified for all of Krondar to hear. "This man has fought valiantly, would you say?"

The crowd erupted in cheers of agreement and praise.

"He's bested every opponent that's had the courage to face him!"

Again the citizens erupted.

"The Rite of Godrick has long been seen as the supreme law of Krondar. As a nation of strength, so too should you be led by strength. I believe I speak for all of us when I say that this man has shown us the essence of strength, not just of muscle, but of mind as well. The rite states seven days of trial. And this man has survived to his seventh. So I ask you, fair people of Krondar, will you allow this man to be your lord? A fair and strong man in every sense of the word. Will you allow him the honor of standing at the head of your ranks? To guide, direct, and watch over you. Will you allow him the privilege to call Krondar his home, a land where he can build and, gods willing, raise a family for generations to come?"

The roar was deafening. The very ground shook from their chants of acceptance.

"As a citizen of this harsh, yet fair land, and former Baron of Dalmoura, would you allow me the privilege and authority to label this man, Lord of Krondar?"

Everything from bread to coin rained from the sky, showering the city in tribute of the naming. Never before had they seen one take the throne. One who had the ability to walk through magic unscathed meant a strong ruler who would see them to victory. For the first time in their lives they saw hope. Hope meant a greater life than simple survival.

"Ravion Santail, I ask that you take a knee!"

The dreuslayer obeyed finding it amusing that moments before he was asked to stand.

Perrimen extended his hand letting the energies of the world around him twist into a faint blue light. They entwined, growing out and solidifying. In the blink of an eye an elegant longsword, etched by the most fantastic looking runes, rested in his hand, outstretched above the kneeling man. "By the laws of this land and the citizens that inhabit it, I name you Lord of Krondar, Master of Barbarians!" Tapping his shoulder with the ethereal blade, Perrimen alternated to the other, ceremoniously dubbing the man before him.

The crowd went wild at the naming of their new leader. Many broke from the group to begin preparations for a grand festival. People fought for the right to host the events, arguing over the most trivial of details.

The well-dressed wizard waved his hand, dismissing the weapon. A silver crown with a red leather lining took its place. "Please rise, My Lord."

Ravion stood, feeling the felt-lined crown fall into place atop his head. A sense of pride washed over him. He watched the flock rush toward him, begging to drape their finest garb over his ruined clothes.

Perrimen turned toward the scattered union. "My people, eat, drink, be merry. Your lord has finally presented himself!"

Several large men carried a thick, wooden throne from one of the buildings. Desire heavy on their faces, they laid it to rest a few steps from their lord, holding position and awaiting his word.

Ravion looked over the throne. It was rough and unforgiving, much like the land it resided over, but it would serve its purpose. Marching toward the seat, he spun around and claimed it. Despite its rugged appearance, it was surprisingly comfortable. Though he didn't intend to get used to it. The position was an honor he'd gladly serve, but standing on ceremony alone was a useless tactic. He was not going to be a ruler of words. He'd lead by example and be a ruler of actions.

Perrimen approached the throne giving a respectful bow. "My Lord, Ra'dulen. I bring a gift for your naming." He reached into his over-sized sleeve and retrieved a finely crafted wooden box. It was long and slender, engraved across the seams by hundreds of tiny runes.

Ravion stared blankly at the mention of the name. No one had called him that since he was a boy. "My Lord, you've extended me enough gifts this day. I fear another may push the boundaries of overcompensation." The sudden lack of ambient noise caught his attention. Ravion glanced around, realizing the townspeople were frozen in place, mid-action. Returning his attention to the wizard, he noted only himself and the man remained free. "I've seen such magics only once before. You've learned much in your absence."

Perrimen didn't say a word. Offering the narrow box he gestured for the man to take it. "That statement holds more truth than you'll ever know. As for this box, let me rephrase. What resides inside is not so much a gift as it is a curse. You're one of a very select few I can trust to keep such an object. It will call to you. It will plead to twist you. You must not let it. You must keep it safe, for if word of its existence spreads others will seek it."

Ravion took the container, staring at the runes. Had he not recognized the etchings he would have though them little more than decoration. "It's written in Eldar?" Silence answering him, he glanced up, seeing the evaporating orange glow. Silently reading the scripture, the words of the ancient language returned to him. *Five there were. Five there shall always be. Let none rise above. But should they, flee!* The box sprung open revealing a thin, wavy blade of black and purple. Ravion closed the lid and stuffed it beneath the layers of fur clinging to his shoulders.

The world around him broke its hold and the townsfolk returned to their tasks, unaware of their lost moments.

Chapter X
Once Lost

The crude boat glided gently along the top of the murky, green water. Krenin plunged the pole into the soft bed pushing himself further along. His eyes searched the surrounding forest. He hadn't seen any sign of company, but couldn't shake the feeling he was being watched. Hoping it remained that way, Krenin pressed again. The boat lunge forward, deeper into alfaren territory. The hearty orcs of the north knew better than to travel alone. He knew better than to travel alone. But what choice did he have? Ensuring his trident badge was visible, he pressed on, hoping it would warrant investigation if he encountered the wood folk. Krenin couldn't recall how long he'd been gone. While time stood still in the arena, the seasons had changed since his last visit to the wondrous forest of Evinwood. It remained beautiful, but there was an unsettling dreariness he couldn't shake. It was as if the trees were less inviting than he remembered, warning him in their silence.

Ahead a large tree had fallen, blocking off the wide waterway. Several smaller limbs had collected against it, forming a barrier across the surface. Guiding his boat to bank, Krenin stepped onto land for the first time since he'd found the river. He'd traveled nearly three days following the water's edge before he'd came across the landing. Had it not been for word of his victory against the dragonkin, Drognau, he had no doubt the orcs would have parted with the small punt. As it were, reputation and coin opened more doors than he could ever know. For the first time, as far as he knew, a half-orc was revered among his kind. And the name just happened to be his own.

Pulling the wooden device to shore, Krenin searched for an area to cross. The thick tree, even in its current state, had to be at least forty-foot tall and there was no telling how deep it had buried when it fell. He couldn't recall any such blockage when the orcs brought him this route, gods knew how long ago. Glancing at the debris, the broken limbs were fresh. The wood hadn't yet dried. And the dirt around the impact site had yet to sprouted grass. That meant it had to have recently fallen. He couldn't help but feel it was an intentional dam. The tree appeared strong, aside from the areas the bark had ripped away during its fall. It was as if someone simply cut it down to block the river pass, greatly delaying travel and offering several ambush points along the way. Of course he was no expert on trees, or anything else for that matter. There just seemed to be something fabricated about this. It seemed too intentional and planned to be anything else.

Sighing heavily, Krenin pressed his booted foot against the flat rim of the boat and stepped down hard. The curved bottom edge rolled, lifting the square shaped nose into the air. Krenin grabbed the rope runs along the sidewalls and pushed his arms through. In a moment, the punt was slung across his back like a wooden shell. Securing the pole he pressed it into the ground and made his way inland, hoping to find a way around the natural wall.

Hours passed and not so much as a slight low area presented itself. Krenin considered trying to climb over, but there was no denying he'd spend more time cutting foot holes than it'd take to reach either end, likely the top as the trunk seemed to be subtly tapering. This had to be the largest tree this forest had to offer and he hadn't even found the leaves yet. The snap of a twig roused his senses. Spinning around, Krenin's brown deep-brown eyes searched the dense woodland. Surely the alfar weren't so foolish as to alert him to their presence. "I know you're here, somewhere. I am Krenin of Marbayne. Ally of your people, I ask for help. Show me where to cross."

A smooth, elegant voice echoed from the trees, closer than Krenin thought possible. It had a familiar sound to it, yet he couldn't place where he'd heard it before. They all sounded and looked the same to him.

"All you had to do was ask. We would have gladly shown you the path hours ago. After all, maintaining our allegiance with The Order is of the utmost importance, now more so than ever. Even if it is to help a half-breed such as you." The tone shifted to distaste toward the end.

Krenin watched a band of alfar step into view. He didn't recognize the face, but the armor danced into his memory. This was the alfar that he'd met with Malakai. The black leather scales weren't an easy detail to forget. "So you show me way across?"

Jaklus smiled. "Not exactly. Your build is incapable of keeping up with us and we don't have time to wait for you."

"But you have time to watch me for hours?"

"Details." The myrkalfar captain gestured dismissively. "Your friend Ravion has made quite the name for himself. And in doing so, he has strengthened our borders. Your border wardens have expanded their territory, and forced the orc pigs into our traps. The few that have escaped traveled east into the wildlands of Vale. For the first time since the orc wars ended, our borders are secure on the south face. Your friend has single-handedly been responsible for that. That alone is why I'm going to help you."

"So Ravion secure the borders? Good for him. Glad he doing something in my absence." Krenin smiled, feeling his lips stretch around his small tusks. He watched the alfar captain nod to one of the others. It was dressed differently. He couldn't be certain if it was male or female. They all looked weak and feminine. The fact the alfar worn no armor and was seemingly unarmed didn't help. Krenin listened to the alfar chant some strange words. An orange glow expanded and wrapped around both him and the caster, swallowing the pair. Krenin's stomach churn as if his insides were being twisted. The forest disappeared from sight, replaced by an open field on the outskirts of a fairly large city. He recognized it at once. This was Fender's Spear. Though it wasn't as run down as remembered. The buildings were patched and clean. The wood planks along the siding had been secured or replaced. For the first time in as long as he could recall, the city was clean. The broken wagons were gone. Actual shops and vendor stands were in their place. It was a city to be proud of.

"Go to the civil hall. You'll find Ravion there." The alfar disappeared in the same glow of orange.

Ink rolled from the tip of the feathered quill, soaking into the fibers of the rough parchment. A single candle rested in its holder, dimly illuminating the newly constructed room. The walls were made of polished cherry and were lined with shelves of books, stands, and tapestries. It was a bit more extravagant than he needed, but the architect insisted. A heavy knock echoed from the other side of the door. Ravion flipped the page, shuffling several others over the top. Resting the quill in its silver holder, he interlocked his fingers and placed his elbows on the desk. "Enter."

The door creaked open revealing a skinny man clad in the silver and blue tabard of Shadgull. He stepped in and bowed deeply. "Lord Ravion, I bring word from Lord Erik De Leon of Shadgull. He seeks audience with the Lords of Dalmoura in regard to his father's murder."

Ravion stood, approaching the messenger. "When does he desire this audience?"

"The next full moon, My Lord. In two weeks' time."

Ravion stopped in front of the man. "Please inform your master of my deepest condolences. The news of Remle's passing was unfortunate. He was a good man. One whom I held the highest respect for. Sadly, I will not be able to attend. Pressing matters of state have occupied my time of late, and I'll be unavailable at the time of your lord's gathering. Perhaps I can meet with him when I pass through Shadgull in the next few days. Otherwise, it'll have to wait until I return."

The messenger nodded, taking a step back. "Understood, My Lord. I shall inform him of your reply, upon my return." He paused, leaving an uncomfortable silence in the dimly lit study. Finding his words, he continued. "My master also wished me to extend his condolences to you in regard to the loss of your friend, Malakai. He has offered to host a grand celebration in his honor, if you so desired. Additionally, it seems Master Gareth and Master Kane have both have vanished without trace. My lord was wondering if you've heard from them. Their absence has been noticed."

Ravion shook his head. "No, thank you, but that won't be necessary. Malakai's loss is regrettable. Though his memory will live on. As for

Gareth, sadly I've not. I haven't seen him since the Dreu War. It's been over a year now. I question his fate, but the old cuss is too damned stubborn to die." Ravion chuckled, silently hoping his friend was okay. "Kane on the other hand had some business up north. That's part of what keeps me from joining Erik."

"Thank you, My Lord. I'll be sure to inform my master of this knowledge. I wish you good fortune in your endeavors."

Ravion nodded. "Thank you, messenger. Be sure to replenish your rations and seek lodging for the evening. You may return to your master in the morning." He extended his fist dropping a handful of silver into the man's palm.

The messenger bowed and backed out of the room, refusing to turn his back until he was out of sight. Waiting for the door to latch, Ravion returned to his desk and uncovered his document. Quickly finishing the missive, he rolled the parchment and blobbed the sealing wax over the lip. Firmly pressing his stamp into the cooling puddle he waited, letting it solidify. Removing the tool he inspected the seal, ensuring the raven perched atop the wolf's head was clearly visible. Tucking the scroll into his vest, Ravion turned to leave.

Reaching the door, another knock echoed. He pulled the ornate, wooden barrier toward him, stunned to find a half-orc upon the other side. "Krenin, my friend. I'm happy to see you. We were worried something had happened." Placing his hand on the half-orc's shoulder, Ravion invited him in. "I was just getting ready to leave, but I can spare a few moments for returning friends."

"Seems much changed since I left." Krenin stepped into the room, looking for a chair large enough for his frame. Not seeing one, he parted his feet enough to stand comfortably.

"Much indeed, though not all has been good. I'm sorry to inform you, but we lost Malakai during the Dreu War. But his death was not in vain. He ensured my survival and managed toppled a dreu city in the process."

Krenin stared at the perfectly seated floor boards. Their intricate grains ran the length of the room, creating an enticing pattern in the wood. It was a comfort from the cut of the words, deeper than any blade could reach. "Malakai a good friend and brother. I'll miss him."

"As will I, my friend. As will I. I wish I had time to hear all about your endeavors. Unfortunately, I'm running a bit behind schedule. I would have a task of you, if you're so inclined."

"What you need?"

"I have a caravan leaving for Marbayne in the morning. Would you do me the favor of ensuring it arrives unmolested? There's a fair amount of information contained in the cargo that I can't risk falling into the wrong hands. I'd feel much better about it if you were to accompany it."

"If it means I don't have to walk home." Krenin gave a toothy smile.

"I don't foresee that being a problem. If all goes according to plan I'll be there in about a week. I'll bring you up to date on everything when I arrive. Feel free to make yourself at home. I, unfortunately, have to run."

"Travel well. See you in a week."

Ravion extended his hand feeling the half-orc lock his meaty grip around his forearm. Pulling him close, they exchanged a brotherly hug and parted. "I'm glad you're home." Ravion spun around and headed for the door.

The golden fields danced in the evening air. Ravion could see the forested mountains in the distance. Ensuring he wasn't followed, he darted across the open and took cover in a rocky outcropping. Studying the rocks he located the hidden trail. Quickly navigating the narrow ridge, Ravion stepped onto the overlook and took position in the center of an odd formation. He could see the spires of the reconstructed keep towering above the sparse trees and jutting stone. Had he not known what to look for they would have blended perfectly into their surroundings.

The moon reached its peak height, beaming its glowing white onto the outstretched ledge. Ravion watched it inch ever closer to its mark, reflecting off the glossy finish of the polished stones, propped in a ring at the center of the rise. The individual beams launched from one to the next, encompassing him. Moving into position, Ravion's body interrupted the pattern and sent a single beam of focused light into the darkened ravine. The reflected moonlight burned bright, revealing the correct path as if it was the only possible option in the maze of trails. At a near run, careful to reach the ground before the light faded, Ravion stepped onto the grassy landscape amazed at the elegance of the sight before him.

The huge fortress grounds stood radiantly in the moonlight just outside an equally large cavern. Ravion approached, making sure he was clearly visible. There was little worry they'd mistake him for an intruder, but there was no sense in taking unneeded risks.

Seeing him, the mul'daron guards snapped to attention and offered a silent salute. They returned to their ease once he passed.

Ravion nodded, acknowledging each one. They were loyal to Senaria. That alone meant they had his respect. Marching toward the entrance with purpose, he stepped into the courtyard. Several stone runs were lined with food of various color and shape. It was unlikely enough to sustain their full number, but it would at least supplement them until the fields were ready for harvest. Making his way along the stone walkway, Ravion watched the heavy, reinforced wooden doors swing open. There was no denying they'd done wonders for the place. Nearly all the rotten wood had been replaced. The moss had been scraped from the stone, leaving an ashy tone behind. Even the damaged walls had been restacked and mortared into place. This keep may as well have been a different construct from the first time he'd seen it.

Ravion stepped through the doors, remembering the face of each guard he passed. Entering the common room he turned and marched toward the stairway running beside the grand hall. He was not here for ceremony. There was no sense in taking the long way around. Cresting the top, he followed the balcony and came to another, smaller set of stairs. A guard stood posted on each side of the closed door. "Is she in?"

"Yes, My Lord. She's expecting you."

Ravion pulled the brass ring, opening the decorated barrier. Stepping inside, he closed the door behind him and smiled at the figure across the room. Senaria stared out the large, open window overlooking the courtyard, grounds, and cavern beyond.

Ravion strode past the polished table running the length of the room. Its chairs were pushed in neatly, showing no one had used it recently. The room was empty and barren, save for the table in the center and the pair of them. He stepped behind her, wrapping his arms around her waist and laying his chin on her shoulder. "Have I told you I missed you?"

"Every time we're apart." Senaria gently touched his cheek. Spinning in his embrace, she threw her arms over his neck and passionately kissed his lips. Breaking away, she stared deep into his eyes, feeling lost in their pensive gaze. "I'm glad you've come. I was beginning to think you'd forgotten about me." Senaria joked, keeping her arms locked around him.

"Never. Nothing in this realm could ever make me forget about you."

"Good! I'd hate to have to march to the ends of Ur just to remind you." She smiled and kissed him again. "I have a gift for you."

"Oh?" Ravion released her and took a step back. "It seems great minds think alike. I've also come bearing gift."

"Really? Well, you first."

Ravion reached beneath his vest and retrieved a red leather tube. Handing it to her, he waited as she removed the end cap and the parchment within. "The deed to this keep and the one thousand acres it rests upon has been put in your name. You're officially a landowner."

She read over the stacked parchment, reviewing each one as if it was the key to her future. Rolling it, Senaria tucked it back into the tube and threw her arms around him once again, hugging tight. "Thank you. I can't begin to explain what this means for us." Kissing him passionately, she smiled her love for the man before her. "Are you ready for my gift?"

He couldn't help but find comfort in her expression. Her every action brought him joy. "Is it a turnip? You know how much I love those." Ravion involuntarily wrinkled his nose at the thought.

Senaria chuckled. "No silly, it's not a turnip. You hate turnips." She marched past him to the head of the table, guiding him by his arm. Reaching beneath the thick, wooden top, she pulled a hidden lever. The table clicked and a drawer popped out of the perfectly matched wood grain. Pulling the compartment open, Senaria reached inside and grabbed a dirty, bloodstained leather satchel. Handing it to him, she waited for him to inspect it.

Ravion glanced over the bag. It was caked in mud, showing it hadn't been opened recently. Where the mud wasn't pressed into the seams he could see a mixture of black and red stains. "Awe, beautiful. You shouldn't have. It's even my favorite color." He smiled, taunting her.

"Very funny, asshole. Open it."

Ravion found the wooden clevis. Flipping the button through the slit, he pulled the flap open and looked inside. The caked mud broke away, falling to the wooden floor. A shimmering black book rested inside, unnaturally clean despite the filth of its container. He pulled it free, inspecting the exterior. Not so much as a speck of dirt clung to the radiating cover or pressed, yellow pages.

"We've broken through the collapse of the cavern and found the catacomb deeps. My scouts encountered a few dreu patrols but nothing they couldn't handle. The lines are broken. For the time in my recollection, the dreu are unorganized and without command. I don't know how long it's going to last, but we're doing everything we can to keep them that way. This book was found by one of my patrols. They were near Derkarha when they came upon something unexpected."

"That's the dreu capital?"

"Kind of. Think of it as one of three capitals cities."

"Okay. What's so unexpected about a book?" Ravion couldn't help but feel like she was keeping something from him. The thought took him back to their first meeting when they didn't trust each other. Unbuckling the leather strap, he flipped past the cover and glanced at the flaky, aged pages. To his surprise, they were completely blank.

"I'm getting to that. This is only part of your gift. I don't know the importance of the book. But it was rumored Nezial had one like it. If this is the same book, perhaps the second part can shed some light on the subject." Senaria let out a sharp whistle.

Ravion heard several footsteps echoed off the stone and wood floors, making their way down the hallway. One of the side doors open, revealing a group of mul'daron scouts. Ravion couldn't recall ever meeting this particular unit. The soldiers escorted a bound man into the room. He was broad but the tattered rags clothing him were much too baggy. A brown woolen bag covered his head and judging by the way it clung his face, he was more than likely gagged as well. Despite the loss of weight and obvious physical changes, there was no mistaking that red glow. "Gareth?"

The soldiers brought him to a stop and pulled the bag from his head. A scar ran along the right side if his face. The damaged eye socket was sunken but the wound had healed. They untied his bindings, letting him carry his own weight. Rangar leaned over to the man and spoke just over a whisper. "As promised, you're a free man now."

Gareth squinted against the overwhelming light. He'd been in darkness so long his eye had trouble adjusting. A muffled voice echoed across the room, too distorted to understand. Despite being disoriented, Gareth felt a comfort that he hadn't expected. He wasn't sure if it was his impending freedom or something else, but for the first time in months, maybe longer, he felt at ease.

"Gareth, what the hell happened to you?" Ravion ran over, inspecting his friend and brother.

"Ravion?" Gareth questioned aloud. "I'll be damned, they were telling the truth. Guess that means I don't have to kill them all now. What if it's all a game? What if they're in my mind? Making me see things?"

Senaria approached, laying her hand on Ravion's shoulder. She was careful to keep her love between herself and the wild dreuslayer. There was no telling what he was capable of and she didn't want to risk him lashing out. "He's still got some fight in him. When my men found him he took out nearly thirty before he collapsed without a scratch. I don't know what he is, but he's got some kind of power I've never seen before. The satchel was in his possession. If I had to guess, I'd say he has some answers."

Ravion was lost in the sight of his friend. He was near a completely different person, yet that vibrant personality still burned bright as ever. Glowing behind that single, unhindered, blue eye. Ravion spun on heel and kissing her as deeply as he could. "You've returned my brother. I'm eternally in your debt."

Senaria smiled. "You don't own me anything. I love you. I want your happiness, nothing more."

Ravion returned his focus to Gareth. "I don't know what you've been through or if you'll even believe what I say. We both know what tricks the dreu can play on a mind. But I promise you this is real. These people are my friends and I hope you can find the truth to that." Ravion pressed a round token into Gareth's hand.

Gareth closed his hand around the badge feeling the engraved surface of a raised trident. Bringing it to his face he focused, letting his sight adjust to the sigil. Looking over the badge, unique among its kind, he studied the markings recognizing it as Ravion's. His gaze shifted back to the dalari scout.

"I believe you." Grabbing hold of the smaller man, Gareth pulled him tight.

Levi Samuel

Chapter XI
The Hawk and the Wyrm

Bits of dust lingered in the air of the neglected council room, displayed only by the beaming sunlight through the stone trimmed windows. The trident engraved wooden table rested in the center of the room, partially obstructed by the dirty, unopened satchel.

Rubbing his hand over the short stubble of his freshly shaven head Gareth paused, adjusting the strap holding his eye patch in place. He hadn't grown accustomed to the feel of it yet, but it made him a bit more sightly. Leaning back in his form fitted chair he listened to the wood creak beneath his weight. Growing impatient, he slammed the front legs back to the wooden floor. A loud crack echoed out, grabbing the attention of the others in the room. "How long are we going to wait?"

Ready to fight, Ravion snapped around finding the source of the commotion. Relieved it was nothing more serious he lowered his guard. "Just a while longer. He said he'd be here." Continuing his ritual he paced back and forth, allowing his usually calm demeanor to dissolve with each step.

The chamber door creaked open revealing a black cloaked figure in the shadows of the upper keep levels. He stepped into the room, unnaturally finding every available shadow to cloak his face.

Ravion froze, watching the figure enter the room. Ready to spring into action he held fast, hoping it wouldn't come to that. Glaring his discontent, he spoke. "Thank you for answering my missive. Would you care to explain why you broke into the vaults?" Unsure if he was making the right decision he slowly approached the table, leaning against the back of his own chair.

A sadistic, yet calm voice echoed from the shadow. "Let's not play coy. You know why I've come." Drawing his sword he smiled, watching the others tense at the sight of steel. Without a word he laid it on the weapon rack. Quickly laying the remainder of his weapons to rest, Lythus lowered the hood, revealing his face to the men and tossing the cloak over the stand. Approaching one of the five chairs he took a seat.

Ravion kept his eyes locked on the familiar face. It didn't disarm him in the slightest. "I know exactly why you're here. You didn't answer my question, Kane."

Lythus kicked his feet up, letting them rest on the well-made table. Bits of dirt and mud fell from the soles of his leather boots, littering the surface. "I don't go by that name. It's Lythus."

Gareth lunged forward, unable to control himself. Getting a better look at the dark warrior he let his words fly. "I don't give a damn if you're going by Remle De Leon now. He asked why you broke into the vaults. You could have easily gained access without attacking the city with a unit of dreu!" The name of the vile race left a distasteful film in his him mouth. Spitting it to the floor Gareth glared at the man, awaiting an answer.

Lythus smiled at the impatient bald man, daring him to act. Seeing it wasn't going to happen, he shifted his gaze to Ravion. "I don't answer to either of you— But, if it will set your mind at ease, everything I've done has been to further the goals of this order. I couldn't simply walk in and take what I needed as Kane. Too many questions would have been raised. I needed the dreu to die at the right time so I let them fight their way into a place they'd be unable to escape and otherwise unable to reach without the proper guidance."

Ravion walked around his chair and took a seat. Choosing his words carefully, he kept his gaze locked on the man. "Your actions, however beneficial they may have been, have shaken our trust. There are matters we must discuss as an order. We have to know you're in this just as much as we are. Between Malakai's death and Krenin's disappearance it's just the three of us. This whole thing falls apart if we can't trust each other."

"I'm not here for your trust. I'm here because you asked for my help. If I wanted trust I'd get a dog. At least I wouldn't have to explain my actions to it at the end of the day." Kicking his boots from the table, Lythus leaned forward and started to rise.

"I'm sorry you feel that way." Ravion nodded.

The hidden doorway along the side wall flew open, revealing the half-orc. Rushing forward, Krenin threw his arms around the heavy, wooden chair and the dark warrior's chest. Bulling him back into the seat, he pinned his arms to the side. Struggling to keep the subdued man seated, Krenin flexed his muscles, squeezing as tight as he could. "Hold still. This be over in a minute."

Rising from their seats Gareth and Ravion approached the occupied chair, taking positions on either side. Ravion reached into Malakai's vacant seat and grabbed a hand full of leather straps. Handing a few to Gareth, they went to work securing the man in place.

Gareth threw the straps around the man's chest, careful to leave room for the half-orc to release him. Pulling them as tightly as he could he locked the buckles and tugged, making sure they didn't have any slack.

Krenin slowly released the man, ready to grab him if the straps didn't hold. Backing away he took position behind the chair, ready to do what was asked of him.

Flexing his muscles Lythus struggled against the belts, hoping he could bulk up and leave enough slack to slip out. Waiting for them to back away he released his hold and tried to move, to no avail. Held tight, he sighed deeply and glanced at his captors. "Really guys? You believe this necessary? Though I must commend you on hiding the pigger. I legitimately didn't know he was here."

Krenin bulked at the slur, but held fast. Spending so much time around humans he'd grown somewhat accustomed to their racism, though it still stung. More so coming from a friend.

Pulling against the bracer on the man's left arm, Ravion grabbed the thin straps and released them, letting the leather covering fall to the floor. "Unfortunately, we do. Did you really think we didn't know who you were? A mysterious masked man that only shows up when Kane is absent. Never mind the glow or the fact that you have the same build. Let's not even mention all the accusations your little schemes have risen. We let you play your little charade, but it's gone too far for too long." Digging around the loose fitted sleeve, Ravion uncovered the peach flesh beneath, spotting his query. Releasing the shirt he took a step back, his fears confirmed. "Damn it, Kane!"

Leaning over the backrest to get a better look, Gareth studied the deep scale shaped scar. Several blackened veins retreated from the mark, disappearing beneath the skin. "Is it as bad as we feared?"

Glancing at the bald man Krenin looked upon the mark, recalling the books Ravion had tasked him with guarding. The pages rushed through his mind, pairing the conversation they'd had hours earlier. Remembering the mark sprawled out in the ancient text he lumbered to his reinforced chair and took a seat. A confused expression on his face he tried to piece the information together, clearly missing something. "What it mean?"

"It's one of the strongest binding spells I've been able to find. Sadly most of the books on this sort of thing were in the tower's library. We got lucky with the information we were able to find. It seems this Lythus figure, best I've been able to translate, has locked itself inside Kane's body. From what I learned from Kane, and judging by the shape of the mark, I'd say we're dealing with a dragon of some kind."

"How do we free him?" Gareth probed the scar, watching the veins react to his touch.

Lythus smirked, watching the young scout turned lord. "You know, you're a lot smarter than you look. Though I'm afraid you can't just remove it. It'd take something that can cut through magic to fully break the binding spell. I'm afraid the only things you had that can do that were in the vault. Had, as in not any longer in your possession." Chuckling at his own joke, Lythus continued. "But even if you managed to obtain one, it doesn't mean I'd be gone. Just that I'd be able to leave. I'm afraid there's not much you can do about that." His amused expression shifted, settling to a stern gaze. "And just so we're clear. If you try, I'll have no problem biting his tongue off." As if the threat had served its purpose his usual demeanor returned. "I'm afraid the only way to get rid of me is for him to do it himself. It's not all bad though. Despite what you may think, I have my uses. Hell, give it some time, you may prefer my methods over his. At least I won't nag you about what's 'morally right' every time a questionable problem requires a questionable solution."

Gareth's gaze shifted from the possessed man to Ravion. "You know, he kind of has a point."

Unable to believe what he was hearing Ravion scoffed, rising from his seat. Walking toward the prisoner he pressed his back side against the heavy table and folded his arms, hoping to wrap his fingers around the kris. Wishing to silence its cries. He was already feeling its absence. "We can't just leave him trapped in there. He's one of us."

"I'm not saying abandon him. I'm saying we use this— this thing for a while and let it sort itself out. That is, after all, how it's apparently going to have to play out anyway. If he has to find his own way out, who are we to interfere? I say we call for a vote. All in favor of using this thing's knowledge to better the order?" Gareth raised his hand and looked to his brothers.

Krenin glanced from one to the other, unsure who to side with. "Makes sense to me." He slowly raised his hand, hoping he was making the right decision.

"I'd raise mine but I'm afraid you've strapped it down. But I feel it should count, I am after all, still a member of this council."

Ravion shook his head. "I can't believe we're considering this." Looking at the possessed form of his friend he stared deep into his eyes, promising more with his gaze than his words could ever achieve. "You're going to do everything we tell you to. If you hesitate or question anything I'll lock you in the vaults myself and you'll rot until you die of old age. If you are indeed what we believe, I'd imagine that would be a very long time."

"Oh, thieves honor." Lythus wiggled against his bindings, mocking a salute in his immobile state.

Sighing heavily Ravion raised his hand. "Vote carries. Krenin, unbind him."

The half-orc stood and approached the occupied chair. Digging his meaty fingers behind the buckle at the man's midsection he reached into his belt, feeling the textured grip of the black and purple dagger in the palm of his hand. In a single fluid motion he sliced into the man's arm, watching the neatly filleted flesh peel away. Krenin pulled hard, yanking both the man and chair toward him.

The meat and skin shriveled around the mark like a branding on cattle hide. The charred, dark gray mass fell free and landed on the chamber floor, breaking apart into dust.

"You double crossing—!"

Using the momentum Krenin punched as hard as he could, sending the chair and its occupant toppling the other direction. It crashed to the floor, the remaining straps holding the man in place. "Call me 'pigger' again!"

Lythus felt bony knuckles smash into his face, launching him backward. It was all pretty clear what had happened. What confused him was the lack of pain. He should have hit the ground by now. Glancing around he realized he was standing. No straps, no chair, just himself and darkness as far as the eye could see. The realization hit him. He knew exactly where he was. Smiling he looked around, searching all directions.

"You should have stayed gone. I was having fun!" He danced around trying to find where the noble warrior was hiding. How anyone could navigate this darkness was beyond him. "Warrior, come out and play!"

A fractured blue light appeared in the distance, growing closer. He could see the brilliant breastplate and sheathed great sword protruding over the man's shoulder. He looked as righteous as ever. It made him sick. Lythus sighed. "I suppose this day would have come sooner or later. I guess we may as well get it over with."

Kane glared his dislike at conniving doppelganger. He stood for everything wrong in the world, and used him to do it. He was going to pay for his crimes. He had to pay. "It took me some time to find my way in this place. It seems it's paid off. What are you?"

Lythus laughed. "That's a simple question, one I'm sure you already know the answer to. I'm part of you, or more accurately, you're a part of me. I'm ambitious. You're stagnant. I get things done. You stand idle, waiting for a sign. It's all rather tedious."

"You're trying to trick me. I would never murder or betray my friends. You're a poison, siphoning the life out of me. Destroying everything I've created."

"While it's true I enjoy toppling your little constructs, I assure you this is no trick! I could have killed you many times over. But honestly, it was too much fun watching you build your little empire only to take it from you. The trouble is we're two sides of the same coin. Without me, you're nothing."

Kane looked down, admitting the truth to himself.

"Unfortunately, the inverse holds true as well. Only one of us can control the body. I thought I'd finally managed to get rid of you during the war, though I must admit that I hadn't counted on you fighting so hard to get back. You're stronger than I'd originally thought. That doesn't change the fact that I'm stronger." Lythus paused, letting his sadistic smile return. Looking into the eyes of his noble counterpart, he continued. "Oh, I'm sorry, did you think you were responsible for anything you've done? That's cute. Everything you are. Everything you have is because of me. Your enemies, your friends, your position, I'm the driving force behind you. I'm the whisper in your ear telling you to seize opportunity. Telling you to attack your foes without hesitation. If I hadn't shown you the way you'd be a lost child wandering the wilderness. Who do you think guided you to this land? Guided you to a traveled road when you knew nothing? It's all been because of me."

Kane felt his emotions swelling inside. He had to act quickly. If they got the better of him, if he allowed them to cloud his mind, he'd make mistakes. He couldn't have that. If he showed the slightest weakness, this— demon could gain the upper hand. And that wouldn't bode well for anyone. "I'm done with your games. If you're truly a piece of me, then prove it. Kill me and claim my body as your own if you can. That's the only way you'll ever keep me from rising up!"

"Oh, if it were only so simple. I can't just kill you outright. I wouldn't be able to have any more fun. I'd be forced to join with you, unable to escape your constant nagging inside my head for the rest of our time. I can't have that." Lythus casually circled the armored man, watching him, taunting him. "No, I seek a more permanent solution. I'm going to break you. I'm going to cut you down at the knees and make you lick my boots clean. By the time I'm done you'll beg me for a mercy that will never come. You're going to lie in wait at my feet like a submissive dog, hoping, one day, I'll reach down and pet you. The longing will drive you mad. You'll become a shell of your former self. You'll be a withered and shrunken husk of a man long forgotten, left to writhe away into an unrecognized lump on this shadowed floor. I'm sure a time will come, long after this world has abandoned your memory, a time when the seven lands have learned to fear my name, that I'll consider letting you see the fruits of my labor. I'll contemplate allowing you to set your eyes on the darkness of a world long past your touch. And on that final day, the day you draw your last breath, I'll remember the promise made this day. And I'll deny you that last question, letting you die without ever knowing what happened to the world you spent so much effort fighting for."

Kane watched him circle like a shark ready to devour its prey. Rebellion grew inside him. He was a wellspring of light in such a dark place. "You'd better strike fast and hard then. For I'll not go down without a fight."

"Ah, there's that rebellious spirit I've come to admire. The very reason I took an interest in you in the first place."

Ready to end the taunts, Kane thought about the sword strapped to his back. He couldn't draw it fast enough. He'd have to improvise. A plan in mind, Kane lunged at the encompassing doppelganger, drawing his dagger and plunging it into the chainmail rings covering his chest. The blade sank to the hilt, stopped only by the silver cross-guard.

Glancing down, a bellowing laugh escaped the dark warrior. Calming himself, he stared his victory into the helpless warrior, watching the defeat work its way into him. "Did you really think I could be killed by such a weapon?" Wrapping his gloved hand around the black and silver banded dagger, Lythus plucked it from his chest. Glancing over the sharpened edges, clean of blood, he dropped it, letting it disappear into the shadowed floor beneath him. Inspecting the stretched rings where the blade had entered, Lythus let out an exaggerated sigh. Shaking his head he waved his hand over the tear. The broken rings reformed, weaving themselves together. In a matter of seconds the torn armor had completely mended itself, removing any sign of the broken links. "I'm afraid you won't be rid of me so easily. I still intend to show you what I've got in store for your friends." Reaching forward quicker than Kane could react, Lythus pressed his finger into the man's head letting the magics flow through him.

Kane tried to evade, tried to flee. It was no use. The man was too fast. He felt a pressure build in his head, throbbing against his skull, begging to be released. Dropping to his knees, Kane grabbed his head, struggling against the torment, helpless to the flood of visions racing through his mind. He watched his body enter the tower, the brilliant armor reflecting the beaming rays of sunlight. He felt the darkness flow from him, tainting the red brick, coercing it to store his corruption. The scene shifted, revealing a village. He felt the necks of children snap beneath his grip. Their pure blood spilled on the ground, coating his boots. He looked into their parent's eyes, watching their hatred form at his sight. He felt the pleasure of their deaths, burning them alive, trapped, and unable to cry out. The scenes shifted again, forcing him to watch murder after murder, each one growing more daring than the last. As if he wanted to be caught. A lingering pain grew inside him. He knew that his face was their final vision. All those people believe him a monster. People that trusted him. People that depended on him for protection. He saw the pain in their eyes. A pain worse than any he'd ever felt. How could he save them? How could he prevent others from suffering a similar fate? Everyone he'd ever known was helpless to the dark radiation seeping from him, slowly corrupting them.

He watched the power flow into a green gem, stolen from Shadgull. Its taint slowly flowed into Remle upon his throne. The crown, taken from the man himself, lay hidden in the cellars of Shadgull City's fortress, awaiting a time it would be found and placed atop the next lord, ready to corrupt him. Every scene played out revealing a small seed of darkness, ready to sprout up and pollinate the world. Even Mortimus, his mentor so long ago, had inadvertently been killed by the shadowed form of himself.

"No!" Kane's vision returned looking upon the creature that had stolen his face. Anger, regret, despair, it all flowed through him. A mix of emotion, swirling about, tested his sanity. *Am I responsible for it all?*

Lythus didn't give him time to process. Continuing on he leaned in, nearly whispering to the defeated man. "Once I've reclaimed your body, the first thing I'm going to do is slice Ravion's throat from ear to ear. He was a useful tool, but his usefulness has reached its end. Gareth on the other hand— He's an excellent puppet. All I have to do is suggest the dreualfar are involved and he'll fall into line."

Kane couldn't take any more. He had to put a stop to it. Drawing his short sword he stood, raising the blade. "You underestimate me."

Lythus laughed. "I've already proven your weapons are useless against me. What do you hope to gain?"

Kane slid the blade under the leather straps along the side of his armor. Slowly dragging the keen edge, it cut. The great sword fell free, disappearing into darkness without a sound. He pulled the breastplate free letting it fall from him. To his surprise it didn't vanish as his weapons had. It seemed to glow a faint light, repelling the shadow around it. "You aren't the only one who's learned how to manipulate the shadow." Closing his eyes, Kane focused on the warmth inside him. It wasn't much, but it was better than nothing. Thoughts of Ravion and Gareth shot into his mind. He couldn't be having this conversation had it not been for them. They were the sail keeping him moving. A bright light erupted from the discarded breastplate, burning the darkness away. Even with his eyes closed Kane could see its radiance. Wrapping his hands around the warm glow he opened his eyes, seeing the pulsing great sword in front of him. The blade was made of the purest white light. Its hilt and pommel equally brilliant. For the first time since he'd arrive in this place, he felt hope.

"That's not possible!" Lythus studied the summoned blade. How could such a weapon exist in a place of darkness? He'd spent more time in the shadow than most, yet he'd never seen anything close to its purity. Only the gods were capable of harnessing such raw power. But which one? The answer filled his mind, sending a slither of doubt through him. *Deidre!* Silently, he called to the god. *I know you're here! Magic like that doesn't just spring up from nowhere.*

As if answering his call, a booming voice echoed in his head. "You've disappointed me, Lythus. You've abused the powers too long."

"What right do you have?" Lythus shouted into the shadow, feeling his anger and fear rise.

"I have every right. You've crossed the line. You've enslaved this child of arcane since he was a boy. You've mixed the magics, both mine and hers. And then you have the audacity to step into my realm and question my authority? It's time you learned your place, wyrm!"

Kane slashed in, watching the beaming blade slice through the shadowed man's leg. Blood seeped from the wound soaking into the thick, black pants. "It seems I've found a weapon that will do the trick."

There was a joy in taunting the man that had gone through so much effort to do the same.

Be on your guard, Deidre. When I'm finished with this fool I'm coming for you. Lightning fast, Lythus drew his sword and jabbed in, bending at the waist. The slightly curved blade rocketed toward Kane, aimed at his chest. Twisting his hips he watched the glowing weapon fly overhead, missing him.

Kane abandoned his strike, bringing the lower half of the blade up to deflect the incoming stab. He heard steel ring out as he knocked the weapon away from him. He side-stepped, dodging a wide blow. Kane counted time between attacks. Finding a window, he calculated. It was more than likely a trap designed to draw him in, only to have him too close to block. Counting through his routine, it never closed. It was a long shot, but he had to take it. He just had to be careful. Traps were something this being was all too skill with, and he didn't intend on being victimized again. Feigning right, the sword outstretched and aimed to stab mid-chest, Kane rapidly dropped the tip and lunged in.

Lythus saw the decoy. He smiled. The bait was taken. Although the blinding light was effecting his perception. He was too close to shut him out. Unable to defend, a sharp pain shot through his stomach. Lythus glanced at the glowing blade, buried in his gut. The links of his chainmail glowed red, burning into flesh. The molten metal hissed and skirted, falling away from the sword that may as well have been forged from the sun itself.

Kane pushed his shoulder into the defeated doppelganger, ripping the sword upward. It split him with ease, tearing the rings apart like a hot knife into butter.

Lythus stood stunned, helpless to the damage befalling him. Weak, his sword slipped from grip. It fell to the shadows disappearing from sight as all the others had.

"I told you, you underestimated me!" Staring deep into the dying figure's eyes, Kane ripped the blade free, watching the imposter fall to his knees. Thick, onyx blood poured from the gaping wound. Kane felt a slight pleasure at the sight. He had more reason than most to hate the man, yet he felt pity more than anything. Though something inside him told him there was more to it than what the dying man had claimed.

Those secrets would have to remain lost. He owed vengeance to the people of Dalmoura, and gods knew how many others long before his arrival. Steeling himself, Kane spun, swinging the blade as hard as he could. It sank deep into his neck, passing through flesh and bone, exploding out the other side in a sickening pop. The force of the blow sent the body toppling over. The head bounced several times, coming to rest a few feet away. Set in his victory Kane watched the final fall of his enemy's chest, feeling a sense of relief wash over him. The sword shrank, disappearing into a foggy gray. He looked around watching the fog dilute the darkness. As if carried away on a light breeze the body faded from sight.

A powerful voice echoed around him, leaving a strange comfort in the mist. "Well done, my son!"

Kane turned to see a large wolf on the edge of the evading shadow. The wolf approached, growing larger by the step. It was nearly dire in size and still growing. Stopping a few feet away, it shifted. The gray hair retreated revealing peach colored skin. Taking weight on its rear legs a man stood and approached the final few steps.

He stood several inches taller and had long, brown hair pulled into a tail. A dark-brown reinforced leather jerkin covered his chest, and matching bracers covered his long-sleeved tunic. He was unarmed, despite the empty sheath resting loosely at his hip.

There was a familiarity to the older man, but it was one he couldn't place. Kane studied the bright blue glow radiating from him, noting the similar traits he shared with Ravion. In fact this man looked like an older, stockier version of his friend. "Who are you?"

The man gave a light smile, both comforting and reassuring him. "My name is Marquel Santail. I'm your father." He gave a shallow bow reminding him of the way Ravion had at their introduction, and hundreds of times since.

He knew it to be true. There were too many similarities between them, though doubts flew through his mind. Hoping his question wouldn't warrant offense, Kane looked deep into the man, searching for answers beneath the surface. "Forgive me, but how am I expected to believe this? I've been in this place a while. I'm familiar with the tricks the shadow plays. This wouldn't be beyond the realm of possibilities."

"No forgiveness needed. You've witnessed much and for that, I'm sorry. I'm also afraid that any proof I can offer would come from a form you've no reason to trust. It seems we're at an impasse, one which requires a choice from you."

"I— I don't understand?"

"I desire my son's return. Many years ago a dragon corrupted him. When the beast entered his body his mind was tainted. It wiped all memory from him, leaving a blank slate of who he formerly was. Fortunately he was found by a noble gentleman who instilled in him morals and virtue. Were it not for this man I fear to think of who he may have become. You have been successful in defeating the beast's corruption. But I assure you, it is not dead. When he told you, you were one in the same, he wasn't lying. It was the corruption that created the emptiness, later filled by an old man's virtues. That became the man you are today." Marquel paused, placing his hand on Kane's shoulder. His eyes trailed from the man before him and onto the fog covered floor. "It pains me to say this, but the corruption cannot be shed until the memories have returned. Until you relinquish my son's body, Lythus's corruption will live on." Bringing his piercing brown eyes to meet the younger man, he continued. "You must both fall before you can truly rise."

Kane sighed heavily. He was beginning to understand what the man was saying. "What happens once the corruption is gone?"

"For you, I'm afraid I don't know the specifics. But my son will reemerge. For Lythus, he's in a weakened state currently, both here and in the physical realm. If nothing changes, he'll regain his strength and continue his path. If you cast him out, he may rise again one day in the physical realm. But that's a problem for another time. He's currently of no threat to the lands you call home."

"I don't know much about dragons, having only met a few. But why would such a beast go through the trouble of possessing your son. Moreover, what would he hope to gain from it?"

"Sadly I'm unable to answer these questions, as I don't fully know. I can tell you that as one of the eldar races, there is more potential in you than you realize. Of the five eldar races, we are each gifted in our own way. Dragons have the gift of foresight. For all I know he saw something in your life that drove his actions. Whether he achieved his goals or not is uncertain. Even the clairvoyant have their limits." Marquel paused a moment, giving a gentle smile to the confused, yet resilient man. "So, may I please have my son back?"

A heavy sigh escaped him. Kane nodded, summoning the focus he'd found earlier. As before, he felt the power form in his hand. It wasn't nearly as strong as it had been. Opening his eyes he glanced at the summoned dagger, forged of a rolling smoke. Finding reassurance in the man's eyes, he spoke. "I suppose it had to happen sooner or later. If you're telling the truth, everything will be alright. If not, at least I won't be stuck in this place any longer." Flipping the small blade toward him he plunged it into his chest, feeling a sharp pain erupt like a thousand needle pricks against his bare flesh. A loud pop echoed in his mind sending doubt throughout his body. Dropping to his knees he felt cold. His body weakened, shaking uncontrollably.

Marquel caught him, kneeling beside the dying form. Holding him as best he could he stared into his eyes, hoping to bring comfort among the flood of pain and fear.

Kane stared into those deep, brown eyes finding concern for his well-being. That was enough to convince him it wasn't a trick. The reassured smile faded of doubt. It didn't hurt as much as he'd expected. Instead it was more of an uncomfortable numb. It started in his fingers and toes, slowly working its way toward his center. He couldn't feel his body. He was little more than a floating, fading head in a sea of fog. His vision was rapidly failing, leaving black blotches here and there. Each thundering heartbeat left another patch. He watched the man disappear and then himself. Once again, he was surrounded in darkness. This time it seemed different. He couldn't see anything. Not even his own body. He was but a thought lingering in an endless ocean.

A blinding light roused him. Memories flooded his mind. Opening his eyes, his childhood in the grove outside Winterhaven fell into place. He recalled Meaius sweeping him up, giving him a dagger. One by one his memories took their place, mixed with those of his lost years. There was so much time he'd missed. How was it possible he could have forgotten so much? The final pieces settled into place, his father's face came to him, and then his mother's. Ravion watched over him, annoyed by his antics. He smiled, recalling he'd only acted out because he'd wanted to be just like him. Finally, his sister came into view. She was beautiful in her own right. If only he'd been able to find her. Wiping the sorrow of his failure away, he took comfort in her memory. Perhaps one day he could make it right. "I'm sorry for doubting you, Father."

Marquel extended his hand, pulling the young dalari to his feet. "I'm just glad you're yourself again. I wish it could have happened much sooner."

Demetrix took his father's hand, gathering his bearings. He glanced at his naked form, unsure how he'd ended up that way. "In this pace my will is law?"

Marquel chuckled. "To a degree. There are limitations in the void. But for the most part, yes."

Nodding his understanding Demetrix closed his eyes, extending his arms. The warmth of clothing grasped him, wrapping layers of cloth and leather around his frame. Inspecting the green and brown armor covering him from shoulder to knee, he smiled his approval. A quiver hung from his side and two slender swords rested in separate compartments beside his arrows. An elegant bow ran down his back, waiting to be strung. The curved wood was wrapped in dark brown leather with green runes running the length of the arms. The waxed string had an emerald glaze to it.

"I'm happy you were able to find yourself, my son. I wish I could spend more time with you, but I fear I must return to the void. There is much I would have of you, but your life is your own. Ravion has made strides to return our people to their former glory. He's on the right path but he'll need your help."

Marquel started to fade. Hurrying his pace he added what little he could. "The alfar are spread thin and many have forgotten the old ways. They'll offer no resistance to the return. The Santail bloodline is but a fraction of our people. We take the aspect of the wolf. With your coming of age you are to carry the wolf as your brother does. Each of us carries the aspect of another animal. Your brother is the raven. Your sister, the phoenix. You, my son, are the hawk— ever watchful and wise. You'll need these tools in the coming years. Use them wisely and do not forget your people. I also wish you to know, your sister bore two children, twin girls. They'll fi—"

Demetrix watched his father fade into nothing leaving him alone once again. Taking a deep breath he felt a warmth he'd long since forgotten. The fog slowly drifted away revealing the council room floor.

Chapter XII
Mirror Mirror

The fractured aura surrounding the restrained man pulled itself together burning bright. Demetrix struggled to move against the leather binds securing him. The toppled chair rested on its back, forcing him stare at those surrounding him.

"Looks like he's waking up." Gareth glared at the bound man hoping their plan had worked. His grip tight around his sword he prepared for the worst.

Ravion watched intently, amazed by the healing glow. Its intensity burned brighter than any he'd seen before. Kneeling, he placed a hand on the man's chest. "Are you yourself?"

Demetrix felt a reassuring calm from the touch. Locking eyes, he stared into his brother's face. "More so than I've been in a long time. Though I'd imagine you need proof before you'll release me."

Ravion smiled. "That would be preferred."

"You go by the name Ravion. Though in our tongue your name is Ra'dulen. Which translates to raven-wolf. If this isn't enough to verify a greater sense of personal knowledge, my birth name is Demetrix Santail, son of Marquel. I was born early-spring in the village of Winterhaven upwards of two-hundred and twenty-eight years ago."

Ravion froze, unable to process what he was hearing. Questions raced through his mind. Leaning in close so the others couldn't hear him, he spoke just over a whisper. "Only one from that point in my life could know any of that. Believe me when I say, if you're lying to me, you and I are going to have issues!" Ravion pulled the tail of the central strap, unhooking it from the buckle.

Krenin lifted the chair setting it upright, while Gareth went to work unbuckling the other straps. He tossed them roughly on the council room table.

Within moments Demetrix was free of his binds. He pulled himself up, standing on his own two feet for the first time in what felt like years. "Ravion, my brother, fear not. I speak truth. The age of dalari draws near. But first, I need a tailor. I feel dirty just wearing this tainted garb." He ran his hands over the chainmail the possessing dragon had dressed him in.

An overwhelming pride swelled within Ravion. Lost in his emotion he grabbed his younger brother, hugging him tightly. "I'm glad to have you back! I feared I'd never see you again." Releasing his hold he stared hard, feeling the bond he hadn't experienced since childhood. "Your clothes can wait, we've much to discuss." Returning to his seat, Ravion grabbed the satchel. He opened the flap and removed the black book from within. Gently placing it upon the table in front of him, he sat quiet, awaiting the others to take their seats. "We've already discussed the nature of this book in private. From what little I've been able to learn it serves as a sort of guide to the creation of this realm. I haven't found all its secrets, nor should I. That much knowledge is too great for any one man to possess. Gareth, would you mind repeating where you came across this book?"

Recalling the day it came to his possession, the bald warrior squinted his single eye at the shimmering binding. "I tripped over the bag when I was fighting the dreu that took my eye. I've explained how I got it many times, but none of it makes sense. It's almost as if the bag grabbed hold of me and held on for the ride."

Ravion opened the book to expose the blank pages within. Flipping from one to another, he showed the empty contents to those in the room. "You alluded that you were able to view the writing on the pages. Would you mind explaining how you managed that?"

"Blood seemed to do the trick for me."

"Blood?" Krenin asked, taken back by the response.

"Yes, blood. A single drop was all it took. It soaked into the page and returned as writing."

"Doesn't seem very sanitary. Oh well." Drawing his dagger, Ravion laid a shallow gash along the backside of his forearm just deep enough to expose the red life fluid. The beading droplets hit the page, disappearing immediately. Almost as quickly as they'd vanished the book sprang to life revealing passages, maps, pictures, and even the occasional spell.

Gareth leaned over, surprised by the scribing red lines appearing on the page. "It didn't show me even a fraction of that. What makes your blood so special?"

Ravion scanned the words paying special attention to the smallest of details. "Because my people, or at least someone very familiar with my people, wrote this book!"

"You're sure this is where you found him?" Ravion stared into the mirror watching the dulled reflection of his friends.

"Absolutely. My mace was here, what other evidence do you need?"

Demetrix ran his hand along the dust covered, polished surface. "What's every portal have?" He turned to look at the others.

"Magic." Krenin answered, giving a toothy smile.

"Two sides." Ravion corrected.

"Exactly. This thing radiates magic unlike any I've felt before, but it's not pulling. It's pushing. If we're translating the book properly this is a portal. One side is here. Where's the other?"

Ravion removed the book from the satchel, flipping through the pages to a specific passage. They refused to hide their contents so long as he held possession of the tome. "All it says is 'The world builder has grown unstable. Tasked by the gods we built the prison, locking it away behind reflections of the past. It was an unfortunate loss, but the good of all creation remains at stake. The doorway shall serve as the only link to our divine providence. May all those abandoned forgive us, for there was no other choice. Should the seals be broken, all hope is lost, for the gods have failed!' It's cryptic, but I can't shake the feeling that the dreu were trying to open this doorway. I can't imagine they succeeded. I'd think we'd know if a dark god was descending upon our world, but we also have to assume they made some progress. As protectors of this land, I believe it falls to us to reestablish any broken seals that may have been damaged."

Gareth listened intently, absorbing the words. "You want to go into some unknown prison with an evil god and make sure he hasn't broken free? You know I have your back but that is the stupidest idea I've ever heard escape your mouth. That's no different than unlocking a cell that holds the vilest of creatures just to see if it was actually locked in the first place. Why risk it?"

An unexpected voice echoed in the small chamber, drawing their attention. "I'm afraid you have little choice." Perrimen stood at the entrance, taking in the sight of the three men and their half-orc. "My apologies, I didn't mean to startle you."

Ravion took a knee, bowing before the former baron. "My Liege, what would you have of us?"

"I would have you stand. I'm not your baron. You really must accept this."

Ravion returned to his feet, welcoming the powerful human. "You'll always be my baron. Regardless of any respect I have for the lords and their titles, I've sworn oath to no other."

"Spoken like a true warrior of the dalari." Perrimen strode toward the mirror, stopping just in front of it.

Ravion watched the man, recalling their last meeting. "What brings you here, if it's my place to know?"

"In truth I came seeking you, all of you. Since the fall of the dreu a vast darkness has set over Dalmoura. It was slowed with the banishment of your alter-ego." Perrimen turned, looking directly at Demetrix. "But it continues to build. I fear time for containment has passed. The source must be stopped or all will be lost. The Tower is no more. They didn't heed my warning quick enough. The base stones were corrupted beyond repair. Perhaps she'll return in time, but alas I cannot promise. A darkness has set in the heart of Shadgull. Tresengal is without an experienced lord. Mount Thuran hides behind their walls, ignoring the rest of us. I'm afraid the last pockets of resistance fall between Marbayne and Krondar. Since one is currently supporting the other, I'm afraid this task falls to your order."

"What would the source of this corruption be?" Gareth interjected, testing the mage. He knew there wouldn't be a direct response.

"That I cannot answer, wish as I may. Sadly I'm just a broken man with little more than a handful of knowledge to pass along." Perrimen returned his focus to the mirror, looking into its dark surface. Running his hand along the edge, he refused to touch it. "The shadow threatens us beyond this speculum. I doubt it can truly be stopped, but if anyone can slow its progression I believe you to be our best chance." Spinning around Perrimen marched toward the entrance, giving his final insight. "As for your current predicament I'd suggest asking your new friends about this mirror's twin. I believe they'll be able to offer more knowledge than I. And Ravion, keep it close. You'll need it." Reaching the entryway, Perrimen paused, looking over the group of dreuslayers one final time. "I wish you the utmost success. We're all counting on you, whether we know it or not." Without another word he stepped into his unhindered door of swirling energy and disappeared.

"I hate when they do that." Gareth shook his head, walking toward the mirror. "I'll never see eye to eye with his brother. Impossible on two fronts now, but I understand he is not his brother. I know you trust him. It's not like they're many dreu left for me to play with here." Gareth placed his hand on Ravion's shoulder. "I'll follow your lead on this one."

Demetrix and Krenin approached the pair, awaiting a decision.

"I don't care what it says! I don't want anything to do with that book." Senaria turned away, refusing to look at the pages.

"It's not my intention to press, I just need to know what you know about the mirrors." Ravion closed the book, shoving it back into the satchel. Pulling a chair, he sat. "Please enlighten me and I'll be out of your hair, never to ask you about it again."

Senaria turned to face him. Approaching, she sat on his lap and wrapped her arms around shoulders. "Don't make promises you can't keep." She kissed his cheek. "You and I both know what would happen the next time I have knowledge you might need."

Ravion found it strange to think of her as one of the dreualfar. She seemed so familiar despite the coldness she often displayed when protecting her people. She was strong and capable. Traits he was all too familiar with. A faint smile breached his lips. "An unfortunate side effect to my position. I'm sorry. I know you don't want to talk about your past, and I don't mean to pry."

She sighed heavily, keeping her arms around him. "The dreualfar have many myths about their creation. One in particular says a dark mirror sucked the magic from their bodies, turning them into warriors of the night. Many variations have come and gone, but that's always the general perception."

Releasing her hold she stretched across him, grabbing the table's edge to keep herself firmly seated. Finding the hidden lever, Senaria watched the edge of the drawer appear. Pulling it open she grabbed a stack of parchment and quickly flipped through, finding one in particular that was torn around the edges and stained with yellow and black. It appeared as if someone had tried burning it. There were several small holes throughout and the corners were nearly gone. Handing the aged sheet to Ravion, she continued. "Shortly after Nezial took power rumors surfaced that someone had found a map to Eldarian. I didn't know if there was any truth to it, at least I wasn't. Not until I found that. I believed it nothing more than a rumor. The council was known to circulate such rumors to promote work among the less willful. Even those of us driven by an unquenchable thirst found solace in the prospect of a life away from battle. We were little more than slaves to the council's will. We'd work ourselves to death in pursuit of a simple life, only for another to come along and pick up where we left off. Many of us learned their tricks and simply stopped playing. But thousands of others had no choice. It kept the council in power, while distracting the rest and keeping us from rising up. So when I found this map I didn't believe what it was." Senaria gestured him to look.

Ravion unfolded the parchment and studied the markings stained into the rough surface. He could see the forest's edge of what he guessed was Evinwood. Near the northwest corner of the forest there was an opening marked by a jutting tower and a freestanding archway beneath it. It wasn't much to go on, but it was better than anything else he had. Folding the map, Ravion returned his attention to her.

"The myth claims that the mirror is in Eldarian. If this map is real that's where you'll find it. Though I must admit, I hope you never do.

Nothing good has come from that place." Pressing her lips against his, she held him for several moments. Breaking away, Senaria looked deep into his eyes. "I don't want to lose you."

"I don't want to lose you either. I'm sorry for asking you to recall darker times. I know those memories haunt you. I swear to you here and now. I won't ask you to do so again, even if you're the only person who has the knowledge I seek. I'd rather go without than to force you to relive that life." Ravion pulled her tight, feeling her warmth. "I'm afraid this is something I must do. I don't know what it will require of me or even how long I'll be gone. Just know that I love you. And I'll be back to you as soon as I'm able."

Senaria stood, allowing him to rise. "Please be careful. I don't want to know a life without you." She wrapped her hands in his, feeling their connection stronger than ever.

"Be safe, my love. If you require anything in my absence send a message to Marbayne. I've left specific instructions with a loyal operative named William Carter. He'll handle any situations that may arise with the utmost discretion." Ravion pulled her close, bringing his lips to hers. It was a lingering kiss, one that nearly stopped time. He didn't know how long he'd be away from her. And if this was his last kiss he wanted it to be a memorable one. Breaking away, Ravion stared into those almond shaped eyes, full of love. "I'll see you soon."

Senaria knew he wasn't being fully honest. She could feel the uncertainty in him. He didn't know if he was going to come back any more than she did. Such was the life of a soldier. Each time they marched into battle they took a chance on it being their last. She forced a smile, reassuring him. "Thank you, my love. I'll dream of you every night you're away, longing for the day you're in my arms again. Please, be careful. You don't know what you're walking into."

Jagged vines wrapped around the black structure, leaving an eerie dread over the dead lands. The ground was cracked in all directions. Little more than dry grass and vicious, barbed weeds sprouted through the desolate dirt, strangling anything they could find.

Krenin stared into the face of an orc statue erected at the entrance of the temple, the only structure that remained completely unhindered by time. "Feels like his eyes follow me." Krenin wobbled back and forth, testing his theory.

"Often times such artifacts are designed to entice that feeling. It makes the observer feel uneasy and therefore easier to manipulate." Demetrix knocked on the statue listening to the solid stone against his knuckles. "See, it's only stone."

"Let's get this over with. I don't like the smell of this place." Gareth stepped through the cracked opening, pushing against the stone door in his path. It opened freely, granting access. Drawing one of his twin cutlasses, Gareth marched into shadow.

Ravion followed closely behind, lost in the architecture around him. He could see the clear signs of his people, but these markings were something else. They flowed like eldar, but the symbols weren't of any dialect he'd seen. Making his way into the ancient temple he felt dwarfed by the sheer space around them.

"See anything?" Krenin asked, searching the room for anything of interest.

"Over there." Gareth pointed his cutlass toward the altar on the far side of the room. One of the nearby doors stood open, awaiting their entry. "Only open door I've seen. I'd guess that's where the previous visitors ventured."

The group crossed the room, finding the small antechamber off the side of the nave. Stepping into the ancient stairwell, the walls flared to life. The mounted scones glowed a purple flame, illuminating their descent around the twisting corridor. Reaching the bottom they passed into the small room. A pile of purple stone lay crumbled in the center and the rear wall was reflective, much like the mirror they'd previously seen.

Ravion felt a strange familiarity with the stone. He could feel the dagger calling to him, begging to be touched. Fighting against its will he stepped past the crumbled stone and approached the ancient speculum. Pressing his hand against the semi-solid surface, ripples expanding from his touch. "It looks like this is the place." Talking a deep breath he walked through, feeling the water-like substance swallow him.

One by one they pressed onward leaving the dark chamber behind them.

Levi Samuel

Chapter XIII
Through the Looking Glass

The stench of decay and dirt filled the room, leaving a sense of dread to linger in the forgotten crypt. The surrounding ancient stones were covered in dark green moss clinging to the crumbled mortar, like ivy following the grooves. Several memorial plots lined the side walls, worn smooth and colored white from age. The patchy gray stones between the hanging moss made the dark chamber feel constricting and isolated. A single arched tunnel, full of disappearing stairs, angled upward from the center of the far wall.

Demetrix ran his fingers along the worn stone, feeling what was left of the carvings. They were too shallow to see and even harder to feel. Seeing Krenin step through the flowing mirror he glanced to his brother. "They're nearly worn off."

Ravion studied his brother's interest. "What?"

"The names and dates. They're nearly worn off. If we could read the markings we stand a chance at figuring out where we are."

"We're not gonna find anything in this crypt. I say we see what's outside, maybe there's a town nearby." Refusing to wait for objections Gareth marched toward the decrepit stairway.

Krenin followed after Gareth, watching the bald man disappear from sight. He ducked at the top of the archway to keep from hitting his head on the low keystone.

"Maybe we should check the book?" Ravion grabbed the leather satchel noticing its lack of weight. Frantically he pulled the flap open and peered inside. Fear crept from the depths of his mind. How could he find his way without direction? "It's missing!" Pulling against the seams,

Ravion searched for holes, unable to find one. Sighing heavily he accepted the fact it was gone. They were on their own. Subconsciously he reached inside his vest, wrapping his hand around the wicked kris tucked away from sight. He couldn't explain it, but holding the blade made him feel less lost. It was as if his worries weren't so severe when the weapon was in his grip.

"It's not in here. And I doubt we can go back to find it. Best thing we can do is keep moving forward." Demetrix watched his brother's face. He was discouraged more than he'd ever shown in the past. There was something larger going on with him. He just didn't know what. Though if Ravion had a secret there was a reason he kept it. He'd talk when the time was right. Approaching, Demetrix patted his shoulder. "Let's go. Gareth's liable to start a war if we don't keep him out of trouble."

Ravion chuckled at the thought, marching toward the arch.

Gareth pushed against the spongy door. The wood was soft and moist, leaving a slick residue on his hands. Stepping into the derelict graveyard Gareth looked around. The trees were tall and ominous. Judging by the lack of foliage on the ground, he guess they were eternally absent their leaves. The wicked branches stretched in all directions showing dark contrasts to the cloudy, gray sky. It was clearly daylight though the sun had trouble penetrating the rolling, dark clouds. Instead it filtered through laying a soft glow over the frigid and uninviting landscape. The weather held a gloomy chill that only autumn could bring. The vegetation littering the ground was just as welcoming, twisted around anything it could reach, strangling it with vicious thick barbs and constricting bands. He recalled the weeds in Eldarian, finding an uncomfortable similarity between the two.

"See a town?" Krenin glanced around clearly unimpressed by his findings.

"Does it look like I've found a town?" Gareth searched the horizon in all directions. It was difficult to make out any structures past the sea of dead trees.

"No!"

Shaking his head at the half-orc's literal interpretation of sarcasm, Gareth found himself missing Malakai. The man was always good for keeping the brute distracted with such simple concepts. Taking a deep breath he continued his search.

The soft glow above the clouds faded at an exceptional rate turning the gray sky into a black, starless night. It happened so fast their eyes hadn't had a chance to adjust to the change. In the distance a branch snapped, drawing attention. Jumping into defensive positions the group drew their weapons, ready to face whatever foes presented themselves.

A low moan echoed through the dark, barren forest sending a cold shiver down their spines. Another followed, and another, each time moving closer. It was clear there was more than one, many more in fact, though it was hard to tell exactly how many.

"Do you hear that?" Ravion asked, searching the total darkness for a source. He wasn't used to his vision in this place. Such a change shouldn't have left him blinded, yet he couldn't see anything.

"Of course I hear it. What the hell is it would be a more suitable question." Gareth scoffed. "Can you see anything?"

"Nope. It reminds me of that spell the dreu use, but that's a small area. I've never seen it on this scale before." Ravion kept his sword at the ready, using the tip to test his reach.

Demetrix held his newly forged swords in front of him trying to focus his vision in the darkness. "I've been in this kind of dark before. We need to keep our eyes open for a mage."

"Krenin don't see anything."

The moans increased, both in volume and quantity. They sounded like they were right on top of them.

Several bright sparks erupted, flaring enough to reveal the head of a torch. Krenin looked out from the flame spotting his friends. "Krenin can see."

"My theory is shot. A torch won't burn through magical darkness." Demetrix offered, searching the flickering dim light surrounded them. Several humanoid creatures were revealed on the edge sight. Their features sunken, leaving little more than rotting flesh clinging to bone. Some were whole while others missed limbs or had their stomachs torn open, revealing gaping holes where entrails had been. The walking corpses varied from human to alfar. Even the occasional orc stood among their number, towering over the rest.

"Undead!" Gareth swung his swords cutting into the closest one. The blade cleaved deep, snapping bone. He jumped back, avoiding the deadly talons clawing at him. "Breaking bone seems to be useless. Any ideas on how to kill them?"

Ravion swiped, aiming for the creature's neck. Dancing around to avoid the claw-like fingers reaching for him, he cut the arm off another. "I've heard you can bash or sever their heads, but I really don't know. I've never actually encountered undead before."

Krenin swung his axe, biting deep into the midsection of one of the orcs. The thick blade tore a large hole in the leather-like skin. Soggy dirt fell from the wound, but the creature continued toward him. Spinning around, his second axe took its head off. The creature's body collapsed to the forest floor, its head landing a few feet away. He watched it stagger from the blow trying to pull itself together, though it didn't seem cognitive enough to pick itself up. "I drop one. It still moving, but not toward me."

Demetrix spun around letting his blades extend. The keen swords cut into the neck of the closest one. Keeping his momentum he sliced into another, sending its head to the dirt. Like the others they fell, but continued to move. "I've encountered undead before. Typically taking the heads off will kill them. But these things, they just won't die. We need to get the hell out of here."

Several flashes exploded in the darkness around them. The blinding light left them staggered, unable to see anything other than a yellow glow. Their eyes slowly adjusted to find a wall of flame on all sides. The undead retreated from the blinding light, leaving the few that were too damaged to walk behind.

Weapons held tight, ready for what was to follow, the dreuslayers watched several humans and alfar drop from outstretched tree limbs. The newcomers landed in the burning trap with them. They rapidly plunged thick spears into the loose heads of the undead, watching the bodies fall still.

"Krenin offer thanks." The half-orc extended his hand toward one of the humans.

Seeing his bulky frame and tusked mouth, they sprang into action. The newcomers surrounded him, their weapons pinned against his throat quicker than he could react.

Ravion approached the group, keeping his hands visible. "Whoa, whoa. I don't know who you are, but if you kill him you're going to have to kill the rest of us. And while we may not look like much I assure you we've seen our fair share of battle. I urge you to ask yourself, is it really worth the loss of your men to make such enemies before you've had a chance to meet them?"

"You speak like an elf." One of the men stepped forward lowering his hood to expose long pointed ears. Stepping toward Ravion, he sniffed. "You speak like an elf. You smell like an elf, yet you don't look like one. What are you doing here?"

Ravion regarded the alfar, unsure what an elf was. Maybe his people existed here? Maybe they were called elves in this land? "My name is Ravion San— Sanson." He recalled the death of his parents, stifling his tongue a bit. "I— My companions and I are from a distant land. Perhaps you could tell us where the nearest town is?"

"Three humans and an orc traveling together? Distant land indeed." The alfar approached the half-orc daring him to attack. "What's wrong with him? He's awful small. And what's the matter with his skin?"

"He's a half-orc. Have you never seen one before?"

"Don't be absurd. Of course I've seen half-orcs. But this— This is no half-orc. Those unfortunate enough to be mutilated by the orcs rarely survive the birthing process. Those that do, wish they hadn't. All orcs, whether half or full, are taken to Idenfal and enrolled in the army. This thing, while it looks like an orc, clearly can't be. It's far too small even for a half-blood and its skin is green."

Ravion stood puzzled at the alfar's statement. Orc skin was dependent on region, yet they were all about the same size, even a half-breed. "I don't know how to respond to that. Judging by your tone, I'd say it best if he weren't an orc. It sounds like they aren't, by reputation, the friendliest of creatures. On the other hand he looks like a smaller version of every orc I've ever met, though not by much."

"You silly human, orcs are gray, not green. I can't say I've even seen a sickly orc that turned green."

Gareth shifted uncomfortably, tired of the questions. "If orcs are gray then I've got something wrong with my eye."

"Green orcs, gray orcs, does it really matter? Can you tell us how to get to the nearest town? We've come a long way and I'm sure you have more important things to do than question us." Demetrix couldn't help but interject, using the opportunity to lift one of the alfaren daggers. He quickly stuffed it beneath his bracer figuring they'd be unarmed in the near future.

"That I can agree with, although you won't be finding any city tonight. These woods are dangerous, particularly in the dark. You'll be coming with us. If you can convince Gailon of your authenticity then perhaps you may be released. As for the question of your orc friend, he's to be restrained and stripped of his weapons. If he resists, we'll kill him. If he attacks, we'll kill him. If he offers anything other than complete obedience, we'll—."

"Let me guess. You'll kill him?" Demetrix smiled at the overly pompous alfar. It was no wonder why so many disliked them.

"Exactly!"

The area carried the scent of cooked meat and spice. The crackle of a fireplace echoed across the quiet room. Several men and women sat about dressed in a variety of clothing. Each one had a weapon nearby, at the ready if needed.

Demetrix sat in one of the crude, wooden chairs watching the man before him. He had a superior demeanor, but carried himself equal to the others around him. What was more surprising was the lack of armor. These people clearly had a hard life. They were dressed as peasants and farmers. That rang one question in his mind. Who were they fighting?

"Let me see if I'm understanding this correctly. You passed through a magical portal into this land. You have no knowledge of the orc armies, nor the shadow legion and their dark god. And to top it all off your plan is to locate and defeat this god, which you have no knowledge of, find another magical portal and return home. Am I missing anything?"

"No, that pretty much sums it up." Demetrix glanced around memorizing the layout.

The human smirked. "Forgive my skepticism, but is it not possible you hit your head sometime in recent history? I mean, let's say I believe your story. That would explain your choice of companions and your attire. But there's the minor detail of magic. The term is not unknown to me, in fact I may be one of the few in this room that have seen it and lived to tell about it. But come on, a magic portal? If such a thing exists the sharliets would have been all over it long before your merry band stumbled upon it."

"I don't know what a sharliet is, but I assure you every word I've spoken has been truth. I've no reason to lie at the moment. Although if magic is as rare as you claim, perhaps I can offer you enough insight to warrant a second thought." Demetrix clapped his hands together, pulling at the fibers of the blue glow surrounding him. Watching them stretch and twist, the colors of the separated strands shifted. A faint green light formed between his hands. Pulling them further apart it grew brighter, forming a single column. Several branches sprouted from the sides, entwining around each other.

The room grew silent, all eyes locked on the spectacle. The stench of worry radiated throughout, growing stronger each passing moment.

"That's enough!"

Demetrix continued pulling, feeling the threads strain against his fingertips. It was nearly ready to serve its purpose.

"I said, that's enough!" The man nodded to the guards standing against the wall.

The two men rushed forward, bringing the pommels of their swords down on the base of Demetrix's skull. He collapsed, the spell dissolving into the ether it'd sprung from.

"Bind his hands and lock him with the others. Bring the tall one out."

They lifted Demetrix's limp form and carried him from the room. A few moments later they returned escorting Ravion.

"Please take a seat." Gailon gestured to the empty chair across from him.

Ravion sat, looking around the room at the fear strung faces watching him.

"I apologize for the manner in which your friend was returned. To prevent a similar outcome, I'll ask up front. Are you capable of using magic?"

"Um— no? I mean I've done some minor healing here and there, but that's not so much magic as it is an understanding of nature. At least if I am, I'm unaware."

"Very well. I'll ask that you don't try any of that here. I warn you, if you deceive me, it's not my hand you must fear. The agents of shadow can sense magic. It would lead them here and I doubt you and your friends are ready to combat an army all on your own. I only wish I was able to explain that to your friend before he tried to cast that spell."

"I wasn't aware he was able to use magic. I'd never seen him do it. Though I'm sure little more than his pride was hurt."

"I hope so. It was not my intention to harm him. I simply could not allow him to continue. Anyway, on to business. My name is Gailon. I lead the third battalion of Elalon's resistance. We may not seem like much, but I assure you this post has stood against all odds for over one-hundred years. If I'm able to keep her that way it'll be time well spent. Would you be so kind as to give me your name? And perhaps explain to me what you were doing when my men found you?"

Ravion studied his movements. His demeanor was relaxed, yet ready to jump into the fray at a moment's notice. This man was loved by his men, at least the few in the room. While it was clear he hid certain points of interest, he was an honorable man by all accounts and could prove a trustworthy ally. "My name is Ravion Sanson. I'd freely include my titles, but I fear their impact would be lost upon you. As for your question, my companions and I stumbled through a dark mirror that turned out to be some kind of portal. We'd just arrived when we were attacked by those undead creatures. Your men showed themselves soon thereafter."

"Your friend gave a similar account, although he mentioned a book that led you to the portal. Do you by chance still have that book?"

"Sadly, I don't. I couldn't find it once we came through. I can't speak from knowledge, but if I had to guess there's a similar book here. What I read in the other one suggested it was an account of happenings in my land. It stands to reason there would be one for this land as well. But again, it's just a guess."

"I see. I don't know whether to wish you luck or recommend you stand down. Any search for such an artifact would be in vain. Most go their entire lives without ever setting their sights on a book. They've been outlawed for as long as I can remember. In fact, most wouldn't know what to do with it if they saw one. Learning to read isn't exactly a high priority when the price of being caught is death."

"Unfortunately when one wants to fight, the ability to read and write can be an invaluable tool in the battle. It seems this land is much different than I'd initially thought. Do you mind if I ask you a few questions about this world?"

"You may."

"You mentioned armies and agents of shadow. With your resistance here would I be wrong in assuming this land is under some kind of siege?"

"You seem to be a man of perception. Your assumptions have struck well. There are many myths surrounding how things got as bad as they are. Though I can't say for certain things were ever any different. I don't know of any who can. Even the eldest of elves would have difficulty recalling facts from that long ago. We've been at war against the shadow since before my birth. Truthfully, I don't know if there ever was a time we weren't at war. The northlands are ruled by the shadow. They're rumored to be seven nightkings, one over each northern province. Each one has their own order of sharliet. Not to mention the orcs that serve them. They revere some dark god claiming to have dominion over all of Irayth. We in the south simply wish to live our lives away from their oppression. But they won't have it. Every year they move a bit further south, claiming more of our lands for their own. Aside from a few pockets of resistance most of the realm has fallen under the shadow's control. I don't give a damn about some attention craving god locked away in the heavens, if such a place exist. It's not the prospect of a god that threatens us on a daily basis. It's those who believe that hinder us so. The resistance has been fortunate enough to keep the shadow from gaining a foothold this far south, but it's a losing battle. If this outpost falls we could very well lose the war altogether. Most of the cities are ruled by the sharliets. As I said earlier, they have the ability to sense magic. No one knows how many sharliets there are, but one thing you should always remember if you encounter one, they're never alone. In this region all the orcs come from Idenfal. They're a vicious lot, bred for war. They take humor in the torment of those weaker than themselves and have been the biggest obstacle we face, as we're outnumbered nearly a thousand to one."

"What can you tell me about this Elalon you mentioned?"

"Elalon is one of the wisest elves I've known. She single-handedly stood against the armies of shadow and freed the forest city of Adariel from the shadow's hold. Once word of her deeds circulated every man, woman, and child willing to stand against the shadow flocked to her aid. It was then the third era was born."

"So you're saying—" The sounding of horns echoed all around, interrupting him. The men and women lounging about the room jumped up, grabbing their weapons as quickly as possible.

"Ravion, I appreciate you speaking with me. I would like to continue this, but it seems we've run out of time. I would appreciate if you would accompany my men back to your friends and await my word. Should you require weapons, they're being kept in the room straight across from you." Gailon drew a long, serrated sword. A pick-like spike protruded from the spine near the tip, leaving the sharpened edge curved like that of an axe. Giving the command he rushed from the room, joining his men.

Ravion made his way to the holding room, ignoring the two men behind him. Busting through the door he spotted Gareth standing near the far wall staring out the smoked window. One of the panes was busted allowing minimal sight into the cloaking night. Looking around he noticed Demetrix lying unconscious on a cloth-covered bench against the wall. He heard the door latch behind him, clicking into place. "Are you able to make out any details?"

"Mere figures in the distance. I can see the glow of several torches. Hard to say how many are around them."

"Most likely orcs. I got a bit of history from the commander. Seems they've been in a state of war their entire lives."

"We should be right at home then."

Ravion walked over to his brother and gave him a light shake. "I've got a feeling this will be unlike anything we've ever faced."

Demetrix shot up, ripping the stolen dagger from its hiding spot in his bracer. "That's a good way to get stabbed."

"I trust your skill. You would have confirmed your target before striking. Good job concealing the blade by the way."

"Sounds like— marching? Why does it sound like marching?" Demetrix rubbed the knot on the back of his head and glanced around the room, regaining his bearings.

"We're under attack. We need to get out of here. This isn't our fight." Gareth broke another section of the glass hoping it would allow a clearer view. "Yep, definitely orcs, though they're either too close, as in within archer range, or they're larger than the ones we're used to."

Ravion's nose wrinkled at the statement. "The bigger they are, the harder they fall."

"You forget, the harder they hit." Gareth chuckled.

"Agreed. Any idea where they stashed Krenin?" Demetrix stood and approached the door. Pulling the handle, the door wouldn't budge. "No surprise here. But they've locked us in."

The dull pitch of horns echoed off the towering trees and ruined buildings. The flicker of torches blazed in the unnatural darkness, shyly illuminating their bearers. If it hadn't been for their number they wouldn't have had any effect at all.

Rezerik looked from side to side inspecting the formation of orcs awaiting his command. They imposed a mighty fear by their mere visage. It wasn't so much the thick armor or the jagged weapons that made them frightening. It was the mutilated flesh beneath that did the trick. Scarred from a lifetime of victories. Each one was branded or cut as a way to identify status among the brutes. Their charcoal gray skin served as a resume that would travel with them regardless of their destination. But the fear they offered was nothing compared to his own. He was one of the few beings the orcs feared. They were bred to fear him. The sound of approaching footsteps roused his thoughts.

One of the sharliets stepped toward the dark horseman and lowered his hood revealing the pale white skin beneath. "Dark One, we've confirmed it's a resistance stronghold. The first squadron has engaged them. The cowards have fallen into their barricades."

Rezerik stared at the intimidated man, taking in the stench of his cowardice. It was a smell unlike any other, but it told him more than enough about the young sharliet. "Good. Send the entire fourth brigade as reinforcement. I need them distracted while I take what I came for."

"As you wish, My Lord." He threw his hood overhead and turned to disappear back into the darkness.

Demetrix stepped back, readying the dagger to strike fast and hard if needed. The door clicked then opened wide revealing Gailon.

"We can't hold them off any longer. If you're going to leave here, you have to go now." The human commander stepped aside and opened the door across the hall. "All of your belongings are in here. Get what you need. I'll lead you to your friend."

They rushed into the room and locating their effects. Quickly securing them they followed after Gailon, hearing the sounds of battle closer than ever. The corridors wrapped around, forming a maze in the large keep. They passed through a narrow stairwell lined with stone and mortar. The bottom was sealed by a reinforced wooden door.

Several brass keys jingled from a large ring in Gailon's hand. He fumbled through them, selecting the correct one. He pressed it into the lock and turned. The door clicked and sprang open.

The dank smell of mildew and stagnant air assaulted them. Stepping into the damp dungeon floor, the chill of the underground soaked to their bones reminding them of long forgotten pains.

"Your friend is this way." Gailon gestured toward the iron cells lining the stone wall.

Following their guide they rounded the corner and spotted Krenin shackled in the center of one of the small cells. He hung limp, his arms stretched overhead by two thick chains securing him to the upper runs of the cage. He was stripped of everything save his breeches. They were held in place only by his muscular hips. He bore several lashes across his back and shoulders, each one coated in layers of dried blood. His bare feet were outstretched, the tips of his toes narrowly touching the cold, stone floor, due only to his collapsed state.

Gareth rushed toward the cell, pulling at the door. Turning toward Gailon he found his anger, begging to be unleashed. "Open it!"

The human fumbled with the keys. Unlocking the cell, he stepped aside, pulling the door with him. Krenin peeked through his heavy, swollen eyelids, spotting his brothers. He tried to pull himself upright, but the chains sapped him of strength. He couldn't lift his head, let alone his entire body.

Ravion stepped into the cell and grabbed the shackles holding his wrist. "Do you have a key for these?"

Gailon reached into his pouch and pulled a small round tube with several barbs protruding from the end. "Here you are." Tossing the key to Ravion, he turned and made for a large chest on the far wall.

Gareth and Demetrix pulled the exhausted half-orc up, taking the weight off his chains. Ravion twisted the strange key, releasing the shackles. Helping him to the bench, they placed him against the wall to regain some of his strength.

Gailon returned holding a leather bag over his shoulder. "Here are his things. I apologize for the inconvenience and condition in which he's being returned to you. While I don't condone the actions of my men in this regard, you have to understand the fear my people have of orcs is not misplaced. I couldn't risk having him loose inside the keep."

Gareth jumped up, stopping inches from the man's face. "I don't give a damn about the fear of you or your people. You've mistreated my friend and I'll not stand for it."

"I understand your discord and I'm truly sorry for the afflictions he's suffered under my command. I did not give the order to have him beaten. I simply wished him restrained and questioned. Some of my men get a little carried away at times." Gailon held out the bag, refusing to back down from the enraged bald man.

Ravion stood, accepting the bundle. "Come on, Gareth. There's no sense in making another enemy when the odds are already stacked so heavily against us."

Gareth held a moment longer, staring his rage deep into the unyielding commander. Knowing his true implications were received he turned, directing his attention to his weakened friend.

"I cannot undo what's been done. But I'm man enough to admit when someone has been wronged. I offer payment for the blood that's been shed." Gailon drew his serrated sword, bringing it to rest in front of him. "It's a poor comparison. But I hope this will help to forgive the wrongs that were done here. I claimed this blade from the first orc commander I ever defeated. I've carried it into every battle since. It's served me well and I now wish it to serve you." He spun the serrated blade around letting the pick slide into its pocket of the sheath. Pulling the leather and wood scabbard from his belt he handed the sword to Ravion. "If you'll excuse me, I need to return to my men for our final stand. You'll find a wooden door under the bed of the last cell. It'll take you into the forest north of here. I wish I could give you more assistance in your quest, but it seems this is where our paths must end. Good luck on your task. May Elalon's grace guide your way."

Chapter XIV
A Way Home

The scent of charred wood was thick in the morning air. Billowing clouds of smoke filtered through the leafless trees in the distance, making the perpetually dark sky seem even darker. The earth shook for miles from the sheer mass of troops clamoring over the decimated site. The dreuslayers stood atop a hill at the forest's edge watching the swarming army overrun the shattered keep. They looked like tiny, black ants in the distance.

Ravion stared at the blazing beacon, listening to the echo of war cries in the distance. A pang of guilt overcame him. He regretted leaving them to their fate. But what assistance could he offer against an army he knew nothing about? If he'd stayed it was likely he'd be among the dead. There was no fear of death, quite the contrary, but he also wasn't foolish. Rushing headlong into eons of conflict wouldn't be the answer to any of his questions. Glancing around he found the faces of his brothers. Something told him they were thinking the same as he. "Gailon told me the orcs would overrun the southern lands if the keep fell. I wonder if any of them made it out?"

Gareth slapped his hand on Ravion's shoulder. "There's nothing you could have done. This isn't our home. We don't know the beasties of this land. I'm sure we'll have many chances to learn 'em. But for now we need to get out of here. We're already in over our heads. No sense in waiting for the tide." Gareth released his friend and bent to help Krenin find his feet. Throwing the meaty, green arm around his neck, he lifted.

The group walked for what felt like hours, though there was no true way to tell how long it had been. The clouds wouldn't part long enough to give them the slightest idea of where the sun was. It wouldn't have done them any good anyway. This land was unlike any they'd seen. Direction was difficult at best. None of the usual identifiers seemed to exist here. Moss grew on all sides of the trees, not just one. They hadn't stumbled upon any pool of water to try the leaf trick. And without the sky, the stars patterns were hidden. That was provided they could identify them here, where ever *here* was.

Reaching a thinning between two patches of trees and a vast plain on the other side, they gently laid Krenin down to rest.

Ravion leaned against one of the gray-barked trees, looking out into the waist-high grain. It grew in thick bundles of thorns that seemed to stretch across in all directions. One thing was certain. It was going to be difficult to cross, much less travel in a straight line. A dreadful feeling crept into him. His hand on the wicked dagger he snapped around, searching the clearing behind them.

"That's the third time you've done that since we left the woodlands. What are you looking for?" Gareth pulled himself up and looked the same direction, not finding anything.

"I've got this lingering feeling we're being followed. I can't explain it." Running his fingers through his lengthening, red hair, Ravion let the notion pass and turned toward their destination. "We should keep moving."

"Aye." Gareth searched the area once more, ensuring there was nothing there. Shaking his head, he pulled Krenin to his feet, securing the weakened orc.

Demetrix moved into position on the other side, easing the weight on the bald warrior. There was no telling how much longer they needed to walk and it seemed foolish to let him exhaust himself when they could be ambushed at any moment.

Ravion sliced through the thick bristles, clearing a path through the field. He hated using his ancestry weapon for such mundane tasks, but it was better than shredding their clothes on the needle-like protrusions. Listening to the dry stalks snap under his boots, he pressed on.

Darkness came and went several times, cycling the seemingly short days in the barren field. Food was scarce, but they'd managed to find a few rabbits to sate them on their journey. Their waterskins were nearly empty, having been rationed two days earlier to conserve it until they found a stream. It was turning into an onerous task. One which seemed would never be filled. Nearing exhaustion they climbed a large hill overlooking a spanning flatland.

The cool breeze carried the sound of civilization. They stared down at a large, walled city. A steady line of wagons and horsemen waited at the closest gate. A handful of orcs stood in front of the portcullis, blocking entry. Two of the brutes dug through the wagons and saddlebags looking for anything of value. Leaving half the contents lying scattered on the ground one of them waved the wagon through, granting entry into the city.

Krenin leaned against the walking stick they'd found for him. He was bruised and sore, but his strength was returning. Feeling his stomach rumble from hunger he eyed the gate, awaiting his friend's opinions. They always had some idea when it came to this kind of thing.

"This may prove difficult." Ravion took in the sight, memorizing the layout as best he could from the higher ground. "Any ideas how we're going to get into town without drawing too much attention? I doubt they'd let us pass with Krenin in tow. Granted he's not like them, they may see him as a sign of weakness and kill him on sight. Or worse, force him to join their army."

Gareth squinted, trying to make out the details. He hadn't mastered perception with his single eye yet. "Aside from the orcs, do you see anyone wearing armor or carrying a sword?"

Ravion shielded his eyes from the dull glow of the clouds, hoping it would somehow grant him a clearer image. "No. Just the orcs."

"Exactly. If this was Marbayne and we were at war would you allow armed and unknown men through the gate? Let me be more direct. Would you let a band of dreu through the gate anytime if they were armed?"

"I see your point." Ravion silently considered his options.

Demetrix surveyed the line. "Why don't we just sneak in? It wouldn't take much. Just cause a distraction and walk through. I'm willing to bet the horses are half-spooked as is."

"I doubt we'd get close enough without being noticed." Ravion glanced at Krenin. "He kind of stands out. We'd need to disguise him. Maybe if they don't see his skin we can pass him off as a large human."

The half-orc rose against his staff. "Krenin only half-human. They not fall for that. Tusks too big."

Ravion dropped to a knee, opening his pack. He pulled a tattered, brown cloak and tossed it to the half-orc. "If we're quick, that should keep the attention off you until we can get close enough to cause the distraction. Do you think you can move quickly when we tell you?"

"Me think so. Legs are still heavy, but should be able to walk. Fast if need to be."

Gareth pulled the jagged sword from his back. "Here, put this under your cloak. If this doesn't go as planned we're gonna to have to fight our way out. We can't go in there with one man unarmed."

Stuffing his swords deeper into the quiver Demetrix slid a leather flap over the top, hiding them from sight. Pulling the pin in the middle of his bow, he folded it in half and slid it into another compartment. Making sure it couldn't be seen, he pulled his cloak around him and locked the golden clasp on the front. "It'd probably be in our best interest to hide all weapons and armor. Like you said, there's no sense in drawing unwanted attention."

Gareth nodded, pulling his swords from their sheath. He found the hidden pocket stitched between the thick layers of his blue and green cloak. Carefully sliding them into place, he secured them so they wouldn't move. Patting himself, he made sure their outline couldn't be seen before glancing at Ravion. The young dalari scout stood fast, an amused expression clear on his face.

"What? I don't hide my weapons. If need arises I'll figure something out. Are we ready?" Refusing to wait for their confirmation, he marched down the hill.

They slowed their pace staying as close to Krenin as possible without drawing attention. If he lost his footing, or his cloak fell open, their whole plan would fall apart. Joining the rear of the line they studied the people around them. As far as they could tell they were all human. A few had cloaks over their heads, making their race a guess.

The stench of manure and dried sweat radiated through the crowded street. These people were barren, lost in their mere existence, never really living. It seemed they had nothing more than the desire to survive. They made themselves slaves to more than the orcs. They were slaves to their cowardice. It was no wonder the orcs had claimed so much of their lands. All these people had to do was stand up and fight, but they never would. It was a hard path. They sacrificed everything and received nothing in return.

Gareth and Krenin slowly made their way around the far side of the line keeping their eyes on the patrolling orcs. Ravion and Demetrix took the inside. Nobody said a word. It was as if they were too defeated to stand up for themselves.

Demetrix glanced around, finding one man's eyes. He looked away the moment they made contact. Demetrix shook his head. If he were the type, he could take anything he wanted and there was nothing these people would do about it. It was pathetic. Sighing his exhaustion at the concept, he returned to his task.

Keeping his eye on the others, Gareth nodded. Signaling his intent, he guided Krenin to within a few steps of the open gate where they waited.

Demetrix watched the orcs carefully. They were abusive beyond need. They destroyed nearly everything they touched, taking pleasure in it. He watched one of them slap an old woman, knocking her to the ground. He kicked her in the stomach, laughing his dominance away. Another approached, taking position over her. Pulling his member from his armored pants he relieved himself atop her, aiming the golden liquid at her face. The dalari ranger stood in shock. *How can these people accept this treatment? They have a choice. They just have to make it!* Chaos erupted behind him. Spinning around, Demetrix noticed one of the wagon hands lying in the dirt. The basket he'd been carrying was busted and the apples that had filled it were scattered about. A sudden shove into his shoulder sent Demetrix to the side. Narrowly catching himself, he watched one of the orcs force his way through.

The brute cracked a whip. The leather tip exploded across the boy's face, splitting flesh and exposing a sea of crimson fluid.

The crowd snatched up the loose fruit as quick as they could, hiding it away from the orcs.

Demetrix was lost in the sight of the boy. He couldn't have been much older than twelve. Pain shot through him, watching the orc bring his plated boot down atop the boy's head. He was dead. There was no denying that. Closing his eyes he turned, hoping to be out of this infernal place as soon as possible. He glanced to Ravion. Receiving the signal, Demetrix slipped the jagged rock from his sleeve and prepared himself.

Ravion watched his brother move into position. Returning the gesture to Gareth, they were all ready. Ravion quickly sliced the leather harness securing one of the horses to its wagon and gave the final signal to his brother.

Demetrix stole a quick glance around making sure no one was watching. Certain of his stealth he jabbed the tip of the sharp stone into the horse's hind haunches, burying it in the muscle.

The horse reared and kicked, launching the near empty wagon into those behind it. The remaining straps caught, yanking against the unsettled mount. The wagon master tumbled to the ground, unprepared for the sudden jolt. In pain and feeling entrapped the horse bucked and kicked, toppling carts and scattering their loads. People scattered, trying to avoid the frenzied beast and spilling carts. While orcs swarmed in an attempt to contain the chaos.

Gareth and Krenin rushed toward the gate letting the mass confusion hide their entry. Ravion ducked one of the flying carts, narrowly dodging a wood and steel wheel to his head. Looking around he spotted Gareth at the edge of the market. Quickly joining him, he searched the docile square, ensuring they were out of immediate danger. "It's kind of gloomy isn't is."

Demetrix stepped through the gate, closing his eyes. He heard the horse draw its last breath. The sound of steel piercing flesh was one he'd never forget. It was unfortunate they killed the beast and even more so that his actions had led to its death. Reaching his brothers, he glared his disdain to Ravion saying more in silence than he could in words. Ravion gave a half-hearted smile, acknowledging his understanding.

Letting the weight off his shoulders Demetrix glanced around, searching the barren market. The few items on display were of little to no value. "How can they live this way? These people have spent their entire lives in fear. I wouldn't be surprised if there were random hangings to keep the population at manageable numbers in the event of a revolution. What are we even doing here? We don't know where to go or what to do. Hell, even if we figure out what we're supposed to be doing how are we going to get home?"

Gareth kept his cloak pulled tight, ready to draw his swords at a moment's notice. "We'll figure it out. Right now, it'd suit us all to have a hot meal and a good night's sleep. We can move in the morning."

"I'd advise you to choose your words wisely while in the open. This city has ears in the most unlikely places." The gravelly voice echoed from the shadow behind them.

They jumped. Spinning around they found a man wrapped in a dark green cloak. The oversized hood hid his facial features.

"I thank you for the words of advice. Though I don't believe we've had the pleasure of being introduced." Ravion gave a respectful bow, keeping his sword hand ready if the stranger attacked.

The man lowered his hood revealing a freshly shaven, middle aged face and a head covered in short, graying-brown hair. His skin tone lacked all pigment, showing he hadn't spent much time in the sun. Though with the constant cloud cover it was a wonder any of these people looked different. "Forgive me, seems I've forgotten my manners. They call me Krizere. And by they I mean that's my name."

"I'm Ravion. These are my brothers; Gareth, Demetrix, and Krenin. Would you mind showing us to the inn? Perhaps we could buy you a drink."

"Ah, thank you for the offer. Sadly, I must decline. I have other matters to which I must attend. I would however like to offer you a proposition." Krizere glanced around, ensuring no one was listening.

Ravion leaned a bit closer to hear what he had to say, but kept enough distance in the event the man decided to attack.

"I can tell you're not from this world. Call it an educated guess, but I've seen that look before. Once upon a time it lingered on my face. I know a place here in town that has exactly what you need to find your way back home."

Gareth crossed his arms, staring the man down. "Answer me this. If you know all this, why haven't you retrieved this item for yourself? You're clearly of able mind and body. What's the catch?"

"You're perceptive. That's good. You'll need it to get home. You're not wrong about there being a catch. I'm unable to obtain what's needed as I'm but one man. As you can imagine, it's quite difficult to find trustworthy allies in this place. But you four, you know how to work together. That's the key to making things happen." Krizere paused, quickly searching the market for eavesdroppers. Locking his sight on an orc patrol he turned his attention back to Ravion. "My apologies. I'm out of time. Continue toward the center of town and you'll come across, The Wounded Stag. Writing isn't so common around here but you'll know it by the broken stag horns over the door. Ask for room two. You'll find everything you need in the foot locker. If you decide to work with me, meet me here, first light, three days' time." Without another word he took a step backward and disappeared between the buildings.

"Well, that was insightful." Demetrix searched the shadows for the man knowing he had to still be there just waiting for a chance to move. He recalled Lythus using the same trick multiple times.

"At least we have a lead on how to get home. I've grown tired of this place already." Gareth turned, gaining his bearings. "The inn is this way."

"Is that it?" Krenin stared out from under his hood studying the run down wooden structure.

"Do you see any other buildings with broken antlers over the door?" Demetrix asked sarcastically, concealing his smirk.

The out of place half-orc searched the surrounding buildings. "I don't see any."

"Never mind. It's a shame Malakai couldn't be here with us. I always underestimated his ability to baby sit."

"That doesn't seem like good idea. How would baby breathe if you sat on it?"

"Point proven."

"Quiet down. You're drawing too much attention." Gareth casually searched the street, hoping they weren't discovered.

"Here he comes." Demetrix gestured toward his brother making his from the pub.

Ravion rushed across the dirt roadway, rejoining the others. Looking around he made sure nobody was listening. "I spoke to the barkeep. I think we may be in over our heads. More so than usual anyway. Not only is room two the entire second floor, but it's already been paid for along with unlimited pleasantries."

Gareth kept watch searching for anyone out of place. Refusing to let his guard down, he spoke. "Sounds like the perfect trap to catch a couple of fall guys."

"What kinds of pleasantries are we talking about? Food, drink, women?" Demetrix couldn't help but smile at the possibilities.

"And then some as it was explained to me. It sounded a little too good to be true. I fear accepting the room would be no different than signing a death warrant. If not for the last meal and luxuries in a town such as this, but for the simple fact that high profiles aren't easily hidden. The moment the orcs come for us they'd know right where we are."

"Maybe they don't have to." Demetrix let his scheming come to the surface in the form of a sinister smile.

"What do you mean?" Ravion shot him a quick glance.

"Well, we all want to go home and this guy offered us a way. Whether it's true or not, we have to check it out. If he's lying, we move on. If he's telling the truth, it's our salvation. As far as the room goes, he just said further direction would be found in room two. Not that we have to lodge there. It seems to me if a few of us partake in a couple drinks and just so happen to make some noise, most of the attention would be claimed. That would allow one of us free rein to explore the upper levels. If that someone just so happened to stumble upon room two, I don't see any harm in observing whatever information may or may not be present. At least then we'd know what we're dealing with and if the price is too high or not."

Ravion glanced at Gareth with a slight shrug. "He has a point."

"Krenin volunteer to drink!"

Gareth shot a stern gaze to the half-orc. "If we were home it wouldn't be a big deal for you to play the distraction. Unfortunately, we're not. We can't risk you being caught if things get out of hand. It's best you hang back as a lookout in the event we have to make a quick exit. I'd feel more comfortable having you as back up if we need it."

Krenin lowered his head. "I understand."

"Who's going upstairs?" Gareth glanced at Ravion, and back to Demetrix.

"Ravion's already made contact with the barkeep. It might be in our best interest if the rest of us remain disassociated. I'm usually up for the sneaky breaking and entering kind of thing. But I wouldn't want to overlook a small, yet important detail and mess up our chance to get home."

"It makes sense for me to follow through since I've already spoken with him. I got a pretty good look at the keys behind the bar. I don't think I'd be able to pick the lock if I go up during a distraction and if I accept the key from the barkeep they'll know someone's claimed the room."

"I suppose I could always sneak away before the fun starts and unlock the door. Then later you can come by and check it out. Just try to do it quickly. I'd hate to open the door for someone else to take what we came for."

"It sounds like we've got ourselves a plan. Krenin, how about you go in before we do and take a seat in one of the corners. I'd like you close, but not in the mix." Gareth handed him a couple silver coins. "Get yourself something to drink."

Krenin nodded and stuffed the coin into his pouch. Adjusting his hood, he staggered across the street and marched through the door.

The stench of stale booze and pipe smoke was nearly overbearing to his heightened senses. The chatter was loud for the time of day. He stood a few inches taller than the tallest human.

Bending his knees, Krenin adjusted to match as close as possible without drawing attention. Finding an open table near the rear wall he pulled out the heavy wooden chair and took a seat, letting the table hide his true height.

A moment later a middle-aged woman with long, red hair approached. She wore a tan dress with maroon top and had a leather corset pulled tight around her waist, causing her bosom to pop. Peering down at the hooded man she gave a heavy sigh. "Name's Melynda. Somethin' I can get ya' to drink, doll?"

Krenin swallowed hard. The thought of what he'd say if he made it this far hadn't occurred to him. Sliding one of the silver coins across the table he quickly hid his green hand and forced his lips around his tusks forcing an impersonation of his best human accent. "I'll have an ale."

"Back in a minute." She snatched the coin and disappeared behind the lingering smoke.

Levi Samuel

Chapter XV
Tribulations

Demetrix darted up the stairs, confident he hadn't been seen. Reaching the first landing he paused. The stairs continued upward running the other direction. Glancing down the corridor he noticed a singular oaken door at the far end. He recalled what Ravion had said about the second floor. That had to be it. He cautiously approached the heavy door held solid in its frame. Ornately casted iron splayed from the hinges and sprawled across the thick, polished planks coming to rest in an intertwining pattern around the latch and knob. Kneeling down he stared intently at the keyhole, having never seen one of its design. Truth be told there were many locks he'd never attempted to open, but he'd witnessed more of the dragon's time in his body than he cared to admit. It couldn't be that hard. All locks are basically the same, save for a few minor changes here and there.

Reaching into the hidden pocket of his armor's inner liner Demetrix found the thin leather pouch housing his picks. Lifting the fold he removed a bar and hook. Carefully placing the bar into the hole, he applied a light amount of tension on the tumbler. Applying a bit more vigor, Demetrix buried the hook into the lock and wiggled it back and forth, feeling the pins. He counted four of them. Going to the furthest one, Demetrix carefully pressed it past the shear point, keeping tension on the tumbler. If he let off for the briefest moment the pin was likely to spring back up. Working his way toward him, Demetrix felt the final pin click into place and the tumbler released. A smile came to his face. He'd done it. Pushing against the bar the tumbler rotated and came to a stop, telling him the pins had reset on the other side. Ensuring his success he grabbed the knob and twisted, letting the door crack open. Peeking inside he glanced around, glad the room was vacant. Carefully, he pulled the door to the seal just enough to keep it from latching into the frame. While it was unlocked there was no sense in taking unneeded chances. Spinning around, Demetrix made way for the stairs. Gareth had a head start and he wasn't going to let him win so easily.

The door creaked open revealing a large, abandoned room. It was fully furnished and seemingly free of dust. Ravion stepped inside, closing the door behind him. Despite the glass windows lining each of the side walls the filtered sunlight did little to brighten the large chamber. He glanced around spotting several lanterns resting upon various ledges about the room. Their shields were free of soot, suggesting they hadn't been used since the room was last cleaned. The thought to light one came to mind. But it would do little more than announce its occupancy. He didn't need the light to see in this place. His vision seemed to work just find in low light. It was the total dark that caused him problems. Scanning the room he noticed the chest lying at the foot of the bed. Slowly approaching, Ravion listened to the floorboards creak under his weight. Kneeling, he slowly lifted the heavy, domed lid making sure there were no trip wires or traps attached to it. Confident in their absence he laid the top back, letting it rest against the polished footboard of the perfectly made bed.

Peeking inside, it was empty save for a rolled, tan colored hide, wrapped several times by a much darker strap. Lifting the roll Ravion unwrapped the hide and pulled it open to find a wooden canister inside. Hundreds of runes were carved into the cylinder, covering every inch of it. He looked for a seam or an end cap, but couldn't find any. The secret had to lay in the runes. Focusing on the strange etchings he felt a warmth wash over him. They were foreign. Nothing about their design made any sense to the numerous languages he'd studied. Yet he couldn't help but feel he should be able to read it. Sighing heavily, Ravion felt it crack in his hands. Inspecting the hollow tube, he noticed several pieces of parchment rolled together and stuffed inside. Removing them, Ravion separated and laid them upon the bed, studying each one for relevance.

A loud crash echoed though the walls, distracting him. Shaking his head he returned his focus to the parchment. "They've certainly managed to draw some attention."

"Indeed they have."

Ravion jumped. Drawing his sword he spun to find a familiar face at the door.

"My apologies. I didn't mean to startle you."

"Krizere?" Ravion paused. "What are you doing here? You said you'd meet us in three days."

"Again, my apologies." Krizere raised his hand, gesturing the weapon down. "I had to be certain you were who I'd hoped. My eyes aren't what they once were. I couldn't risk being mistaken. I'm glad to see I wasn't." He pointed to the scattered parchment behind the armed man.

Ravion lowered his sword and glanced back. "I've gone over each one and haven't found anything that's supposed to help us."

Krizere folded his cloak over his arm and took a step closer. "That's because the parchment is of no use to you. Simple maps I've drawn over the years. Much like literature, maps are a rare commodity. They're next to useless if you don't understand how to read them."

"Why'd you send us here if these have nothing to do with the way home?"

"The parchment isn't why I sent you here. Their case is. Think of it as a test. The runes scribed into that cylinder are of an ancient dialect from my homeland. I scribed them long ago as a personal keepsake. I knew I was the only one from my land here, so I imbued the very dirt of Ur into the runes. Only one who has walked her fields can open it. As I said, I had to be sure of your validity before I agreed to aid you."

Ravion sheathed his sword and stacked the parchment. "Now that I've passed your test—." He paused, rolling and pressing them into the tube. Pushing the two halves together the seam disappeared. "What would you have of me?" Ravion choked his annoyance away. It would cloud his mind and that wouldn't aid him.

"I understand your frustration. But I assure you, you're much closer than you think." Krizere pulled a chair and took a seat. "Hidden beneath this city is a vast library. One of the last this land has to offer. The book keeper has one in particular that we need if we're going to find the portal. The problem lies in the fact that he won't give it freely."

"What's he want in exchange?"

"Short form, the magistrate's scepter."

"How about long form?"

Krizere sighed, resting his elbow against the wooden armrest and pressing his cheek against his knuckles. "Magic here is more of a curse than a blessing. Those who possess it shine like a beacon. Sooner or later someone will alway comes to answer its call. When you're the sole guardian of not only one of the last, but one of the largest libraries in the land, magical tomes can be difficult to hide." Sitting up, Krizere continued his tale. "Long ago the keeper had a rod that was capable of shielding magic from the sharliets. A few decades ago a foolish young boy stole the rod. When he tried to leave town the magistrate's guard stopped him. They took the rod as payment for alleged crimes. The keeper has since resorted to less effective means of hiding the library, though it's only a matter of time. Let's just say if the wrong person arrives before we do our way home disappears forever."

"So you're saying the rod has to be returned to the library. This librarian would be willing to give us the book then?" Ravion took a seat on the bed, listening to the story through the commotion going on below them.

"I believe he'd be more susceptible to negotiations if it were returned. Though I can't guarantee anything."

"Great. So we're still working with uncertainty." Ravion sighed. "Where can I find this rod?"

"The magistrate of this fair city has some extracurricular activities she'd prefer didn't become common knowledge. One of these activities is embezzling from the city coffers. The rod, once it was taken from the boy, caught her eye. I'm sure it's stashed with the other treasures she had hidden away."

"Let me get this straight. You want me to break into the magistrate's private stash of illegal goods and rummage through to find a magical rod. Which I'm sure is illegal to possess as well since magic in general seems to be frowned upon. Once we have it, we have to find a hidden and illegal library so its guardian *might* give us a book that *might* lead us to the portal so we can get home? Am I missing anything?"

"You missed the fact that breaking and entering, the book itself, and the possession of a book are also illegal. And the portal home is probably someplace we shouldn't be either. Which makes it trespassing, which is also illegal."

"Is that all?" Ravion chuckled. "Well, I suppose I've faced worse odds. I can't seem to think of any right now, but I'm sure I have at some point."

"You'll do fine. You've made it this far unscathed. When I found the mirror I was unarmed, unprepared, and wearing rags."

"Perhaps you could tell me how you came to learn so much about this?"

Krizere smiled, adjusting the collar of his tunic. "Well, that boy in my story. He grew up."

Another crash rang out, shaking the walls. "What in the nine hells are they doing now?" Ravion for the door. Quickly reaching the stairs he froze seeing several orcs at the door dragging a limp Krenin across the floor.

"It seems you're a man down. Can't say I'm surprised, sending a half-orc in as a decoy. I'd recommend you go in tonight. When you're done, I've a feeling this city will be crawling with orcs. And if you wait for morning it's unlikely your friend will be able to join you." Krizere patted him on the shoulder and marched past, disappearing down the steps.

Demetrix glanced from his cards, watching Ravion dart up the stairs. Shifting his gaze around the room, no one else seemed to care. His sight ended on Gareth sitting across from him. He gave a gentle nod, hoping the others at the table wouldn't notice. He picked three cards from his hand and laid them face down on the table. "I'll take three." Sliding them toward Gareth he stole a glance at the eyes around him, taking comfort in their focus on their own hands. Flexing his wrist, he slid one of the cards into his sleeve and pulled another.

"What do you think you're doing?" Gareth shouted across the table, dropping his own hand so all could see.

"What are you talking about?"

"Don't play me a fool. I saw you slide that card into your sleeve." Gareth grabbed the young rogue's wrist and twisted, exposing the hidden cards.

"Huh? I wonder how that got there." Demetrix smiled, unable to steel his face.

"I don't contend with cheaters." Gareth released his grip, bringing his other hand around in a fist.

Demetrix anticipated the hit. Throwing his weight into it he fell atop the table and rolled, grabbing the edge to topple it with him. Cards exploded into the air flying all directions. The room hushed, watching the spectacle before them.

Gareth stormed toward the prone archer, ready for reimbursement. Demetrix kicked out, hooking Gareth's leg. He pulled, watching the one-eyed warrior buckle beside him.

Gareth let his legs fold. Falling quicker than he intended, he reached out, grabbing one of the empty chairs. Shoving with all his strength it crashed into another table, toppling it.

The men jumped, enraged by their ruined game. In the excitement one spilled his mug on another. That one, in turn, hit him. Moments later the tavern was in full brawl.

Gareth felt someone grab his cloak, pulling him into the air. Unable to get his feet beneath him he crashed back down, hearing a large mass fall beside him.

Demetrix saw one of the large men grab hold of Gareth. Throwing his weight he kicked out, catching the man's legs. His knees buckled and the man fell, dropping Gareth. Angry patrons filled the room, breaking chairs, throwing tables, and using anything they could find to cause pain to the others.

Krenin stood, swinging his half-full tankard into the face of one of the larger men. The wooden mug collapsed against him, sloshing the bronze liquid across his tunic. The man landed hard on the floor showered in bits of wood and stale ale.

Demetrix whipped his legs around transferring his weight and landing on his feet. Grabbing hold of Gareth he pulled him to his feet just in time to dodge a swing from one of the enraged brawlers. "I think it's time we get out of here. Things are beginning to get out of control."

"Agreed!" Gareth glanced around the room finding the half-orc near the door. He stood out, like a beast among sheep. The patrons gave him a wide girth, uncertain if they wanted to engage anything that resembled one of the orcs. "Krenin, time to go!"

The half-orc walked toward them, unmolested. They made their way through the barroom toward the kitchen. Rushing down the narrow hall, they turned into the storeroom. Gareth shoved a shelf to the side, revealing a wooden hatch in the floor. Demetrix grabbed the hole in the wood and pulled it open. Quickly jumping down, he rolled to the side and waited for the others.

Gareth heard a loud crash. He spun around, seeing two of the large orcs slam one of the tables into the wall. One of the humans fell to the floor, his head crushed. There was no question the man was dead. "We've got orcs." Hurriedly, he jumped into the crawl space.

Krenin stepped toward the hole. Sizing it, he wasn't sure he'd fit. It was almost as wide as his shoulders. If anything it'd be extremely tight. He readied to jump hoping it wouldn't hurt too badly. He still hadn't fully healed from his time in the cell. Something grabbed his arm pulling him the other direction. Muscling through he tried to continue, but it was no use. Whatever had him was stronger than he. Stealing a glance, a startling image stared back at him. It was clearly an orc, though its skin was the color of charcoal and hundreds of scars marred every visible patch of flesh. He wasn't sure, but he could have sworn the eyes flashed red for the briefest moment although they were clearly a dark brown now. Before he could move, a head-sized fist rocketed toward him, knocking his vision into blackness.

"It was all for a gods damned test?" Gareth fumed, clenching his fist in anger. He could feel the air around him tense.

Demetrix sat atop a wooden crate digging the tip of his dagger into the grain. "I wonder what they'll do with him?"

Ravion peeked out the doorway of the abandoned shack, watching the last of the orcs leave the tavern. "I don't know, but whatever it is, I don't think it'll be good. We need to get him out of here, but first we have to find this rod. We can't risk breaking him out before we go in. It'd draw too much unwanted attention."

"So we're just gonna let him rot?" Gareth slammed his fist into one of the thick, wooden supports. It cracked under the blow. He inspected the wood, surprised he'd hit it that hard.

"We have a few choices. We can put it to a vote. We can let him sit for the night while we go after this rod and hopefully get the direction we need. It's a typical heist scenario, which will more than likely end with some heat. That means added security when we go after Krenin. Or we can try to go after him now, which might be expected since they know he wasn't alone. If we take that route it's guaranteed we won't be able to get the rod for quite some time or at least until they've forgotten about us. Either way we're against the hourglass. I personally vote we get the rod first and then Krenin. It's a simple retrieve, extract, and escape plan. Which seems easier than having to wait gods know how long until they stop looking."

Demetrix wiped the tip of his dagger and sheathed it. Taking a deep breath, he spoke. "I don't like leaving him in there any more than you guys, but I agree with Ravion. We can't risk breaking him out before we have everything this town has to offer. If we do so prematurely we might as well kiss our chance home goodbye."

Gareth glared from one to the other unhappy with their decision, though he understood their reasoning. "Fine, but we are going to get him out. He's in there because I jumped prematurely. If I'd waited a little longer we could have fought our way out and he wouldn't have gotten pinched."

"You can't blame yourself. We had a plan. It worked as best it could under the circumstances. Had it been you or I that got caught they might have killed us outright. At least with him being what he is, it buys us some time." Demetrix had his own regrets, but they wouldn't serve his purpose. Moving forward, he jumped from the crate and approached the door.

Ravion glanced out of the hole in the roof staring up into the ever-cloudy sky. "Night's about to fall. We need to move soon."

Krenin awoke feeling a sharp pain in his wrists. He struggled, but couldn't move. Opening his eyes he looked around, seeing several of the larger orcs standing over him. He was splayed out on his back, his arms stretched and bound to a thick plank under him.

The orcs grabbed the plank and lifted him upright. His weight shifted, putting all of it on his arms. He felt his shoulders separate, threatening to pull out of their sockets. His wounds tore open from the tightened skin. Blood began trickling down his back. The increasing pressure of the jagged iron barbs dug into his wrist, cutting flesh. The orcs slid the beam into place, sinking the peg of the vertical post into a hole near his skull. They let go, letting the crucifix teeter slightly where it crossed.

Krenin felt his strength waning. He hadn't been hanging for long but already it felt like an eternity. The sun was beginning to set in the distance, not that it could be seen through the constant rolling clouds. It was the approaching tide of darkness that heralded its coming. The flare of torch fire caught his attention. The orange glow was somewhere behind him, out of sight. Krenin struggled to see, but it was beyond his reach. A figure approached, clinging to the shadow. One of the orcs held the torch standing in silence, like a dog obeying its master. The orange glow reflected on the razor edge of polished iron extending from the man's hand.

"This warvich was found in your possession. Where'd you acquire it?"

Krenin squinted in the growing night trying to get a better view of the man and weapon. Catching it at just the right angle he recognized the jagged sword Gareth had given him. He opened his mouth, finding his lungs heavy. Clearing his throat he forced the words. "Found it on the ground." He couldn't see the man's face, but he could tell he was smiling.

"Now is that anyway to begin a new relationship? What if I told you I know where this blade came from, and it really doesn't matter how it came to your possession. I just wanted to see if you'd tell the truth." He paused for nearly a minute before selecting his next words. "I'll make you a deal. If you can defeat five of my finest warriors, I'll allow you to keep this sword."

Krenin felt the desire swell inside him. But at what cost? Even if he had the blade there was no chance he was going to be allowed to return to his brothers. And in his weakened state, was it possible he could face five of these monstrous orcs and survive? He spat what saliva he could muster at the man, knowing he was out of range. It didn't matter, the insult was enough. "Give me that blade and I stick it up your ass!"

"That's what I like to hear. That inner fire that burns so bright in one yet to be broken. It'll make you loyal once your will is mine." The man tossed the warvich into the dirt. "Bring him down. I want to see how bright that fire actually burns."

The unnatural darkness filtered into the courtyard obscuring all movement outside the glow of wall mounted torches. Demetrix snuck behind the unsuspecting man. Reaching out he tapped the guard on the shoulder. When the man spun, Demetrix punched him in the larynx, silencing his screams. Quick as he could he tackled the man, wrapping him up. Arms locked around the guard's throat he squeezed, feeling him go limp. Demetrix picked himself up and drug the man into one of the shadowed corners, laying him to rest as quietly as possible.

"Took you long enough." Ravion smiled from across the walkway, gesturing to the unconscious guard behind him.

"It's been awhile, cut me some slack." The younger dalari turned and gestured from beneath one of the mounted torches.

Gareth walked toward them. "I don't understand why we can't just kill 'em. It'd be twice as quick and less likely to bite us in the ass."

Ravion sighed "We've gone over this. We don't know which side this magistrate falls on. If we kill her guards that's another enemy we don't need to make. I'd rather face the wrath of a pissed off politician over a stolen item than have them come after me with thoughts of vengeance for lost men."

"You're kidding me, right? You've met just as many men of power as I have. Rarely have any of them given two shits about those under their employ. Typically they're just as likely to kill them themselves for failing to protect their interest."

"Now's not the time for this conversation." Demetrix charged. Dropping to his knees he slid across the polished, slate floor. He pulled his bow, tripping two guards rounding the corner. Standing up he hooked the strung bow around one's head, using it to slam him into the other.

Ravion rushed forward. Tackling the remaining guard, he choked him out.

Gareth watched helplessly, seeing a third guard round the corner. The man's sword was raised and ready to pierce Demetrix's back. "Look out!" Instinctively his hand shot out, as if he were going to physically stop the attack. He felt the man's throat in his grip. Squeezing, the pulsing body squirmed against him. Gareth watched him go limp. Shaken, he released watching the unconscious body collapse to the floor.

Ravion and Demetrix stared in wonder at their friend.

"Um? What was that?" Ravion asked, his puzzled expression asking the same question multiple ways.

"I don't know. Things like that have been happening since I lost my eye."

Ravion stared intently at his friend, amazed by what he'd just done. "I assume this is what Senaria was talking about? Whatever it is, it's not magic. I've seen my fair share. You need to learn to focus it. Can you imagine what you could accomplish if you knew what you were doing?"

"I hadn't thought about it like that."

Demetrix stood. "I agree. You need to learn to control it, but now is not the time. We need to keep moving. The next patrol won't pass for another twenty-two minutes."

Levi Samuel

Chapter XVI
The Heist

Krenin hit the ground, his legs buckling from the impact. Approaching footsteps demanded his attention. Glancing, he caught the keen edge of his sword in the glow of torchlight.

One of the orcs carried the blade, tossing it in the dirt before him.

Krenin lunged, wrapping his fingers around the appropriate sized grip. He spun, letting the jagged blade cut into the unsuspecting orc. It didn't make a sound, staining the dust in a pool of crimson blood. Krenin rolled his wrist, recalling the blade to his control. He stared his rebellion into the shadowed figure. "One!"

The man gestured, clearly amused.

Another orc approach, carrying a smaller version of the sword Krenin possessed, though this one had a shield strapped to its back.

Keeping the man in the corner of his eyes, Krenin unfocused his vision, allowing a wider span of sight. The last thing he needed was someone approaching from his blind spots.

The orc rushed and swung, flinging the shield into position mid-stride.

Krenin raised his sword knocking the smaller weapon away from him. He took a few steps back, careful to keep an eye behind him.

The orc continued forward, locking the shield against his arm. He hammered the smaller warvich against the wood ringing out a deep thud. A vicious smile formed between his thick tusks and he charged, slashing twice before thrusting the shield out to bash the smaller green orc.

Krenin knocked the swipes wide, but wasn't ready for the shield attack. The reinforced wood crashed into him, knocking his arms into his body. He tried to recover, but the orc was already upon him.

The larger orc swung, putting all his strength into the single attack, hoping to cut the green orc down before he could recover. He heard steel ring out. Stealing a glance he was amazed to see the greater warvich locked against his own, halting the power attack. *How did he do that? I'm stronger, bigger. Puny orc is disadvantaged! No way he strong enough to stop me!*

Krenin strained against the blow, his legs threatening to break against the force. It was nearly more than he could handle. Pushing against the attack he readied to deflect the shield. Krenin stared into the brute's eyes noticing something he never expected. Surprise. He could use that to his advantage. Watching the orc's shoulders he saw the first sign of movement, alerting him to the incoming attack. As anticipated the shield flew forward. Krenin held fast, absorbing the forceful blow. He had to keep the sword locked until he was ready. Seeing the orc over extend into the shield, he spun on knee and broke away from the smaller weapon. It cut helplessly into the dirt. Abandoning his weapon, Krenin locked his meaty hands around the crude, wooden shield and ripped it away from its master.

The orc wasn't prepared for that.

Twisting his upper half, Krenin slammed the wooden device into the orc's face. It splintered against the blow. Swinging again, the shield cracked completely, splitting into two layered chunks of wood and steel.

The orc stumbled back, unable to regain his senses. The smaller sword fell from his hand, landing in the dusty road.

Refusing to miss the opportunity, Krenin brought one of the shield halves up, jamming the jagged and broken corner into the orc's chin. The brute fell backwards, unable to rise.

Krenin straddled the defeated orc. Slamming the point of the broken shield, it pierced the orc's throat, nearly severing its head. Krenin tossed the broken shield aside and secured the smaller sword. Inspecting the spiked handguard, he punched the dead orc shredding flesh. The excitement of the arena coursed through him. Pausing for the briefest moment he saw a reflection in the still eyes of his victim. Refusing to wait, he brought the smaller sword around jabbing the wide tip through the approaching orc's waist.

The orc cried out in pain, dropping to his knees.

Krenin ripped the rending sword free, amused by the disemboweled orc's final moments. It was trying to lift its own warvich in a feeble attempt to stab him. Krenin released the smaller sword, locking his fingers around the dying orc's wrist. He squeezed as hard as he could, feeling the bones crack beneath his grip. Easily overpowering the failing strength Krenin twisted, feeling the bones give. A sickening pop echoed and the hand went limp, held only by skin and muscle. Still locked around the gruesome sword, Krenin forced the broken limb around, shoving the weapon into the orc's neck.

The orc fell backward bleeding out and suffocating. It was still before it hit the ground.

Picking himself up, the half-breed marched toward his sword and pulled it from the dirt. Facing the shadowed man once again he took a deep breath and straightened his spine in rebellion. "Three!"

Two orcs charged in, weapons drawn and ready to cut the green-skin down. One of them swung a pike toward his head.

Krenin dodged the weapon, knocking it away from him. Unprepared the other orc slam into him. Both he and his grappling counterpart crashed into the dirt. Krenin's sword slipped from grip.

Refusing to give the green-skin chance for recovery, the orc punched.

The hardened leather gauntlet smashed into his face. It was all he could do to stay conscious. His neck pop from a second blow. Timing it out, Krenin waited for the next attack. Seeing it en route he bucked, throwing the unsuspecting orc overhead.

The orc face planted in the dirt. Picking himself up, he glared at the smaller, more agile orc.

Krenin rolled, narrowly avoiding the bladed tip of the pike. It plunged into the ground, burying the head. Using the opportunity to his advantage he tightened his stomach and rolled toward the imbedded weapon, throwing all his weight against the wooden shaft. The added force threatened to rip it from its wielder's hands. The wood flexed and snapped, showering the half-orc in sharp splinters.

The disarmed orc roared his discontent and drew his warvich.

Rolling to his knees Krenin sprung up, waiting for the orcs to be upon him again. He was unarmed, out manned, and unsure how he was going to survive this. They were stronger, but he was resourceful. This was going to be a battle of opportunity, nothing more. Readying himself, he waited for their approach. Catching movement out the corner of his eye, Krenin spotted the unarmed orc swing. He ducked, causing the creature to miss him entirely. Dropping low, he kicked, knocking the orc's legs from beneath him.

The orc dropped from the unexpected kick. Rolling, he regained his balance and popped back up on his knees. Abandoning pause, he swung, punching the half-orc in the face.

Krenin stumbled backward, seeing the second orc approach, warvich raised and aimed to decapitate. He had to do something fast or it would all be over. Spotting the broken shield in the dirt, Krenin dove for the kneeling orc, grabbing his chainmail shirt and pulling him close. He slammed his forehead forward in hopes of landing a solid blow.

The orc threw his hands in defense. It was no use, the blow smashed into his nose, forcing tears from his eyes. Unprepared and off balance, the orc tumbled, propelled by his attacker.

Passing his defenses, the impact coated Krenin's face in a spray of blood. Holding tight, he fell backward pulling the orc with him. Krenin landed hard on his back, the orc atop him. Seeing the incoming attack, the half-orc pushed the heavy orc into the air, hearing the falling sword penetrate. The orc gasp in pain, the wicked blade protruding through the dying orc's chest, restricted only by a few unbroken rings of chainmail.

The towering orc thrust the sword deeper, hoping to impale the green-skin.

Krenin didn't have many options. He was trapped beneath his meat shield and his final aggressor was in position to finish him. Seeing his only option, he shoved the dead orc, using the force to move himself. The orc and protruding sword hit the ground beside him. Wasting no time, he swung as hard as he could, punching the standing orc in the ankle.

The orc howled in pain, his ankle cracking beneath the powerful blow.

Krenin hit again, weakening the orc while carrying his momentum. He slammed into both legs, grabbing the broken shield from the dust.

Unable to withstand the force, the orc collapsed and landed hard in the dirt.

Krenin climbed atop him and batted him across the face with the shield fragment. It broke from the impact, splintering into pieces. Seeing the broken pike beside them, Krenin grabbed the jagged spear. Securing it, he shoving the splintered wood into the side of the orc's head. The needle like slithers cut through flesh, burying themselves. The harder he shoved, the weaker his enemy got, which meant the deeper the splinters pierced. Feeling all resistance give way, a final jolt buried the wood deep in the orc's brain. The orc was beaten but not dead. Not yet. Releasing him, Krenin stood, turning to face the cloaked man. He was the victor once again. A gladiator fighting for the crowd. Only this time his arena didn't have walls. Glancing at the dead orcs, a sense of honor overcame him. Returning his attention to the man he wondered what was going to happen next. "Five!"

The man smiled, only his mouth shown in the torchlight. "Well done. But he's not dead yet. Finish it!"

Krenin glanced at the orc. There was no fight left in him. He was likely to die from his wounds. Even if he didn't he'd never be functional again. Several gashes along his face bled from the cuts and pricks of the wooden needles. The gaping hole in the side of his head, housing the remnants of the shaft, displayed ridged bone and muscle. Even brain where it had pierced the ear. But the man wasn't wrong. The orc wasn't dead yet. Unable to stop himself Krenin straddled the orc, placing his knees against his shoulders. Grabbing hold of the blood-soaked spike, he ripped it free. He couldn't help himself. He had to obey. His body acted of its own volition. Krenin watched, helpless to his own assault. Flipping it around, he stabbed the bladed head deep into the orc's throat. Twisting the broken weapon he hooked it around his esophagus and pulled, bringing flesh and meat with it. He could taste the blood in his mouth. It was sweet. Sweeter than anything he'd tasted before. Jabbing the tip into the orc's skull, he picked himself up and turned around.

Gareth strained against the awkward weight. He held both arms overhead, struggling to balance the smaller man. "What do you see?"

Demetrix balanced himself against his wobbly base. Peering through the glass window he watched the inhabitants on the other side. "Shhh."

"Don't 'shhh' me. I'll drop your ass."

Ravion chuckled. "Perhaps it'd be wise to wait for him to come down before he tells us. Wouldn't want to risk them hearing."

Gareth sighed, bracing himself against the wall. "This would be much easier if his ass didn't weigh so much."

Ignoring his comments Demetrix dug the tip of his dagger beneath the wooden seal, prying the brass latch open. As quietly as possible he lifted the window, hoping to hear them better.

A heavyset woman, dressed in layers of out of place clothing sat behind a large, oaken desk. She pulled a bag from one of the drawers and handed it to an excessively thin man. "Put these with my other trinkets. I'll not have them fall into the hands of that sharliet."

The man took the bag. "Do you think it wise to maneuver while he's here?"

"So long as those loyal to me keep their mouths shut there's no reason to fear. He'll be gone before long and we'll be back to business as usual." She gave the man a stern gaze, more warning than anything.

"As you wish, Magistrate. Will you be requiring any more of my services this evening?"

"Yes, actually. I want you to locate the men that escaped the tavern brawl this afternoon. Find out who they are and take care of them. I can't have a couple of renegade resistance fighters stirring up trouble in my city. It doesn't inspire confidence with the sharliet."

"As you wish." He heaved the bag over his shoulder and stepped out the door.

"Oh, and Marcus, need I remind you what happens if you fail me?"

"No, Magistrate."

Demetrix softly closed the window and signaled Gareth to bring him down.

The bald warrior lowered him, letting him fall the last few feet.

"It's her. One of her henchmen confirmed it. She's greedy as far as I could tell. Gave a bag full of stuff to one of her men and told him to put it with the others. She said she didn't want it falling in with the sharliet, whatever that means."

"Both Gailon and Krizere have mentioned them. They act as the commanders of the orcs. I didn't learn much, but they're widely feared. If one is here we need to be that much more cautious."

"That goes double. She told her man to find us. Said to 'deal' with us. Apparently, they think we belong to the resistance."

"Sounds like we need to pay her a visit before her assassin does us." Gareth smiled at the thought of removing the collar he'd been leashed with.

"You may be right about this one." Ravion glanced at the window. "How do you advise we get in without a scene?"

"We might as well walk right in the front door. We know how to get out from here. The window isn't that far. We can jump if we have to." Gareth sized the drop as an afterthought.

Demetrix scanned the area. "I've got an idea."

A gentle knock echoed through the small room. She stood from her desk and marched toward the door. "What is it? I asked not to be disturbed." Pulling the door open with a vengeance she glared at the man on the other side. "What?"

Ravion smiled. "Good evening, Magistrate. Might I trouble you for a moment of your time?"

She froze, feeling the cold steel against her throat.

Gareth stepped into view, guiding her inside. He pushed her into one of the wooden chairs and took position behind her, keeping the blade firm against her flesh.

Ravion stepped in behind them, closing the door.

"I've never seen you before. That leaves you to be common thugs or rogue resistance fighters come to pick the bones." She glared at Ravion letting her distaste radiate.

"You're wrong on both counts." The young dalari casually walked across the room and opened the window. He turned and took a seat behind her desk. Pressing his elbows against the polished top, he interlocked his fingers and smiled. "You're in possession of something that doesn't belong to you. We simply wish to obtain said item and we'll gladly be on our way."

She struggled against the edge of the dagger, feeling a small amount of blood trickle down her neck. "What are you after?"

"I'm glad you asked." Breaking his hold, Ravion sat back in the chair. "It seems at some point in your career you came across a rod. Not just any rod, though. This one is special. I'm told you put it with your private reserve. So I'll make you a deal. Give us what we came for. We'll leave and you'll never see us again. Hell, you can even try to send people after us if you'd like. I'd prefer you didn't, but I can't stop you. Or we can do it the hard way. My friend's been itching to kill someone all night, but I really don't want the cleaning bill. And I'm sure you don't want to experience that amount of pain before the end."

She forced as much hatred into her glare as she could muster. He had a calmness to him she hadn't seen before. His demeanor reminded her of the few sharliets she'd had the misfortune to meet. If only there was a way to hire him. "You seem to have it all figured out. You've gained all the bargaining chips, with the exception of one."

"And what might that be? If you'd be so kind as to inform us." Ravion gestured subconsciously. "After all, the presence of choice is kind offerings. We're not barbarians." He chuckled to himself thinking of his title.

"I recall the rod of which you speak. You'll be saddened to learn that it isn't here." She smiled victory. There was no way they'd be able to take her to the vault without discovery, regardless of how many guards they'd killed.

Ravion smiled. "Well it seems you have us in quite the predicament." Refusing to let a single word betray him he continued. "But, let me ask you this, if I may?" He waited patiently for her response.

"It seems I don't have a choice."

"Oh, don't be like that. There's always a choice, just sometimes not a good one."

She paused in uncomfortable silence. "You may." He was infuriating, yet she couldn't help but like him. Perhaps if the tables were turned she could enjoy his personality a little better.

"What are the contents of your vault worth to you?"

"What?"

"The contents of your vault. The place you stash your stolen treasures. What are they worth to you?"

"I'm afraid I don't understand what you're asking"

He let his head drop, showing clear disappointment at her inability to follow. It wasn't nearly as fun when you had to explain everything. Reaching into his pocket, Ravion removed a golden ring with a green gem set into it. Tossing it to her, he walked to the door.

She caught the ring, recognizing the etching in the stone. "Where'd you get this?"

"Your vault of course. Where else would I have gotten it?" Ravion opened the door and stepped around the corner. Returning a moment later, he guided the slender man into the room. He was bound and gagged, his white tunic in stark contrast to the dark brown vest over it. Ravion set him against the wall, letting his subdued form slide to the floor. Shutting the door he returned his focus to the older woman. "I'll repeat again. What are the contents of your vault worth to you?"

"Marcus, you fool, you led them to my vault?" Her voice was venom, spitting anger at the man.

Ravion stepped in front of the woman, leaning close so she could look him in the eye. "Madam Magistrate, I won't ask you again."

She pointed to the far wall. "Behind the tapestry you'll find a hidden stash. It's in there."

Ravion lifted the cloth banner and ran his hand along the wall. Finding the seam he traced it out, identifying the door. Pushing one side, the wall rotated revealing a small room full of trinkets. A scepter rested on a table, half buried by gold and silver. Lifting the ornate tool he turned and held it up for her to see. "Is this it?"

"Yes." Knowing her usefulness was at its end, she closed her eyes expecting death to follow at any moment.

Inspecting the carved wood and golden studs, Ravion walked to the window and tossed it out. "Madam Magistrate, it's been a pleasure doing business with you. Your vault is secure. We haven't taken anything you don't know about. As much as I'd love to stay and chat, I recommend you use what little time you have left wisely. Get yourself and your treasures to a secure location. An anonymous message has been sent to the sharliet about your dealings with the taxes of this fair city. You have the option of pursuing us, but I fear it wouldn't be the best use of your time." He climbed up the perch and jumped out the window, landing on the cobblestone beneath.

Gareth sheathed his dagger and followed after, disappearing from sight.

Demetrix stared down the shaft of his arrow, watching the magistrate and her bound servant. She jumped up, running toward the window. He let loose his arrow, sinking it into the wood between her arms.

She fell backward avoiding the vicious bolt, searching for its source. "Marcus, get yourself untied and gather my things. We have to get far from this city."

Chapter XVII
Parting Ways

The torch lit streets were barren, aside from the occasional orc patrol. Demetrix stood on the ledge of the two-story building looking out over the city. One of the patrols was a few blocks away and moving closer. He'd have to be quick if he was going to avoid them. Gauging the distance he stepped off, freefalling to the dirt covered street. Forcing his body to obey he went limp just before impact, absorbing the shock through his legs and into his chest. Nearly crouching on the road he jumped up, letting his body realign from the force. Dusting himself off Demetrix turned, seeing the glow of torches flickering along the wall. He had to move or they would see him. Running the half block to their hideout he gently knocked on the wooden frame, keeping it from echoing out in the night. Waiting in full view he watched the door crack. A single eye peered at him.

Ravion stared through the slender gap finding his brother waiting patiently in the open. Quickly releasing their makeshift latches he pulled the door inward, granting access. "Any sign?"

Demetrix stepped through the portal and spun, latching the door before speaking. "She's fled the city. Took a sewage tunnel on the temple side of town to get under the wall. It'll take us closer to the Blackguard barracks, but I think we can use the same one to escape."

"Where does it lead?" Gareth stepped into the faint glowing light beaming through the hole in the thatch roof.

"Best I could tell it empties into a marsh about a mile away. It's hard to be certain, but there is clearly some kind of a bog that direction. I did notice the Blackguard was nearly abandoned. And the patrols are out in force. Though they seem to be avoiding that direction. It seems almost as if something is deterring them, like they have orders to stay away."

Ravion checked the latches, making sure he hadn't missed one. Leaving the door he took a seat atop one of the wooden crates littering the rundown shack. "We'll keep that in mind. Were you able to find Krenin?"

"I did. He's being held just outside the trade gates. For now they have him tied to a post, but he's still alive and seemingly in good health. Although I don't know how much longer that'll last. There were only a handful of guards watching him, but it looks as if they're going to move soon. They're stocking a caravan not far from him. I think we may be able to fight our way in, but we'll have to hurry. We'd probably have better luck if we can convince some of the townspeople to aid us."

"We can't plan for that. It leaves too many loose ends. Besides, this land has a full army standing in opposition to the orcs. If their own people can't convince them to stand, what chance do we have?" Gareth fumed. "We need to get this damn book and get Krenin so we can get out of here, permanently. We can't rely on anyone other than ourselves. That's the only reason we've survived this long."

"Calm yourself, Gareth. You're not wrong, but we must also hear each other. Time and again, we've rose above the odds and emerged victorious. This will be no different. But we have to trust each other. Only when all thoughts and opinions are heard, can we bring order to chaos. We—" Ravion froze, hearing footsteps outside the door.

A gentle knock echoed through the room.

Ravion drew his blade and approached the door. Cautiously he pulled against the knob, letting the door open just enough to peek out. It held firm against its latches and blocks, reinforced by the tension. Squinting through the crack he saw a scrawny human, maybe in his early twenties. He was dressed in tattered rags that draped over his small frame.

"Are you Ravion?" The young man asked, staring into the darkness from beneath his dark brown cowl.

"I am?"

"I have message from Krizere." He extended a sealed scroll toward the door, keeping it at arm's reach from the crack.

Wait for it! Wait for a clean shot! Strike fast and hard!

Gareth felt the familiar sensation wash over him, hearing the thoughts of the man. Seeing Ravion reach for the latch, Gareth charged. "No!" Abandoning all caution he slammed into the door. The makeshift latches broke under the force. He busted through sending splintered pieces of door into the alley and tackling the unknown man.

The boy fell backward, dropping a concealed dagger.

Gareth brought his forehead down, smashing it into the boy's face. Drawing his own dagger he plunged it deep into his chest, watching the life fade from his eyes.

"What the hell was that?" Ravion snatched up the parchment, searching the night for witnesses. He could hear the patrols in the distance. There was no way they didn't hear the crash. "Why'd you kill him?"

Gareth picked himself up, dusting the dirt from his clothing. "He was gonna stab you when you took the note."

"How do you know that?"

"I don't know. It's one of those things that's been happening. I could hear his thoughts, feel his emotion. He was nervous. Afraid he wasn't going to be quick enough. I just ensured he wasn't."

Demetrix stepped out, looking at the body. "We need to get out of here. There's no time to hide him, and I'm afraid the door is beyond repair."

Ravion sighed. "We're being playing. Nobody should have known where to find us." Breaking the seal he unrolled the blood-soaked letter and read aloud. "Ravion, I'm afraid I won't be able to meet you tonight. I've fallen in with a bad crowd and don't think I'll be around long enough to accomplish our mutual goal. I can't risk my captor's coming across this missive and discovering what you seek. If you receive this, take the key to the place we first met. You'll find your way from there. The final message from, Krizere of Tulgar."

Demetrix quickly rummaged through the dead man's pouch looking for anything that might aid them. "Guys, look at this." He pulled the man's sleeve back so they could see his arm. The flesh was charred and blistered, as if he'd been recently branded. The mark nearly covered the width of his arm, depicting a horned head looking out over the world.

Gareth surveyed the jagged brand studying the contours. "What do you suppose that is?"

Ravion rolled the missive and stuffed it into his waistline. "I remember seeing it in the book. It's the mark of Izaryle, though it doesn't matter. We've been compromised. I'll grab the scepter. Gareth and I will find the library. Demetrix, keep watch over Krenin. If they move him, follow suit. We'll catch up when we can."

"Wake up, green-skin!"

Krenin felt a boot rocket into his ribs. The sharp pain threatened to rob the air from his lungs. He opened his eyes to see one of the orcs standing over him. "Kick me again and I'll rip your leg off and beat you with it." He was surprised he'd fallen asleep, yet he couldn't deny that he felt better than he had in weeks.

"Ha! Puny orc think he so strong. You not scare Kull." The orc laughed. "Get ready for travel. You goin' to Idenfal. Gonna be trained like an orc."

Pulling against the shackles Krenin sat up. "I'll never be like you!" Working his way up the post, he got to his feet.

"You no have choice." Kull grabbed the chains and gave them a sturdy whip, dislodging them from their hold. Pulling the half-breed away from the post he approached a caravan. Several orcs stood in-line, chained to the one in front of them.

Krenin couldn't help but notice the difference in these orcs. They weren't seasoned warriors. Most of them were starved and under clothed. He tried to fight against the orc's hold, but something worked against him. His legs move of their own accord, making him follow suit. He felt a watchful presence. Glancing around, he saw the man from the night before. He stood at the gate, his hood overhead. Despite the gloomy, morning light the man seemed the have an unnatural shadow around him. Krenin's eyes shot to the jagged sword hanging loosely at his hip. He knew it intimately, recalling the man's promise to him.

The larger orc drug him into position. Krenin glanced at an orc lying in the dirt. Judging by the thin bits of skin clinging to his mutilated form he'd been drug for miles, probably dying somewhere along the way.

His escort removed the shackles from the deceased orc, kicking him to the side. The malnourished body easily rolled out of the way. Kull pulled the half-orc into the gap and fixed the shackles to him. Sinking the pins in the holes he locked a large pair of tongs around the sides and squeezed, pressing them into place. Kull yanked against the chains, ensuring they were set. "Stay on your feet or you get drug. We won't stop until nightfall." Grabbing the next section he repeated the routine, ensuring all the orcs were secure. Making his way to the coach, Kull climbed onto the bench and released the brake. Bringing his whip around, he cracked it behind the horses. They broke into a trot causing the wagon to lurch forward.

Krenin felt the chains go taunt, yanking him into a jog. Pacing himself, he caught up. Beads of sweat formed on his forehead, threatening to drip from him. Reaching the open terrain he stole a quick glance at the shrinking city walls. In the distance he spotted a familiar face among the top of the wall, watching him fade away.

Demetrix studied the retreating shipment of orcs. "This just got complicated." Attention mainly on his friend he glanced around, making sure he wasn't being watched. Pulling his hood overhead, Demetrix jumped from the wall, landing the dust-covered road. Carefully making his way through the row of lingering orcs he followed after the wagon, watching it shrink into the distance. He had to let it go for the time being. Once he was free of the city's eyes he could move much quicker. Until then, caution was needed.

Snowflakes fell from the sky, piling atop the already accumulated mass. On the outskirts of a small village, the orc leading the caravan detached the dead orcs and shortened the chains. He attached a few new additions in place and prepared to move again.

Demetrix watched the caravan from the distance. He couldn't risk going into town. The further they traveled, the less friendly people seemed, not that they were friendly in the first place. It wouldn't serve anybody if he were to get caught. Time was beginning to lose its bearing. He'd followed them for upward of sixty days, having lost track a few weeks ago. Despite the frigid temperatures, Krenin seemed to be holding strong. Demetrix had reached the edge of their encampment a few nights ago in hopes of freeing his friend, but had been forced to retreat due to the wargs they'd picked up in the last village. He was running out of time and his rations were getting low. He'd already resorted to hunting small game and melting snow for water, but the orc presence was growing. He wouldn't be able to stay with the caravan, undiscovered, much longer. Pulling his cloak tight to block out the biting winds, Demetrix prepared for the next stretch of the journey.

The crack of a whip set the horses in motion and the caravan pulled away, dragging its cargo with it. It trudged along, deeper into the frozen northlands. Next stop Idenfal.

Krenin listened to the crunch of snow beneath his booted feet. He was fortunate. Most of the prisoners were barefoot and wearing nothing but loin cloths. He hadn't had much time to talk to any of them. And the wagon master put a stop to it the few times he'd tried. Best he could tell most of them were being taken to Idenfal for punishment. He hadn't learned the details, but it seemed they were all guilty of disobedience in one way or another. He tried not to think of what their fates would be, though a few of them had suggested public execution. He found it strange they would go through so much effort to transport if dead was their fate. It seemed so much more convenient to simply execute them on site, but he'd never understand these orcs. They were a different breed than those he was used to. The howl of the wargs drew his attention.

Demetrix caught a brief shadow out the corner of his eye. Searching, he noticed a few figures standing just past the edge of the tree line. From this distance he couldn't make out their features but there had to have been at least twenty of them. As best he could tell they were watching something.

Redirecting his attention to the caravan he noticed a few of the figures lying in the snow, waiting for the caravan to near. Excitement gripped him. If they were ambushing, this could be his chance to free Krenin and return to his brothers. Stringing his bow, Demetrix readied an arrow. Watching, refusing to betray his position to anyone, he waited.

Commotion echoed all around. The caravan was in chaos. Krenin hastened his pace, trying to keep with the panicked horses. Several humans and alfar appeared from the snow, catching him off guard. In seconds, they'd completely surrounded the wagon, halting the horses. There was too much going on. Krenin couldn't see if they killed them or simply cut the harness. But one thing was certain. The wagon wasn't going any further until this was over with.

The assortment of men and alfar struck with precision, tearing into any orc they saw.

Krenin dodged one of the alfar, seeing him charge. Bringing his shackles up he blocked the strike, knocking the blade wide.

The alfar recovered and struck again.

Krenin saw the orc ahead of him fall. Using the added slack he threw the chains around his attacker's sword, wrapping it up. Pulling as hard as he could, he ripped the weapon free of its master's grip.

Wasting no time, the alfar pulled a dagger and pressed again.

Krenin stared in wonder, hearing the thud. An arrow plunged into the side of the alfar's neck and exploded out of the other side. The alfar collapsed into the snow, staining it red. Staring at the fletching, they looked familiar. He'd seen their design before but the details escaped him, like something else blocked that memory. Searched the white hills, the chaos around him called his attention. Krenin felt something hit his back.

It burned like nothing he'd felt before. A spearhead protruded from his chest. A gentle flow of red fluid trickled from the wound. He probed the injury, curious to how he wasn't dead. It seemed he'd gotten lucky. The spear rested just below his collar bone barely missing his lungs.

Demetrix grabbed another arrow and nocked it. Taking aim he released, watching the arrow spin through the flurries. It arched and struck his target, sending the human into the powdery precipitation. He hated having to kill them, but they were going after the wrong target. A horn echoed in the distance. Looking to the horizon, Demetrix saw the strangest thing. An army of orcs approached, fast. They were riding what appeared to be giant wolves, similar to those in tow but much larger. Another horn sounded, less guttural than the first. The collection of humans and alfar scurried to retreat into the trees. Demetrix searched for the figures he'd seen moments before, but couldn't find them. It was as if they'd simply vanished.

The wargs closed the gap surrounding the caravan, while the second wave charged after the ambushers. They caught up in a matter of minutes, tearing into them in the most gruesome fashion.

Demetrix couldn't bear to watch. Nobody deserved to die like that. There was something horrendous about being eaten alive. A snap echoed behind him, too close and loud to have been an accident. He was caught. Cupping his bow in open hand, Demetrix slowly raising them overhead. It wasn't much but at least he could show he was no threat.

"Good boy."

A blade gently rested against the back of his neck. One of the alfaren scouts stepped into view and took the bow and quiver while another patted him down, ensuring he didn't have any other weapons. Demetrix stole a final glance at the caravan. His heart sank. Krenin was hunched over, lying in the snow. A pool of blood expanded around him. He'd failed. His friend was dead.

Stepping from the darkened alleyway Ravion approached the edge of the market square, recalling the exact location he'd met Krizere. Looking around, he was happy to see they were all alone. The orc patrols seemed to be focused elsewhere, granting him a bit of comfort in the dread inspiring night. Pulling the rod into view he raised it high, watching the golden studs reflect a nonexistent light. A dull white glow flared from the studs, forming a single beam that burned the darkness away. Taking a deep breath Ravion stepped into the alley, watching the walls brighten from the unnatural torch. Reaching the middle it faded, leaving him alone in the dark.

A thin orange line appeared in the wall beside him. It opened wider revealing a doorway. Firelight flickered on the other side, illuminating an elderly man in the shadow. Ravion was lost in his appearance. Despite his age he was surrounded by a familiar glow he'd grown accustomed to seeing. Though this man wasn't like Demetrix or Gareth. He had a white aura, seemingly divine in such a dark place. A gentle voice escaped the man, comforting him in the strangest of ways. "Summon your friend. I can feel him lurking in the shadows."

Ravion smiled at the ruse. Turning the direction he'd come he gave a quick wave, signaling Gareth.

The stocky warrior emerged from the shadows and stepped into sight.

The door opened fully, exposing the man to the warriors. He was dressed in white and silver robes and carried a gnarled staff that seemed to match the man in both age and texture. He was exceptionally spry despite his elderly appearance. "Come in before you're spotted." He stepped aside, granting entry.

They stepped into the small room, taking position in the open center. The hovel was furnished enough to show occupancy and little else. There was a single bed and a small table set with a wooden cup and platter. A kettle hung over the fireplace, removed from the heat. A pair of dirt stained stockings rested above the mantle.

The old man sealed the door and quickly secured the heavy latch. Lifting a thick beam he set it in the hooks and slid a rod through to keep it from coming out.

They found it a bit extreme, but considering this man was supposedly hiding what was believed to be one of the last libraries it was understandable why he went through such precautions.

Finishing his routine the old man quickly moved past them, using his staff to balance his weight. He reached the far wall and pushed gently against the near empty shelf. It slid quietly to the side exposing a stairwell leading into the underground. Refusing to wait for them he stepped through the opening and disappeared behind the wall.

Ravion and Gareth followed after. The architecture was beyond amazing. It had to have been constructed when the city was built. There was no other logical reasoning for the sheer brilliance the stones depicted. Not to mention how difficult it would have been to build such a place in private. They knew that one from experience during the construction of Dreuslayer Keep. Caution had to be taken to ensure no one person learned too much about any particular part of the structure. That would have led to a weakness in its defenses. Instead they hired each one for a small part, keeping any of them from truly learning any key developments. Reaching the bottom of the stairs they paused, awaiting the man.

He retrieved a brass key ring that was secured to his waist by a thin, silver chain. Fumbling through the keys, he sought one made of an onyx material. Placing it gently into the lock he twisted, hearing the door click. It sprang open revealing darkness on the other side. "Welcome to the last library of Irayth. If you'd be so kind." He held out his bony hand, covered in wrinkles from age.

Ravion hesitantly extended the rod, unsure if he was making the correct choice. But what options did he have? Answers could be granted here. That was more than worth the risk.

The old man took the scepter and held it up as if he were inspecting the etched details. The glowing beam of light reemerged, only this time it flowed away from the head forming into a solid orb of light. It hovered in front of them burning away the shadow in all directions. The old man gave a simple gesture, watching it float away. It slowly floated past the first rows of shelves. The orb split into three smaller spheres. The two break offs shot into basins resting along the side walls. The area came to life illuminating thousands of books untouched for years. The remaining orb continued on repeating the process again, and again. Each time lighting the section in its entirety. Reaching the far wall the final slither flew higher than ever, taking position in the middle of the curved ceiling. A blanket of white spread over the massive chamber, forming a dome over everything.

The sheer size of the library had them trapped in a sense of awe. There were so many books here, all hidden from the world above. There was no way any single person could hope to read even a fraction of them in twenty lifetimes.

Ravion shook himself from the possibilities this library contained. Focusing on his task, he turned to face the man. "We've come for—".

"I know why you've come. You're the travelers from the realm of gods. Ur I believe you call it. Your arrival has been long foretold. It has been passed down from guardian to apprentice since the library was built." He walked to an empty podium and inserted one of the strange looking keys into the locked drawer. A resounding collection of clicks echoed out. Watching the retainer bars retract and sink into the sides of the stand, the drawer sprung open. He reached inside and removed a sleek, red bag trimmed in black. Laying it to rest atop the stand he untied the drawstring and pulled a book free. "You'll need this where you're going. But I warn you, do not let it fall in with the agents of shadow. If they get their hands on it, your world will be forfeit."

"We understand." Ravion stepped forward, examining the book. Unlike the other, this one was covered in runes, tooled into the cover. It was bound in dark, red leather and the pages looked to be edged in gold. He ran his fingers along the runes tracing them out. "These aren't like the other book."

"I'd imagine not. The guardian tomes were created to track key elements in each of the nine realms. This realm was not supposed to be inhabited. Therefore a book was not initially made for it. But things don't always go as planned. Izaryle's corruption took hold quicker than any could have anticipated. The creators fell, many of them rising to become the first order of Sharliets. They used their magics to establish rule, trapping the rest of us in this life. Those few that resisted came together knowing one day the binds would weaken. It's believed they created this book, recording everything that had happened, and everything that would happen. One of the creators was chosen to protect it at all cost. That one became the keeper, collecting books and hiding them away for the day order would be restored. Unfortunately, I fear it's far too late for that. This realm has been too long in darkness. The best we can hope for is a bloody war that weakens both sides. Perhaps, many years after that, some semblance of peace can be had."

Gareth waited impatiently, uncaring about ancient tomes or the knowledge surrounding him. "Where can we find the mirror?"

"Why, Idenfal of course. It's located in the lowest levels of the nightking's castle. But you can't just walk in. It's the strongest bastion of shadow this side of the icelands. You'd never make it inside."

"Has anyone ever tried?" Gareth asked, challenging the glowing man's statement.

"Well— No. Most don't have the courage to try. And those that do rarely make it out of the city alive."

Ravion shot a glare to Gareth. He had to learn to choose his battles. It wouldn't serve them to pick a fight with their only ally. "Do you happen to have a map to Idenfal and possibly the layout of the castle?"

"I can help you with direction to Idenfal, but I'm afraid the castle is unknown to me. To my knowledge nobody who's gone in has ever made it back out. Though I suppose you have one benefit over the rest. If you succeed you won't have to worry about making it out." The man hobbled to a standing case. Opening the door he reached in and retrieved a large piece of worn parchment. Rolling it, he extended it to Ravion. "That'll get you there. Keep the mountains to your left. If you do that, you'll be heading north.

Ravion stuffed the book and scroll into his pack. "We understand. Thank you for your assistance. Should the tides ever change and you're able to leave this place you can seek refuge in a land called Marbayne. Your debt will be repaid." He gave a respectful bow. Turning around Ravion made for the stairway, Gareth at his heels

The keeper watched them leave. Placing the scepter in a bronze holder he closed the drawer, speaking to himself. "If the tides ever turn I fear my purpose here will be long finished." Sealing the door he followed them up the stairs. Removing the locks he opened the door, allowing escape. "Good luck storming the castle. I hope you're able to accomplish what you came for, but a word of caution. Regardless of what happens there must always be a nightking."

Levi Samuel

Chapter XVIII
Lost Time

The forest was dark and gloomy. Yet it held an odd comfort. It wasn't so much the outstretched limbs overhead blocking out the little light made it through. Nor was it the constant roll of clouds, or the continual downfall of snow. It was an eerie presence, lingering in the shadows, like he was being watched. Of course he knew he was, but that wasn't the point. There was something else, something ancient and powerful. It felt tranquil, yet deadly at the same time. Putting the feeling to the back of his mind, Demetrix followed his escorts through a wall of thorns. They passed through as if they weren't really there. Chancing fate, he followed after, surprised by the illusion. The most serene and beautiful city he'd ever seen rested on the other side, awaiting exploration.

It was elevated off the forest floor by hundreds of thick, stilt looking beams carved from the still living trees at their base. Luscious, green ivy stretched across the white marble-looking wood, climbing its way to the elegant rails. The suspended platforms stretched out in four teardrop shaped balconies. A white series of towers shot to the heavens in the center, arched and contoured perfectly between one another. If a fortress city could be described as perfect, this one qualified.

Lost in the sight Demetrix realized he had stopped. It was short lived. One of his captors shoved him into action, forcing him onward. He obeyed, continuing toward the magnificent structure. They led him under one of the towering rises and approached the thickest of pillars. It was as if the low light was playing tricks on him. Out of nowhere a spiraling ramp appeared, wrapping its way up and disappearing into the underside of the ceiling.

Reaching the top, elegance grew. Not only was it a sight to behold from afar, but close it rivaled no other. This city glowed bright in a land of dark. Every beam, pillar, and wall was the color of pearl, unmarred by a single smudge of out of place dirt. Platforms lined the manicured gardens, forming walkways between the smoothed buildings he hadn't seen from the ground. Every so often pearl vines grew from the emerald green grass, intertwining around one another and separating at the top, forming an odd cage of sorts. A glowing blue orb floated freely inside each one, illuminating the landscape in all directions. Lost in the sheer magnificence of it all Demetrix hadn't noticed the group of alfar approach him.

"Captain Taroul, what have we here?"

Demetrix turned, hearing a voice made of honey. As beautiful as the city was, it didn't hold a candle to her radiance. A thin white dress covered her slender frame, revealing much of her shoulders and back. The long, pointed ears shot through her straightened brown hair. She carried no weapon yet her muscle tone suggested she was familiar with a blade. He felt his heart race beneath his chest, finding it hard to be in her presence.

"My Lady Elalon, we found this one in the Fields of Shanar. We ambushed an orc caravan headed for Idenfal. He killed two of our men from Kenoar Pass."

"Kenoar Pass?"

"Yes, My Lady."

She arched an eyebrow, looking the prisoner over. "Let me see his bow."

One of the alfar stepped forward, handing her the wooden instrument. The limbs were cover in a runed, brown leather and held in place by tightly wrapped forest-green sinew. The braided string matched the sinew, strung on one end.

She took the weapon, examining its construction. Quickly stringing it she drew, inspecting the flexed wood. Letting the tension fade, she unstrung it and returned it to the alfar. "That's a nice weapon. Did you make it yourself?"

Demetrix didn't know what to say. Lost in her beauty, he found the first words that popped into his head. "Uh— yes?"

Elalon smiled at his discomfort. "Release him." Directing her words to the archer, she continued. "Walk with me. And know, any hostility shown toward any of my people will be met with swift and unforgiving justice." She turned and strode away.

Demetrix hesitated uncertain why she would trust a perfect stranger, not that she didn't have enough security in the event of an attack. He followed after her.

Seeing he was at her side, Elalon led him through the center archway and into the main keep. "You're quite the shot. Kenoar Pass to the Fields of Shanar is a one in a million shot and you did it twice. I could use an archer like you, but I'm troubled. You don't seem like an agent of shadow. Why did you kill two of my men? Surely you understand the danger the orcs pose, yet you interfered in a successful ambush resulting in a greater number of casualties."

Finding his ability to speak, Demetrix chose his words carefully. "I regret having to kill those men. I didn't want to. They were attacking the wrong target."

"Wrong target? There were humans? Elves? The orcs don't typically take prisoners to Idenfal."

"I'm afraid you misunderstand. One of my companions was captured and loaded onto the caravan. I'd been tracking them for quite some time when your men attacked. I had no problem with that. When they went after my friend, I had to step in."

"I understand protecting your friend. I'm sorry my men got in the way of that, but I feel like you aren't telling me something. Unless your friend was an orc he shouldn't have had anything to fear of my men."

Demetrix paused, uncertain if he should tell her or not.

Elalon stopped, turning to wait for him.

"Krenin is half-orc, though not of this land. He's not like the orcs here."

"I find that somewhat hard to believe. I've never met an orc that didn't raid, rape, and pillage for the pleasure of it. Much less one that was capable of having friends."

"Have you ever seen a green orc?"

"No!"

"You've never met an orc like Krenin then."

"Well, even if your friend is different I fear he won't be for long. Once he reaches Idenfal he'll be trained to forget everything he's ever known. If he survives that, they'll rebuild him to be like them. It's a safe assumption that your friend is gone."

Demetrix took a deep breath. There was logic in her words. Resuming his pace he took position beside her once again, walking wherever she was leading him. "I fear he won't make it that far. He was wounded when I was captured. He's probably dead by now. Even so I owe it to him to make sure. And if by some miracle he lives, I have to try to rescue him."

"I can't fault that. It's that very attitude that spawned the rebellion and makes us different than them." She passed through the inner courtyard and into the center most building. It shot into the sky, seeming to reach the clouds.

Demetrix found it strange. The size of this place should have made it visible for days in any direction, yet he couldn't recall seeing it prior to being here. "How are you able to keep this place from being overrun?"

"We have the area cloaked. From the outside it reflects back, making it seem as if it's not here. It's taken hundreds of years, but the orcs won't come into the forest. Our survival is dependent upon discrepancy. We never attack from the same place more than once and we never lead our enemy to our gates." Following the twisting corridors, she stopped outside a single door.

Demetrix stood upon the red carpet lining the hall. The walls were mostly bare, save for the groomed ivy and other plants hanging here and there. He stared at her, uncertain why she stopped here of all places.

"You're welcome to reside in this room while you're here. If you need anything you can find a guard at either end of the hall, or you can find me to the right and at the end. I'll have all your gear returned to you. Please take a moment to clean up. I'd appreciate if you'd join me for dinner."

He hadn't expected any of that. Blushing, he thought as quickly as his mind would let him. "It would be my pleasure." Giving a shallow bow, Demetrix mimicked Ravion curtsy.

Gareth twisted the arrow, probing deeper into the wound. "Don't play games with me. You know who I'm talking about!"

Wiping the blood from his longsword Ravion sheathed it and picked up the heavy bow. He approached and knelt beside Gareth, staring at the defeated and bloodied orc. "Getting anything yet?"

"He was just about to tell me where they took him." Twisting the shaft a little harder Gareth forced the head into meat, watching it tear the hole wider. He pressed his knee into the muscle of the orc's arm, constricting the veins and keeping it numb and unable to function. Straining to focus he forced his will into the brute's mind. He could feel the defying thoughts, urging him to dig deeper. The answers were there, he just had to find them. Images of battle and blood filled his mind. He could see this orc's desire. It was almost as if he was a slave to his own bloodlust.

The orc howled in pain, feeling the iron head wedge itself between his ribs. "I don't know! Why don't you ask someone else?"

Ravion glanced at the fleeing humans. Most of them wanted nothing to do with this. The few that watched kept their distance for fear of retribution. "This isn't getting us anywhere. We need to get moving. I'm sure another group is on its way by now."

"Almost." Returning his attention to the orc Gareth continued. "I know you're dumb, but you're really going to tell me you don't remember seeing a smaller, green orc within the past few days. I mean, come on, the way I understand it he's the only green orc this land has."

The orc was silent for a few moments, clearly searching his memory. "I saw green orc months ago. He taken to Idenfal. Trained as orc."

"Impossible, he was taken from the tavern just yesterday." Gareth felt the orc's mind unlock, revealing all his secrets. The orc's telling rang true. *How is that possible?*

"Kill me if want. Changes nothing."

"We've learned all we're going to from this one." Gareth brought his dagger down, cutting into the orc's meaty throat. It gargled in protest, drowning in its own blood. "Tell me, how could we lose a few months in a single night?"

"You don't believe him, do you?"

"I was able to see into his mind. He wasn't lying."

"Interesting. The only thing we've done was go to the library. I've heard stories of certain places that remain outside of time. I suppose that would make sense as to how they keep the magic from being detected."

"I guess. If it's been a few months where do you think Demetrix or Krenin are?

"It's hard to say. Though it seems our answers await in Idenfal. The sooner we get there the sooner we find out what the hell is going on." Ravion tossed the orcish crossbow over shoulder. The crude weapon was unwieldy, but it was good to have distance if they needed. "The tunnels are this way."

Ducking into the alley, they disappeared from sight.

A cool cloth rested against his forehead, absorbing the beading sweat pouring from him. Lying on a wooden table his eyes shot open, taking in the sight of the hide covered hut. Krenin watched the heat waves rise to the open top, melting the bits of snow that dared float into the hole. The room was warm, he knew that much. Yet he remained cold. Trying to sit, a shooting pain erupted in his chest.

"Rest. You not ready yet."

Krenin turned his head to find a gray-skinned orc standing a few feet from him. He held a stone bowl in his hand, working a wooden pestle inside. The contents crunched, echoing a coarse grinding sound. Straining against the pain, Krenin inspected his chest seeing where the spear had pierced. The wound was swollen and black, packed by a faint green, near white paste. Thick yellow fluid bubbled around the edges. "What happen?"

"You run through. Lucky from the look. Nothing important got hit, but the poison took toll. You got infected." The orc approached and wiped away the bubbling fluid.

"How'd I get here?"

"Warg riders brought you. Only three survive. The shadow lookin' out for you. Warchief say you important. Don't want you to die without honor."

"Warchief?"

"You meet in time. Rest now. You take care of pups tomorrow. Go to train when healed."

Laying back Krenin watched the heat roll from the opening, feeling his strength fade away. Closing his eyes he drifted off to sleep.

The following day Krenin sat up, feeling the wound pull. It was numb, but didn't hurt any less. The deep purple skin had faded, returning to a bruised green. Pulling the wool shirt over his body he hooked the wooden buttons running the chest, pulling it together. It was a few sizes too big, but it was better than nothing. Stepping out the leather flap Krenin felt the cold assault him. It burned his lungs and froze his nose hair. The light bits of moisture clinging around his mouth instantly froze. The sounds of combat echoed all around. Searching all directions, Krenin found himself in the middle of the largest orc settlement he'd ever seen. Even the capital of Tulgrimm was nothing compared to this, though it was more pleasant to look upon.

In the distance there was a huge stone castle surrounded by a wall. A large mountain range wrapped around engulfing much of the stonework. The orc buildings were crude in comparison, but equally magnificent. The majority of the space was taken by a series of pits. Most of them filled by orcs locked in melee. Each one wore little more than rags, though their supervisors were dressed in full armor.

A wolf's howl caught his attention. Recalling his duties, Krenin noticed what looked to be a rather large stable, though it didn't have the typical corral he'd grown accustomed to seeing in such places.

The churned snow beneath his feet was packed tight, refusing to make a sound. Pressing a heavy soled boot into it Krenin took his first steps, nearly stumbling. Catching himself he took another, finding his rhythm. Rounding the corner, the most fantastic sight came into vision. The largest dogs he'd ever seen ran from one end of the pen to the other. They were nearly twice his size and covered in a variety of patterns.

"You there, greeny!"

Krenin turned finding on orc standing beside one of the massive beasts. He ran a thick bristled brush through the warg's fur, removing clumps of hair.

"Get over here and do this." He laid the brush on the table and moved, letting the half-breed move where he'd been.

Krenin picked up the brush and pulled it through the coarse hair. He was amazed at how thick the fur was.

"When you done, there's more."

For several days Krenin collected mats of fur, stuffing it into heavy sacks. He'd wondered what they did with it, but his questions were soon answered.

Krenin heaved the final sack onto a wooden cart, watching the wooden wheels carry it away. Following his supervisor as quick as his body would allow, they traveled to the edge of the orc city.

"Unload the sacks and dump the fur into that barrel." The grizzled orc abandoned the cart and wandered off toward one of the other huts.

It didn't take long to finish his task. Awaiting the warg master, Krenin watched one of the orcs pull several handfuls of fur from one of the other barrels. He dropped it into a metal container and poured molten wax over the top, tapping on the side every so often. Capping it with a plate, he pulled a lever. The metal container tilted on edge, moving away from the flame. It flipped on end and fell into the snow with a hiss. The orc grabbed another container and positioned it where the first had been. Breaking the seal he removed the plate and reached in, pulling a blanket like sheet from inside. Laying it over a mold he pressed it into shape and tossed the finished piece onto a piled cart.

Krenin saw everything from clothing to training dummies piled high. It seemed they used the fur for nearly everything. Inspecting his own clothing, he noticed the pressed fibers intertwined.

"Come on, greeny. We have cleaning to do."

Krenin glanced back noticing the warg master had returned. The scent of strong alcohol radiated from him. Moving as quickly as he could, he grabbed the handles of the cart and guided it. Following his supervisor, they returned to the pit.

"Clean pens of shit, but stay away Uma. She due for pups and you don't mess with 'em."

Krenin grabbed the shovel and squeezed between the runs. Tending his duties he heard the first sounds of birth from the far pen. Laying the shovel against the barricade, he stepped through to see what was going on. Leaning against the rail he watched eight pups squirm around the straw filled pen. Their fur was clean and wet, suggesting she'd already cleaned them. They fought to get at her. He was amazed by their size. Even newborn they were already the size of small dogs. An unusual movement caught his eye. He saw one of the pups dig its way from beneath the others. It was much smaller and was having trouble finding its mother. Krenin recalled his orders but he had to do something. It needed to eat. Climbing through the rails, he scooped the pup into his hand and positioned it at one of the unused nipples.

The pup latched on and started eating. Standing guard, Krenin made sure the others didn't force it away. He waited patiently, ensuring it had its fill.

"I told you to stay out!"

Krenin spun, seeing the enraged orc. "That one couldn't get food. I help him."

The warg master glared over the run, looking at the pups. "It's a runt. No use to us. Like you! It won't survive the training. Take it out and kill it. Better die quick than suffer its whole life."

"You want me to kill it?" Krenin couldn't believe what he was hearing.

"That's what I said. Take and kill it!" The orc glared his command, daring the half-breed to argue.

His head low, Krenin scooped the puppy up and stepped through the runs. He heard it whimper, begging to be returned to its mother. Stepping outside he locked his arms around the pup, shielding it from the frozen wind. Carrying it to the side of the building he stared into the animal's searching face. He watched its nose flex, learning his scent. "I can't do this!" Looking around, he made sure no one was watching. Burying the pup in his shirt to keep it warm he marched across the snow as quick as he could and entered his hut. Laying the pup in his bed he covered it in the warg fur blanket. "I'll come check on you when I can."

Returning to the pit the warg master gave him a questioning glare. "Is it done?"

Krenin lowered his head. "Yes!"

"Good. Get back to cleaning the pens."

Demetrix stood at the edge of the highest balcony overlooking the forest city. He could see the peaks of Idenfal in the distance. Listening to the soft footsteps behind him, he waited for her touch.

Elalon placed her hand on his hip, laying her chin against his shoulder. "Wondering where they are again?"

"I am. They should have been here months ago."

"I think I may have something that could help. We stopped a contraband shipment this morning. It had a few items the shadow doesn't need." Elalon gently pulled against him, silently begging him to follow.

Demetrix followed her down to one of the lower levels. Twice as many guards stood over this area as any other he'd seen in the city. Elalon waited for the double doors to open. Stepping through, she approached a wooden chest resting along the far side of the room.

Demetrix scanned the room, curious to what was so important. Shelves lined the walls. Tables stood here and there. Chests and crates covered every surface, carved extensively with alfaren runes. "What is this place?" He didn't need to ask. This was similar to their vault back home. It was the duty of a protector to lock away powerful artifacts. Sometimes keeping them out of the wrong hands meant hiding them from the world.

"This is where we put all the magic items we find. It's the only room we've been able to ward against the sharliets." She opened the chest retrieving a head sized orb wrapped in a bronze colored cloth. Laying it on the central tables, the only table not filled by like chests, she gestured him over. "I haven't seen one of these since I was a child. Even then, they were rare." Uncovering the orb, she kept her eyes off the reflection.

"What is it?" Demetrix studied the crystal surface, unable to find a single flaw or imperfection in it.

"It's a seer's stone. It has many uses but for you it can show where your friends are." She wrapped her arms around him, pressing her lips to his. "You just need to place your hands on it and think of what you want to see. If it's capable, it'll show you."

Returning her kiss, Demetrix looked deep into her eyes. "Why do you do all of this for me?"

Elalon smiled. "You're unlike any man I've met. I could have continued on alone but I choose not to. Despite your little quirks, which I enjoy, I see strength in you. I believe you're capable of great things and I want to be beside you when you realize it too." Gently grabbing his wrists, she guided them to the sides of the orb.

The clear stone was warm to the touch, but fogged around his grip. Demetrix stared into the reflection. *Show me Ravion.* The image briefly distorted and became clear once again. Ravion approached a village gate. Gareth marched behind him. They didn't appear a day older than when he left them, yet in the past months his own hair had grown several inches and a lengthy brown beard clung to his face and chin.

"I recognize that village. That's Tiermoar. It's about a month southwest of here."

Demetrix released the orb, letting the image fade. Turning to face her, a renewed hope radiated from him. "Do you know of any way I might be able to get a message to them?"

"I can think of a couple."

The pub was near empty. Only a few men sat here and there enjoying their drinks. The fireplace crackled, sending a few glowing embers to the stone platform it rested upon.

Gareth stepped through the door, searching the faces within. Happy to see a lack of orcs he approached the bar and leaned against the counter. "Need two rooms for the night."

Ravion followed after, taking position beside his friend.

The barkeep tossed the rag over his shoulder and reached under the counter, grabbing two keys. "That'll be four kerilum."

The two men paused, hearing the currency.

Ravion reached into his belt pouch. "Will you take gold?"

The room went silent. Everyone turned to face the newcomers.

The barkeeper leaned in close, whispering to them. "I wouldn't say that so loud around here. We ain't seen gold in these parts since I was a boy. Shadow runs pretty strong through here. You're liable to end up with an orc warvich in 'yer gut before the night's out. Go around back. I'll meet you there." Increasing his tone he near shouted, making sure everyone heard him. "We don't use no resistance money 'round here. Get out! Find somewhere else to sleep!"

Ravion was a bit confused, but picked himself up and left. Gareth studied the man for a moment, unsure what was happening. Shaking his head he turned and marched out.

Reaching the back door they waited patiently. A click echoed through the wooden barrier. It opened revealing the barkeep. "Sorry 'bout that. Couldn't risk any of them reporting back. Here's 'yer keys. Since ye ain't working fer the shadow I'll take two silver if you got it."

Ravion pulled two gold pieces. "Take this. If things get rough you may need extra for repairs."

"Thanks much. Come on in. There's a ladder in the store room that'll take you upstairs. I'll send a girl up in a bit to see if ya' need anything."

Ravion nodded his appreciation and stepped inside. Finding the ladder he quickly climbed up and stepped onto the balcony overlooking the room below.

Doors lined the outer wall on two sides. Checking the markings etched into the keys they found the two rooms furthest from the stairs, they were blocked from view by a false wall.

Stepping into their perspective lodging they closed the doors behind them.

Ravion lay on the bed looking up into the vaulted ceiling. He recalled Senaria, letting her scent flow through him. The warmth of her skin seemed so close, yet so far away. Looking upon her face in his memory he closed his eyes, hoping to dream of her. A tap at the window roused him. Sitting up he glanced out, seeing a hawk perched upon the seal. Standing, he approached and unlocked the wooden frame. Sliding it up in its track the bird flew into the room, shedding a few of its smaller feathers. It landed on the back of the chair, waiting patiently. Ravion noticed a small piece of parchment wrapped around its leg. Untying the sinew he unrolled it, studying the ink stained markings.

R, I'm glad you're well. When able, meet me at High Point Bluff. Travel north, keeping the forest within sight to the right. You'll know it when you see it. D.

Levi Samuel

Chapter XIX
An Orc of a Different Color

Krenin ran his hand through Uma's fur. She'd grown accustomed to him while she was nursing. He held the tankard against her, working his fingers to drain what milk he could into the cup. Listening for the warg masters he peeked inside, ensuring he had enough. Quickly climbing between the rails, careful to keep from spilling it. Hearing movement outside he quickly stashed the mug behind the feed bags and grabbed his shovel.

The warg master came through the door. "The warchief believe you well enough to train. Report to Commander Mac'thar!" He passed the half-orc and disappeared into one of the rear pens.

"Yes, sir!" Wasting no time, Krenin laid the wooden handle against the rails, grabbed the concealed tankard and stashed it beneath his shirt to keep it as warm as possible. Stepping outside, he made his way across the frozen landscape and into his hut. A smile came to his face seeing the gray and white tail wagging back and forth at his sight. Krenin stared into those icy-blue eyes, feeling a sense of joy wash over him. The pup had nearly doubled in size since it had been hidden away in his hut. Krenin grabbed the hanging cow bladder from the wall support. Quickly pouring the still warm milk he sat down on the bedroll and held it up, letting the pup bite down on the end.

The bladder was empty in no time. Delightfully wagging it tail, wide paws scraped at the half-orc, trying to climb into his lap.

Krenin lifted the pup, straining against the growing weight. Gently scratching him behind the ears, Krenin felt a joy he'd never known. It was short lived. "I have to go train. You stay here and be quiet. Don't want them finding you." Setting the young warg on his bed he stood and made his way out the leather flap, feeling the rush of cold surround him. Stealing another glance into the small dwelling he looked upon the beautiful fur coat, wondering how much longer he could keep it a secret.

Making his way to the training pits Krenin approached the armored orc standing near the front.

"Green-skin, grab sword and fall in. You behind, have lots to catch up."

Krenin picked up one of the crude, rusty weapons lying on the rack outside the pit. Stepping between two of the unarmored orcs he took position and turned to face the commander.

"Begin!"

Krenin didn't have time to raise his blade in defense. The orcs surrounding him spun around, bringing their dulled weapons down upon him. He hit the ground feeling the ice melt beneath his flesh. The blows continued to rain, too numerous count.

Hearing a commanding shout they stopped, returning to their idle state.

Krenin weakly picked himself up. He could feel his bruised and broken skin throbbing in the cold but he would survive. No bones were broken, though it didn't mean he wouldn't hurt for many days. Staggering back into position he readied his sword, hearing the commander give the order again. He raised the blade in defense stopping the first attack he saw, though there were too many to block. Again he collapsed to the ground. Hearing a familiar echoing shout, they backed away from him.

Days turned to weeks, and weeks to months. The half-orc stood in formation, ready for the vicious assault. They'd stopped attacking him every time, trading for the new arrivals, but he still fell victim on occasion.

Listening to the commanding shout Krenin raised his blade, deflecting the first sword. Wasting no time he knocked a second away from him, and a third. Spinning around he held them off, keeping his attackers at bay. For the first time, he'd completely held them off. Realizing his success, Krenin brought the sword low, knocking the legs out from under one of the orcs. Shoving another over the first they toppled, granting him wide girth. Securing his station, Krenin locked all others out.

"Halt!"

Glancing to the commander Krenin lowered his sword and snapped to attention, awaiting orders.

The commander approached, stepping in front of the green-skin. "Took you long enough." Increasing his tone he turned away and addressed the unit as a whole. "If you can't protect yourself, you can't protect the orc to your side. Remember this. One day it could save your life." Returning his attention to the half-orc he spoke in a softer tone. "Fall out. You go train with Warlord Grundar."

Krenin turned and laid the dulled weapon on the rack. Passing the chow pit he grabbed a large hunk of boar meat and took a small bite, continuing toward his hut. Opening the flap, the large warg sat idle on the bedroll. The fur blankets had been shredded and strung across the room. Shaking his head Krenin stepped inside, making sure no one saw the hidden dog. Sitting in the bed, Krenin held the meat out.

The warg gently took it and jumped to the dirt floor where he proceeded to destroy it.

Krenin glanced at the crate lying against the wall. The layer of straw was compacted and covered in filth. It was ready to be changed. The dog was producing more and more waste each day. Krenin ran his fingers through the thick mane, watching the collection of gray and white fur bunch between them. "We gonna' have to hide you somewhere else soon. You getting too big to stay in here."

Abandoning what was left of the meat the young warg's ice-blue eyes stared up at him. The pup laid his head across the half-orc's lap and plopped against him.

Krenin patted his side, listening to the hollow sound echo beneath his hand. "Perhaps we sneak out in a few days. That give me time to get stuff." Footsteps approached the door. Jumping up, Krenin rushed to the leather flap and stepped out to see one of the gray orcs a few steps away. Quickly closing the flap he waited for the orc to speak.

"Warlord Grundar waits for you. Said to get there now or suffer the lash."

Krenin nodded, watching the orc turn and head off. Stealing a final glance at the flap he turned and headed after the orc, trying to think what his excuse was going to be.

Reaching the pit, Krenin noticed several orcs dressed in armor and carrying sharpened weapons. There were a few that carried a small number of scars upon their flesh. Compared to their commanders' battle-scarred bodies they were minor. But markings in general made them superior to the orcs he'd been training against. Spotting the warlord standing near the front of the pit, Krenin approached and bowed his apology.

"What take you so long to get here? I've no time to wait for foolishness." The warlord glared at the small orc, clearly not happy about his presence in general.

"I had to shit. Thought it better to do before coming."

The orc arched an eyebrow. Shaking his head he gestured to the large hut standing alongside of their area. "Go get fitted. You gonna' fight like an orc, you gonna' look like an orc."

Krenin nodded and rushed toward the open canopy. Despite the chilling wind and constant snow the open sided structure was surprisingly warm. He searched the collection of forges seeing all kinds of weapons and armor lying here and there. Looking for anyone to talk to Krenin approached the first forge-man he saw. "Warlord Grundar sent me. Said to get fitted."

The smith glanced from his work, scanning the smaller orc from head to toe. "You awful small. What he want, kid armor?" The orc laughed at his own joke. Gesturing to one of the piles of various pieces he steeled himself, letting his laughter die off. "Dig through those. Find the closest. We modify and make fit."

Nodding acknowledgment Krenin searched the pile, finding what he could. The women's armor was a closer fit to his smaller stature. He suspected they'd give him a hard time over it but it was better than nothing. He brought the pieces he found to the smith.

The orc took one look and busted into laughter. Calming himself he forced words. "Come back at nightfall, I'll have them ready for you."

Krenin returned to the warlord. "He said come back later."

"Very well. Take this and fall in." The large orc extended the greater warvich to him.

Krenin wrapped his hand around the weapon recognizing it immediately. He couldn't recall where he'd seen it before, but he knew it was his. Moving toward the rear of the collected orcs he took position, ready to defend himself if they turned to strike.

The reforged armor fit perfectly. Krenin stretched in the heavy plate. It moved as if he weren't wearing it at all. Testing his flexibility he heard some of the other orcs chuckle at his expense. He didn't care. It was comfortable and had done a fine job protecting him. That was all that mattered. Taking position in the center of the pit he watched the orcs standing around the outside ring. He rather enjoyed these exhibitions. They gave him a chance to expand his single combat skills and silence anyone who spoke out against him. Already he'd climbed through the ranks, yet there were many who still doubted him. It didn't matter. Soon they'd all respect him. Raising his warvich, he awaited the command.

The warlord stood on an elevated platform overlooking the spectacle. Banners whipped in the chilling winds, attached to jagged posts buried in the ice-covered ground. Raising his hands for all to see he called the defending champion. "Sergeant Vorak Shadowhelm, enter the ring."

Krenin watched one of the seasoned orcs approach. He carried a smaller warvich in each hand and his thick armor was stained black. He recalled seeing this orc fight before. He was vicious, refusing to give the slightest quarter.

"Anything goes. Last orc standing claims status. Loser descends to the afterlife with nothing. Begin!"

Vorak charged, both swords raised and ready to cut the half-orc down.

Throwing his warvich in defense Krenin deflected the first strike and side stepped, letting the second fly past him. Spinning around he narrowly raised his sword in time to block the incoming attack. Looking into his opponent's face he saw a calm unlike any he had seen before. This orc hadn't begun to test him.

Vorak smiled. The green-orc had been lucky thus far. That ended today. Keeping his main-hand locked against the greater warvich he brought his off-hand up, ramming the jagged guard into Krenin's jaw. The green-skin stumbled backward. Sword in hand, Vorak removed his blackened helm and swung it, bashing him in the face.

Krenin fell backward slamming into the densely compacted snow. Grabbing his face, sticky, warm blood poured from the wounds.

The orc raised his blades evoking a cheer from the surrounding spectators. Circling, gaining their praise, Vorak returned his attention to the prone half-orc.

Anger burned inside him. This orc was going to pay. Abandoning his sword Krenin jumped and charged, throwing his shoulder into the orc's midsection.

The impact knocked the swords from his grip. Flying backward, propelled by the green-skin, Vorak landed hard in the snow. No sooner than he hit the ground, his neck popped, jarred from a sudden impact.

Krenin's thick, green fist slammed into the side of Vorak's head. Bringing his other around, it rocketed the other direction. Krenin's eyes locked on the dark-red blood trickling from the deep gouges where bone and skin were closest. He could see the white sinew beyond the meaty tissue. Slamming his forehead down, Krenin shattered the orc's nose with a crunch. Rising from his beaten opponent, he took pleasure in the inflicted pain. The orc hurt him. It was only right he did the same. Spitting a mouthful of blood on the weakened orc, Krenin turned and marched toward his sword. If he was going to finish the job, he was going to sate its appetite. Lifting his weapon, Krenin spun, hearing a deep howl echo from the across the pit. The orc had climbed to his feet, chin outstretched and pointed to the sky.

A matching howl echoed in the distance.

Krenin could hear something massive getting closer. Thundering footsteps sounded near, shaking the ground. A dark flash shot through his vision ending at a huge warg standing in the pit, positioned between him and the orc. The snarling, pointed teeth threatened him. He looked deep into the warg's blackened eyes seeing no submission. This warg wasn't going to back down and neither would he.

The beast lunged, knocking him from his feet. Krenin felt its dagger-like teeth sink into his arm. Howling in pain he pressed the flat of his blade against the warg's chest, pushing it away as best he could. The vicious maw snapped, inches from his face, trying to tear him apart. Krenin could see the orc fast approaching, ready to kill him while his defenses were down.

Another howl echoed, this one much closer.

Krenin felt the weight suddenly leave him. Glancing over he saw two dogs toppling over one another. His pup hunkered close to the ground, fur on end and teeth ready to kill. It sprang, tearing into the other.

The black warg snarled, scratching and pawing, trying to get at the smaller animal. It was no use. The younger pup was quicker, more agile. It tore into the beast's neck shaking its head viciously, trying to rip out anything vital.

Krenin was lost in the battle. The pup he'd rescued, rescued him. He had to help. The larger warg would surely kill him if it got one bite in. His attention was stolen seeing the orc approaching from his side. A smaller, jagged sword was aimed and flying at his head. Instinctively Krenin ducked, bringing his own sword around. It caught the orc in the stomach. Ripping the weapon free he watched the steady flow of blood drip from Vorak, soiling the already stained snow.

The orc dropped his sword, unable to keep his grip on the weapon. He was rapidly weakening. Hearing a yelp Vorak glanced over, seeing the smaller pup sink its maw into his mount's throat. It collapsed, ending his pet. Defeated, he looked upon his successor anticipating the final blow.

Krenin slashed wide, letting the jagged edge cut through his opponent's chest. Refusing to leave it to chance he twisted the blade and brought the pick down. It sank deep into the orc's skull lodging itself in place. Krenin watched the star-glazed eyes of the dying orc. They stared back at him, crossing and rolling up. A mixture of drool and blood fell from Vorak's mouth. He dropped to his knees, the remainder of his strength fading rapidly.

Krenin ripped the blade free. hearing a suctioning pop as the pick was released. Turning to find his pup he stared in pride, watching the smaller animal bite into the already dead warg. It ripped out another chunk of meat, feasting on its victory. Approaching the pup he scratched it behind the ears, realizing they were surrounded. Raising his blade, he prepared for the worst.

The surrounding orcs stared in silence, lost in awe of the victors. A single voice echoed above the silence. "A fine victory. One worthy of note."

Krenin searched the crowd finding the unfamiliar voice. He stood stunned, watching the warchief step into the pit.

"Let this be lesson to all. Never underestimate your opponent. You never know the resources they possess. Even the weakest foe can emerge victorious given the right opportunities." Gesturing to the half-orc the warchief continued. "Stand down, Krenin. You fought a fine battle this day. And emerge, Sergeant Krenin, slayer of Shadowhelm!"

The orcs erupted in cheer, lost in the primitive heat of battle. "Krenin! Krenin! Krenin!" The echoing roar of his name was deafening in the sea of orcs.

Pride overflowing, Krenin raised his warvich overhead, enticing their praise. It felt good, hearing them chant his name. He'd never had a people of his own. It'd taken a while, but these orcs finally accepted him.

The warchief extended his hands, silencing them. "The status you earned has perks, one of which is a battle warg of your own, though it seems you already acquired one."

The pup stared at his only friend, those icy-blue eyes piercing his soul. Krenin found the blood matted fur around its maw somewhat humorous and unnerving at the same time. Scratching the pup behind the ears he listened to the warchief continue his speech.

"Your warg may reside in the pens, where it will receive the utmost care. Now, step forward, Sergeant and receive your station."

Several orcs broke through the crowd carrying a litter into the center. They sat the large platform down and disappeared back into the warrior mass. It had wind breaks on three sides and a huge throne fixed to the center. A moment later they returned carrying a smaller one. Laying it atop the first, beside the throne, they took position on the sides.

Krenin looked at the device. The smaller was covered in burning embers. Best he could figure it was designed to provide heat in the open cold, though he found one thing odd. He could see the hilt of an unusual dagger sticking from the coal.

The warchief marched up the fixed steps and plopped in his heavy chair. His nearly white mane blew in the snowy mixture, blending in with the weather. He wore black fur over his shoulders and carried a large axe with a spike sticking from each end. It hung at his side, suspended by a single leather strap. The gray of his face and arms was marred by hundreds of scars, displaying years of victory and conquests. Waving the young, green orc to approach, the warchief reached to the embers and secured the hilt of the buried dagger. Pulling it free, a thin blade glowed bright orange.

The orcs grew silent, watching the ritual. Many of them had gone through it several times, though the younger and less experienced stared longingly at the green-skin.

Krenin stabbed his warvich into the snow and patted his warg's head. The pup sat, happy to return to his treat. Walking toward the warchief, Krenin marched up the steps, stopping in front of the venerable warrior. Standing tall as he could, Krenin stared straight ahead, knowing his test was only half over.

The warchief stood, placing his hand atop the green orc's head. Gently raising the glowing blade he pressed into his face, following the contours of his cheekbone.

Krenin felt the sizzle before it even touched him. The smell of his cooking flesh made him sick but he had to endure. To show weakness in this moment of honor would bring disgrace upon him. He tensed, feeling the burning edge carve from his nostril and up under his eye. The frozen winds burned the fresh wound like no other, but he felt pride in the status.

"Behold, Sergeant Krenin, Slayer of Shadowhelm!"

The orcs erupted in cheer once again.

The warchief plunged the blade back into the flame and leaned close for the green-skin to hear. "Enjoy tonight. Tomorrow, you and your warg report to Warlord Morrek. You being sent on a hunt."

Levi Samuel

Chapter XX
Ties That Bind Us

The dim glow of daylight faintly shined upon the elegant skylights atop the towering keep of Adariel. The crystalline windows collected and amplified it, sending warm beams down to the polished marble floor below.

Demetrix marched, listening to the echo of his boots off the vastly empty walls. Approaching the great hall the towering, white doors opened as he neared. Alfaren guards stood patient, refusing to say a word. Continuing past he entered the chamber, feeling the light upon his face for what seemed the first time in over a year. Despite its feel, he didn't care for visiting the hall. It was too big. Too— empty. The dwindling population made him feel like he was alone in the world. A funny concept considering he'd spent much of his life alone. Perhaps that was the problem. He'd spent too much time alone, he was ready to have company. Setting his feelings aside Demetrix marched across the seamless floor and approached the three thrones, perched upon the dais.

Elalon sat to the left, scanning stacks of parchment piled high on a pull about table. Glancing from her reports, a smile breeched her face. "I'm happy to see you. I was beginning to think you'd never visit me here." She laid the parchment in such a manner that she could pick up where she left off. Pushing the table away she stood and threw her arms around the young dalari's shoulders, softly kissing him.

Returning the kiss, Demetrix stared into her eyes, regretting what he had to say. "I'm afraid I must leave."

The pair stood in silence a brief moment, one that lasted an eternity.

"I know." Elalon gave a half-hearted smile. "Your brothers should arrive any day now. It's best you greet them."

"I fear it's more than that. We were searching for a way home. If they're headed this way that means they succeeded, at least enough to have a plan. I don't know what that will entail, but I fear it means I'll be away from you for a long while." Demetrix placed his hands against her sleek hips. "For what it's worth I've enjoyed my time here, getting to know you. I only wish I'd met you sooner, so that we had more time."

"Shhh." Pressing a finger to his lips Elalon quieted him. "I'll not have you saying permanent goodbyes. This is a hard land. People die here every day. Most don't have the opportunity for such luxury. I'll see you again. If not tomorrow, then a thousand years from now. But I'm certain I'll see you tomorrow." Smiling she reached back, grabbing one of the papers she'd set to the side. Pulling it between them, she held it so he could see the writing.

It was encrypted, but she'd shown him how to decipher it. Reading aloud Demetrix listened to the details, he was otherwise unable to pick out silently. "Two humans near the forest, a day from High Point. One wearing an eye patch, the other, long red hair. Neither appear to be agents of shadow." Breaking his gaze from the parchment he returned his attention to her. "That describes Gareth and Ravion!"

"I thought it might. I received that missive early this morning. They should be here just before nightfall. If you'll allow it I'd like to send a unit with you. They'll regard your orders as if they were my own. Collect your friends and return here. If it's our final night, I'd like to have you completely. Tomorrow, you set out, supplied and ready to do what you must."

"Yes, ma'am!" Demetrix smiled and kissed her.

Screams echoed from the wooden barricades. Humans scurried, trying to escape the crude hovels. Bellows of smoke rose from their thatch roofs. The easy tinder quickly engulfed in flame.

Krenin brought his warvich down. The serrated curve along the edge sank deep into a woman's skull. Her head popped under the pressure, splattering blood across his face. Licking his lips Krenin tasted the sweet fluid of victory. He didn't know why he enjoyed it so much. It wasn't wreathed in honor. These people were unarmed and yet he cherished their demise. They were inferior to him, inferior to the orcs. The weak deserved misery. It was their place. He was an orc, strong and worthy of ruling. Glancing over he spotted his pup ripping the innards from one of the lesser beings. Taking pride in the sight he marched over and scratched the young warg behind the ears. He was still smaller than the others, but perfectly sized for him. "That's a good boy, Xarg."

The pup wagged his tail in approval, licking his master's blood-soaked fingers.

"Sergeant, this one knows something." One of the larger gray orcs approached, dragging a human across the dirt road by his shoulder length, brown hair.

Krenin looked the man over. He was in his later years though he showed no accumulated muscle mass. It was as if the man had never swung a sword.

The orc forced him to his knees. "Tell him." The orc's common was severely broken.

"I— I just run the inn. Didn't know they was wanted for anything!" His lips quivered and tears ran down his face, soaking into his dirty twill tunic.

The orc smiled letting his guttural orcish words resonate in the half-breed. "It cries like a baby. Perhaps we should end his suffering?" Fingers entwined in the human's hair, he jerked the man off the ground, exposing his throat.

Krenin knelt in front of the human. How could they tolerate being so weak? It was disgusting. "Where they go?"

"Th— They didn't s— say. Tho— Though I think I hea— heard one of 'em mention Hi— High Point B— Bluff." He wept openly, unable to ignore the pain. Nearly all his weight on scalp, it threatened to tear free.

Glancing to the commander Krenin saw the nod. The axe-like tip of his sword plunged into the man's throat, cutting through meat and bone. A sickening pop echoed and the man's head came free, ending his pitiful sobbing. The body hit the dirt, bleeding out through the open wound in his neck. Standing to his full height Krenin absorbed the carnage around him.

The larger orc flung the head, watching it roll toward one of the weak structures. "Give the command, Sergeant!"

"Your command, Warlord." Clearing his throat Krenin shouted over the chaos. "Burn the buildings. When they come out, kill them all. Leave none alive who harbor fugitives!" Grabbing one of the torches he tossed it onto the straw roof beside him, watching it smolder and ignite.

The entire block was aflame. Soon little more than piled embers would remain. Dead and dying humans littered the streets, left to bleed out where they fell. A light snow drifted from the sky settling on the blood-red streets.

Krenin watched the last woman fall to his brethren. He didn't understand why they took the time to mate with her first but it didn't matter. She was dead now. With a satisfied smile he shouted. "People of Tiermoar. This what happens when you shelter enemies of shadow. Next time, we not be so merciful!" Sheathing his warvich he gave a low whistle, watching Xarg happily approach. Grabbing the leather heel mounted on the warg's back, Krenin kicked his leg over and found the comfortable saddle. Turning away from the city he patted the noble beast, signaling he was ready.

Warlord Morrek rode beside him. "High Point Bluff, he say?"
"Yes!"

The larger orc pointed to the outlined forest in the distance. "It on north face. We reach in few days."

Krenin nodded his understanding. Signaling his mount, Xarg launched, leaping across the dirt and snow mixture in bounds. The pup was happy, running freely. He was faster than the other wargs and didn't sink so deep in the snow due to the lighter weight.

The other warg riders sprang into action, falling in behind the green-skin.

"Are you sure we're in the right place?" Gareth squinted against the blinding snow. It was hard to see anything through the constant furies.

He felt the numbness in his toes. It was one thing when they were dry, but the days of walking brought sweat. And with it new misery when they stopped. Pulling his thick cloak tighter around him, Gareth hoped it would block out some of the chill. He wasn't dressed for such weather.

Ravion unrolled the tiny scroll, reading the brief message. "This has to be it." Reaching into his pack he pulled a crude sight glass and checked the landmarks, hoping to get a better idea of where they were. In the distance he could see the faint outline of a huge structure built into the mountain face. Handing the glass to Gareth he continued. "If you look seven degrees left of that tall peak, you can see an archer turret. You think that's Idenfal?"

Gareth rubbed the scruff growing atop his head, knocking the snow build up free. It offered mild resistance, doing little to block out the cold. Pressing the glass to his eye he found the stonework, scanning as much as he could. "I'm not sure, but it'd make sense. That map shows we should be pretty close. It's hard to tell, but I think that's a training ground to the left. If anything, I'd guess that's where we'll find Krenin. Provided he's still alive."

"At this point we can only hope. He's strong, but we don't know what they've put him through. I've seen some pretty gruesome techniques that could make the most resilient of men break."

A familiar voice echoed from the trees behind them. "It's not his wellbeing we have to worry about." Demetrix stepped into the outcropping.

They turned, hearing the young dalari. His armor had been modified to withstand the cold north. A thick fur liner poked from around the edges and his shoulder pauldrons had been extended, covering more of his arms. The heavy canvas cloak was pulled around him, clasped in the center by a golden leaf. Most shocking of all was his dark brown hair. It hung near shoulder length, blending into his equally long facial hair. He carried a pack and had his bow and quiver over his shoulder.

Ravion approached, grabbing his forearm in a hugging embrace. "It's good to see you. Look at how long your hair's gotten. You look like you've been doing well, particularly in the midsection." He poked at the slightly bulged belly of his armor.

Gareth stepped forward, hugging him. Breaking away he gave a playful shove. "Good to see you. I'm glad we got your message."

Demetrix chuckled. "I was beginning to fear they'd shot the hawk down before it found you." Dropping the pack he pulled out two fur hides, nearly emptying it. Tossing one to each of them he slung the pack and continued. "We have lodging for the night. Tomorrow we make for Idenfal."

"Lodging? Where?" Ravion questioned, searching his brother's face.

A collection of alfar and humans stepped into the open, revealing themselves.

Ravion counted twenty of them. "Resistance?"

"Yes. Their stronghold isn't far. Though don't trust your eyes in the forest. It has a tendency to play tricks on the mind."

Gareth sighed. "Great, another thing to mess with my mind."

An ear piercing howl echoed through the air. The humans and elves took defensive positions.

"Orcs? They were followed!" One of the alfar announced, nocking an arrow.

Demetrix abandoned the pack, following suit.

Drawing his sword Ravion shed the fur hide, finding it in his way. He was much colder without it, but lack of mobility was too great a price to pay for comfort.

Gareth drew his swords, readying himself for the fight.

A group of warg riders breached the crest, flying over the snow at a remarkable speed.

Demetrix counted at least thirty of them. "Aim for the wargs. There's better chance to wound the orcs when they fall."

Arrows flew through the air disappearing into the approaching horde. The first few wargs toppled end over end, losing their riders in the snow. The dismounted orcs were slow to pick themselves up. Those that did quickly fell to the continuous flow of arrows.

Ravion took a step back, looking over the drop off. He could barely see the bottom. "Take as many out as you can. Let the second wave through! If they come in fast enough, they'll run right off the edge."

Gareth looked back, understanding Ravion's plan. He was too cold to move quickly, but perhaps there was something he could do about that.

He closed his eye. Imagining the orcs as dreu he found his rage. Letting it build, a barrier wrapped around him. He already felt warmer. Forcing the image with all his might, Gareth thrust his hand outward, straining against the force flowing from him. He could see the wave of clear energy shoot forth, forming a squat wall across the snowy hill.

Many of the wargs tripped over the invisible barrier, face planting in the white powder. Their yelps and cries of pain echoed above all else. Seeing his brethren topple, Krenin urged Xarg faster. Heeling him gently the warg leapt, clearing the unseen wall. Several of the other orcs followed suit. They were nearing their target, ready to end the resistance in this one key attack.

"Ready spears!" Krenin shouted, pulling one of the wooden poles from the side of his saddle. "Launch!" Rearing back he flung the weapon ahead of him, watching it soar into one of the elves, pinning him against a tree. Several others flew through the air. Some hit, some missed, disappearing among the trees and snowfall.

"Krenin?" Ravion stared at the devoted green, half-orc. There was something different about him. A blood lust showed in his eyes unlike any he'd seen before. He wasn't just drawn to it. He enjoyed it. He'd seen that look before, but never so strong as to block out the man that carried it. "Krenin, stop!" The half-orc barreled toward him, threatening to trample.

Krenin charged toward the human— or elf. He wasn't sure what it was. The face looked familiar, but they were all pretty much the same. At least this one had the courage to carry a weapon. Maybe it would put up a worthy fight before he let his pup feast on the entrails. Launching another spear he knocked one of the archers off his feet, sending him back and pinning him to one of the trees. Out of spears he drew his warvich, ready to cut into the man-elf.

Ravion knew it was too late. They were too close. He had to do something now. If he didn't, Krenin would strike. *I'm sorry, my friend!* Ravion rolled at the last minute, jabbing his sword straight into the air. He felt resistance against the razor-sharp edge and warm blood coat him.

Xarg howled in pain. Krenin felt the pup go limp. It tripped, burying itself in the snow. Coming loose from the saddle, Krenin slammed into the ground. Unable to stop himself he slid, seeing the rapidly approaching cliff edge. He was moving too fast. Flying over the ledge, he felt weightless.

"Krenin!" Ravion charged toward the edge, watching the half-orc disappear from sight. Sliding to a stop, his heart sank. There was no way he could have survived the fall. Yet he couldn't see any bodies in the distance, but that didn't mean anything. Enough snow could have covered the body. Or if it was ice, he could have broken through. Sighing heavily, Ravion picked himself up and spun around. There were still orcs to contend with and they were going to pay for the death of his friend.

Demetrix dodged one of the spears. It impaled one of the humans. Side stepping he fired an arrow into the orc's side, knocking it from the saddle. The warg slid, falling over the icy cliff.

Ravion jumped out of the way and moved closer to the trees. He didn't intend to follow Krenin over the edge. Coming up behind the archers he leapt from cover, slamming his shoulder into a mounted orc. It toppled into the snow.

The orc sprang up, drawing his warvich. Lunging at the human, he missed.

Ravion jumped back, deflecting the strike. It almost knocked his sword out of his hand. Seeing the orc reserve his strength for a powerful attack, Ravion prepared.

The orc charged, releasing a shrieking battle shout. He swung his warvich with such ferocity it would break anything it touched.

Ravion brought his sword to block. The enchanted steel flexed under the force, but stopped the attack. Refusing to give the orc another chance he jumped, letting the orc's strength betray him. He crashed to the ground. Flipping overhead, Ravion plunged his sword into the brute's back, piercing the thick breastplate. The orc fell forward, gasping his final breath.

Gareth launched one of his swords end over end. He could sense the invisible force around the blade, carrying it toward his destination. The sword stabbed into an orc, tip first, burying itself to the polished handguard. He calmly walked toward the snarling warg, shoving his remaining weapon into the beast's maw. The warg yelped and collapsed. Ripping his sword free he turned, searching for any others.

Demetrix counted the men Elalon had sent with him. There were only nine remaining, but all the orcs were dead. It was a heavy loss, but one the resistance could count as a victory. "Gather the wounded. Let's back to Adariel before more orcs show up!"

Music echoed throughout the elven city. Elves and humans alike danced in all directions. Tables were covered by elegant, white cloths displaying a plethora of color. Roasted boar, fresh fruit, arranged vegetables, and many desserts were splayed out for all to partake.

Ravion and Gareth sat at one of the tables uncomfortably watching the people around them.

"You're sure it was him?" Gareth arched his exposed eyebrow at the outfit of choice by one of the humans. It was strangely tight and tailored of a dark brown. Frilly white lace exploded from the collar and wrist holes, seemingly on purpose. Shaking his head he returned his attention to Ravion.

"I am. If it weren't enough that his skin was green, I got a good look at his face."

"That's unfortunate. I always liked the dummy, regardless of how many times he annoyed me."

"As did I."

Demetrix approached the table. He was dressed in fine silk of emerald and brown.

Elalon followed closely behind, her hand in his. She wore a radiant and flowing gown matching in material and color to Demetrix.

"Ravion, Gareth. I'd like to introduce you to Lady Elalon, leader of the resistance and last of the royal elven line." He leaned in and whispered. "That's what they call alfar here." Guiding her around to meet them he stepped aside.

Ravion stood and gave a delicate bow. "Lady Elalon, it's a pleasure to meet you.

She bowed in return. "The pleasure's all mine. Demetrix has told me so much about you."

"I assure you it's not all true." Gareth chuckled, half meaning his statement.

"I should hope not." She jested, softly hitting Demetrix in the arm.

"What are you guys doing here? Go out, drink— be merry. Elalon has already had supplies set out for us. We'll leave at first light."

Gareth looked around the open platform locking his sight on one of the human women at the drink table. "You know, this is the first time we've been able to unwind since we got here. I believe I will partake of the festivities." He stood and marched toward the girl. Spinning around, he shouted over the music. "I'll see you gentlemen in the morning."

Ravion chuckled, watching Gareth initiate contact. Returning his attention to his brother and Elalon, he found their urging faces staring back at him. "What?"

"You need to unwind. There's plenty of time to sulk later."

"I'm not sulking. I'm observing. Someone around here has to have their wits about them. What if the orcs seek retribution?"

Elalon gestured to the sides. "My guards are keeping watch. They'll handle any situations that arise. If it's bigger than their ability, the rest of us will have time to clear our heads and prepare."

"I appreciate the sentiment, your majesty." Ravion smiled, hoping the statement didn't come across as abrasive. "But I have more than tonight to think about. I'd rather get a good night's rest and be ready for whatever we may face tomorrow."

"I understand. Have a wonderful evening. If you need anything, you have but to ask." She pulled against Demetrix, urging him to follow. "Now, if you'll excuse us, we have some—" She paused. "—things to work out."

Ravion smiled understanding her intention. "Have fun, you two. I'll see you in the morning."

Chapter XXI
The Long Walk

Jagged steel scrapped against the icy cliff face shaving layers from the frozen formation. Krenin struggled to keep hold of the leather wrapped handle of his sword. Numbness had set into this knuckles. Pulling himself up he kicked into the crystalline surface, fracturing it. The mirrored finish distorted, leaving white cracks where his boots hit. He buried his toes into the damaged section, pressing his back against the crevice behind him. Wedged into place he ripped the blade free, stabbing it into the ice above him. His arms were growing tired. Glancing up he could see the ledge. Gritting teeth he repeated the process, seeing the powdery substance within reach. He threw his thick, green arms over the edge digging through the snow, searching for anything to grab hold of. Finding what felt like a tree root he pulled, hoping it would hold his weight. To his relief, it did. Dragging himself to the top Krenin dusted the snow from his chilled armor.

Bodies littered the elevated bluff. Orc, human, elf, warg— they remained scattered where they'd fallen. A light powder had collected atop, but it seemed the snow had stopped shortly after the battle.

The exhausted half-orc staggered through the knee-deep accumulation, searching for survivors. It didn't matter what race, they would serve his needs. A red stain caught his attention. His knees buckled at the sight. He saw gray and white fur, partially covered, lying just ahead of him. Icy blue eyes stared back at him, cold and glazed. Tears poured down his face, freezing instantly. He crawled on his hands and knees, pulling himself toward Xarg. It seemed the closer he came, the further the pup was. An eternity passed. He finally reached his only true friend, the one that loved him no matter what. Gripping the mixed fur, Krenin pull tight to the loving animal. Examining the wound he noticed he'd been cut from chest to tail, gutting him in a single slice. Replaying that moment in his head he knew who was responsible. The human looking elf was going to pay. Krenin pulled the damaged harness free of his pup. He didn't bother unbuckling it. The straps had been cut. No, it was best to preserve it in its current state. That way the man would remember what he'd done. That memory would be his last. Stern gaze locked, Krenin heaved the leather and metal to his shoulder and searched for the tracks leading into the forest. There weren't enough bodies here. The survivors had to have retreated somewhere and he would find them.

Stepping onto the thinning snow around the forest's edge Krenin heard a grunt to his right. Glancing over he saw a few orcs huddled around a small fire. They were wounded, but maybe they could serve his purpose. After all, if he was going to catch up and find these humans he didn't have time to return to Idenfal. His revenge would be swift. It would be methodical. It would be without mercy.

Approaching, Krenin looked upon the group of orcs. There were only six remaining. Measuring each of them, none but himself held any true status. "Get off your asses. We have humans to kill!" Refusing to wait he turned and made his way into the forest.

The amplified morning light beamed through an overhead window illuminating the large bed stationed in the center of the room.

Demetrix awoke, feeling it upon his face. A milky, white arm was wrapped around him taking comfort in his embrace. He hated to wake her, but it was time. To abandon her without word seemed cruel, despite her feelings toward goodbyes. Carefully moving her arm, he crawled out of bed and quickly stepped into his black, woolen breeches. Leaning over he kissed Elalon's forehead, watching her sparkling blue eyes peek open.

A smile breached her lips at his sight.

"Good morning, beautiful. Did you sleep well?"

Wrapping her arms around his back she pulled him close, kissing his lips between words. "Better— than— ever!"

Demetrix gently pressed his forehead against hers, lingering above her. "That's good." Closing his eyes, he dreaded what he was going to say next. "I—."

As if she were reading his mind Elalon spoke, silencing him. "You don't have to say anything. I know you have to go. I wish we had more time together, and perhaps one day we will. But for now, you've given me my wish. I got to see you *tomorrow*." She moved her head, kissing his. "Go. Your brothers are probably waiting for you."

Demetrix smiled, looking into her face for what could possibly be the last time. "I love you."

"And I you."

Pushing himself up, Demetrix grabbed his tunic and boots and slowly walked backwards toward the door as to keep her in his sights for as long as possible.

She laughed at his silliness. "Go! You're going to be late."

Smiling at her he spun around and disappeared, pulling his shirt overhead.

"Took you long enough! What'd you have to do, clean your armor?" Gareth joked, picking at the fur liner sticking from beneath the leather plates.

"I said I'm sorry. What do you want from me?" Demetrix adjusted his quiver, ensuring he could reach his arrows and swords with ease.

Ravion chuckled, seeing it was getting under his brother's skin. "It's not like we had a set departure time or anything. I mean, if you want to go back to bed for a few hours, we can wait."

"If you guys keep fucking with me, I just might."

"Relax, we're just giving you shit." Gareth punched him in the arm. The blow was absorbed by the layered leather. "We're glad you finally got some. Only took traveling to another world to do it, but hey, our brother got laid."

"You know what? I fucking hate you guys!" Demetrix heaved his pack and marched toward the forest's edge.

Ravion and Gareth laughed, watching him storm away.

Strange noises echoed all around. The orcs huddled closer together, following their commander through the haunted forest. One swung his axe, batting at a seemingly attacking apparition. He searched, puzzled, unable to find any sign of the missing beast.

Krenin glanced back, glaring his anger into the frightened orcs. Returning his attention to the overgrown trail he adjusted the heavy harness, securing his grip around the blood-soaked leather.

The trailing orcs felt his rage burn through them. There was something primal about it. As if he had not a care in the world other than the urge to kill. It was both inspiring and alarming. Though a great many orcs spent their lives aspiring to find such a state. Entering battle free of worry or care made the perfect warrior. If their commander had reached this state there wasn't anything to stop him, at least not without heavy losses. Trekking onward they ignored the phantoms, fearing the green orc's wrath over what the forest could offer.

Krenin threw his hand into the air, halting the weakened orcs. Peeking through the trees, he could see a massive city standing in plain sight. How had he never seen it before?

The orcs searched the trees, unable to find any reason for their halt. Did he smell something? Scratching their heads, they waited for his command.

His lips tightened around his tusks. He would taste the blood of those within the city. Though he didn't have the orcs required to penetrate its walls, nor the rope to scale her sides. A flicker of movement caught his attention. Squinting into the distance Krenin spotted the man responsible for Xarg's death. His blood boiled. His palms grew sticky, longing to wrap around his sword. He wanted nothing more than to charge across the open and cut the man down. Stealing another glance at the city he realized they were too close. If he took another few steps he'd be within sight. Turning to face his men Krenin spoke in perfect orcish. "The men we after are just ahead, though we too close to the elven city. We have to go around. When they dead we come back with full might of shadow to crush resistance for good."

The orcs wanted to cheer, still uncertain where he was referring to, but it wasn't their place to question. Nodding their agreement they followed, letting him lead the way.

The snow was much thicker on the mountain side than it had been in the hills. The three stood atop one of the bluffs overlooking the gargantuan city before them. Even at this distance it towered high overhead and stretched as far as the eye could see. The coin sized snowflakes didn't help matters. The darkened outline was all they could see. Not the gate, not the turrets, and certainly not the watchmen undoubtedly present.

Ravion looked through the makeshift glass searching for any sign across. It helped a bit, but much was still hidden from view. Scanning the outer wall, acknowledging the full expanse of the castle grounds, he noticed a wide bridge spanning across the deep chasm to the other side. The lingering snow made it difficult to see, but it was clearly there. Tracing the road to the wall he was able to make out the blackened and sealed gate. Twin spires shot into the sky on either side overlooking the approach. It seemed there was no way across without being seen. Lowering the sight glass he turned, addressing his companions. "I found the gate, but there's no way we can make it. Not without some kind of cover."

A brief shadow danced across the corner of his eye. Curiosity fueling him he stepped closer to the ledge, bracing against a small tree. Adjusting his sight he twisted the dense glass, gaining better detail over the amplified image. A lone horseman turned, following a twisting, narrow trail along the side of the chasm. He rode out of the shadowed crevice and onto a small road branching from the near side of the bridge. Tracing the horseman's route he noticed a slight glimmer in the dark. An icy bridge, hidden far beneath the surface reflected the sparse glow of sunlight. "There may be another way into the castle."

"What do you see?" Gareth asked, uncertain of anything in his near-blind state.

Handing the sight glass to the one-eyed man, Ravion continued. "Do you see that rider down there?"

Gareth positioned the tube and adjusted the quartz. He found a man mounted atop a horse galloping along the main road. He was gaining unnatural speed, yet the horse seemed to be able to keep the pace. The man wore a black cloak, its hood covering his face. Each step the horse took revealed the pale-white face of a man. His form was bulky suggesting he was wearing thick armor. The edge of a scabbard could be seen hanging from his side. "Yeah."

Demetrix focused, feeling his sight clear and seemingly zoom in to focus on the man. "Yes."

"He didn't cross the bridge. I think there's another path. Down there, in the shadows."

Gareth turned, searching the direction Ravion had suggested. "You sure? I'm not seeing anything."

"Come on, I think I know how to get there." The young ranger pulled himself away from the edge and into the tree line. Climbing to one of the higher bluffs he noticed the trees were beginning to grow sparse. Aligning his position to one of the faded windows in the upper spire he stepped to the edge and peeked down.

"Where are you taking us?" Gareth locked his arms around one of the trees, regaining his footing against the steep snow-covered rocks.

"Look." Ravion pointed into the chasm.

Demetrix braced himself against a tree and leaned over. He saw a thin, icy pass stretching across the endless ravine. It was narrowly wide enough for a single horseman to cross without falling into the void below. A trail snaked along the cliff face disappearing into a wide cavern in the depths. "I wouldn't have seen that." He admitted, admiring his brother's find.

"Had it not been for that rider, I wouldn't have. It blends in perfectly."

"Well, I'll give you a job well done for finding it, but how are we gonna get to it? These rocks would be hard enough to climb without my fingers being numb. Mix that with snow cover and I think it'd be a quick drop to a final stop." Gareth kept his hold on the frost covered tree, refusing to lean over the edge.

"We'll just have to be careful. It's either this or we give up trying to get home." Ravion admitted, hoping it would spur the once bald warrior into action.

Demetrix dropped his pack and removed a long bundle of rope from the side. "Would you say that's about eighty feet to the bridge?"

Ravion stole a quick glance, judging the distance. "About. Certainly no more than a hundred."

Demetrix sized a foot between his hands and measured the twisted hemp. Counting silently he estimated roughly one hundred and fifty feet. Sighing, he placed the two ends together and quickly ran the rope through his hands ensuring it folded evenly. "We'll have to be careful. I don't think there's enough to reach the bottom, but it won't be too far a drop. Just make sure you don't slip when you land." Approaching one of the thicker trees, Demetrix looped the fold around its base. Running the tails through, he pulled tight, making sure it would hold. The tree didn't budge. Nodding his contempt, he swiftly whipped the tails, watching them fall over the edge and disappear into the depths below. Holding the rope for Ravion he stepped aside. "You want the honors?"

Snaking the rope over one boot and under the other Ravion inched toward the edge, keeping it taut. Feeling his weight leave the ground he gently swung away from the bluff, suspended over the gaping chasm below. Hands loose around the hemp, he lifted his foot and slowly slid toward the bridge. Reaching the bottom he locked his grip, extending himself as far as he could. His feet were just barely able to toe the slick surface. Letting go he bent at the knees, absorbing the minor shock. Careful to keep his footing, Ravion backed away, scanning the area.

"You're up." Demetrix handed the rope to Gareth.

Gareth cautiously took it, fighting himself to let go of the tree. He looked down at the increasing distance and back to the young dalari. Swallowing hard he glanced again.

"Go on. We don't have all day."

"Give me a damn minute!" Gareth snapped, refusing to take his eyes off the distance.

"It's not that bad. Just hold onto the rope and set your feet. Over one, under the other. If you need to slow, step down. The pressure will stop you. To speed up, lift your foot slightly. It's pretty simple."

Closing his eye Gareth positioned his feet, keeping a death grip on the thread-like line. Trembling, he opened his eye again to look at the rope around his feet. It was much thicker than it felt, though it didn't set him at ease. "Like that?"

"Yeah." Demetrix lunged forward, shoving him over the edge.

"You motherfucker!" Gareth clenched tight, holding to the rope with every part of his body.

Demetrix stepped toward the edge and looked down, seeing his friend gently swaying back and forth. "All you have to do is lift your left foot and you'll slide to the bottom."

His face hurt. Clenched so tight he could feel tears squeeze from his good eye. The words reached him, but his body wouldn't comply. "I can't. I can't!"

"You're telling me a big, strong warrior like yourself can rush into battle without a second thought, but he can't handle sliding down a rope?" Demetrix couldn't help but laugh.

"I'm gonna kill you when I get down from here. You know that right?"

"Well, I guess it's a good thing down's the only way you can go. Unless you've learned to fly?"

Forcing himself to peek at the depths below, keeping his death grip, Gareth felt nauseous. The slight spin was making him uneasy, as if the more he twisted the quicker the rope was going to break.

Demetrix drew his dagger, stepping toward the ledge. "I hate to do this, but I'm going to count to ten. If you haven't started sliding by the time I get there, I'm going to cut the rope."

"Don't you fucking dare!"

"One, two, three—." Demetrix placed his dagger against the braided hemp, making sure Gareth could see it. "—four, five—."

Gareth slowly lifted his foot. The rope slid through his grip, slowly guiding him toward solid ground. Within seconds he reached the bottom, toeing the icy surface. Trembling, he scooted as close to the wall as he could, refusing to get near the edge.

Demetrix put away his dagger and grabbed the line. Abandoning all caution he jumped, letting a free-fall claim him. Watching the rapidly approaching ledge he hooked his feet and pressed down, slowing himself enough to tighten his grip. Moments before impact he locked both hands and feet, stopping him instantly. The rapid descent stretched the rope nearly an additional foot. Stepping off, he let go. The rope sprung away from him, suddenly free of the weight.

Lost in impulse Gareth stepped forward and swung, catching the young dalari in the side of the head. Justice flowed through him. Had he not dropped he would have hit him again. Anger fueled, Gareth scooted his feet an inch at a time across the thin layer of ice. The slippery material comprised the entirety of the bridge.

The pain throbbing through his frozen ear was but a pinprick to the uncontrollable laughter rolling from him. Demetrix stared up at the enraged dreuslayer, forcing his laughter to subside. "I hope you feel better now."

Ravion chuckled, pulling his brother to his feet. "You know you deserved that, right?"

Chuckling to himself Demetrix watched Gareth reach the other side. "Yeah, I kind of did. Did you know he was afraid of heights?"

"Why do you think he spends so much time under ground?"

His eyes got big, as if he'd just uncovered some big secret. "Is he a dwarf?"

An angry shout echoed across the ravine. "I'm not a gods' damned dwarf! Get over here before I plant my boot in your ass!"

Whispering, Demetrix added to the annoyance. "He's angry. Must be a dwarf thing."

Ravion shook his head, instantly regretting their plan.

Quickly crossing the bridge, they joined Gareth on the other side.

Levi Samuel

Chapter XXII
Out with the Old

Metallic dust rose from the stiff, golden pages, gleaming in torchlight. Ravion meticulously flipped through them, searching the etched words. A golden sheen danced across his face, renewed by each page. Scanning as fast as his eyes would allow, he froze, holding the raised page near its threshold. He recognized the words, but their meaning eluded him.

Gareth leaned against the chiseled walk, feeling the heat from the torch overhead. Glancing over the young dalari's shoulder he sighed heavily, showering him in a nagging disapproval. "Do you really think now is the time to be reading that?"

Refusing to look up from the foreign words Ravion turned another page. "Ask yourself this. Would you rather have some idea as to what we're facing when we find the mirror? Or be forced to figure it out during a fight? I believe it'd be rather difficult to read a book while dodging a sword."

Gareth groaned, pushing himself off the wall. Pacing across the narrow tunnel he kicked his drying boots, watching dust fall from the rough surface. "I suppose you're right. Gods, what's taking him so long?" Spinning around he fell against the section he'd been leaning and slid down, taking a seat next to Ravion.

"Have patience, my friend. He'll be back soon enough." Flipping between two pages, Ravion noted a similarity in text. The ancient writing was fascinating, though a bit dry at times. "I wish I knew who wrote these books. They put some serious effort into them."

"Probably some wizard with too much time on his hands. I'd even wager he used a magic quill to do all the work. Lazy bastard!"

Ravion chuckled, shifting the book so Gareth could see it. "The words are carved, Gareth. Besides, not all casters take shortcuts. I've known quite a few that refuse to take the easy route for fear of becoming dependent on their magic. Those few have my utmost respect."

"Blah! Just because they never showed you their fixations doesn't mean they didn't have 'em."

Ravion shook his head, knowing he'd never win this argument. Hearing footsteps, he shifted his attention toward the entrance.

Demetrix stepped into the torchlight, lowering his hood. "It's done. We shouldn't have to worry about anyone coming up behind us."

"Finally! Can we go now?" Gareth jumped up, straightening his cloak.

"Someone seems a bit impatient." Demetrix pulled the torch from its holder and smothered the flame.

Using the final bits of light Ravion closed the book and stuffed it back into his satchel. Pulling himself up he stretched, listening to his back pop.

An unwelcome snap caught their attention. Jumping to the ready they stared into the face of a middle-aged man wearing black robes. His receded hairline left a slight peak at the center, accentuating his pale-white skin.

"I thought I saw a torch flicker. What have we here? Three— humans." He paused, sniffing the air. "No. Two dalari and something I've never smelt before." A wicked smile came to his lips. "You've come to pay homage to the shadow, haven't you? I must say, not many of your kind are left. Thought we'd found them all. I guess not. No worries though, you're here now. I'll be happy to deliver your sacrifice." He kicked his cloak behind him letting it fall to the center of his back. Drawing a broadsword, he centered it on his mass and took a deep breath.

Ravion was taken back by the man's knowledge, as well as his demeanor. "What is it with these guys? They're so cocky. Okay, so I tend to talk—"

"A lot!" Gareth interjected.

"But am I really this sure of myself when I do it?"

"Yeah, you kind of are." Demetrix nocked an arrow and took aim, waiting for a clean shot.

"Really?" Lunging forward Ravion drew his sword, hearing the metal collide. Spinning around for another attack he felt something brush his leg. "Be on the lookout, something else is here."

The sharliet easily deflected the strike. Twisting the wide blade he sprang into action, slashing at Ravion. The attack was short. He side stepped and readied another strike. It was one thing to combat a single opponent, but three at once would prove difficult unless he could keep them bottle necked.

Ravion leaned back, avoiding the blow. This man was skilled in the ways of the blade. He was already in position to disrupt their efforts, forcing them to work around each other. Feigning left Ravion spun and attacked opposite, hoping to use the man's tactics against him. Falling back he spoke, encrypting his words. "Retnec, Xirtemed. Thgir og ll'I, tfel ekat, hterag."

Understanding, Gareth drew his blades and stabbed at the pale human's left side. Dipping the blade, he rolled his wrist and switched hands. The sharliet wasn't quick enough to deflect the second strike. The tip stabbed through the black cloth covering the man's torso. It rang out, signifying something solid. "He's got armor."

Exhaling slowly, Demetrix forced his body into submission. This shot was too critical to miss by even the slightest margin. Two inches on either side of his brothers' heads remained clear. The odds were stacked slightly out of favor, but he was confident he could pull it off. Closing his eyes he visualized the target, blocking out all other obstacles. Taking a second breath he opened them, verified, and let loose the string. It rolled off his finger tips and rapidly sprung forward. The arrow buckled under the sudden force. Correcting itself the wooden shaft wobbled slightly and took flight, catching the air in its fins. The feathers began to spin, slicing through the air with remarkable speed. The tip was dead on, ready to impale its target. Just a few more feet and it would strike him between the eyes. His heart pounded in his chest. If only it could arrive before his bothers moved. Watching in earnest, waiting for the killing blow, the arrow stopped mid-air for the briefest moment. His success was stolen. A circle of red formed around the obscured shaft and the arrow hit the ground, embedded in some kind of strange, invisible beast. Stepping forward Demetrix watched the creature come into view, drawing its final breath. The arrow had pierced its nostril and exited the rear of its fur-less head.

Hearing the yelp and thud, Gareth stole a glance back, spotting the huge beast lying dead behind him. "What the hell is that?"

Demetrix stared at the creature, lost in its appearance. It appeared to be some form of dog, though none he'd ever seen before. Its gravelly skin was black, looking almost of scale. The eyes were lifeless and dark. It had the stench of decay about it. An unusual hiss escaped, as if the air was escaping the wound. It melted before his eyes, disappearing into nothing but a handful of cave dust. Shaking his head, Demetrix grabbed his arrow and readied to fire another shot.

The sharliet stabbed and hooked his blade, forcing both warriors to react. Instantly withdrawing he stepped back, building a cushion of space between himself and the trespassers. "You're gonna' pay for that!" Extending his gloved hand, archaic words flow forth. "Thgif siht dne ot rewop em dnel, thgilp s'tnavres ruoy, thgim tsekrad!"

Demetrix felt his chest tighten. He couldn't explain it, but he knew the man had a hold of him. The pressure was squeezing the life from him. His heart raced, constricting itself quicker by the second. He wouldn't be able to take much more. Losing feeling in his arms he watched his bow hit the ground, springing away from him. An impact reverberated through his body. He was lying on the crudely chiseled floor, convulsing. He foamed at the mouth, clutching his chest, unable to give his torment voice.

Ravion looked from the caster and back to his brother. His skin was turning blue. He had to do something and quick. "Hey!" Reaching beneath his cloak he flung a simple dagger. It flew true, aimed at the man's chest. He didn't move, didn't acknowledge it— didn't flinch. Ravion watched the small blade hit head on. It narrowly touched his shirt and shot to the side, landing on the floor. *What the hell? How'd that miss?*

Gareth closed his eye, focusing his will on the assailant. Whispers filled his head. Whispers and shadow. He couldn't understand the words, but the intent was clear. He had to stop it. Forcing his rage to the surface, Gareth turned toward Demetrix. Keeping his eye shut he envisioned the air around the ranger. Stacking it like blocks he created a thick shield, blocking out the dark energy flowing toward his friend. He felt the invisible grip collide with his wall, trying to find a way through. Unable to find flaw, it retreated and disappeared.

What? Why'd it stop before I crushed his heart? The sharliet sniffed the air, searching for something. They haven't used magic. Why'd it fail? Lost in the moment, unable to understand what happened, fear overcame him. Had Izaryle withdrawn his blessing? Did he want these intruders alive?

A sharp pain erupted in his chest, cutting his thoughts short. Glancing down he saw a purple and black handle protruding from him. "Impossible. No blade can pierce—"

He collapsed, unable to speak another word. The pain was immense. It burned to the depths of his soul, as if it was being devoured. Then all was gone. He couldn't feel anything. No pain, no joy, no sorrow. He was simply a void floating in the ether of creation.

Raising his head to the sky Krenin sniffed the air, feeling the cold freeze his nose hair. The scent was gone. Gritting his teeth his tusk ground together, containing his rage. There was only one place it would be expelled and that wasn't here. Searching the snow he spotted a partially covered footprint. The torrential snowfall was rapidly covering them. Knowing they wouldn't last much longer he followed, seeing a second pair join them. And then a third. Jumping from one set to another, he stopped at the edge of the tree line. Turning back, he waved his orcs to join him.

They approached, cautiously navigating the slick slopes. Reaching the cliff's edge they paused, seeing the single rope disappearing over the edge. Krenin leaned over, spotting the bridge below. "It look weak. One at a time." Refusing to wait he grabbed the rope and quickly slid down. Making his way across the icy path he drew his warvich and stopped just outside the cave. He hated waiting, but the others were needed if for nothing but fodder.

One of the orcs watched, seeing Krenin make his way across. Grabbing the thin braid he stepped off and slid down, using his hands to control his speed. He hit the rocky outcrop harder than he'd intended. Grabbing the rope he gave two hard pulls, letting the others know he'd reached the bottom. He waited, watching Grem mount. Seeing him in position, he turned and started across the bridge. His leather soled boots made it hard to navigate the slippery surface.

Grem grabbed the rope and pulled hard, making sure it was sturdy enough to hold his weight. Content with its tension he leapt backward, letting the rope slide across his back side. Watching the landing he squeezed, slowing himself. Stepping off he turned and started across the bridge, seeing Murroc reach the far side. No sooner than his boots touched the slick surface his feet came out from under him. He landed hard on the narrow ledge and toppled over the side, disappearing into the darkness below.

Krenin sighed, seeing the orc vanish. "Be careful, we can't afford to lose you all!"

The next orc waved his understanding. Pulling against the rope he quickly descended and stepped onto the bridge, careful to keep his footing. He froze, feeling the bridge shake violently. Looking back he saw the crossway began to crack. He was too far away to run for it, not that it would do him any good. He was more than likely to slip and fall over the edge. Pausing, he waited, unsure what to do.

Sarok slid down the rope, feeling it bounce under his weight. Curious, he squeezed, stopping himself midway. He looked up to see if the one of the others had mounted. The braid twisted in his hands, slowly spinning him around. Hearing the ice crack he watched in horror as it stretched across, splitting beneath him. He had nowhere to land and it was unlikely he could go back up, at least not without adjusting his grip.

An echoing pop radiated through the chasm and the bridge disappeared into the abyss, his brother along with it. "Pull me up!" Sarok shouted to the two remaining orcs. He felt them grab and lift. Rising nearly a foot he felt the rope stretch beneath his grip, triggering the thought of his demise. Glancing down he saw the other end disappear into the shadow.

Krenin stared out watching the fear ridden face of Sarok, dangling helplessly halfway down the rope. He heard it pop like a whip, ripping it free from the tree at the top. The rope shot out, the frayed end slicing through the air. One of the braids caught his face sending pain through him. He hit the ground, unable to contain it. Watching the rope disappear into the darkness he realized exactly what had happened. "This was a trap!" Pulling himself to his feet Krenin reached up, feeling the blood on his fingers. Licking it, it tasted of vengeance. He lifted the harness from the snow and turned toward the dark tunnel. "Let's go. The others no use to us now!"

The carved tunnels dissipated taking the form of bricked stone. Before long they were marching through what appeared to be a part of the castle dungeon. The occasional scones reflected the labyrinth of corridors and passageways, but it was eerily quiet. Aside from the sharliet they hadn't seen another soul since arrival, though that was partially by design. Voices meant trouble so they avoided them when they could.

"I wish we'd found him before going after the rod. This place gives me a bad feeling. It makes me feel guilty for failing to free him." Demetrix stopped at the doorway, listening for any movement. Continuing past he scanned the distance, an arrow at the ready.

Ravion ducked under the collapsed beams lodged against the wall. "We're all feeling that way. It's like the stone is whispering doubt, making us weak. Just ignore it. We'll be home soon enough. Besides, there was nothing we could have done differently. I've replayed it in my head many times. If we'd rescued him first, we would have had orcs on our tail the entire time. I doubt we would have been able to handle both orcs on top of the guards. Not to mention the amount of death we would've had to deal were that the case."

"Sometimes a high body count has its advantages. For starters, people don't want to get in your way. If we had the reputation to back it up, I doubt the magistrate would have been as apprehensive with her aid." Gareth smiled recalling the fear he'd placed in the woman.

"Even we can't stand up against a full army in unknown territory— Wait! This way." Ravion pointed down one of the adjoining passageways.

"How do you know?" Demetrix redirected to take the lead once again.

"I'm not sure exactly. I just feel it. Like the book is telling me."

"That damn book's talking to you now?" Gareth raised his eyebrow, concerned.

"Not exactly. It communicates with me, but not in the traditional sense."

"In what sense then?"

"I don't know. I just feel a connection. Like I know what the pages say before I read them. I don't know how to explain it. I just know the mirror is this way."

"Do you think it's wise to take directions from a book that tells you what to do?" Gareth stared at him, waiting for a response.

"It's not telling me what to do. And it may not be wise, but it's all we've got right now. I don't see what the big concern is."

"The big concern is I don't want you flipping sides in the middle of a fight. Corin knows what that cursed book would tell you to do. And I'd hate to have to mess your pretty face up." Gareth laughed.

"As would I. I wouldn't be able to get your ass out of trouble, were that the case. Besides, I don't think it can possess me. It just communicates with me through— emotion."

"Well if you get a wild hair up your ass and feel you have to express emotion with your sword, warn me first. I'd like the opportunity to fall on my own blade." The larger warrior gave a light chuckle, ducking one of the settled rafters.

Demetrix rounded the corner and stopped. "Guys."

Ravion froze, staring down the long corridor and into the open doors at the far end. He could feel the mirror staring back at him. "This all seems a little too easy."

"I agree. Weapons out?" Demetrix raised his bow, ready to fire if needed.

"Weapons out."

Ravion and Gareth drew their swords and slowly followed the youngest of them through the dark catacomb.

Reaching the chamber they stared in awe at the sights before them. The twelve pillars lining the side walls lay broken on the floor. They recalled the ancient temple realizing this was nearly the same, aside from the dilapidation. The usual ever-changing faces were fearfully blank, radiating a sense of dread. The ancient runes were worn away showing little more than minor etches in the crumbled stone. The onyx temple seemed drained of its ore leaving the once masterfully carved stones in ruin. They looked as if they would crumble with the slightest touch.

Continuing through the room they headed toward the mirror. Ravion searched the murky image just ahead. A familiar voice echoed through the ancient chamber.

"I see you've made it."

Ravion spun around seeing the aged man. "Krizere? What are you doing here? I thought you were captured."

"Well, not exactly. I had to make you think I was detained. There was no way the keeper would have given you the book if he knew I was working with you. And I think we can both agree that I couldn't just tell you everything up front. That would have revealed too much of my plan. And revealing too much, too early, is a good way to fail. If I haven't learned anything else in my years, I've certainly learned that lesson." He opened his arms, offering greetings. "I'm glad you're here. And I apologize for my deception. You're a little too clever for your own good. Had I given you more than a piece at a time you would have found some way to derail my plans and I couldn't have that."

"Ravion, what's going on?" Demetrix steadied his bow, unsure if he should release his arrow or not.

"I'll let you know as soon as I know something."

Gareth stormed toward the elder man. "What in the hell is the big deal about sending us on this wild goose chase. You got Krenin captured with your damned test. Now he's dead. Your hair brained schemes have cost us dearly. Got us traipsing through—" He suddenly was flying through the air. Slamming into the far wall, several of the aged stones crumbled beneath the force. Hitting the floor Gareth rolled over and began to pick himself up.

"Does he ever shut up?" Krizere smiled, keeping his hand in front of him. "Anyway, where was I? Oh yeah. I was about to give formal introductions." Waving his hand his appearance altered. The earth tones of his simple, yet well-made clothing, faded away to be replaced by black and silver robes. His armor flared out, locking itself around his growing form. The jagged leather covered him from neck to knee. Vicious spikes formed on the pauldrons, arching out to threaten anyone who got too close. His hair drained color and elongated leaving a platinum white in its place. The humanoid features twisted and grew dark. Within a heartbeat the once pale skin was black as night, revealing two glowing green eyes "Rezerik is my true name, but you may call me Nightking."

The sight of the dreualfar sent Gareth into a rage. Strength renewed, he jumped up, glaring his hatred. "I was ready to kill you before. Now I'll be takin' pleasure in the task!"

Ravion's hand shot up, stopping the enraged warrior. "Gareth, hold. There's something different about this one. He's not like the others we've faced."

"He's a dreu, how much different can he be?" Drawing his swords, Gareth anticipated what he was going to do.

"We can't risk rushing in half-cocked." Ravion pleaded, wishing he could keep his eyes on both of them at once.

"Ravion, we've got bigger problems." Demetrix motioned to the entrance.

Krenin and another orc stepped into view.

Krenin marched toward the center of the room. Barely containing himself he plucked the ruined harness from his shoulder and launched it onto the floor. A bellowing battle roar echoed from him shaking dust from the walls.

"Krenin, I don't know what you've been through, or what you've faced, but you need to quit fuckin' around and get over here to help us." Gareth waved the half-orc over.

Stretching his lips around his tongue, Krenin spit their harsh language at the short-haired man. He was a warrior, that much was clear, but he was going to die just the same as the elf-man. "Don't dare speak my name. Do it again and I cut it out!" He raised his warvich gesturing the action.

Without hesitation he charged, bringing his sword down upon the large man.

Demetrix fired, sinking his arrow into the gray orc. Nocking another he watched him approach.

The orc plucked the first missile from his gut. Snapping the thin wooden shaft, he dropped it. Raising his sword, he stomped toward the small archer.

His aim true, Demetrix released a second shot, watching the arrow plunge into the orc's eye socket. The force rocked his head back and he crashed to the floor.

Ravion drew his longsword, advancing toward Rezerik.

"Are you sure you've got what it takes to handle me? You have no clue what I'm capable of. I might be more than you're prepared to handle."

"It's a risk I'm going to have to take. You're in between me and getting home."

"Funny you say that. You're in the exact same position." Rezerik extended his hand. The air around it shimmered briefly and a heavy morning star appeared in his grip. Letting the weight of the head fall he used the momentum to carry the mace around.

Ravion deflected the blow, feeling the impact in his arms. He flew backward landing hard against the wall. Forcing the roll he stopped on his hands and knees. Realizing his sword was missing he searched the room. It lay at the nightking's feet.

Scanning the room Demetrix watched Ravion slam into the wall. He reached into his quiver, grabbing his shorter blade. Flipping it around so the edge was facing up, he hooked the notched pommel over the string and drew back as far as he dared. Releasing, he saw the sword fly straight toward the dreualfar.

Rezerik wrapped his morning star around, knocking the projectile away from him.

Gareth charged, ducking the spiked head of the morning star. He slashed into the blackened armor, but couldn't tell if it penetrated or not. Slashing again, he stole a glance at his brothers. Demetrix needed his help. Forcing his hatred aside he disengaged and charged Krenin, knocking him aside.

Demetrix nocked and fired another arrow. It disappeared overhead, knocked off course from an unexpected impact on the lower arm of his bow. Seeing a green hand he hooked the bottom around the half-orc's wrist and twisted, binding it in the string. Releasing his bow Demetrix pulled his remaining sword, letting the half-full quiver fall to the ground.

Ravion charged forward and dove, grabbing his sword. He rolled avoiding the deadly spikes headed toward him. Kicking himself out of the way, the stone crack beneath the powerful blow. Using the opportunity to his advantage Ravion jumped and stabbed as many times as he could, watching the enchanted blade glance off the nightking's armored ribs. It refused to allow the narrow blade through.

"There's a reason I chose you, Ravion. You possess something your companions don't. It's not that you're dalari."

Ravion paused, backing away from the dreualfar.

"Yes, I know of the dalari. At one time I was counted among their number. Long ago before I felt the call of Izaryle. That's not it. I choose you because you've tasted power. You can relate. In fact, in a different lifetime you and I might have been kindred spirits."

"I'm nothing like you. I'm not controlled by power. I was strong enough to control my thirst. You–– You're just a coward afraid to let go of something that will never be yours. Not truly anyway."

Rezerik laughed. "Well, there you are right. This power will never be mine, but I've got the next best thing. Once I get home I'll be the vessel for Izaryle. What's the old saying? If you can't beat them, join them. I'll be sure to eradicate every last dalari in your honor when I return."

Ravion felt a pang of guilt swell within his chest. Swallowing hard, he raised the sword and stabbed. The sword's tip pressed firmly against the unnatural armor. He saw the blade flex as he had hundreds of time before. This time it buckled and snapped, sending jagged pieces back toward him. He collapsed, feeling his will crack like the unbreakable sword. An armored hand grab him, easily flinging him across the room. He crashed only a few feet from the mirror.

Seeing Ravion fall Gareth abandoned the half-orc and charged, hoping to reach him before the nightking landed the final blow.

Twisting his warvich Krenin cut the bow in half, freeing his arm. He glared at the young archer. This filthy excuse for a warrior had killed too many orcs. It was time to dull out punishment. Raising his warvich he flipped the blade, angling the pick so it would sink into his weak skull. Gazing upon the weakling one final time, Krenin let the blade fall. *What was that?* His eyes locked on a small leather sigil at the man's waistline. It was colored green and had a black trident carved in the center. He knew that mark! Memories rushed into his head. A man's face came to view. Malakai? The realization hit him. Jerking the blade he felt it connect. With growing fear he glanced at the archer, feeling his guilt subside. The blade had missed its mark, though it hadn't missed entirely.

Demetrix felt the pop long before he heard it. Pain shot through him, too great to truly comprehend. He stared at his destroyed leg, unsure what to do. It was twisted and mangled beyond repair. The shattered bone where the pick had buried itself was little more than a gory paste. The vicious weapon had torn him from knee to foot, the blood-soaked pick protruding through the bottom of his boot. Warm blood flowing freely, a numbness set in leaving his vision fuzzy and blurred. His head hit the stone floor and darkness overcame him.

Gareth stopped himself. Stuck between the fate of his brothers. Spinning around, he slammed into the half-orc, landing atop of him. He punched, feeling his knuckles tear open against the rough stone floor. He was free of thought and anger, though the power clearly flowed through him. A resounding pop echoed in his head. But it had no meaning. He punched again, the half-orc's head whipping the other direction. Staring at the green body, a thick bulge formed in his neck. *What have I done?* He grabbed Krenin's shoulders, pulling him up. Trying to rouse him, he knew it was no use. His head hung limp. Sighing heavily he laid him down and picked up his swords. Demetrix was wounded, but he was out of harm's way for the moment. Ravion didn't have such luxury.

The air escaped his lungs. Ravion stared into the mirror seeing the nightking's reflection approach. He crawled toward it hoping he could pull himself up.

"I trust you've already read the book? I'd hate to have to explain this next part to you." Rezerik kicked him in the ribs. The sheer force flipped him to his back. "I was never willing to pay the price to open the portal on this side. That's why I needed you, my kindred spirit. You'll take all the risk while I receive all the reward." Reaching down Rezerik grabbed hold of Ravion's head and lifted, pulling him upright. Pressing him against the mirror's frame, he knelt in front of him.

Ravion gasped, reclaiming enough air to speak. "You can't make me!"

"That's where you're wrong, dalari. I can and I will." A wispy black smoke flowed from Rezerik's mouth. It danced through the air as if it were sentient. Searching, it traveled toward Ravion forcing its way into his nostrils.

Unable to move, Ravion felt the power spark inside him. It seemed familiar. Akin to how the dagger made him feel. The dagger! Looking down he could see the skin on the back of his hand start to darken. His hair grow began to grow. The few strands he could see started to fade. "No, I'll never be like you!" Shaking himself, he forced the change to subside.

Gareth slammed into the nightking, jabbing his curved blade up under the thick breastplate. Warm fluid ran down his hand, coating him in the darkest blood he'd ever seen. Forcing all his strength into the weapon, Gareth twisted and snapped the blade from the hilt, leaving it trapped inside the wound.

Rezerik gasped, feeling the blade rip through his insides. Weakened from the exchange and the unexpected attack his power started to wane.

Ravion stared into the wounded nightking's eyes. "Want to know why I'm nothing like you?" He choked, feeling his body return to his control. "I have friends who watch my back." Ravion slipped the kris from beneath his vest and jabbed it into the dreualfar's temple.

Rezerik's eyes crossed, feeling the blade pass behind them.

Retracting the kris, Ravion pushed the dying dreualfar away. He stared blankly at the still form, dreading what he knew was to come.

Gareth extended his hand and pulled him up.

Ravion got to his feet. He watched the body explode, coating the room in the same black smoke he'd expelled moments before. It collected where the body lay. He knew it was coming. There was no stopping it now.

Gareth went to work picking up the broken pieces of Ravion's shattered sword.

As if targeted, the smoke surrounded Ravion, forcing its way down his throat. He felt the power spread through him, though he controlled it, not the other way around. Exhaling slowly he turned, watching the mirror come to life.

Gareth stood, hearing what sounded to be a rolling tide behind him. Turning toward the mirror, he noted the swirling vortex of energy. "Looks like the mirror's open. Guess we can go home now." Gareth handed the sword fragments to his brother.

Accepting them, Ravion glanced at Demetrix, lying unconscious on the ground. He'd lost a lot of blood. Handing the kris to Gareth, he sighed. "Get Demetrix home and lock this in the vault. We can't risk it falling into the wrong hands."

Gareth took the wavy blade, stuffing it into his cloak pocket. Pulling the unconscious archer up to his shoulder, he lifted him and walked toward the mirror. Pausing, he turned to look upon the seemingly stronger version of his friend. "Aren't you coming too?"

Ravion casually walked away from the mirror, refusing to look back. Calmly he spoke, letting his words resonate within the temple. "Sadly, no. There must always be a nightking. Maybe I can slow this Izaryle from reaching our world." Passing through the enlarged doorway he raised his hands, giving a gentle motion.

The stone crumbled, sealing the entrance behind him. A thick cloud of dust spread out, hiding the remnants of the ancient doorway.

Levi Samuel

Epilogue
And Then There Were None

Thick layers of dust coated the trident carved table at the center of the council room. A stale, musty odor lingered in the air refusing to dissipate. A series of maps were unrolled and sprawled out covering on half of the once polished surface.

Weight resting firmly against the solid top, Demetrix stared intently at the inked landmarks, straining his eyes to comprehend their meaning. "Where's the battle taking place today?" He glanced to his informant.

"Culhaven and Aeron were hit pretty hard. Many of the women and children were hidden within the fishing vessels, but most of the men were slain." William replied, wearing his lieutenant's badge proudly. The green background was in great contrast to the silver lined trident.

"Are the wardens en route?"

"They are, My Lord, though they were delayed in Gamora. We lost two detachments in the assault, but order was restored. They reported a day's travel from Fender's Spear. Enemy on the run. Unfortunately, they slipped away. There's no telling where they've gone from there, but we'll find them."

"Keep looking. There's been enough death already. I won't have the people of these lands thinking we can't protect them. I also want a list of the fallen. It's our responsibility to ensure their families are taken care of."

"It will be done. On another note, my progress into the Black Lotus is going well. They've used nearly all the coin I brought them. The war's been hard, forcing them to lay down their weapons and focus on their people. It shouldn't be long before they're back in business."

"Very good. As per our arrangement, I expect a list of every hit. I don't want a gnat falling if I don't know about it."

"Understood, My Lord!" William grabbed a rolled piece of parchment and a small brown bag lying beside the maps. Lifting the flap he stuffed both into his satchel.

Demetrix watched the young spy gather his belongings. He would make a good leader one day, though he had much to learn. "Travel well, until we meet again."

Standing tall, William extended his arm, awaiting his lord.

Pressing against the gnarled cane, Demetrix took a step closer and gripped the man's forearm. Feeling the return, they gave a light shake and broke the customary embrace. He watched the man scurry out the door.

Gareth marched through, passing the lowly rogue on the way out. Nodding his acknowledgment he spotted Demetrix standing over the table, his focus returned to the maps. "Erik paid me a visit today."

Refusing to look away Demetrix listened to his friend approach. The larger warrior's presence pulled memories of pain to the surface. "What'd he want?"

"He expressed desire to retain his father's arrangement with us. He wouldn't put it into so many words, but he also has his sights on Krondar. I've got a feeling he's after more than free trade."

"I wouldn't put it past him. He's impulsive and a bit possessive. I fear it's only a matter of time until he shows his true colors."

Gareth agreed, glancing at the maps claiming the young ranger's attention. "More attacks?" He leaned over, inspecting the marked areas.

A heavy sigh escaped. Breaking his focus Demetrix glanced up, studying his friend's aging face. "Unfortunately. We haven't even figured out who they are yet. Every emissary I've sent has been sent back less a body. The messengers are refusing to take the job even at a hundred krons."

Gareth chuckled, pulling an apple from his pouch. "I can't say I blame 'em. Hard to spend money when your dead." He took a rather large bite of the juicy red apple, crunching between words.

"I can't fault them for not wanting to risk it. In a polite world we'd all abide by the same standard rules. Don't kill the messenger. Don't leave your comrade behind enemy lines. Some people just can't play in polite society." Demetrix wiped a few drops of apple juice from his map.

Swallowing prematurely, Gareth locked eyes on the young lord. "You got something to say?"

Abandoning the table, Demetrix pressed against the cane, turning to face Gareth. "I understand he told you to bring me back, but— Oh, just forget it."

"No, you've got something to say, say it."

Demetrix sighed, fully aware this conversation wasn't going to end as he hoped. "I don't understand why you let him stay."

"He does what he wants. I did what he asked me to. I can't help that you're pissed about me saving your life." Gareth stated flatly, taking another bite of apple.

"I just— forget it. I'd have better luck talking to a tree.

Gareth shrugged. "Like you said, 'Don't kill the messenger'."

Demetrix stared long and hard at the warrior. Shaking his head, he forced the subject change. "Speaking of messengers, what do you know of a woman, Senaria? I found an old letter from her in Ravion's things. She's also listed in his will. I remember him mentioning her, but it was brief. Aside from mention in his journal, there's no formal records of her elsewhere."

"Who?" Gareth asked, inspecting the half-eaten apple.

"Senaria. From what little he wrote, she's the leader of a group called Mul'daron. He was rather vague as to who they are. According to his report, it looks like he commissioned enough supplies to build a fortress for them. He used the same tactics we did building this place. So unless he built another Dreuslayer Keep somewhere in Krondar, there's a lot more to his lordship than he told us."

Gareth turned around, looking at the drastol statue of the barbarian leader standing behind Ravion's chair. Scanning the others he looked upon Malakai, and trailed to Krenin, recalling the half-orc's fall. He glanced from his likeness, returning his gaze to Demetrix. "There is a keep, just before the mountain pass that leads to the coast. The people there, I took for alfar. They were the ones that found me after I lost my eye. There was a woman present that day. I never thought to ask, but I could tell he held her in high regard."

"That settles it. I need to make a trip to Krondar. If he sheltered them, he had good reason. I'd need to learn what that reason was if I'm to do the same."

Gareth licked the juice from his fingers. "I'd accompany ya', but I have other matters to attend."

"Drinking and whoring aren't matters."

"They are if you're retired."

Demetrix shuffled the maps and parchment cluttered about the table, his aggravation growing in the chaos. There was so much to do and little time to do it. The world had changed so much in his absence, yet in many ways it remained the same. Finding the document he'd been searching for he pulled the forms from the pile, quickly rolling and shoving them in his pack. Krondar was a long journey and he didn't intend on forgetting anything.

A knock at the council room door roused him. "Enter."

One of the guards stepped through the cracked barrier, snapping to attention. "Highlord Demetrix! Another emissary from Mount Thuran has arrived requesting your attention. Should I send him up?"

Demetrix closed his eyes, sighing annoyance. Returning his attention to the guard he pressed against his cane and hobbled toward him. "I have more important matters to tend than some petty grievance from a land that wants nothing to do with us." Shaking his head, he continued. "Show him the refectory. I'm going to end this once and for all."

The guard turned and disappeared around the corner.

Slowly, Demetrix made his way to the balcony and took position to see the man approach.

The emissary strutted along the manicured pathway through the bailey. Head held high, he refused to give the slightest acknowledgment to anyone that didn't bare a noble status. His personal escort marched a few steps ahead while the guard Demetrix had spoken with trailed slightly behind.

The escort stepped to the side, taking position inside the archway leading to the dining hall.

The keep guard moved to the other side, allowing the man to enter alone.

Stepping from the balcony, bracing himself against the banister, Demetrix guided himself down the winding staircase, studying the puffed courier.

The man entered the refectory and took a seat, ignoring the few servants here and there.

This arrogant pup was in the wrong place for such a superior attitude. That was one thing he wouldn't tolerate from anybody. In Marbayne, the poorest peasant was shown equal respect as the lord. It wouldn't change this day. Nearing the bottom step Demetrix spoke, letting his voice carry over the near empty hall. "What's your name, emissary?"

The man jumped, hearing the highlord's voice. Spinning around he waited for the crippled man to reach the bottom step. Impatiently awaiting his approach he gave an exaggerated bow, more a show of protocol than respect. "Leandar Muales, My Lord."

"Take a seat, Leandar. I don't have much time, but since you've made such a long journey I'll hear your words." He suppressed a smile, mocking the man's length of travel. Mount Thuran was perched in the mountains to the west of Marbayne. It wasn't a difficult or long trip, being reachable within a day.

One of the servants rushed into the room and laid a golden platter on the long, oaken tabletop. It was covered in sliced meats and dried bread layered out to display each piece, while protecting the one beneath it. She bowed respectfully to the emissary. "May I take your cloak and cover, sir?"

Another servant placed a silver goblet in front of the man, pouring a golden liquid into the cup. The man shed his layers, refusing to lower himself by speaking to her. The two disappeared as quickly as possible, watching for their services to be needed again.

Demetrix pulled one of the chairs and took a seat, facing the messenger. "You must be parched from your trip down the mountain. Have your fill, we can talk afterward." Adjusting the wooden walking stick against his leg, he felt the pressure relieve slightly. Interlocking his fingers he rested them against his stomach and leaned back, impatiently watching the man stuff his face.

The emissary gorged, leaving little room for anything else. A loud belch escaped his mouth and he pushed the platter away. The woman rushed over, claiming it. "Would you like more, sir?

Leandar rubbed his belly, leaning against the high-backed chair. "No, my appetite is sated. I would, however like another glass of mead." He held the goblet up, spilling a small amount of the syrupy liquid on her dress.

She lifted the pitcher, lying not but a few feet away, and filled the cup. Laying it to rest once again she turned and disappeared.

Demetrix stared his discontent at the man, silently containing his rage. This disrespectful, glorified messenger would only lower himself to talk to the hired help if he needed something and was rude about it at that. He waited for the man to take another long draw of the freshly filled goblet. Timing it, he spoke, forcing the man to answer with a full mouth, lest show disrespect to his superior. "Now that your appetite is sated, what is it your queen has ordered you to say?"

Leandar searched for the words, thrown off by the invitation to dine. Buying as much time to swallow as he could, he cleared his throat. "My Lord, I was sent to inform you—." He retrieved a worn parchment from his pouch and unrolled it. Reading the missive aloud, he kept his eyes on the scribed words. "Demetrix Santail, with Lord Ravion's absence and your right to succession granting you entitlement to the lands of Krondar, you are hereby in violation of treaty seven-two-seven signed by the Coalition of Countries, stating that no one man may assume lordship over multiple lands without the previous consent of the CoC. In light of this violation, I offer you compromise." Leandar paused and swallowed hard before continuing. "Surrender the lands known as Marbayne to Mount Thuran or we will unleash our newest weapon against your city. If you accept these terms, you and your men will be allowed to live in peace without change to your lifestyle. You will fly the banner of Mount Thuran and submit to her majesty's rule. Sincerely, Cuariss Feiara, Royal Consort to Queen Kallop Feiara."

Demetrix sat quietly refusing to show any gesture that would give away his thoughts. Swallowing his anger he carefully considered his options. Staring blankly at the messenger, refusing to blink, he watched the man shift uncomfortably in his seat. Decided on his response he calmly spoke, forcing his emotion into the pit of his stomach. "Your queen oversteps her bounds."

"My Lord, I have everything in order. All the details are with me. If you'd like to view the treaty for yourself—."

Pulling himself upright in the chair Demetrix raised a finger, silencing the man. "I know what the treaty says. My name is written upon the parchment, same as the other lords. There's one small factor in which your queen has overlooked. Despite my title of highlord, which by definition states that I rule multiple lands, if she'd bothered to do any research past her greed, she'd note that I'm not the sole benefactor to the deed of Marbayne, nor Krondar." Rising from his seat he forced the pain away, hearing his cane clap loudly against the slate floor. He felt as if the unhealed bones inside his leg were grinding against one another, threatening to tear themselves apart. It took every ounce of resolve to put full weight on the injured leg and pretend as if he weren't filled with crippling pain. Refusing to show any form of weakness Demetrix stepped toward the man, towering over him. "Now yes, I rule Marbayne as a glorified steward, an appointed position by the council. But I do not own her lands. The Order does. It takes a majority rule of the council to determine any decisions. Of the five members, only two remain. Without full on war, resulting in the complete decimation of my people, you're out of luck until the other seats have been filled. As for Krondar, Ravion's Will did not grant me lordship over the barbarian peoples. That honor went to one, Senaria Mul'daron of Krondar. It falls to me to aid her in this duty. So with respect, I suggest you get your ass back up the mountain and give your queen a message from me."

Demetrix leaned in close, letting the pain fuel his rage. "If she ever thinks of sending a single man to my walls over this bullshit again, I'm going to personally march to that cesspit you call home and put a leash on the bitch myself!" His anger boiled like a poison trying to escape his body. Unable to stop himself he kicked the chair out from under the emissary, feeling the bone snap under the exerted pressure. "Get the fuck out of my lands!"

Leandar crashed to the floor unsure of what had just happened. He jumped up, looking at his mead stained tunic. Visibly shaken, he dusted himself off and ran for the courtyard.

Demetrix held strong, watching the arrogant prick scurry for the exit. Seeing him pass out of sight he crashed to the floor, letting his wounds overcome him.

Staring at the missive, the path revealed itself as the words described. The moonlight revealed a perfect trail through the rocky outcropping. Carefully making his way down, Demetrix felt the molded rawhide around his leg. It rubbed the sensitive skin, chaffing terribly. Ignoring the discomfort he pressed on, pushing against his cane and selecting where he was going to step. In no time he reached the bottom, lost in the sight of the massive keep before him. How he hadn't seen it from the high rise was a mystery, but not one worthy of his attention. Approaching the outer wall, he froze, lost in the sight of the blue aura surrounding the man. "Wha—? How do you exist?" He knew they weren't true dalari, at least not in the manner he knew of them. But a rose by any other name remained a rose. This one had simply been taken apart and put back together. From the look on the guard's face, he had no idea what he was talking about.

"Highlord Demetrix?"

"That I am."

"Lady Senaria is expecting you. This way please." The guard turned and stepped through the sealed barricade.

Demetrix followed, too lost in the discovery of this nest to pay attention to the structures around him. How many are there? He felt like a child receiving presents for the first time. In this case it was the restoration of his race. Ravion did it. He found them! Unable to contain his smile he followed the man through the restored archway and into the courtyard. They were everywhere. Some trained with sword while others expressed themselves in art and music, learning their individuality. It was a wondrous sight to behold. Without realizing it he was already inside the keep.

Making his way through the winding corridors, he was led to an upstairs reception hall. Taking a place at the end of a long table, he paused, awaiting his announcement. A woman stood, looking out the window at the far side of the room, her back to the door.

"Highlord Demetrix Santail to see you, My Lady." The guard bowed and left the room.

Senaria turned, looking upon the young lord. He was several inches shorter than Ravion and had dark brown hair opposed to the red she longed to see once again. But his features held similar appearance. He, however, wasn't Ravion. "You said you had news of Ravion?" Senaria prompted, gesturing toward one of the chairs. She walked nearly half way across the room and took a seat not far from the one she'd suggested.

He didn't know how long he'd been staring, but judging from her expression he was making a fool of himself. Giving a slight bow, Demetrix collected his thoughts and took a seat. Reaching into his satchel he retrieved a sealed scroll and slid it across the table to her. "I thank you for seeing me. I must say this place is extremely difficult to locate without guidance. Well done on that." Shifting to formal business, he took a deep breath and gestured to the sealed scroll. "As you already know, I'm Ravion's brother. I regret to inform you that we underwent a trip not long ago. Sadly this was a trip Ravion will not be returning from." He could see the pain in her eyes. She sat in silence, burying her feelings.

"Is— Is he dead?" She adjusted in the wooden chair, wishing she could release the pain building inside her. It was the worst pain she could imagine. Yet there was hope.

"He wasn't when I last saw him, but I can't say with certainty if that's changed. As far as I've been told, he made the choice to stay behind." A spark ignited behind her eyes.

Senaria remained silent, listing to what he had to say. If Ravion chose to say, there was good reason for it. She would see him again even if she had to go to him.

Allowing her a moment to process, Demetrix continued. "In addition to this news, I wished to inform you that you were named in his Will. It's a little strange, exercising a man's last testament before his passing, but in this case, it's unlikely he'll be returning." He waited for her to unroll the scroll. "What you hold there is the deed to the lands of Krondar. He left its lordship to your care. I'll assist you as best I can, but my time will also be needed in my own lands. Should you require anything, please send message to Marbayne. I'll answer when duty permits."

She looked up from the document, studying his face. "We just met, why would you assist me?"

Caught off guard by the question, Demetrix selected the best response. "My Lady, Ravion was my brother. I don't know how you two found each other, but in going through his things I learned that he was extremely fond of you. That piqued my interest. For that reason alone, I offer my support. But then I got here and I saw your people. Had I not felt obligated beforehand, I would now."

She raised an eyebrow at the statement.

"I don't know what Ravion told you about our kind, and I don't wish to confuse you in any way but your people seem to have a strong connection to mine. Ravion must have seen this, which I'm sure had some part in his motives. Ravion aside, this explains my motives. If your people are indeed related to mine, and I believe they are, I'll do all I can to aid you." Demetrix pushed himself up, steadying against the wooden supports. "My Lady Senaria, it's been a privilege meeting you. I hope to share words again in the near future, but I'm afraid I must return to Marbayne. The attacks have moved fairly close to these parts. I'd prefer to reach Shadgull before nightfall." Taking his own weight, he gave a final bow and turned, leaving her to her affairs.

A gentle breeze blew across the forested courtyard. The clash of swords echoed through the trees, calm and precise.

Demetrix limped his way down the line of soldiers looking upon their seemingly young faces. In truth his didn't appear much different, but he was beginning to feel his years. Stopping in front of a young girl, narrowly old enough to apply for the border wardens, he scanned her from head to toe, studying the blue glow radiating from her. "What's your name, recruit."

"Rayel Santail, sir!" The young scout stood amidst the row of eager warriors, each one ready to prove their worth. She wore a brown leather skirt and matching armor. Twin short swords hung from her sides and fiery red hair ran down her back.

"Santail, huh? What brings you to Marbayne, Rayel?" Demetrix waited for her response, as he had the previous soldiers. This one was different. She claimed name. If she truly was who she claimed to be, there would certainly be a place for her. But he had to be sure.

"I aim to better myself in the ways of battle in hopes of ascending the ranks so that I might fight by my uncle's side."

"What's your uncle's name, recruit?" She looked up at the crippled archer, unsure if she should answer correctly. "Ravion, sir." The assurance in her voice carried through the trees.

"Very good, Rayel." Turning, he stopped in front of the next recruit. Staring him in the eyes, he began again. "What's your name, recruit?"

"Perrin, sir."

"What's your business here, Perrin?"

"I hear this is the place to train in the ways of magic since the tower left, sir."

"You've come to the right place. Do you think you've got what it takes to be among the elite magi we have to offer?"

"I do, sir!"

"Very good, Perrin. We'll make a battlemage of you yet." Demetrix went down the line, learning all the new recruit's names and faces. It helped know the men he led. Their deaths didn't sting as bad when he could put a face with the list. Finishing his introductions he opened a wooden chest and pulled out a handful of black sigils. Each one had a white trident carved in the center. Tossing one to each of the recruits, he closed the chest and paced in front of them. "These mark you as an initiate in The Order. Have it with you at all times. With improvement you'll receive a new badge and benefits. Let it be a beacon for you in times of need. Your brothers and sisters will always be there for you, just as you'll always be there for them. Wear it with pride. You're dismissed."

The group broke up, disappearing to their various duties.

"Rayel, might I have a minute?" He hobbled to the young scout. "What do you know of Ravion?"

"Sadly, not much. I met him briefly before he had to go on some important mission. I was in Krondar not long ago and they hadn't heard from him. Has he returned?"

"Sadly, no. And he's not expected to. Let me ask you this. I've known Ravion for a while now. He never mentioned anything about siblings. How do you tie in?"

"My mother told me about him before she died. She said she thought he was dead. They got separated when they were little. Reputation of the Dreuslayers traveled to my homeland in West Korenthia. My mother suspected it was Ravion, but she couldn't be sure. After she died, I tried to find my father and sister. A merchant told me he might have taken position at the tower, but it was gone before I arrived. Then I learned this was the birthplace of the Dreuslayers and I had to find out for myself. May I ask you a question?" She continued, refusing to wait for a response. "How do you tie in? I know you're dalari. I can see your glow. Aside from you, and Ravion, I haven't seen any others."

"It's a long story full of many complications. Short form, my name is Demetrix Santail. Son to Marquel Santail and brother to Ravion and Alexzandra. This would make me your uncle as well. Walk with me and I'll answer any questions you have."

Demetrix stared out the window overlooking the bailey, and the city beyond. He watched the new recruits training against the dummies, recalling a simpler time. Lost in thought he didn't hear the door open.

"You spend an awful lot of time lookin' out that window."

Hearing Gareth's voice he turned, finding the man sitting against the edge of the table. "It helps me think. I look down at the men and women striving to be better than they were the day before. I see hope. Hope for the future. Hope that we've made a difference. I see their faces, free of mar and regret from years of battle weighing heavily on the soul."

"I didn't come here to listen to you unburden yourself. I came to give you a lead on your raiders." Gareth pulled a dagger from his hip and began scraping dirt from beneath his fingernails.

Demetrix chuckled at the warrior's abruptness. "I enjoy these little chats. Won't you take a seat and tell me all about it?" Forcing sarcasm into his words he limped toward his chair.

"I've already got one." Gareth smiled motioning at the table beneath him. Waiting a moment, ensuring his point was made, he stood and marched to his own seat. "I can't prove it yet, but Erik has some hand in the attacks. I stopped by the pub in Shadgull last night."

"And by stopped you mean you stayed all night."

"I'm telling the damned story! Anyway, I was making my way upstairs with a fine young lass. When I passed by the back room, I saw Erik and his second— oh, what was his name? Jem." Gareth raised his finger, denoting remembrance. "They were dressed in all black, talking to a guy about a special dagger. I couldn't stay real long for fear of drawing too much attention—"

"And by that you mean you were distracted by the girl you previously mentioned." Demetrix suppressed a chuckle, seeing the irritation build in his friend.

"Do you want to hear what saw or not?"

"By all means."

"You sure? Cause I can keep it to myself. I'd hate to waste your time."

Sighing heavily Demetrix waved him on, all humor lost. "Please proceed."

"Where was I? Oh yeah, I didn't wanna draw too much attention, but I know a deal when I see one. I did manage to see a drawing of the dagger before my entertainment drug me off. I knew I'd seen it somewhere before so I stopped by the vaults before coming here." Gareth reached under his cloak and drew the thin, wavy dagger of black and purple. He extended it toward the ranger. Releasing it, it settled in Demetrix's palm.

Demetrix took the kris, examining the runes running along the blade. "You think this is what they're after?"

"I do. And if they're willing to kill their own citizens for it, something tells me they'd stop at nothing to get it. I'd hate to see the aftermath if they learn we have it."

"I wonder what's so important about it?"

Gareth watched in earnest. "Ravion killed the nightking with it. I don't know its history before he had it. Ravion said to lock it away and keep it safe. On his word alone we can't risk Erik finding it."

"I remember small pieces of Lythus talking about the dagger. He wouldn't ever say much, but I could tell he was afraid of it. I'll send for Perrin. He's quickly making progress. Maybe he can tell us a little more."

"I'd express caution. We don't know what this thing does or why he wants it so bad. Best I've been able to find was a report of a dagger that can grant unlimited power to its wielder." Gareth stood reclaiming the mysterious blade. "I'll return it to the vault until we have more answers."

A blinding light exploded, illuminated the room.

Demetrix shielded his eyes, turning to see the source floating above the council table. "Gareth. Are you seeing this?"

"Aye!"

"Ravion?" Grabbing his cane Demetrix stood, stepping closer to the glowing silhouette. "Ravion?" There was no mistaking the face staring back at him, though he seemed darker than he recalled.

The light grew wider forcing them to look away. It wrapped around, surrounding them in a warm embrace. They couldn't see anything it was so bright.

Hearing the commotion on the other side of the council room door, William approached. It wasn't alarming, but it didn't belong. Slowly reaching out, he pushed the door open and peeked into the seemingly abandoned chamber. "My Lord? Are you here? I just received word the Black Lotus were offered a sum of two thousand gold for your head."

A loud clap echoed out.

William stepped into the room. He saw the wooden cane lying upon the floor. "Highlord Demetrix?" Making his way to the table, keeping his eyes open for any sign, he inspected the gnarled wood. A purple sheen caught his attention. Abandoning the worn cane he secured the wicked dagger lying beside it.

William, claim me!

Hearing the whispers in his mind, he felt a jolt shoot through his hand. Turning toward the door, dagger in fist, a purple glazed reflected in his eyes.

The story will continue in Izaryle's Key

Be sure to stay up to date with the newest Eldarlands books at
http://www.levisamuel.com

Please leave a review at your online retailer.

Author's Notes

I'm going to risk making an ass out of myself and assume you've read Izaryle's Will (Eldarlands – Heroes of Order Volume One) prior to stumbling upon this one. If you did, you should already know that the story started many years ago in the mystical lands of the Misted Hills. That's the name of the Springfield chapter of the Eldaraenth© Live Action Role Playing (LARP) game. I met some of my closest friends within that fantasy world contained upon that small farm north of town.

We'd get dressed up in our finest garb (or whatever we were able to find/make that had a proper feel to it). We'd don a variety of weapons and armor, and we'd hop into the mindset of our various characters.

Once there, the events of such an alluring and fantastic world shaped us in every conceivable way. We were the characters. Their actions were our own. We faced character rivalries, bandit attacks, and hundreds of other scenarios that could have arisen in any fantasy setting.

I'd be lying if I said we never instigated said problems, depending on what I felt was needed at the time. On more than one occasion my friends and I would find out what the primary group of adventurers was after for any particular encounter. We'd track down their objectives and, depending on what we felt was best, we'd either make it easier or harder for them. There was one event in particular where the adventurers found themselves in needed of the hammer of a specific dwarf character. They weren't the most political of bands and we knew they would simply kill the dwarf and take the hammer. So, we did what was right. We tracked the group, created some obstacles, and slowed their progression so we could get a few steps ahead. We then found the dwarf and proceeded to spend the remainder of the weekend protecting him all in the aim of preserving his life. With minutes to spare, and the supposed heroes nearly defeated, we delivered the dwarf where he was needed and completed the main objective. He happily performed the forging that was required of his hammer. And considering he wouldn't have given up his tool, even if it cost him his life, we created tension for the heroes, and entertained ourselves along the way.

We weren't always the good guys, but we were never the bad guys, at least not to our own perspectives. Every action we took, good or questionable, was for the sole purpose of protecting the world we'd all grown to love. But this series of books is not directly related to the game world. It's simply inspired by a few of the more interesting characters. This series is its own world. The events here-in were created my me, in my imagination, and should not be confused with the details that occurred in the Eldaraenth world.

I released this trilogy of books once before, in October of 2016 at a small convention in Evansville, Indiana. The staff and guests of Tri-Con feel like family. I was happy to have been accepted into their ranks, and grateful they allowed me the opportunity to release my book there. I managed to nearly sell out, which is always a goal I strive for. Most of the time I succeed, but on occasion I bring a few books home. I'm extremely grateful that so many have believed in me enough to read my work. Though I'm aware that most of you are here for the story rather than me. And I'm okay with that fact. I enjoy writing. Having readers is more than enough reward.

It's you fantastic readers that made my launch a success. But that small feat aside, it was nothing compared to what I discovered upon my return home. My new book (the past rendition of this book) had climbed the charts of Amazon's Top 100 Hot New Releases. For nearly a month, I checked it multiple times, day and night. Each time, I recorded the status. Some days it climbed, other days it fell, but it was on the list and that's what mattered. But there was one small detail that made it better than all the rest. At one point this book had climbed the ranks and taken position above J.K. Rowling's newest book, Fantastic Beasts.

I hate name dropping. I feel it's little different than ride someone's coattail in measure of your own success. But in this case I was ecstatic that my book was not only on the same list, but I had somehow ranked higher. I love with the Harry Potter books. In fact, I've probably read them more times than I have any other title aside from my own work. I have immense amounts of respect for her and her work, and I hope one day my name can reach even half as far. In fact, as an indirect tribute I named one of the chapters in this book, Fantastic Beast in honor of that achievement.

In all the excitement of this, there was one unexpected detail I was forced to take a long, hard look at. Statistically speaking, when a book spikes the way mine did, it puts the author on a time limit to release the next book. Otherwise momentum is lost, and that can result in a massive flop immediately following a massive success. That means I had extremely limited time to get the next book finished and ready to release. In my preliminaries, I had roughly 3 months to finish the next manuscript and be ready to go to print. Which is supposed to cause a secondary spike on the first book, which in theory would carry this one with it. I have yet to authenticate this, but everything I've found suggest the pattern is legit.

But writing a new book so quickly isn't always possible. Especially when the author works a full-time job, is a single parent, and has many other responsibilities to maintain. I had another book I'd been working on, which had to be finished before I could direct my attention toward this one. I went through the entire manuscript and did a near complete rewrite in two weeks. Once I'd finished that I sent it out for what felt like the twentieth time. Though in reality, it was more like the fourth. That's a down side to working with traditional publishers. Everything works on their time instead of mine.

So, with little time to spare, I went to work writing this book. I had a small part of the story left from the original A.R.C. But it was broken and in need of a complete rewrite. I did the only thing I could do. I set myself a goal. It had to be completed no later than December 31, 2016. I pushed myself every day for two months. And in the end, I made it. I finished the final words of the last chapter on December 30th and sent it to my editor. He did his thing while I went to work writing all the filler materials, such as the words you're reading right now. But enough about what I did to get it written.

As I stated earlier, this book was originally the second half of book 1, a much smaller and condensed version of it, but it was there. If you were one of the few unlucky enough to ended up with a copy of the advance reader, and tried to read it, you have my apologies for the atrocious combination of words within those pages. I was pretty bad back then.

Both books, one and two, were originally planned as one story. When I was working toward publishing book 1, my editor at the time pointed out that I'd made a common rookie mistake. I was seeing the world so vividly in my own head that I'd forgotten the reader couldn't. This left a story with no real feeling to it. I had characters and interactions, but the world had no texture. You couldn't feel the wind upon your face, or see the billowing smoke rolling from the chimney above the inn.

Realizing this, I learned what I needed to do, which the smartest path was to split the book right down the middle and build upon the foundation of each half. I added thousands of details, created new content, and managed to bring the characters a little closer to reality. I took two broken stories, equal parts of roughly 40k words, and shaped them each into a believable world that was just under 200k words total. In the two months I spent rewriting this book, I ended up writing several entirely new chapters, all the while polishing and adding details to the world around the story. I made it so much denser than it was. I gave the characters stronger motives, I made them love, and I made them hate. They became real, making them feel like the people I'd used for their inspiration. And if I did everything right, you, dear reader, should hate me from time to time. But I hope I'm redeemable as everything I've done was for the purpose of moving the story. I created what I believe is my best work yet.

As many of the characters are based on real friends of mine, I encountered moments when I had to call those friends, regardless of the time. On more than one occasion, I heard a tired and sleepy voice answer the phone in a raspy "Hello?". It wasn't that I enjoyed waking them at all hours of the night. I had to share my excitement and emotions. These characters became real. And like real beings, I had to express the torment and joy they put me through. I would wake my friends and get onto them for their character's actions. I know they had no more control over their character, written by me, than I have over their physical bodies, But I felt obligated the inform them of the shit their character was pulling, which often got a good laugh. Though not all encounters were bad. In fact, many were humorous, or annoying, or some other part of the emotional range. I laughed. I cried, I felt tears of joy. Hell, just the other night (When I originally wrote these notes) I had a scene where some of the characters were bantering back and forth. It had me in tears of humor and ridicule, forcing the emotions of the character based on me to the front of my mind. It pulled me back to a point when such banter was a regular occurrence. I felt as my character did. And I had no choice but to call my friends, laughing about the entire encounter. If no other part of this book is well received, I believe that one will be. There is true emotion within those few words, which tell the story of a brotherly love that only the closest of people have developed. I believe I've done a fair job of tapping into that relationship between my closest friends and I. This is my best work yet. It's dark, gritty, loving, forgiving, merciless, and with any hope, alluring.

In conclusion, I thoroughly enjoyed this book and I hope you will too. I've created a world here, one which will be thoroughly explored in future works. The characters may change, but there are many more stories to tales to tale. You'll learn more about the eldar races, the gods, the monsters, the heroes, and many others. I have an entire series of twenty plus books planned, I just need the time to write them. Time that I hope to gain by doing this full time. But the only way I can make that happen is with your support. You've already purchased this book and for that I thank you. But there is more to be done. I urge you to take a moment to leave a review at any online outlet which you've found this book. And if you'd like exclusive access to a free book set within this world, please subscribe to my newsletter. http://eepurl.com/dxRUvL

Thank you in advance and I look forward to bringing you many more hours of entertainment.

Levi Samuel
December 2016 – Originally Written
September 2018 - Revised

www.ingramcontent.com/pod-product-compliance
Lightning Source LLC
Chambersburg PA
CBHW070056030726
47506CB00002B/491